A LEGACY

OF

MAGIC

&

MONSTERS

KRISTEN JENNINGS

Edited by Cara Lockwood (Edit-my-novel.com)
Cover Design and Illustration by Azura Arts @azura.arts
Interior Formatting by: Vellum

Trade Paperback ISBN: 979-8-9929437-2-6
Ebook ISBN: 979-8-9929437-3-3

First Edition October 2025

To my younger self: be loud, bold, and unequivocally yourself. Because you are worthy of love exactly as you are.

Content Warning

- Loss of parent(s) off-page
- Death of a close friend
- Open door sex scenes
- Discrimination against certain groups within the kingdoms
- Attempted (and successful) murder

 ONE

Sunrise at the Royal Palace was Audra's favorite time of day. As the first pink and orange rays of light touched the verdant green tree branches and burned away the cold morning mist on the lawn, the day took on a glow that made her believe in endless possibilities. Uninterrupted, Audra could enjoy her first cup of tea at the table on her balcony while the light warmed her fair skin, peaceful and quiet.

Or, at least it was usually uninterrupted. This morning, Audra found a piece of parchment folded under the cutlery, closed with a wax seal pressed with a crescent moon surrounded by three stars. The symbol of the mages of Ymira. Like its predecessors, the letter bore no inscription on the front and the contents would no doubt contain a similar line of inquiry. With hands that trembled like a sapling in a storm, Audra broke the seal and read the two lines of text.

> *You deserve to live with people who do not make you hide who you are. Magic is your birthright. Come home.*
> *-V*

Each letter arrived without warning, written in the precise, clean penmanship of V, an enigmatic character who revealed nothing of themselves while detailing a startling understanding of Audra's life. As a child, the anecdotes about her parent's courtship and lives before she was born offered glimpses of joy during dark periods of grief. Yearning for a familial connection, Audra replied to those early letters with endless questions that were met with an urge to visit Ymira, kingdom of the mages. As her guardians, King Keld and Queen Isadora forbade the trip and cautioned her against replying to a stranger who would not even offer their full name. After that, Audra stopped replying to the letters and their frequency decreased until they only arrived after incidents where Audra released magic. Varied in length, the message of the letters were always clear: V wanted Audra to go to Ymira and learn magic.

The implication that the royal family did not love her for who she was was absurd. Magic was discouraged in both Solven and their neighboring kingdom, Feldor, but it was not forbidden. Past the northern mountains, the kingdom of Kalmere outright forbade magic and executed anyone seen practicing it. But here, Audra did not need magic. Protected by solid walls and trained soldiers, with tutors and all the books she would ever need, Audra had everything she ever wanted. And she had bigger things to worry about today than an ominous letter.

After all, this was the day that Prince Graham returned from the Hunt. A tradition started during the age of darkness over two hundred years before, each member of the Guard was tasked with hunting a netvor on the eve of their twenty-first ageday. Unleashed through dark magic, these monsters preyed on the kingdom's people and could only be vanquished by a member of the Guard. Identified as children through a series of tests that revealed their increased strength and senses, Guards pushed their bodies to develop the skills necessary to kill creatures designed to lure humans to excruciatingly painful deaths or turn them into monsters themselves.

The Hunt was the final test after years of training. Kill their first monster, and they received the honor and responsibilities of a Guard. Failure to kill a monster meant death, for no Guard returned to the castle if they were unsuccessful in their Hunt. As crown prince, Graham's primary responsibility was to protect the people of his kingdom, and he began training as soon as he could hold a sword. Four days ago, Graham embarked on his Hunt with his half-brother Kasteel, and they were expected to return tonight for the ceremony that would officially mark Graham's ageday and responsibility as a Guard.

Audra watched Graham train for this day her whole life. As the king's ward, she was educated alongside Graham and Kasteel, but that education did not extend to the Hunt. When she first came to live at the castle, Audra fawned over the brothers and shadowed their every move. At eleven and seventeen, respectively, Graham and Kasteel resented the constant shadow that Audra presented. Trailing after them in lessons on geography, languages, and politics, eight-year old Audra worked hard to make sure she did not fall behind. The only time that she failed was when the princes started training for the Guard. From the start, it was clear that Audra did not possess the enhanced strength, speed, or endurance necessary to kill netvor.

Although she would never complete a Hunt herself, Audra knew the danger that Graham was in and the fear for his safety kept her tense and anxious each day he was away. Growing up together at the palace, Audra and Graham's proximity in age and shared interests in history and nature often resulted in them reading together in the meadow and exploring the castle together, building a close friendship. Over the years, their friendship grew into something more, at least for Audra, and her heart ached each day they were apart. She had to fight past the tight knot of her stomach to keep down food, the churning thoughts in her head making her stomach roil with nausea. *What if he is injured? What if Graham dies?* Or worse, *what if he finds a lyswen and it turns him into a monster?* Those thoughts kept Audra awake long after she had gone to bed and were the reason she sought solitude this morning. Even though Graham was reserved and distant lately—something that worried Audra more than she wanted to admit—he was the one person who understood her and supported her when she accidentally used magic.

"It really is quite sad to watch," a pinched-faced girl with pale hair and peaches-and-cream complexion remarked to a group of young nobility at an outdoor tea party a few years before. "She has no clue how pathetic she looks. Following the princes around as if she were actually their friend, not just a charity case taken in because their parents were friends. If I were

her, I would be so embarrassed. It is obvious that the princes only tolerate her because their parents tell them to."

She delivered the last remark with a pointed look in Audra's direction, the rest of the table laughing with their friend. Furious, Audra met the girl's stare, hating that the words might be true. Worse still, they were laughing at her pain and, as a tingle sensation built in her arms, Audra wished that they would stop. Seconds later, tea spilled down the front of the girl's gown, almost as if she had slipped when bringing the cup to her face. But Audra knew she had caused it. Recently, small bursts of magic were responding to her emotions, despite the king and queen's insistence that she keep it hidden.

Worried that someone would notice the tea had not spilled on accident, Audra turned and fled from the party. Needing a place to calm down, she went to her favorite spot in the gardens. Snake-like vines covered the garden wall, hiding a small alcove from view. Spongy moss covered the ground, providing a natural seat, and low-hanging branches of a nearby tree brushed her shoulders as she sat. Almost completely sealed off from the world, Audra could escape the bustle of court and be alone here.

Or, as the rustle of leaves behind her revealed, until Graham found her. Taking a seat beside her, Graham leaned back on his elbows, chestnut-brown hair shining in the flickering sunlight through the shade of the tree. Eyes the color of slate met her moss-green eyes behind thick lashes, a hint of a smile brightening his olive-hued skin.

"I know I should not have left like that." Audra pressed her face into her bent knees to hide. "I will apologize to the queen later."

"You think I am here because you left that awful party early? I came here to check on you. I heard what that girl said." Graham bumped her knee with his own, encouraging her to peek at him.

Could her day get any worse? Audra was mortified to know that Graham overheard the girl, not that she had been quiet. She wished he had not followed her here. At least then she would not have to worry that he would tell her the girl was right.

"She was a miserable gossip with nothing better to do than make others as miserable as she is. Do not listen to a word she said. We—I—do not see you that way. You belong here as part of our family."

Warmth climbed from Audra's heart to her face, turning her cheeks

*pink with happiness. Graham's eyes widened slightly as he looked at her,
before turning away with a small cough.*

"Did you make her tea spill?"

Audra winced. "It was an accident. Your mother would be disappointed to know I used magic again."

"I am sure my mother will agree the girl deserved it."

"Still, I am not supposed to use magic."

*"Which is a shame. It is not like you would ever really hurt anyone,
and it is part of who you are. You should be proud of it."*

"Really?"

"Of course. When I am king, I will make it so that all mages can practice magic in Solven. That way, you would not have to hide it anymore."

The sounds of rustling fur and the soft stretch of bones caused
Audra to turn in her chair, blinking away the memory. Padding through
the open balcony doors was Isik, a clever and mischievous fox, and her
dearest companion. Fur the color of the snow-capped mountains and
eyes as dark as the jagged mountain-peaks, Isik was a sixteenth ageday
gift from the royal family.

"Good morning, sleepyhead," Audra cooed to her beloved pet. "Did
you get enough beauty rest?" Stopping near her feet, Isik tilted his head
and narrowed his eyes as if offended by the question. "My apologies,
your highness," Audra taunted with a mock bow. "I forgot that you are
not a morning person. Or animal, as it were." Standing from her chair
with a stretch, Audra scratched Isik between his ears and started toward
her bedroom. "Come along. I am sure the king and queen are waiting
for us in the breakfast room."

Her dressing gown flowed around her feet as Audra crossed the
bedroom to her wardrobe, the plush texture of the rug keeping her feet
warm over the stone floor. Built generations before, when the kingdom
was little more than clans fighting amongst themselves for access to
resources, the wing of the palace where Audra resided was built entirely
from stone crafted from the mountains. Cold in both winter and
summer, Audra appreciated the rich history of her room, knowing that
it protected the first rulers of Solven and kept the occupants' secrets
within the weathered stone.

Behind the painted landscape of wildflowers and songbirds that decorated her dressing screen, Audra removed her nightgown, letting the silky material puddle on the floor while she stepped into a peony-colored day dress. She was eager to start the day, and waiting for confirmation that the Hunt was successful made it difficult to focus on daily life.

As she turned to head out the door, her gaze caught on the letter from Ymira again. It taunted her where it sat, still open, on the metal table, one corner of the page curling upward in the slight breeze. Not wanting a maid to find it while they were cleaning up her tea, Audra snatched it from the table and tossed it in the fire.

After all, magic created the netvor, and with Guards to protect the people, why would anyone need the help of mages? Their practice of magic was a well-protected secret and anyone wishing for magical assistance had to travel through the Weld forest and the perilous path through the mountains to reach the territory of mages. A journey for the desperate.

The broken.

The weak.

Audra had no reason to think of the territory of Ymira and the magic she possessed. She was protected and safe in the castle and would eventually be Solven's princess. It was everything she wanted. Everything she needed. Not even a personal invitation to learn about magic from an individual who called themselves the High Mage could entice Audra to leave Solven. Not even the six invitations she had received over the years.

Her life was perfect, and nothing would change that.

Two

With a flounce in her step and a pair of new cream slippers embroidered with the same flowers as the color of her dress, Audra made her way out the door and down the corridor, Isik close on her heels. Running her hand along the dark wood of the banister, Audra gazed at the artwork lining the hall, reflecting on the years of memories she had here.

The daughter of one of the king's oldest friends, and strongest commanders, Audra spent time each summer at the castle, playing and studying with Graham and Kasteel while her parents fulfilled their responsibilities in court. Naturally, the encouraged proximity created a close bond between the three and over time it became clear that while Kasteel saw Audra as a younger sister, Graham did not. Tragedy struck one summer when a sickness swept over the land, draining life from infected people like a leech, and Audra's mother perished from the illness. Grief-stricken, Audra and her father did not return to the castle for two years, during which time Graham determined that girls were gross and he no longer wanted to play with Audra. When her father was killed defending the king, it was the queen who insisted that Audra remain at the castle as the royal ward.

Shaking away thoughts of the past, Audra turned into the breakfast room and curtseyed to the waiting king and queen. "Good morning, Your Majesties."

Isik slipped around her to his plate waiting in the corner, spoiled by the fresh fish caught and prepared just for him.

Much like her father, King Keld was a tall, barrel-chested man with a figure accustomed to hard work. His wavy, russet hair was tied back in a high bun, and the matching beard was neatly trimmed. Never an idle man, the little free time he had between dealing with the concerns of the kingdom was spent among his people, working the fields or building homes and markets, lending a pink tone to his ivory skin.

"Good morning, Audra. I hope you had a pleasant night's rest." He returned her greeting with an affectionate smile. Keld treated her like family from the day she met him.

"I certainly hope you slept better than I did," Isadora said from the table, rubbing between her dark brows. Despite her claims for sleeping poorly, her ebony hair was shining as it lay in thick curls down her back, chestnut-colored eyes bright against her warm, olive skin. "Half the night was spent praying for my sons' safe return and the other half was fretting over the guest list for the ball. Having your assistance planning everything has been a relief to me, Audra. You are showing an aptitude for navigating the complex life planning royal events."

As the younger princess from Cordille, a kingdom across the sea from the continent of the three kingdoms, Queen Isadora was a wise and compassionate woman, teaching Audra everything she knew about navigating royal life and building a strong court. The one skill that Queen Isadora had difficulty imparting on Audra was the ability to control her emotions. Presenting a calm, dignified presence to the country was crucial to maintaining peace, as the queen always explained, but Audra had difficulty masking her emotions. Verbal outbursts when she was frustrated with a lesson or angry at a bully had decreased as she grew, but Audra could never manage to mask the small flare of temper when involved in a heated debate or the frustration with other nobles jockeying for position with the royal household. And the small bits of magic released in those instances never hurt anyone, right?

Scents of fresh wildberries, sweet cream, freshly baked bread, and roasted meats drifted from the various breakfast dishes elegantly placed on serving trays. The sensory stimulation reached Audra's nose, causing a low rumble in her stomach.

"I slept as well as could be expected. Thank you for your concern. If there is anything I can help with, please let me know."

"There will be time enough for us to go over the day's schedule and ensure everything is ready for the ball. But first, let's eat before the bear in your stomach decides to make an appearance." With a wink to Audra, Keld motioned the staff forward to remove the covers from the dishes on the table. Deciding on a small sample of each dish and a bracing cup of tea, Audra watched as the king personally served his wife food. Once finished, he placed a kiss on the back of her hand and they both began to eat. Years ago, Audra asked him about the puzzling habit.

"Because she is my equal, my beloved. Elskede. Isa shares the weight and responsibility of a kingdom with me. I want to ease her burdens and it is my joy and responsibility to ensure her happiness in all things. With all my beloved Isa does for the kingdom, I want to show her my love no matter how small the task."

A small sigh escaped Audra's lips as she watched Keld and Isadora, wishing that she could share such a moment with Graham.

"The bear and I thank you, but I am sure it would be no hardship for you to vanquish any creature that invades these halls," Audra replied with a pointed look to the tattoos gracing the king's arms, one for each netvor he had killed. Looking at the tattoos reminded Audra of what Graham faced on his Hunt, and sparked new worry over his safety. "I just hope that Graham is equally as adept."

"Graham has prepared for this moment his entire life and has Kasteel with him. No harm will come to either of them." Keld shared a look with his wife. It was no secret that the queen and king encouraged a relationship between Audra and Graham.

"I remember when it was Keld's Hunt and ageday ball." Queen Isadora's eyes took on a glassy quality as her mind drifted to the past. "You looked so severe and focused, arms crossed and frowning. Almost as if you expected something to attack."

"I was forced into fancy clothes with no weapons, paraded around women vying for a crown. Of course I was uncomfortable," Keld grumbled as he took another bite of food.

"Of course, dearest. You were very brave to go through that awful process." Audra coughed to hide her laugh at the banter between the couple. Although he was an intimidating man, capable of felling trees or beasts with ease, Keld was actually quite romantic and revealed a soft side only for his wife. Isadora was equally as fierce, having raised Kasteel on her own for several years after the passing of her first husband, and defending herself against people who sought to take advantage of her precarious position in Cordille.

"Will Graham find it unbearable, do you think?" Although Audra and Isadora spent months planning the ball, Audra was embarrassed to realize that she had not given much thought to Graham's feelings towards the event. They organized a banquet with his favorite dishes, mixed with offerings from visiting kingdoms, selected flowers and linens that matched his silver eyes, and the entertainment consisted of several acclaimed performers and musicians. She had assumed he would see the culmination of their efforts and be elated.

"With you and Isa planning the ball, how could he not enjoy it?" Keld said reassuringly. "I didn't find the entire event completely unbearable. It's how I met the love of my life." Isadora traveled from Cordille with her younger sister to Solven for Keld's ageday celebration. Their father had hoped that Isadora's younger sister would catch the eye of the future king and that their marriage would strengthen the alliance of the two kingdoms. "I saw Isa through the crowd and instantly knew that she was it for me."

"He asked me to dance and then we walked through the gardens, talking about anything and everything. Hours passed and only felt like minutes. We shared our aspirations and hopes for the future. I felt like I had known you forever."

"It only took one night for me to know Isa was my destiny. It just took her some time to catch up to what I already knew."

"Time gave me the opportunity to know you better. To ensure you were the best choice for Kasteel and me. I could not let myself be blinded by how handsome you were."

Keld laughed heartily. "Were? Good to know I married you before I lost my looks."

"Hush you." Isadora lightly smacked his shoulder with her hand. "Age has only improved your features."

Placing her chin on the arm resting on the table, Audra smiled as she listened to the story she had heard over a dozen times. The courtship of the king and queen was well-known throughout the kingdom. Traveling minstrel groups performed adaptations of their once-in-a-lifetime love story. It was something that Audra wanted for herself. The beautiful dress, romantic music, and first dance that would lead to happily ever after. Tonight's ball was the perfect opportunity. She just needed Graham to arrive.

As if her thoughts called him into existence, a footman swept into the room, bowed to the King and queen, and announced, "Your Majesties, the princes have been spotted. They return from the Hunt."

Silverware clattered to the table as Audra dropped her fork, finally hearing the words she was waiting for. Gaze whipping from the footman to the king and queen, Audra's pulse raced with the anticipation of seeing Graham again. He was unharmed, returning from the Hunt in triumph. He had to be, or else the footman would have phrased the return differently. The urge to leap from her chair and run to Graham coiled in Audra's muscles, her hands gripping the edges of her chair to remain seated until dismissed.

"Excellent! Let's go and welcome them home." Setting down her napkin, Isadora waited for Keld to pull out her chair before taking his hand and motioning for Audra to follow them.

Not a lengthy walk compared to her daily stroll through the garden, the journey from the dining hall to the courtyard felt endless as Audra walked behind the king and queen. Her feet itched to move faster and bring her to the moment where she would lay eyes on Graham and verify his safety herself. The front doors to the castle were crafted from the black cherry wood that grew in the Weld forest and were carved with figures depicting the joining of the clans under the first queen's reign. Standing on the stone landing before the doors, Audra was reminded of the importance of the Hunt that Graham was returning from.

A large courtyard lay in front, surrounded on all sides by the walls of the palace and a set of steel-enforced gates that protected the entryway from attack. Along one wall were the stables, the smell of hay and horses wafting on the breeze. The position of the stable provided quick access to mounts for messengers and soldiers who had to leave at a moment's notice. Across the courtyard, along the other wall, were barracks to house the soldiers protecting the castle. Several of the soldiers taught Audra to play cards with them, and she enjoyed their easy-going banter and relaxed manner that was a stark contrast to life at court.

Looking out past the gates, the silhouettes of Graham and Kasteel grew closer and their features became distinct in the morning sunlight. Riding a gelding the same obsidian-color as his wavy, shoulder-length hair, Prince Kasteel entered the courtyard first. A bright smile lit his olive skin as he turned towards his brother.

"Still not fast enough to beat me, little brother! You'll have to do better than that to succeed in the Guard."

"Hah! You only won because your horse has a lighter load to carry." Swinging down from the saddle, Graham passed the reigns of his dapple-gray gelding to a waiting stable hand. The brothers shared a laugh born from years of friendly competition.

"Welcome home, sons," the king's voice bellowed across the courtyard, his arms held open for an embrace as the princes made their way up the curved staircase to the landing. "I am glad to see you both safely returned from the Hunt."

Each son dutifully received a crushing hug from their father, Keld's massive arms squeezing them close in an outward show of his relief at their return.

"Thank you, father. I am glad to be home. You didn't have to greet us, though. We would have found you for the ceremony." Although she was standing mere steps from the king, Graham's eyes refused to meet Audra's. He was probably just tired from the Hunt, she reasoned, not wanting to give fuel to the worry tightening her throat. At least she was able to drink in the image of him with leisure. Days in the sun added copper highlights to Graham's wavy brown hair and a light tan graced his skin, as if the urge to caress his skin was too great for even the sun. A cursory sweep over his body showed no critical injuries, but Audra's fingers twitched with the desire to personally check. Heat swept up her body at the thought of removing Graham's clothing to check for wounds, gaining access to the cords of muscle she had seen when he trained shirtless on hot summer days.

"...have we not, Audra?" Queen Isadora looked at her expectantly and Audra fought her way out of the fog in her brain caused by thoughts of Graham shirtless. Pink stained her cheeks as she prayed that her thoughts were not apparent to the others.

"I apologize, Your Majesty. I was overcome with relief at the princes' safe return that my thoughts escaped me. What was it you were saying?"

"I was just telling Graham all about the ball we prepared and how much work you put into it to make it perfect for him." Isadora gave her a knowing look. In recent months, Graham was rarely home, leaving little time for him to learn about the ball—or spend time with Audra.

"My sincere thanks, Lady Audra. I'm sure the celebration will be one to remember." A short incline of Graham's head punctuated the statement, more formal than he ever addressed her. Still, he avoided her gaze.

"It was my pleasure, Your Highness. Was the Hunt a success?"

Something in her question caused Graham's body to tense, his gaze snapping up and connecting with hers. As their eyes met, Audra's breath caught in her lungs, like trying to breathe in a chilly wind. Colored like raging storm clouds, Graham's eyes were typically unguarded and twinkled with mirth. Now, however, Audra caught a flash of pain and sorrow in his eyes before he shuttered the emotion and turned away.

"It was." Turning towards his parents, Graham inquired on matters of the kingdom while he was away.

Heavy silence filled the air and cold replaced the heat that Audra felt when first seeing Graham. Gone was the man who talked with Audra for hours about a book he read or brought a basket of her favorite berries that he found when training in the forest. Confused by his sudden change of attitude, Audra looked at Kasteel for guidance.

"It's good to be home again. Sleeping on the cold ground and listening to this one snore reminds me how much I miss the comforts of home." Kasteel playfully elbowed Graham before sweeping Audra into a hug and spinning her around. "And I missed you, of course, Sprite!"

"I missed you too, you big oaf." Clinging to his neck, Audra pulled Kasteel tighter, having missed the comforting warmth of his friendship.

"Of course, we all missed you both." Queen Isadora swept first Graham and then Kasteel into hugs. "And as much as we look forward to hearing the tale of your adventure, you both reek of sweat and horse. Go inside and prepare for the ceremony." With one last bow and a kiss on their mother's cheeks, Graham and Kasteel walked into the castle.

"I should go check on the preparations for the ceremony." Turning towards the castle, Keld stooped to kiss his wife and then turned to address Audra. Noting her furrowed brow and frown, the king pulled her into a hug. "Don't worry about Graham's behavior. The Hunt has a way of changing people and he is most likely tired from the journey."

"Keld is right. Graham will need time to process everything he experienced the last four days and will come to you when he is ready. In the meantime, we have a ball to prepare for." Linking their arms together, Isadora pulled Audra back into the cool halls of the castle. But nothing could distract Audra from the cruel thoughts that circled her head like vultures waiting for a kill.

What if he's never ready?

THREE

In the hours that passed while Graham prepared for the ceremony to become a Guard, Audra participated in the queen's rituals to prepare for a ball. Verifying the placement of the decorations and quality of the food and drinks. One thing she tried not to do was dwell on Graham's odd behavior. Each time Audra's thoughts wandered to their awkward reunion, her heart dropped into her stomach, thoughts buzzing as she wondered if she said or did something wrong. Did he feel ambushed by her presence, not having a moment to rest when arriving home? When they bade farewell before his journey, Graham had not seemed to mind her waving him off as he rode out the gates, even going so far as to kiss her hand when he told her she would see him again soon.

Each time her thoughts distracted her, Audra found herself putting plates back on the banquet tables upside down, or unfolding napkins that were perfectly ordered. When Isadora caught Audra staring out a window, vase of flowers in hand, the queen sent her to go relax in her room.

After soaking in a tub filled with jasmine-scented oil, Audra walked to her dressing table to get ready for the ball. Her hand froze on the bell pull when she noticed the thin black envelope cradled between the silver hairbrush and matching jewelry box that were gifts from her mother. Gifts from a mother she had few memories of. A woman who was a descendant of the original mages, a bloodline passed to her only child and the reason for the letter that now lay on Audra's table. Two letters in one day did not bode well.

Aren't you tired of pretending to be someone you are not?
-V

"I am not pretending. I love my life and I do not need you and I certainly do not need magic," Audra said while glaring at the paper. Isik lifted his head from where he was curled up on her bed, searching for the subject of her conversation.

The letter drifted to the floor, forgotten, when a lady's maid arrived to help Audra with her hair and dress. The rhythmic clop of horses' hooves and the clatter of carriage wheels rolling across the cobblestone courtyard drifted through Audra's open windows as guests arrived at the castle. Each arrival meant that the ball would start soon, the eager anticipation swirling in Audra's chest steadily climbing to a peak. She felt perched on the edge of something incredible.

Finally, the result of months of planning was here.

Audra let out a small gasp as she looked in the mirror. The soft glow of the magelights—magical inventions were appreciated even while mages were not—illuminated her white dress, causing it to shine like a pearl. Small green vines with blue flowers, the same flowers as those on the royal crest, were embroidered along the hem, sweeping the floor and twisting around her ankles as Audra twirled in place. A lace-covered bodice cinched her waist at the top of the full skirt and continued upwards in a high neck, leaving her arms bare. Her ash-brown hair was transformed into a braided coronet that framed her oval face, small crystal flowers delicately woven within the braid to catch the light. Blinking slowly at her reflection, Audra saw excitement and anticipation reflected in her moss-green eyes.

Waiting for Kasteel to come escort her, Audra went to her bookshelf and pulled out a well-worn tome on Solven's history. While the majority of the books in her room belonged to the royal library, this one was a gift from Graham.

"Happy Ageday, Audra." Graham handed her a parcel wrapped in green cloth tied with a gray ribbon. "I found it in a shop in Oshea." A trip that Audra hadn't been allowed to go on. Villagers in Oshea reported livestock disappearing in the night and asked for a Guard to investigate. As an opportunity to learn how to track netvor first-hand, Graham went with two experienced Guards to assist in tracking the monster, although he was not permitted to help kill it since his Hunt had not taken place. Gone for a week, Graham had missed Audra's seventeenth ageday.

Pulling at the ribbon and removing the cloth covering, Audra savored every moment of opening her present, particularly because it extended the rare opportunity to spend time alone with Graham. After breakfast, he had invited her for a walk through the gardens, stopping at a trellised arbor covered in light blue flowers and closed buds that shaded the bench sitting below it. The fragrant scent of the blooms perfumed the air around them as Audra's fingers stroked the cover of the leather book.

"Myths and Mysteries: a History of Solven. It is beautiful, Graham." Audra's breath caught as she opened the book to reveal painted illustrations of historical events. "Thank you. I will treasure it always." Clasping the book to her chest, Audra turned to face Graham.

"You deserve beautiful things."

A breeze ruffled her hair and Graham captured a wayward strand, tucking it behind her ear. Audra kept perfectly still, just in case she was dreaming that Graham's hand lingered on the curve of her ear after releasing the hair. The movement brought their faces closer, mere inches apart, and if one of them moved closer, their lips would touch. Her heartbeat quickened, eyes drifting shut as she felt Graham's breath against her lips. This was it. They were finally going to kiss. She would finally know how his lips felt against hers.

A bird took flight off the branch of a nearby tree, the rustling sound breaking the spell around them. Clearing his throat, Graham stood and held out his hand to help her rise, allowing her to lead the way back to the castle. Overjoyed at the compliment, Audra kept silent to prevent spilling her feelings as they went their separate ways, Graham hailed by a passing courtier and Audra to her lessons with the queen.

Lost in the memory, Audra almost missed the rap of knuckles on her door. Dressed in a burgundy vest with tarnished gold buckles lining the front, and black pants with knee-length boots, Kasteel lounged against the opposite wall, tattooed arms visible. Striding across the hall, he bent to kiss Audra on the forehead before saying, "You look beautiful, Sprite. Cleaning up suits you."

Punching his arm, Audra tossed back, "I was going to say you almost look like a prince, but your manners are certainly un-princely." Joking with Kasteel eased some of the nerves that were clawing her stomach and she laughed as he rubbed his arm and pretended to wince.

"Me? Un-princely? That doesn't sound like me at all." Kasteel wrapped her hand around his bent arm and led her to the ballroom.

His arm was warm beneath her touch, the inked images winding from his shoulder to wrist reminding her of Graham's ceremony. Starting with a pattern of three interwoven lines, the symbol for protection, wrapped around the top of the bicep, for each netvor they killed, a Guard would receive a four-pointed diamond tattoo with the symbol of the netvor in the middle, slowly filling in their arm until it looked like they were wearing armor. When they fought, armor did protect them, but for ceremonies and gatherings, they went sleeveless to inspire people. Audra was sure that it did not hurt as a way to attract bedmates either.

"How did the ceremony go?" She watched him out of the corner of her eye.

"It went well, and don't even try to ask for more than that. You know I can't give details." Kasteel's tone was final as he gave her a side-long glance. "Just try to enjoy the evening, okay? You deserve it."

"Fine," Audra said with a sigh, knowing it was impossible to get more information from him. As they neared the ballroom, her nerves returned in full force. "Will he like it? The ball, I mean." *Will he like me* was the question she was afraid to ask but desperate to know. Before this morning, she was confident that Graham would enjoy the evening, but after his odd behavior towards her, Audra was uncertain.

"He'd be an idiot not to," Kasteel said as he squeezed her hand in reassurance. "I know he seemed...detached earlier. Don't let that spoil your evening. What happened on the Hunt is still fresh in his mind, but

I know that he cares for you. You put a lot of work into this and should be proud no matter what anyone else says. If you like the ball, then that's all that matters."

"Thanks, Kasteel."

"Anytime, Sprite." With a nod toward the herald, Kasteel stepped back and gently nudged her through the open doors.

FOUR

A loud hum of voices filled the air as Audra stepped through the doorway, quieting briefly as she was announced. After years of living in the castle, it still surprised Audra at the level of interest the nobility viewed her with. Her careful descent on the staircase was monitored by visiting emissaries, local nobility, and gentry alike, since her position with the royal family was well known in Solven. Viewed as Graham's most likely choice for a bride, people were equally likely to curry favor with her as they were to attempt to steal her place. Especially tonight. Keld shared his first dance with Isadora at his Hunt ball, as did his mother before him, and her mother before. With how frequently the king and queen shared how important that first dance was to them, Audra knew that if Graham gave his first dance to her, their future was secure. She just had to make sure she did not trip and make a fool of herself before then.

Looking through the parted crowd, Audra followed the path they created straight toward the dais where the king and queen sat on their throne-like chairs, Graham at their sides. Although she saw them every day, Audra's heart pounded in her throat as she curtsied on shaking knees.

Do not fall. Do not fall. You have done this a million times. Audra silently cheered as she raised from her curtsey and addressed the king and queen. "Your Majesties. It is an honor to be here this evening." Her voice sounded stiff.

"The honor is ours, Lady Audra. We hope you have a wonderful evening." King Keld held back a smile, maintaining the appearance of treating her how he would any other guest.

"Thank you," Audra replied, turning to Graham and dipping into another curtsey. "Happy Ageday, Your Highness, and congratulations on your Hunt. May Hellig grant you continued strength, wisdom, and love this year." A ripple of shock crossed Graham's features before he masked it, and Audra worried that she had overstepped. Although it was not an outright declaration of her feelings, wishing him love was bolder than she had ever been.

"You gift me with your kindness, Lady Audra," he said, formality dripping from every word out of his mouth. Audra assumed he was following the king's lead, not wanting to show outright favoritism in front of the other guests. "Please, enjoy the evening."

The nobles closest to the dais, though not close enough to risk the safety of those on it, strained to hear the exchange, quickly glancing away as Audra turned to face them and joined Kasteel at the edge of the crowd. After her entrance, there were only a few guests waiting to be announced, and Audra watched as they greeted the royal family, half paying attention to the exchanges. The other half of her attention was focused on Graham, searching for hints in his expression to reveal if he was enjoying the night.

Like Kasteel and the king, Graham wore a sleeveless shirt, a light blue woven with gray, sharpening the steel of his eyes and the light tan of his skin. Silver buckles trailed a line down the shirt, shifting with his movements. Dove gray pants hugged his thighs like a second skin, and Audra's face flushed as she saw that they left little to the imagination. But the fresh line of ink, skin red and swollen while it healed, drew her gaze like a beacon of light in the dark. From a distance, she could not tell what symbol was etched into his skin, revealing what manner of creature he encountered during his Hunt, but it emphasized the curve of his arm, the strength he was capable of.

"Princess Esha of Feldor." As the herald announced the last guest,

Audra turned towards the entryway, surprise coursing through her body. She did not know that Feldor was sending a princess to the ball. Did the queen and king know? They must have known. Did Graham know?

A foreign princess could not have gained access to the kingdom without Keld and Isadora knowing. Then why would they have not told her? Audra tasted the bitter tang of disappointment and hurt at the realization that they kept it a secret. Watching the princess' measured walk toward the dais, Audra was able to get a better view of her as she drew closer. Tall, with thickly-braided black hair tucked behind her ears to showcase elaborate gold earrings, Princess Esha was stunning. An intricately beaded shawl draped over her arms, the golden fabric matching the dress that flowed like water over her body before pooling at her feet, complementing her bronze complexion. Each step carried her on an effortless glide toward the throne, no movement wasted on the journey.

"Your Majesties," she began, the rich alto of her voice matched her graceful bearing. As she curtsied, Esha adjusted her shawl, revealing gold bangles on her wrists that created twinkling music as they moved together. "You honor Feldor with your invitation. My family extends their congratulations on this happy occasion."

It is not fair that one person is so beautiful, Audra thought unkindly, wishing that Princess Esha had stayed in Feldor. Completely focused on her own reaction to the princess, Audra missed the sharp breath Kasteel took when he saw Princess Esha, his eyes drinking in the sight of her like a man finding water after days in a desert.

"You honor us with your presence, Your Highness." King Keld greeted her with the same level of courtesy shown to other guests.

"Your Highness." She turned to address Graham. "I wish you every happiness this year."

"Thank you. With a blessing from you, how could it be anything but happy." Graham's full smile caused Audra's heart to sink. This was not how the night was supposed to go. Eligible princesses were not supposed to show up unannounced. Well, at least not unannounced to her. And that smile, full lips parted to reveal his dimples. That smile was not meant for other women. An ugly, churning sensation started in Audra's stomach as she watched the princess curtsy and then move to stand next to the Feldorian emissary. Uncomfortably close to where Audra was standing.

Gaze drawn back to the dais by metal catching the light, Audra watched as Keld addressed the crowd.

"Esteemed guests, treasured friends, and loyal subjects. We welcome you on this special night. Today not only commemorates the twenty-first ageday of our son, Graham, but also the start of his responsibilities as a Guard."

Seamlessly weaving through the crowd, staff presented goblets of sparkling wine on silver trays.

"He has demonstrated courage and honor, and is ready to embrace the responsibility of defending his people. I'm so proud of you son," King Keld said as he turned toward Graham with damp eyes. "Join me in toasting your Crown Prince, Graham!"

The crowd raised their glasses as one, toasting the prince with the eager joy of people watching the future of the kingdom flourish. With one smooth motion, Graham swallowed the wine and the praise, fingers clenched tight against the glass.

"Are you sure he is alright?" Audra turned her face slightly and lowered her voice so that only Kasteel could hear.

"He'll be fine, just winding down from the ceremony. I promise." Kasteel's response was meant to reassure her, but Audra noticed that he kept a close eye on Graham's movements.

Passing his empty glass to a waiting server, Graham swept his arm in a wide arc, cueing the musicians positioned in an alcove.

"Maestro, some music, if you please. I believe the people were promised a ball." His words sent a laugh through the crowd. Then he turned and the opening notes of a waltz followed.

Audra spent years imagining this moment perfectly. Graham started down the marble steps, gaze intent and a smile lifting the left side of his face to reveal one dimple. Soft, purple-tinted moonlight filtered from the arched windows lining the sides of the ballroom, muting the sharp angles of Graham's jaw. A series of rich, clear notes flowed through the room from the cello, a violin repeating the notes shortly after like a dancer mimicking their partner's movements. Graham was the center of her universe and each of her senses flooded with him. Her heart pounded in a staccato beat, the rapid *thump-thump* drowning out the sounds of those around her, creating white noise. *It's him. It's him. It's him,* beat her heart. Audra's vision narrowed on his languid approach, blurring her peripheral vision into nothing but shapes and colors where people used to be. Although he was not close enough to confirm, Audra swore she could smell his unique scent of freshly-tilled earth, smoke, and cinnamon, a heady combination that always had her leaning closer to him. He was twenty steps away.

Ten.

Five.

Then his arm extended as his feet closed the distance. Reaching his hand out and bowing over the hand in its grasp.

Princess Esha's hand.

As if time slowed, Audra watched as Graham led Princess Esha onto the dance floor, her heart beating at a sluggish pace. Each inhalation felt like ice was splintering in her lungs, the pain of watching the couple like a physical wound, raw and gaping. Static noise was replaced by the dull roar of blood rushing through her body. Her dress felt tight and itchy, the skin underneath clammy. Audra tried to avert her gaze, but her eyes were frozen as they watched the couple twirl across the floor. It was as if her brain and body disconnected, her eyes fixed on Graham, even as tiny shards of her heart broke apart with each turn around the dance floor.

"Audra. Audra!" A sharp pinch at her elbow brought her focus back as Audra glared at Kasteel with tear-filled eyes. "I know you're hurt and this isn't how you thought the night would go, but you need to breathe and focus."

Kasteel subtly indicated to the lights closest to her dimming. "Control your magic. The entire court, among others, is watching you right now. You need to make them think you expected this. Don't give them your pain as a weapon to use against you." Sucking in a deep breath, Audra glanced at the crowd from the corner of her eye. People were watching her and murmuring behind fans and gloved-hands.

"I want to leave." Audra's voice wobbled at the request as she stuffed the emotions flooding her into a box. Maybe if she shoved them back far enough, she would not feel anything.

"I know, but if you leave now, they will see it as a weakness. You have to wait, pretend like it doesn't matter. That's the only way you win." Tucking her arm around his, Kasteel gave her a gentle smile. "I'll be with you the entire time."

Audra swallowed around the lump in her throat and took several steadying breaths. Kasteel was right. Her pain was not entertainment for the bored members of court. As long as she kept it hidden, no one would know how humiliating this was. *Besides,* she thought to herself, *it is just one dance. He probably thought dancing with Princess Esha first would strengthen the relationship with Feldor. I am sure Graham will dance with me next.*

But he did not. Pain turned into ire as she watched him dance with eligible lady after eligible lady, not once offering Audra a dance. It took all her concentration to breathe slowly through her nose and out her mouth, controlling the magic that wanted to lash out in response to her pain. Pain at the king and queen for inviting the princess. Pain at Graham for dancing with anyone but her. It was a relief when the first guests began to leave, allowing Audra the opportunity to slip away without bringing attention to herself. Wanting to be rid of any memory from the night, Audra fumbled with the buttons of her dress, tearing the fabric and ripping away buttons in her haste to be free of its confines. What had started as an optimistic manifestation of her dreams was now a tattered heap of cloth on the floor, surrounded by scattered hairpins. Looking at it unlocked the pain that Audra fought to keep hidden all night, so she curled up in her bed, holding tight to Isik, and cried.

<hr>

IN THE LATE hours of the night, Audra woke with a pounding headache and raw throat from crying. It seemed rude to wake one of the castle staff at this hour for something she could fix herself, so Audra put on her robe and left for the kitchen to warm a pot of water for tea. After years of exploring the castle, Audra needed no light to guide her way and she let the curving wall of the dark stairwell guide her path to the kitchen. Soft light from an open door pooled at the base of the stairs, and the sound of raised voices met her ears. Unsure who else would be awake at this hour, and not wanting to explain her own puffy-eyed presence in the kitchen, Audra slowly crept forward, intent on learning the identity of the other occupants and listening for their departure. Her pulse spiked when she heard the unmistakable drawl of Graham's voice.

"I've grown tired of your incessant nagging. Either join me for a drink or leave."

"You've had quite enough to drink already," Kasteel replied. "I know something happened on your Hunt, but it doesn't give you the right to act like an ass. Talk to me, brother. I want to help you."

"Help me? There's nothing wrong with me." A strangled laugh followed Graham's words. "This is about Audra, isn't it? It was just a dance."

"It wasn't just a dance and you know it. She expected you to propose tonight. She's loved you her whole life."

Hidden in the shadows, Audra held her breath, betrayal piercing her heart at having her feelings revealed. True as it was, Kasteel had no right to share her feelings.

"Is that what she truly wants? Our parents have pushed Audra in that direction our entire lives. Everyone has built up our relationship like a big fairytale, but did they ever stop to ask what she actually wanted? One dance wouldn't have changed anything."

"Then you should have talked to her first, not humiliate her. I'm not saying you have to marry her, but she deserves an explanation." Kasteel's shadow moved to place a comforting hand on Graham's shoulder.

"If you know so much about what she deserves, maybe you should marry her. One prince is hardly different from the other." Shoving aside the hand on his shoulder, Graham grabbed his bottle of wine and strode into the darkness. Rubbing a hand down his face, Kasteel bit out a curse before collecting his lamp and following his brother.

Darkness swallowed Audra as she fled from the stairs, seeking the reassuring comfort of her room. But it had never truly been her room. Everything in it belonged to the royal family of Solven. Audra was at the mercy of their generosity. A generosity that might end once they knew their son would never love her. She would never be Graham's wife. The thought made her physically ill, her body curling over itself, protecting the shattered pieces of her heart from falling out. As if by holding tight, it could force the pieces back together, making her whole again.

Staying here would kill her. If she had to watch Graham fall in love with another woman, Princess Esha the likely candidate, it would destroy her.

"I can't stay here." Audra let out a frustrated groan and began to pace. "But where would I go? I don't have any money. Nothing worth selling."

Realizing that she did have something to sell, Audra rushed to her dressing table. Inlaid with amethysts shaped like a four-pointed star, the silver brush and jewelry box from her mother had to be worth something. Feeling the crush of parchment under her feet stopped Audra before she reached the table. The letter from earlier mocked her from the ground, silently proclaiming that V was right. Audra was nothing but a pretend princess. But as she held the letter in her hands again, the previous message faded, and in its place was exactly what Audra needed.

Come home, Audra.

FIVE

Mages were not a common sight in Solven. Or anywhere for that matter. The small kingdom was located along the northern mountains of Solven's borders, but the mages of Ymira kept to themselves. People who sought the aid of mages returned with tales of secret rituals and harrowing journeys. Tales of children disappearing once they displayed magical talent. Similar to the shrouded mystery of the Guard ceremony, acts of magic were shared only among mages. On the rare occasion that a mage traveled, it was always in a pitch-black carriage with the curtains drawn to conceal the occupants. Audra now waited for such a carriage outside the castle gate, Isik at her side. Once she communicated her desire to travel to Ymira, V provided simple instructions.

> *I will send someone to collect you at first light. Wait outside the castle gates. Pack light.*

Packing was the easy part of the journey. Her valise held a few pairs of clothes, the book on Solven's history, and the gifts from her mother. Leaving a sealed envelope on her desk for the queen, Audra's steps were heavy, the knowledge that she was leaving the only home she knew was a weight on her shoulders. Each hallway and corner that she passed held a myriad of memories, sliding down the banister with Graham and Kasteel, sneaking desserts from the kitchen, staging mock battles in the spacious corridors. This was the last time she would smell the familiar scents of furniture polish and scented powder for cleaning, breakfast foods cooking in the oven, and banked fires. For ten years this was her home, but not any longer.

Emerging from the forest was Audra's future. Two midnight black horses pulled the carriage, mist swirling around them as their hooves hit the ground. It was unnerving how quiet the carriage was, the wheels rolling smoothly over the road without a single groan from the wood. As it approached, Audra noticed a small window at the front of the carriage, apparent due to the lack of driver. *Maybe the horses are magic,* she thought as they stopped precisely when the side door was level with her face. The only marking on the otherwise unadorned carriage was a silver plaque engraved with a crescent moon surrounded by three four-pointed stars. Wondering if she should open the door herself, since there was no one else in sight, Audra startled when the door swung out suddenly.

A long curtain of ink-black hair tipped with the color of the deep ocean was the first thing Audra saw. One pale hand with honey under-tones pressed against the door while the other pushed back the fall of hair to reveal a set of dark blue eyes glaring at Audra.

"Are you getting in or not? We don't have all day." The woman spoke with a slight rasp. Her voice sounded like it belonged to someone who had not experienced much joy in their life.

Greeting apparently over, the door began to swing closed. Reacting quickly, Audra grabbed the door, holding it open for Isik to jump inside.

"Wait," she said, and gestured to her bag. "What about my things?"

"Put it on the back. I'm not here to wait on you, princess," the woman huffed. The door closed with a slight shudder.

After securing her valise, Audra braced her foot on the carriage step, sparing one glance back at the castle. Could she really leave the only home she remembered? A fresh wave of tears pooled in her eyes at the memory of Graham's cold words and Audra roughly wiped them away before climbing into the carriage. Learning about magic was better than staying at the castle as an unwanted guest.

The horses began pulling the carriage around the moment she sat in the plush forward-facing seat. Isik was already comfortable, curled in the corner of the cushion with his head resting on his front paws. Contrasting the plain exterior, the interior of the carriage was tastefully appointed. Frosted glass lamps were mounted in each corner, their muted light providing a cozy atmosphere. The polished ebony wood gleamed in the lamplight, complementing the navy velvet seats. Each side of the carriage had windows lining the top-half of the door and side panels, and Audra watched as they passed through the entrance to the forest.

Although she knew it would have been painful to stay, watching the familiar sights of her childhood home grow distant filled her with melancholy. Leaving everything that was familiar felt like putting on a new pair of shoes, tight and stiff at first, but time and use would make it comfortable. That was what she hoped at least.

Pasting a pleasant smile on her face, Audra clasped her hands in her lap and waited for the mage to introduce herself. Moments ticked by with Audra staring at the side of the woman's face while she stared out the window. Maybe mages were not taught etiquette and she did not know it was polite to introduce herself first? No matter, Audra would just have to make the first move.

"My name is Audra. It is a pleasure to meet you."

A disgruntled look slid her way, as if Audra had interrupted her musing.

"Leah." Having provided the necessary response, she turned back toward the window.

Refusing to let the dismissal deter her, Audra attempted to start a conversation again. It was that, or continue to wallow in heartbreak.

"When I received the letter from V, I was not sure what to expect. Can you tell me about them?" She was infinitely curious about the mysterious entity behind the letters.

"You will meet her when we get to Ymira." This short reply was spoken towards the window.

Forcing cheer into her voice, Audra pressed on. "I look forward to it. How long have you lived there?"

"Look—" The sharp tone compared to the relatively bored note of her other responses, took Audra by surprise. Crossing one knee over the other, Leah regarded Audra from the opposite seat. "I know this is all new and exciting for you, and as happy as I am to guide you through this experience—" The words dripped with sarcasm. "—I had to travel at an ungodly hour to get you and would appreciate some peace and quiet so I can rest. Entertain yourself."

Audra's jaw snapped closed. Message received. This mage, Leah, was not interested in being her friend, nor being civil.

Fine. Audra was sure that she could make other friends. Not that she had much experience with it since Kasteel and Graham were her only two friends at the palace. Thinking about them brought fresh tears to her eyes and she tried to quickly blink them away. She did not need Leah noticing and complaining about her emotions disrupting the peace and quiet.

Glad that she had the foresight to pack a book, the one gifted from Graham, Audra pulled it out of her skirt pocket and settled into the seat to read.

The First Queen of Solven

Before she united the clans under one banner and formed the kingdom of Solven as our queen, Bria belonged to a warrior clan. Strong and fair, she led her clan with fierce protectiveness, constantly striving to enhance their position. It was said that Bria would spar with no less than eight opponents, could lift a tree trunk with one arm, and would personally tend to the sick and wounded. While her prowess on the battlefield was legendary, Bria was equally known for her ability to anticipate potential conflict and prevent it through alliances and trades. There was nothing she feared.

Until the dreaded black-blooded monsters began appearing. The first recorded sighting of a netvor is lost to time—if it ever existed at all—but it is well documented that Bria was the first to actively seek out the creatures. After a netvor attacked Bria's village, killing several people before a group of warriors were able to defeat it, she contacted other clan leaders and asked if they had encountered similar beasts. Soon, stories of violent attacks, done by horrible creatures, spread throughout the villages. Determined to root out the origin of these monsters, Bria took several of her strongest warriors to search for answers. After traveling for several months, they tracked down a rumor that revealed a horrible truth. Dark magic from a mage named Dyrun infected malevolent people, turning them into monsters.

For the first time, Bria felt fear. The abominations were already incredibly strong, requiring multiple warriors to take them down. Two of her warriors were killed in a battle against one, and countless innocents were slaughtered. She wondered how they could stand against a mage powerful enough to create such monsters.

Feeling hopeless, Bria prayed to Hellig for guidance and was blessed with a vision. In it, Bria was guided to a cave that was only accessible through a mountain pass. Stopping for the night at the base of a mountain, the warriors asked what they were searching for.

"A way to become strong enough to stop those creatures," she said.

The next morning, Bria and a few of the warriors woke up feeling stronger and faster than they had before, eyes glowing ice blue. Armed with their new power, Bria and her warriors, the first Guards, began rallying their allies and forming new alliances, determined to eliminate the netvor and Dyrun.

Stretching her arms above her head to remove lingering stiffness from sitting in the carriage, Audra looked at the imposing mountain face before her. After several hours of travel and pausing occasionally to stretch their legs, they cleared the forest and were welcomed by the sight of the miles of lush fields and farmland that lay at the foot of the mountain. Vibrant hues of green created a patchwork quilt, divided by the winding path of a river.

"That river flows from Maneseen Lake, where our village sits. If you follow its path, you'll find where it disappears into the mountains. Beyond that is Ymira," Leah explained as they filled jugs of water for the remainder of the journey and let the horses rest.

Once they were back in the carriage, Audra asked, "What is Ymira like?"

"Like nothing you've heard, I'm sure. We don't make sacrifices or kidnap people. We value our privacy and protect our way of life. Ymira is a place where mages are safe to practice magic. We have farms, craftspeople, and entertainment just like you're used to. You can hike through the mountains or swim in the lake on warm, summer days. In the winter, we gather in homes drinking warm wine and sharing stories around the fire." Talking about Ymira softened the tense lines in Leah's face.

"It sounds beautiful." Hearing about the place she would call home eased some of Audra's fear of the unknown.

"It is. Different from what you're used to, though. Mages survive by being self-sufficient. No staff to clean up after you."

Audra huffed in frustration. "I know how to take care of myself." She had not learned four languages or an entire continent's worth of etiquette by sitting on her hands.

"We'll see about th—" Interrupted by a sharp jostle of the carriage, Leah paused and tipped her head towards the window. The packed-dirt road was replaced with a rocky path that followed the curve of the river up into the mountains. Craning her neck out the window, Audra swallowed past the fear blocking her throat at the steep incline the path followed, obscured by low clouds. To make matters worse, the sun had begun its descent, and what light the horses could see by would vanish. Darkness provided the perfect cover for netvor to attack.

Audra's voice cracked as she looked away from the window. "It seems unwise to continue traveling at night. Maybe we should stop and continue the journey in the morning?"

"We are perfectly safe...Just keep watching the road." The complete lack of alarm in Leah's voice calmed Audra slightly. With the horses' heads as her focal point, Audra watched as they slowly reached the crest of a hill, unable to see what lay ahead. As they cleared the turn, the air around the horses shimmered like oil on water.

Like curtains parting, the view changed from the precipitous climb to a stunning valley. Orange light from the setting sun filtered between the mountain peaks, bathing everything it touched with a warm glow.

At the eastern edge of the valley lay Maneseen Lake, its gently flowing water reflecting the light like stars. A small manor resided on the northern edge of the lake, surrounded by a village to the west. Tendrils of smoke rose from cottage chimneys dotting the farms to the south.

"How is this? Where did it...?" Audra trailed off, head pivoting to the path behind them, now appearing as an innocuous trail. "And do not just tell me 'magic.' I know that."

"At least you aren't as empty-headed as you look. That's promising. We just passed through the ward. Similar to a gate, it keeps out unwanted visitors. Those wishing to find Ymira start on the same path we did. If they approach the ward with ill intent, they will find themselves wandering through the dangerous paths of the mountain until they leave or perish." There was no remorse in her tone for their deaths. "Those with good intent, or possessing magic, are able to approach and are greeted by a mage. I sent a note to inform the patrol of our arrival so they would not stop us. Passing through the ward alerts the High Mage of our arrival."

"That was thoughtful, thank you." Travel-worn was not the first impression Audra wanted to leave. "How has the ward lasted so many years?" Even magelights, charged with magic, faded after several years.

"The mages on patrol monitor the ward for fluctuations and repair any places where the magic is thin. It takes immense focus and power to maintain the wards, something only powerful mages can accomplish."

Any amount of magic seemed powerful to Audra, but she supposed that was just because she had much to learn. As the carriage continued down the sloping path towards the lake, Audra leaned against the window to get a better look at her new home. Wildflowers sprouted from the ground, covering the rolling fields in a kaleidoscope of colors. Curving with the base of the mountain were tall evergreen trees, their thick branches providing shade for the plants beneath them. The fresh smell of tilled earth, decaying leaves, and scented plants carried memories of playing in the woods as a child, reminding her of Graham and causing her heart to clench painfully.

"It is incredible," Audra whispered reverently. For all its grandeur, the royal palace was removed from nature, dedicating space for training grounds, stables, and opulent rooms. Even the royal garden lacked the raw connection to nature that Ymira had.

"Just wait until you see Rauha Hall." Leah's mouth curved up slightly. "No castle in the world can compare."

We will see about that, Audra thought to herself. After all, she grew up in a castle and it seemed unlikely that a manor house could be more impressive than that. Though there were many words Audra could use to describe Leah, hyperbolic was not one of them. When it finally came into view, Audra had to force her jaw not to drop in wonder.

Rauha Hall was three-stories of weathered, ruddy-colored bricks. Curved edges and rounded roofs softened what could have appeared as an imposing structure. Instead of pushing nature out, it was integrated with the hall. Boxes of flowers and shrubs bloomed beneath the windows. A large garden sat on the eastern side of the building, ending with a curved tower covered in vines. Trees stood guard along a pebbled-covered path, leading the way to the open courtyard. The longest side of the building faced the lake, reflections of the water rippled across large windows. Rolling to a stop before the stairs to the front door, Audra agreed that Leah was right. Rauha Hall was unlike any castle she had ever seen.

"Usually, you would be expected to assist with taking care of the horses after the journey, but the High Mage is expecting you. And she doesn't like to be kept waiting." Leah hopped off the carriage step with muttered directions on how to find the High Mage's room.

Audra barely had time to remove her valise before Leah turned the horses toward the stables, the sharp staccato of their footfalls ringing through the night air. Isik barked a sharp note of displeasure at being so rudely dismissed, hopping out of the carriage behind Audra.

A simple wooden door stood at the top of stairs, its iron handle cold in Audra's hand. It opened soundlessly to a polished entryway decorated with embroidered tapestries. On the left was a stone staircase with a mahogany banister, carved with images of the surrounding forest and mountains that continued up the second and third floors. The center of the room was open, the heat of a fire warming Audra's skin, the small seating area welcoming her tired feet. Ignoring Audra's hissed words to stay nearby, Isik promptly walked off to explore his new home. The murmured sound of people talking somewhere above her reminded Audra that she could not rest until she met with the High Mage. Too preoccupied with wondering what the mysterious V was like and how she would fit in at Rauha, Audra hardly paid attention to her surroundings, nearly tripping on the stairs when she reached them.

Maybe I should have tried to train more with the soldiers. Audra's breathing was ragged after climbing three flights of winding stairs. Taking several deep breaths, Audra adjusted her hair and clothing before knocking on the door.

"Enter," a smooth voice called from inside the room. Standing behind a large wooden desk, looking out a window with hands clasped behind her back, was a tall, athletically-built woman. Finely dressed in an embroidered black jacket covering black pants, the High Mage was nothing like Audra expected. Although this was only the second mage she encountered, Audra expected her to look more...well, magical. The person in front of her could have been anyone from the kingdoms. Her brown hair was dusted with gray and cut close to her head, highlighting a square jawline and light-brown skin.

"You must be Audra," the woman said as she turned. "My name is Valeria, High Mage of Ymira." Her voice reminded Audra of a crackling fire, warm but dangerous.

Not quite sure what the protocol was amongst mages, Audra gave a small curtsey. "Thank you for having me. Your home is lovely."

"There is no need for that." Valeria flicked her hands like she was brushing the air. "You will soon find that life in Ymira is not as formal as you are used to." Gesturing to one of the chairs in front of the desk, Valeria continued, "Please, sit. I'm sure you are tired from your journey."

"I enjoyed the views along the way."

"A tactful way to imply that the company left much to be desired." Valeria's smile softened the harsh set of her face, small creases forming beside her brown eyes. "Leah does not make the best first impression and has a difficult time making friends. Nonetheless, I hope you can work past that as the two of you will share quarters along with another mage."

Audra had her doubts about getting along with the prickly mage, but she knew it would not end well for her if she did not at least attempt to be cordial. Leah had lived here for years and her word would carry more weight than Audra's should a disagreement occur. "I will do my best."

"See that you do. What you gain from your time here is completely up to you. Everyone in Ymira worked hard to get where they are, and I expect no less from you. Your age and lack of understanding of basic principles of magic are less than ideal." Valeria held up a hand when Audra opened her mouth to defend herself. "But we will not allow that to hold you back. You have immense potential and if you apply yourself diligently, I am confident that you could be one of the most powerful mages of our time."

That seemed impossible. Audra was intelligent and worked hard, but powerful? It was not a word often associated with her.

"May I ask you a personal question?" Valeria passed her a cup of tea and Audra nodded.

"After years of hiding your magic and refusing my offers to train you, you finally accepted. Why?"

Audra pulled at a loose thread of fabric on her skirt while she sought an answer that would satisfy Valeria without drawing attention to her humiliation. "It seemed like a better choice than the one waiting for me." Just the thought of facing Graham after his rejection had her stomach turning.

"Learning that the prince did not share your feelings must have been difficult. I'm sorry."

Tensing in her seat, Audra wondered how Valeria knew what transpired. Based on the appearance of the letters, she assumed there was a magical way to spy on people.

"You do not have to lie. Your letters made it clear that you never wanted me to be a princess. I am here now, you should be happy that you got what you wanted," Audra snapped.

"Just because I wanted to see you reach your full potential, not settle for a life chosen for you, does not mean I cannot understand your pain." Valeria's chastisement was softened by the empathetic look in her eyes.

Almost as soon as the words exited her mouth, Audra felt guilt at her anger. "You are right, that was disrespectful. I apologize." It was not

Valeria's fault that she was hurt. Just as quickly as the anger built, it fizzled back into heartache.

"Thank you. One of the first things you'll need to practice is controlling your emotions." A slight strain was evident in Valeria's tone. "Magic is closely tied to one's emotions, feeding off the intent behind them. Just now, your magic reacted to your pain and anger. It radiated off of you in a misguided attempt to protect you. With your lack of training up until this point, it's a miracle you haven't caused a disaster."

"I spilled tea on a lord once." A small giggle escaped her lips at the memory. Valeria's throaty laugh caught Audra by surprise.

"He probably deserved it," Valeria said. "You sound just like your mother when you laugh."

Audra sat forward in her seat, not wanting to miss a word that Valeria said. There were so few people who could share memories of her mother and Audra greedily absorbed every piece of information. "Really? You knew her?"

"Of course, I did. Didn't anyone tell you? She was born in Ymira, as was I."

Tingles of excitement worked their way through Audra at the thought of returning to the place where her mother was born. Would she walk the same paths her mother did? Learn the same things?

"She died when I was little, and it hurt my father too much to speak about her. Did she study magic too?"

"Unfortunately not. Blessed by Hellig in many other ways, your mother did not have the gift of magic," Valeria replied. "My father and I lived in the house next to your mother's family in the village. She was one of my closest friends. As the years went on, it became apparent that she was not gifted with magic, and the disappointment weighed on her. When she was your age, your mother left Ymira to live amongst the people of Solven. It was the last time I saw her."

Eyes downcast at the memory, the elder mage frowned and turned towards the window.

After a long pause, during which Audra wondered if she should leave, Valeria switched topics. "Starting tomorrow, I will begin instructing you, but before you retire for the night, I wanted to conduct a small assessment of your capabilities. That way I can see where we are starting from." Valeria waved her hand and a pale crystal floated from a nearby shelf over to the desk, settling in front of Audra. "I want you to focus on the crystal and make it float."

"How?" Confusion laced her tone as Audra glanced from the crystal to Valeria.

"Magic is an expression of your will. Feel the magic inside you, harness its power, and then guide it to lift the crystal."

Furrowing her brows, Audra turned her thoughts inward. Using magic was something she had only done unintentionally. What did Valeria mean "feel the magic inside you?" How was she supposed to know how it felt? The longer Valeria stared at her, the more nervous energy filled Audra. She directed her focus to her heartbeat, the wounded organ revealing no underlying energy. A bead of sweat slid down Audra's back as she shifted in her seat. *What if I can't find my magic? Will they make me leave? It is just lifting one crystal Audra, do not embarrass yourself.* Pulling her lower lip between her teeth, Audra's eyes strained as they focused on the crystal. *Move!*

"That's enough Audra," Valeria addressed her while leaning forward to remove the crystal from the desk.

"No, wait! I can do it. Please give me another chance," Audra implored.

"I said that is enough," Valeria's firm tone silenced any argument Audra had. "You can try again tomorrow."

"Tomorrow? You mean I get to stay even though I failed the test?"

"One attempt does not equal failure, Audra. You will try again and again and again until you succeed. Failure only occurs when you stop trying. Do you understand?"

"Yes."

"Good. Now, you had a long journey today and should rest before your training begins tomorrow. Breakfast is at seven and I will collect you once you finish helping clean the dishes. Leah is waiting for you at the bottom of the stairs to take you to your room."

Dismissed, Audra rose from her chair and bid Valeria a good night. Despite Valeria's reassurance that her training would continue, Audra felt lingering disappointment at her inability to lift the crystal. If she could not control her magic, would she fit in Ymira any more than she did at the palace?

As soon as she saw Audra, Leah began walking in what Audra could only assume was the direction of their bedroom. Grateful that the other girl was disinclined to talk, Audra kept track of which stairs they used and the turns they took so that she would not need an escort just to reach her bedroom. They stopped in front of a door at the end of a corridor on the second floor. Gesturing for Audra to enter first, Leah stepped back as Audra opened the door and took a step into the room.

"You're here!" A blur of curly black hair and gangly limbs knocked into Audra before she fully entered the room. "I heard the carriage arrive and wanted to greet you, but Valeria said you had to meet with her first and that I should wait here for you instead. So I waited and waited and now you're finally here!" The small figure's words came tumbling into Audra's shoulder, increasing in speed and volume until Audra was worried that the girl had forgotten how to breathe.

"It is a pleasure to meet you," Audra spoke around the constricting hug. "Are you my third roommate?"

"Yep!" The girl beamed at Audra with a wide smile and luminous golden brown eyes that were stunning against her dark brown skin. Based on her still-growing limbs and slightly rounded face, Audra guessed that the girl was a year or two younger than her. "My name is Taara. You are going to love it here. We hardly ever get new mages and it's even better that you get to share a room with us! And—Oh. my. GOSH! It's so cute!" Taara's squeal was close enough to Audra's ear that she thought it would damage her hearing. Turning to see what caused the burst of excitement, Audra saw Isik sitting on the floor, letting Taara smother him with affection.

"Meet Isik. He loves it when people scratch his ears, and if you catch him a fish, he will be your friend for life."

"Then I will just have to catch you as many fish as possible," Taara said with a kiss on his forehead. Isik looked smug, what could almost pass for a smile pulling his lips up. "How did you get him?"

The joy of the memory was overshadowed by sadness. "He was a gift from the royal family."

Taara sprang back up, looping her arm through Audra's. "Valeria said that you lived in a castle! Can you teach me how to be a princess?"

A sharp pang resounded in Audra's chest at the reminder of her lost dream. It hurt to think about everyone she left at the palace, but Taara watched her expectantly, her body practically buzzing with energy.

"Well, I—" Audra began.

"At least let her put her stuff down before you begin the interrogation, Taara." Leah strode past Audra into the room. Whether Leah knew that the topic made her uncomfortable and meant to spare her from it or not, Audra appreciated the interruption.

"Right, sorry, Audra." Taara winced. "Leah has to remind me when I get carried away. This is our room." Arms stretched wide, Taara spun in a slow circle, encompassing the small room. Along each wall was a small bed, pointed towards one another in a triangle, accompanied by a nightstand and wardrobe. A series of magelights hung from the ceiling at different lengths with windows spaced evenly throughout the interior walls to provide light. Taara pointed to the bed on the right. "That is your bed. I hope you like it."

"I am sure it will be fine." Audra smiled at Taara's infectious enthusiasm. The bed was smaller than she was used to and it would be her first time sharing a room with others, but it looked comfortable enough.

Watching Audra stow her limited possessions, Taara informed Audra that she could purchase anything she needed in town. "I am afraid I will have to make do with this. I do not have any money for new clothes."

A soft snort came from Leah's direction. "It must be a tragedy for you, going from having everything to having nothing."

Leah's sardonic tone was grating on Audra, but she did not have the energy to argue with her that evening. Plus, she promised Valeria that she would try to get along with the prickly mage. Ignoring Leah's comment, Audra turned toward Taara.

"Would you show me where the washroom is? It's been a long day and I would like to clean up before heading to bed."

"But it's still so early." Taara deflated a little. "We have a small washroom through that door, but just wait until you see the hot springs in the cavern. They're so big you can swim in them!"

"That sounds incredible! I really appreciate all your help tonight, Taara." Audra felt bad for dampening her spirits. "And I am looking forward to getting to know you better."

"Me too! Have a good night, Audra."

"You too, Taara." Closing the door, Audra quickly cleaned off and prepared for bed. Slipping beneath the covers, Audra closed her eyes and tried to let the exhaustion of the day drag her into a dreamless sleep. Instead, her brain tortured her by flashing memories of Graham, the ball, and the conversation in the kitchen behind her closed lids. Clutching Isik against the gaping cavity where her heart used to be, Audra let her tears flow, quieting her sobs to not disturb her roommates.

SIX

Breakfast was served in a small dining room that overlooked the green lawn leading to the lakeshore. Audra looked around the tastefully decorated room, green striped wallpaper and dark wood paneling creating a comfortable atmosphere. The smell of freshly baked bread, sweet fruit, and grilled meat hit Audra's nose and caused her stomach to grumble despite the queasy grief that made eating difficult. Isik sniffed around the edges of the room, whining softly when he could not find his usual bowl of food. Heart breaking at the sight of her beloved fox looking lost, Audra quickly put together a plate of edible food for him. Leah mumbled something about spoiling the animal, but Audra ignored her. After filling their plates, Audra, Taara, and Leah sat at the long table across from two mages who looked around Leah's age, only a few years older than Audra.

Setting down his cup of tea, the mage dressed in a loose, basil colored shirt and fawn pants smiled at Audra and leaned forward in his wheeled chair. "So, you must be the girl everyone's talking about. I'm Eli, nice to meet you." His round, rosey face and curly, golden hair gave him an endearing appearance that was complemented by a wide smile.

"Eli's incredible at making salves and potions," Taara supplied from Audra's left.

"You'll have to visit the garden. It's magic all on its own. Putting your hands in the soil, tending to each leaf and—"

He was interrupted by a man with golden skin and perfectly coiffed black hair. "If we let Eli continue, he would talk about plants until your ears fall off." He inclined his head toward Audra. "Silvan. Welcome to Rauha. Maybe things will finally liven up now that you're here."

"I am really not that exciting," Audra replied.

"Oh, please." Silvan waved off her statement with a well manicured hand, his eyes sharp. "Valeria has been trying to get you here for years. There must be something interesting about you." He leaned forward, his silver shirtsleeves resting on the table. Unlike the relaxed dress Audra had encountered in Ymira so far, Silvan's style was more suited to a courtier. A finely embroidered vest fit over his shirt perfectly, not a single wrinkle marring its appearance over midnight black trousers. "So, what was life like at the palace?"

Audra shifted in her seat as four sets of eyes focused on her. Hurt cast a shadow over even the happiest of her memories at the palace, and she worried about her ability to share without crying. "It was great. Most days, I would study with the queen or a tutor, read, plan royal events, and take walks through the garden."

"Sounds a lot like what we do here," Leah commented. "Not all that exciting."

"Yeah, except we don't live in a *castle*," Silvan replied dryly.

Audra was desperate to change the topic of conversation. "Can you tell me more about what life is like at Rauha?"

Eli and Silvan, Adura learned, both lived at Rauha Hall. While they were talking, a few older mages filtered through the room, grabbing food and quietly sitting amongst themselves.

"For most of us, we work in areas that best suit our abilities. There are artisans, potion makers, and armorsmiths that create goods for sale within Ymira or trade with traveling merchants. Some of us—" Eli gestured toward Silvan and Leah. "—guard the wards and cultivate the crystal cavern, where the crystals for lights and charms come from. Taara, and I guess you now, study with elder mages."

"You're all about the work, Eli. Some of us also like to have fun." Silvan nudged Eli playfully. "There is a pub in town and we have festivals to celebrate major events. Those with artistic talents occasionally put on shows or exhibits, which would be more fun if we were allowed to show off outside Ymira."

Leah huffed. "Yeah, those *with* talent. No one wants to hear your attempt at playing the lute again."

It was slightly overwhelming watching the group interact. They were obviously comfortable around each other, sharing quips and laughing as they recalled previous festivals. Unlike the polite conversations at court, this group interrupted each other, laughed loudly, and lacked artifice. Audra felt like an outsider looking in, lonely and a little jealous at the group's affection for one another.

Glancing at the clock, Silvan winced and stood. "As much fun as I'm having, I'd better get going if I'm going to get to my watch on time." The rest of the group said their goodbyes and left for their respective duties.

"You're helping with kitchen duty, right?" Leah waited for confirmation. "Follow me and try to keep up."

Audra watched as Leah stacked plates, gathering her own stack and struggling to balance the uneven tower. "A little help over here?"

Leah rolled her eyes and set down the dishes she was carrying to show Audra how to properly stack them. "I forgot how useless princesses are."

"I am not a princess."

"Could have fooled me." Leah led the way to the kitchen, where they placed the dishes on a counter before going back to the dining room to remove the empty serving trays. "Scraps go into that bucket for compost. Do you know how to dry?"

Audra shook her head. "Can you not use magic for that?"

"Of course, *I* can. Can you?"

"No." Audra glowered behind Leah's back.

"I'm not using magic to get you out of your share of the chores. Besides, I have my own work to do." Each dish rose from the pile as Leah used magic to draw them into the sink and scrub them off, sending the clean dishes to a new pile by Audra. Together, they worked in silence until the kitchen was spotless. Surprisingly, even though Leah finished with her portion of the chores first, she stayed until Audra was done. Probably to make sure that Audra did not shirk her responsibility.

"Stay here until Valeria comes to get you," Leah said and then walked out of the room.

Well, goodbye to you, too, Audra thought as she watched Leah depart. Arms tired from the unaccustomed work, Audra was glad to sit on a chair by the fire while she waited for Valeria. The spots of water on her dress were evidence of her lack of experience drying dishes, and Audra appreciated the opportunity to dry off before she started training. At the sound of heavy footsteps, Audra stood and turned toward the open doorway as Valeria entered the room, dressed in another all-black ensemble.

"Good morning, Audra. Did you enjoy breakfast?"

"Yes, thank you. The view of the lake is incredible."

Valeria clasped her hands at the waist. "I am glad you think so, because that is where our lessons will take place. There is plenty of space for you to learn to control your magic without harming anyone." Leading the way out the side door, Valeria gestured for Audra to exit first. Just outside the kitchen was the small patch of herbs that Audra noticed on her arrival. Meticulously cared for, each row was evenly spaced with small posts indicating what was growing. As they curved around the building, Audra tipped her face towards the sun, allowing the rays to warm her skin.

Something brushed against her leg and Audra looked down to see Isik rush past, bounding across the lawn.

"Friend of yours?" Valeria raised an eyebrow when Isik returned to them and nipped at her pants.

"More like family. Sorry about him. Isik must have extra energy after being in the carriage all day yesterday." Audra wished that she had a toy to throw for him. But Valeria surprised her, using magic to lift some leaves and send them off into the forest for Isik to chase. Before he raced off, Isik rubbed against Audra's ankles and looked at her as if checking she was safe.

"What a curious creature," Valeria said as they watched Isik disappear into the forest.

"He does like to explore, but he knows when to come back." Stopping just before the grass turned into the rocky shore, Valeria gestured to a woven blanket laid on the ground.

"I was actually referring to his attachment to you. Many animals are drawn to mages, our connection to nature through magic linking us together, but for Isik to almost sense your emotions is remarkable."

"It may seem silly," Audra mused, "to think that he understands me, but Isik has comforted me and been a friend when I had few others."

Valeria watched her closely. "It is only silly if you think it is. Do not let others dictate how you feel. If Isik is your family, then embrace it. Life is too short to wither away under the expectations of others."

Mulling it over, Audra tried to merge this advice with the lessons of her childhood. Was that why Graham rejected her, because she did not meet his expectations? Life as a royal was lived in the spotlight, and people were constantly judging every action and word. It became second-nature to mask her true feelings behind a polite facade. Was it necessary, or just what she was used to?

"I hope you don't mind." Valeria cut into her thoughts. "But I would like to get to know you better before we begin. Understanding your motivations and experiences will help me develop lessons that fit your needs."

Swallowing around the nervous lump that formed in her throat, Audra hoped her smile did not reveal her unease. "Whatever you think is best. I am curious to learn more about you, about all magical topics really." Maybe if she asked enough questions, they would not have to talk about her as much.

"I would be surprised if you didn't. How much experience have you had with magic?"

While explaining her limited use of magic, Audra watched the gentle roll of the lake's surface catch the light. Based on the letters she sent, Audra was surprised that Valeria did not know every detail surrounding her magical outbursts.

"So, in each instance, your use of magic was unintentional?" Audra nodded in confirmation. "Did you ever try using magic intentionally?" Valeria's voice was as soothing as the ebb and flow of the water, the morning breeze rustling her loose black pants and tunic.

"No, I did not think using magic was necessary."

"Why?" There was no judgment in her tone.

"It...I..." Audra paused to think it over. She remembered an instance where she began stirring her tea with magic while with the queen. Recalling Isadora's reaction, Audra responded, "Because I did not need magic when there were Guards and soldiers to protect me."

"I see. Did you not want to use the gift Hellig gave you?"

"I never saw it as a gift." Audra tucked her knees into her chest and wrapped her arms around them. "Most of the time I used magic, it hurt people. Not badly," she was quick to add, "and while it is not banned in Solven, mages are not exactly welcome. It was easier to just ignore that I could use magic."

"Did the prince have anything to do with that decision?"

Audra began tugging at a loose thread on the blanket, hoping that choosing to remain silent would bore Valeria into moving on from the conversation. With each minute that passed, Valeria's neutral expression remained unchanged and she showed no inclination to talk. "He actually wanted me to use magic, but I would rather not talk about it."

Respecting her request, Valeria moved on. "I want you to remember something very important, Audra. Magic is part of who you are, and when you reject it, you reject part of yourself. By suppressing your magic, it allows your emotions to overpower any control you might have."

Valeria guided her into a seated position, legs crossed with her palms resting upright on her knees. "You need to sift through your emotions and empty your mind to find the core of your magic. Close your eyes and let your thoughts drift away."

Eyes closed, Audra tried to empty her mind. But each brush of wind against her face or call of a bird drew her attention away to focus on the new sensation. How long did she have to do this?

"Focus on your breathing. Inhale for three...two...one, and exhale for three...two...one." Valeria breathed steadily through her mouth. "With each thought that crosses your mind, acknowledge its presence, then dismiss it."

After four breaths, Audra felt a piece of hair drift across her face and tickle her nose. Rubbing it, Audra wondered if she had a ribbon to tie back her hair. *Focus*, she reminded herself, *address the thought and let it go.* That worked for several more breaths, before she heard something splash in the water and wondered what it was. The pattern continued for some time, until Audra started shifting from side to side. Cracking open one of her eyes, she watched Valeria to see if they were done.

"Excuse me, Valeria, how much longer are we going to sit here?"

"Until you no longer think about how long we've been sitting here."

"But I do not feel any closer to finding my magic. Are you sure this works?"

With a slightly exasperated sigh, Valeria turned to face her. "There are no shortcuts to learning magic, Audra. Your emotions are clouding your ability to find your center. By learning to empty your mind, magic will not have to fight to get your attention. Once you find your magic, it will get easier to summon it."

"But I do not even know what I'm searching for. What does it feel like?"

"What does it feel like to be happy? Or sad? Or any other emotion? You'll know when you find it."

Audra frowned at the cryptic message. She will know when she found it? That was definitely not helpful. How useful was sitting in silence, focusing on her breathing? There was nothing magical about that. At this rate, it would be years before she even figured out how to find her magic.

"Trust me, Audra. I know this seems pointless, but I promise it will help."

Oh, no. Did she say that part aloud? "Okay."

Folding her knees under her, Valeria rose gracefully. "A mage named Darius taught me these techniques after a very difficult time in my life, when I was angry and had little control over my magic. With time, I know that they will help you too. In the meantime, we can work on your stamina. Each mage is blessed with varying potential for magic. Some hold small amounts of power inside them, and others vast oceans of power. There is always more to learn about magic, but one truth that has never changed is that each mage's capacity for magic is finite. The more you learn and grow, the more magic you can use without reaching the edge of your capacity."

"How will I know when I reach the edge?"

"The same way you know you are close to your limit when exercising. Your limbs will tire, your body will drain of all energy, and you could lose consciousness if you push too far. Push past your limit, and it could be the last thing you ever try."

Audra paled at the thought. Now that she knew what it was like to use magic, the thought of accidentally going too far filled her with unease.

Standing, Audra watched as Valeria guided her through a series of poses, pulling muscles in her body that she had never felt before. It took all of her focus to remain standing as Audra twisted her torso over a lunge and Valera reminded her to breathe.

Audra cursed when she wobbled from a one-legged stand and fell to the ground.

"Just stand up and try again."

So she did.

THE SUN WAS BEGINNING its descent when Valeria dismissed Audra, informing her that they would meet each morning by the lake after her chores. Her legs and arms were vibrating with exhaustion as she made her way back to the castle. Valeria made the exercise look easy, but Audra's aching muscles suggested otherwise. Looking at the stairs, Audra wondered if she really needed to visit her room before dinner. Would it look bad for her to crawl up the stairs so that she did not have to move her legs? For a brief moment, she imagined curling up on one of the couches on the first floor and not moving until the next morning.

"How was your first day?" Eli wheeled next to Audra.

"It was really good," Audra replied with a fake smile. "How was your day?"

"Most of the day was spent in the greenhouse, so it was great. I know we just met, but you don't have to say you had a good day just to be polite." Eli used a lift to join Audra on the second floor, turning in the direction of her room. "I know what it's like trying to fit in, so I won't judge you if the day wasn't great. Valeria is teaching you, right?"

Audra nodded. "Meditation wasn't easy for me either, but it does get better."

"Thanks Eli. It definitely wasn't what I expected when I thought about learning magic. Especially not the exercise. My body is so weak, I am worried that once I sit down, I will never be able to get back up," Audra said dryly.

Then she glanced at Eli and realized the implication of her words. "Oh! I am so sorry Eli. That was insensitive of me."

Audra felt shame slide down her throat at the thoughtless words.

Eli chuckled before saying, "I know what you meant, so don't worry about it. Being in a chair is part of who I am and I'm not ashamed of it." He slowed to a stop in front of her door, his voice kind. "I know you weren't saying it to be rude."

"I'll be more thoughtful with my words next time. Thanks, Eli." Audra bid Eli farewell before walking into the room and slumping against the closed door. This day had not gone the way she expected. She thought that magic would come easily and her inability to focus enough to channel magic was disappointing. Whenever Audra was angry or upset, magic came without thought. Now, when she needed to prove that she belonged here, Audra could not even figure out how to bring it to the surface.

"Rough day, princess?" Leah closed the book that she was reading on her bed.

"I will manage," Audra sighed and pushed off the door, heading toward her closet for a change of clothes. "And, again, I am not a princess."

"You certainly dress like one. How did training with Valeria go?"

As she reached for a clean dress, Audra's arm ached at the stretch. "It was unexpected, but I am sure it will get easier with time. Now, if you will excuse me I would like to bathe and then rest before dinner."

"Go right ahead." Leah gave a mocking bow and returned to her book. "Just don't rest too long. We're on dish duty after dinner."

After cleaning the dried sweat from her body and changing into fresh clothes, Audra lay on her bed and tried to rest. Unfortunately, her mind refused to quiet and paraded memories behind her closed lids. Without the distraction of being around others or physical activity, her thoughts returned to the events that led to her arrival in Ymira. Remembering Graham dancing with Princess Esha and confessing his disinclination to marry Audra sent hot lances of pain through her heart. Her breathing became ragged and tears slipped from the corners of her eyes. She just wanted to stop hurting.

Breathe in and breathe out. Valeria's calm voice filtered through her thoughts. Focusing, Audra drew in steady breaths, then released them, dismissing each thought that interrupted the practice. Still far from perfect, it did help dull the anguish. So Audra continued until she was able to drift into sleep.

The next morning, Audra woke to find a set of flexible pants and loose top at the end of her bed. Having conversed little at dinner the previous evening and retiring to bed early, Audra frowned at the thought of someone entering the room to deliver the clothes while she slept.

"Those will help you move easier." Leah was putting on her own pair of pants, made of a sturdier fabric than the ones Audra was holding. Her change in attitude from mocking to reluctantly helpful was suspicious. "We wouldn't want you hurting your pretty face." There was the response Audra was anticipating.

"Don't be mean, Leah." Taara flopped onto Audra's bed to pet Isik. "She won't get hurt training with Valeria."

Audra's relief was short-lived.

"You're right, you can't get hurt if you can't even use magic." Leah's look of satisfaction seared Audra as she walked out the door.

"Don't listen to Leah. I'm sure you'll be using magic in no time. It just takes some practice."

"Thanks, Taara. To be honest, I thought it would be easier than it is. Did everyone else have difficulty in the beginning?" At least if she was not the only one it would make Audra feel better.

"Valeria says that everyone has their own difficulties to face. What's easier for me might not be for you, and that's okay." Taara squeezed her hand gently. "You just have to keep trying." She flashed a bright smile as she stood and pushed the clothes into Audra's arms. "Hurry up and get dressed, or we'll miss breakfast."

Silvan, Eli, and Leah were already seated when Taara and Audra made their way into the dining room, plates full of food before them. Fluffy white clouds decorated the sky and muted the bright sunlight shining through the windows. Issuing greetings to the group, Audra filled her plate and sat down to eat. To her surprise, there was a plate of food waiting for Isik in the corner, and when Audra asked the group about it, Leah's cheeks turned a suspicious shade of pink. Exercising the previous day increased her appetite and Audra was glad for the excuse to keep her mouth occupied while she listened to the group's conversation.

"We had another family come to the ward yesterday," Silvan shared. "A cobbler, her husband and two daughters. They realized the eldest had magic when she began levitating tools when working."

"Does that happen often? New mages coming to Ymira, I mean." The turn of conversation fascinated Audra. No one in Solven or Feldor knew exactly how many mages existed, and until coming to Ymira, Audra had never met another person who could use magic.

"Not really." Silvan glanced around the group. "Usually we get a few people at the wards each year, but only one or two stay."

"Why do so few stay?"

"Because some have families who love them," Leah said from the opposite side of the table.

"What does that mean?" Audra glanced around the table to find the others averting their gaze, staring at their plates or the artwork on the walls.

"Only magic users are allowed in Ymira." Leah refused to break eye contact. "The rest of the family cannot cross the wards, so they have to choose. Leave their child where they might be safe, or refuse to separate and return back to their homes."

"That is cruel, making a family choose like that." Audra was aghast at the prospect.

"It's how it's always been," Leah said with a shrug. "We stay safe by staying together, keeping out all outsiders. There is too much risk that Kalmere could infiltrate Ymira in their quest to kill all mages."

"So what did the family choose," Audra asked Silvan.

"They chose to stay together and returned home."

Despite the prospect of the family remaining together, Audra felt resentful of the choice that was forced upon them. It was no choice at all.

"Some have it a lot worse, princess."

Audra gripped her fork tightly at hearing Leah's favorite nickname for her.

"Some mages are too scared to make the journey, others fear persecution in their kingdom and choose to stay hidden, and still more are killed when their powers are discovered. Some find themselves abandoned when they show signs of magic, discarded like the waste their families think they are and forced to make the journey alone." She pointedly stared at Audra. "Not everyone is lucky enough to gain Valeria's attention and receive an escort here."

If she had not been watching Leah closely, Audra would have missed the wet sheen in her eyes before Leah pushed back from the table and stormed out of the room. Silence filled the space she left. Appetite gone, Audra gave up the pretense of eating and put down her utensils.

"I am sorry if I brought up an uncomfortable topic. I did not mean to upset anyone."

"Don't take it personally. It's just a sensitive topic for Leah." Eli gave her a sad smile. "Outsiders are purposely kept in the dark regarding how Ymira's run. No one expected you to know about the mage-only policy. Most people don't find out until they get here."

A subdued Taara spoke up from Audra's side. "When I first used magic, my dads were worried that I wouldn't be able to hide it. Magic isn't forbidden in Feldor, but mages are treated like outcasts and sometimes killed by bad people. They knew that I would be safe in Ymira, but didn't know they couldn't stay with me." Her voice wobbled as she told the story, the pain of separating from her parents evident. "It was because they love me that they wanted what was best for me, even if it meant not seeing me again."

"If the wards prevent non-magic users from entering, why not allow a mage to go with the family to train them? Why separate the family at all?"

"Because that's not how it's done." Silvan rolled his eyes. "We don't agree with it either, but the elder mages decided long ago that this would keep us safe, so that is what we do. As if allowing the kingdoms control over how they treat us keeps anyone safe. We have more power than they could dream of. They should be the ones afraid of us."

Audra did not want anyone to fear for their lives. "But if we could—"

Eli held up a hand to interrupt her. "You don't have to convince us, Audra. Valeria enforces the rules and if you want to stay here, you'd better follow them."

Chastised, Audra sat back in her chair as she watched the others finish their meals and depart for the day. When she arrived in the kitchen after picking up the dishes, Audra saw no sign of Leah. *I guess that means I am on my own today.* Hands on her hips, Audra debated where to begin. She learned how to dry dishes the day before and had watched Leah use magic to wash the dishes, so how difficult could it be?

Wet patches of water and soap bubbles covered Audra as she rushed from the kitchen over an hour later. If only Isadora could see her disheveled appearance. Pulling the clinging fabric away from her skin, Audra hoped the sun would dry her quickly. Cleaning the dishes was more difficult than drying them and required a fine balance to prevent dropping the item or stopping water from sloshing over the side, a task that Audra moderately succeeded at. It also took significantly longer than she expected, and she hoped that Valeria had not been waiting long.

"I am sorry I am late," she said as she approached Valeria and sat next to her on the blanket.

"Do you often apologize for things that are out of your control?" Her question caught Audra off-guard.

Puzzled, Audra replied, "But it was my fault." Then she explained the morning's events.

"While your words might have reminded Leah of a painful memory, it was her choice to leave the room and her choice not to assist you with the chores you were both assigned. You can only take responsibility for your choices and actions, not others'." Audra pondered that thought as Valeria continued, "Additionally, you can't be late when we never set a time for your lessons."

"Is there a time you would like to start?"

"No, as I told you yesterday, we will meet each morning after your chores are done no matter how long they take."

Audra sighed at the prospect of having less time to practice magic if she was stuck cleaning dishes for hours.

"Why are you in a rush?"

"I just thought the point of me being here was to master my magic and yet I have not learned anything." She paused, waiting for Valeria to fill the silence, but when she did not Audra continued on. "If I do not start learning something, if I cannot prove that I belong here, then what was the point?"

"Do you regret coming to Ymira? I will not keep you here if you wish to leave."

"No, but..." Audra watched the clouds drift across the sky while she determined how to put her feelings into words. "I came here because you said that you saw potential in me. What I had planned for my life did not work out, and if this does not work either, then what am I supposed to do next?"

"No one knows what their future holds, Audra. Life often takes you down uncertain paths and opens up new parts of yourself to explore. You don't have to figure it all out now, or even years from now. If you are only here because you're trying to prove yourself to someone else, then you will never be satisfied. Learn magic because *you* want to, Audra."

"I do want to." She sat up straighter on the blanket.

"Why? To get over the disappointment of your previous life?" Despite the sensitive nature of his questions, Valeria's posture and tone remained as relaxed as the drifting clouds.

Irritation wormed its way through Audra. She was trying to move past her time in Solven, avoiding thinking of Graham and the pain of learning he did not love her. Not that it was working, based on the crushing pain that lingered in her chest.

"Disappointed? What's there to be disappointed about? Did I prepare my entire life for that moment? Sure. Would it have been nice to at least be acknowledged for my hard work? Of course." With each word, a churning sensation built between her lungs and spread to her limbs. "But to not even receive the decency of telling me to my face that he didn't want to marry me, that he didn't even love me? I'm not just disappointed. I'm furious."

Valeria nodded and placed a warm hand over hers. "So why do you really want to learn magic?"

"Because I want to prove that I'm worth something! Maybe if I could do magic and had power of my own, maybe then he would love me." Tears pooled in her eyes and spilled onto her cheeks.

"You don't need to prove anything to be worthy of love. It's okay to hurt, Audra. But don't let that change how you want to live your life. Look around you." She drew Audra's attention to the wind—a magical wind—swirling around them, picking up blades of grass and fallen leaves. "You are capable of so much more than you ever thought possible. This power you have, it's a gift meant for you, not anyone else."

"But I cannot control it. I did not mean to use it."

"Listen to me, Audra. You can control it, and I am going to help you. Just like we did yesterday, close your eyes and focus on your breath."

Now that she was aware of the wind around her, Audra had difficulty focusing on anything else. Sensing her agitation, the wind howled past her ears. With each snap of air across her face, Audra's breathing hitched, fueling the wind as her panic mounted.

A cool hand clasped hers. "Acknowledge the thought and let it go," Valeria reminded her.

Audra spent several minutes trying to focus her thoughts and steady her breath, resetting after each distraction and willing her mind to remain in the moment. Slowly, the wind settled to a soft breeze, flowing around them like a caress.

"Good. Don't suppress what you were feeling. Instead of focusing on your breathing, I want you to pinpoint where the emotion is coming from. Tell me when you get there."

Valeria's rough hand squeezed Audra's reassuringly. It was not difficult to locate the source of the anguish. There, in the center of her chest, was a gaping maw where her heart used to be. A phantom knife pierced her chest with each thought of Graham, pain and anger pulsing with each heartbeat. The all-consuming power of it blocked out everything else and triggered a spike in power.

"It's too much. It hurts too much." Audra wanted to hide from the throbbing wound.

"Breathe through it. Life is full of painful moments, but also beautiful ones. You can't keep ignoring how much it hurts and you can't make it go away. Acknowledge it and release the hold it has over you, just like focusing on your breath. Once you can separate the emotions, you will feel your magic."

Self-preservation encouraged Audra to avoid dwelling on the negative emotions, to hide behind a wall so thick that no pain could touch her. But that would not help. Staying physically and mentally busy had only served to let the anguish gather its strength, like a weed slowly curling around a flower as it choked the life from it. Audra was taught to tamp down any negative emotion and cast off any sign of magic.

No more.

Feeling deeply was not wrong. She could cry when she needed to. Laugh when it felt good. As long as it did not control her, succumbing to despair and allowing it to overtake everything else, she would survive. No, she would do better than that. Audra would thrive. Sitting with her emotions, whether they be pain or jubilation, was normal. So Audra sat.

And she remembered.

What Graham chose to do and say was his responsibility. All she could control was how she reacted. Losing her first love would always hurt, but she could move past it. This time, when she focused on the ache in her chest, she did not allow the memory to overtake her. Audra allowed fresh air to fill her lungs, lifting her chest skyward, and as she breathed out, she visualized the pain leaving her body like a toxin. With each successive breath, she repeated to herself, *I am enough, exactly as I am.*

I am enough, exactly as I am.

I am enough.

Exactly as I am.

She sunk deep into herself, diving beneath the crashing waves of grief, pain, and anger to the calm water below. Huddled deep within a crevice of her soul was something new, a feeling like a cornered animal, tired of being pushed back again and again, suffocated from being repressed. She had rejected this part of herself for so long that it hardly recognized her anymore. For so long, she held back this part of herself, and it was hurting her. More tears slid down her face, but this time the outpouring of emotion was not because Graham did not love her, but because *she* did not love herself.

Magic was part of her, and by rejecting it over and over, she could never accept herself for who she truly was, and it ravaged her soul. Reaching internally for that coiled ball, Audra imagined cupping it in her hands and holding it close in a loving embrace. *Never again*, she promised herself. Never again would she hate a part of herself. She would learn to love herself, faults and all, starting with this broken piece. It was then that she felt it, the faint warmth of a cooling ember, doused by the flood of emotions, but not vanquished. That was the core of her power.

Resilient. Bright. Hers.

"Oh," she whispered reverently, "that's what it feels like."

And with a gentle exhale, Audra wrapped the wind around an invisible hand, pushing it out towards the lake before bringing it back, tickling her hair and lifting the edges of her shirt. Smiling, Audra turned toward Valeria, puffing her skin with air before letting it go.

"There you are," Valeria said proudly.

Seven

Going through her own training reminded Audra of days spent watching Graham train with the Guards and the once fond memories were tinged with sadness and a spark of anger.

"Want to try something?" Casting a shadow over where she was seated beneath a tree, Graham stood in front of her and gestured to the circle designated for sparring. Graham was starting to fill into his long limbs, muscles taking over the angular shape of his youth. Her own body was now gently curved, and Audra's awareness of Graham sent a tingly feeling into her core.

Setting aside the book on Feldorian customs that she was reading, Audra sighed. "You know I cannot. I do not have the enhanced strength of a Guard."

"You will not need it for this." At the eyebrow raised in contradiction, Graham continued. "Strength is not just physical. Now come on, what I have in mind will not hurt you." He reached out a hand to help her up, and Audra was powerless to do anything but put her hand in his. She trusted him.

Leading her to the center of the ring, Graham illustrated several stances to defend from attackers. When she tried to replicate the poses, Graham stood close, the scent of cinnamon and sweat causing her to lose focus. Asking for permission to touch her, Graham helped move her limbs into the correct position, indicating the most vulnerable parts on a person's body. Once she had a grasp on the stance, Graham stepped in front of her and sank into a defensive position.

"Alright, show me what you have got."

"What? No. I am not going to hit you." The thought of injuring him was abhorrent. She was learning these poses to spend time with him, not from any desire to fight.

"You will not learn how to do it if you do not practice. Besides, it's not like you could actually hit me." He goaded her into action, knowing that she was competitive.

With a look of fierce determination, Audra struck, only to meet the flesh of Graham's palm.

"Good for a first try. Do not forget to keep your wrist straight or you could injure yourself."

Adjusting her stance, Audra threw another punch. It was satisfying to hear the smack of her hand connecting with Graham's palm. So, she did it again. And again.

"I think you have got that part down," Graham said after countless punches. "Just do not forget to aim and you should do fine. We can go over more tomorrow."

"Why?" Sweaty and flushed from the exertion, Audra thought this lesson was a one time whim of Graham's. His sudden desire to teach her how to defend herself was suspicious, and she watched his face closely while he answered.

"Because everyone should know how to defend themselves. You should never feel trapped and helpless and I would feel better knowing that you can keep yourself safe. Anytime you like, we can practice." Happy to spend more time with him, Audra met him late each morning, practicing before sitting under her tree with a book to watch him complete his training.

Audra later learned that Graham had overheard a group of young nobility talking about her at a recent dinner party, remarking on how she had grown up into a beautiful woman they would not mind finding in a *dark hallway. Enraged, Graham had invited the group on a tour of the royal armory, where they got an up close and personal look at his favorite weapons along with a subtle threat that if he found out any of them had forced their attention on an unwilling partner, they would find out exactly what those weapons did.*

Though she had initially found the practice dull and pointless, Audra grew accustomed to meditation. It calmed and balanced her thoughts, and although it would never be one of her favorite activities, she could tell that it was helping her latch onto her magic faster. Guiding the magic through her body into something tangible was like trying to catch a fish with bare hands. Slippery, time consuming, and a test of patience.

When Audra initially expressed concern over Valeria's training regiment, citing her physical limitations when tested for the Guards, the High Mage listened to her concerns intently. Valeria responded with her own questions, inquiring what types of training she had tried before.

"Guards are born with different anatomy than mages and non-magical humans. While their training would have been incompatible with you even if you lacked magic, I suspect that your body reacted so strongly because of your magic."

"What do you mean?"

"People are born with the enhanced abilities to become a Guard, yes?" Audra nodded. "And they are tested as children to determine if they have those gifts?" Another nod. She was given more than one test, hoping that her abilities would manifest with time. "It is impossible for you to have been born with those abilities. Not with the magic inside you. Magic created the original Guards, and it is a type of magic that allows them to use their gifts."

"W-what?" Audra's jaw dropped open at that news. "That cannot be true. Guards do not have magic."

"I am not surprised the old rulers of Solven hid that knowledge, but that is no excuse for you not to learn about it now. There are some books in the library on our history. Leah knows which ones. The magic that aides Guards is different from ours, but it is magic all the same. Since your magic manifested as a mage, it could not also manifest as a

Guard. By trying to force it to be both, it reacted negatively and caused physical pain. What I have designed for you should not stretch beyond your physical capacity, which means your magic will not react. Instead, this will help you build stamina and patience, but we will take as many breaks as you need. Stop me immediately if you are in pain."

Audra's legs were wobbly by the time she returned to Rauha, but she could not return to her room yet. First, she needed to stop in the library. Hopefully she could find the books without needing to ask Leah for help. Following Valeria's directions, Audra navigated her way to the third floor, pulling open a plain wooden door with a brass handle shaped like a tree. The library was decorated simply, matching wooden shelves lining every available inch of the four walls. Two tall windows broke up the shelves on the far wall, providing natural light that was supplemented by magelights hanging from hooks along the shelves. Stepping into the room, Audra turned in a circle to take in the variety of books lining the shelves. Her feet pad across a plush carpet patterned with a map of the kingdoms, and her eyes caught on the constellations painted on the ceiling.

Beautiful. Audra could imagine spending weeks in this one room alone.

The sound of a throat clearing broke Audra away from her study of the books.

"Can I help you find something?" Leah was seated in a low chair, reclined with a book in her lap.

So much for avoiding the grumpy mage. "Yes, actually. Valeria said you would know where to find books relating to the history of mages, specifically on how magic was used to create Guards."

Gently setting her book to the side, Leah pushed up out of the chair and flicked her black-and-blue braid behind her as she walked towards the shelves. For several long minutes, she searched in silence, pulling books off the shelf and handing them to Audra. Happy to keep silent after their last awkward exchange, Audra trailed along after Leah, reading the spines of books on the shelves to see what else she might like to read.

"You've been doing well. Learning magic, I mean." Audra's head jerked toward Leah at the unexpected compliment. If not for the red-tipped ears peeking through her hair, Audra would have thought Leah was insincere.

"Thank you. It has actually been a lot of fun. I am sorry for upsetting you at breakfast."

Leah turned with a sigh, placing a worn leather book in Audra's hands. "You didn't know. It's...not something I like talking about. Sorry about skipping out on helping with the dishes. It won't happen again."

Hopefully she meant the bad attitude, and not just the chores, but Audra did not want to expect too much.

Tapping a finger on the book, Leah shifted the conversation back to the original subject. "Start with this one. It's a journal from one of the original mages, Safrina. It goes without saying that this book is extremely valuable to mages. Do. Not. Ruin it."

Having completed her task, Leah turned and strode back to her chair. Barely resisting the urge to stick her tongue out at the other mage, Audra went back to her room to read. The initial entries were the typical musings of a young person, detailing Safrina's adolescence with her sisters, Annika and Pennifrin. Audra skimmed through those pages until she found entries related to the study of magic.

Magic has existed since Hellig created our world. It flows through the fabric of the world and there have always been a select few blessed with the ability to harness it. This gift—like all gifts—should not be taken for granted. My sisters and I were born with such gifts. We knew so little about the powers we possessed, and left our home to try and find others like us.

We have made a few friends in small villages and on the road these last few years. Annika is a natural at getting people to talk to her, and she is working to set up a method of communication between us all. That way we can continue to share ideas even from a great distance. There is one mage that travels with us now, a handsome mage named Dyrun. He heard about our travels from a friend we met in a village, and sought us out so that he could join us. It is nice having another companion to travel with. I love my sisters, but traveling exclusively with them can grate on my nerves. Dyrun is charming, witty, and powerful. Some of the magic he performs is awe-inspiring. He has become a good friend to me, offering encouragement and helping record what we have learned about magic.

Audra placed a ribbon in between the pages of the journal to mark her place. Frowning, she wondered how Dyrun was not immediately recognized for the evil churning in his soul. That he was able to pass as Safrina's friend for years was disturbing and sent a shiver down Audra's spine, the waning light adding to her disquiet.

EIGHT

Days of training had Audra returning to her room feeling like a wrung-out cloth. There was satisfaction at completing the exercises Valeria prepared for her, both her magic and muscles growing stronger, but with it came aches and pains that Audra was unaccustomed to.

"I know what would help," Taara replied after Audra complained about a particularly stiff muscle. "We should go to the hot springs after dinner. The water is amazing and so relaxing." The younger girl had quickly endeared herself to Audra with her enthusiasm and joy for life.

"That sounds divine." Audra linked their arms as they walked to dinner.

"Leah makes a potion that changes the color of the water so that it looks like a rainbow! And it smells really good too. You're going to love it."

"Oh, I am not sure Leah would want to share that with me." Despite their shared room and chore assignment, Audra had trouble warming up to Leah. After their conversation in the library, the two girls barely spoke to each other.

"Of course, she will! Leah," Taara called out as they approached the table, "we're going to the springs tonight. You have to come with us!"

"Really? I *have* to go?" Leah lifted an eyebrow.

Taara was undeterred by Leah's unfriendly tone and flopped into a chair to drape herself across the table in front of Leah. "Well, we want you to go."

Glancing between the two of them, Leah waited a moment before saying, "Fine." Audra was surprised at the response, thinking that she would not be interested in something as frivolous as soaking in iridescent water. But when Taara cheered at her acquiescence, Leah smiled briefly before turning back to her meal.

The path to the springs was narrow and wound down the side of the hill Rauha Hall sat on. Drying leaves crunched under Audra's worn boots as they followed the path with the aid of a lamp Leah carried, its swaying light casting shadows around them. Tall trees created a canopy above them, starlight twinkling between the gaps. Without the disruption of human voices, the melodic cries of nocturnal birds and insects filled the air. Each step and rustle of fabric felt intrusive on the peaceful setting.

Behind a makeshift barrier of rocks was a small pool, curls of steam rising from the water. Folding their clothes and placing them on rocks, the girls stepped into the pool. Audra hissed as her foot dipped into the hot water, the temperature biting at her cooler skin before easing into a soothing caress. Sighing, she sunk the rest of the way into the water, leaving only her head exposed to the night air. The water swirled with every color imaginable, the result of Leah's potion. It was pretty, and Audra was about to compliment the blue-haired mage before Leah's voice called out from across the small pool.

"Does this live up to your royal standards, princess?"

Rolling her eyes, Audra replied, "I asked you to stop calling me that."

"Why? Does it bother you, *princess*?" Leah's mocking tone was particularly grating against the peaceful night air.

"Leah, please." Taara glanced nervously between them.

"It's okay, Taara." Audra held up her hand to stop her from interrupting again before glaring at Leah. "What is your problem with me? I have been nothing but nice to you since we met and you have insisted on calling me names and treating me rudely."

"I thought you would be happy with the name. After all, everything you wanted in life was to be a perfect little princess," Leah sneered. Ripples of light reflected from the moon and stars danced across her face, highlighting the resentment simmering in her eyes.

"There is nothing wrong with wanting that!" Audra's voice shook with anger. She was tired of people questioning her past, putting her down for having that dream. "Just because it was not a choice that you made does not make it wrong, and I do not deserve your scorn for it." Her chest heaved with each breath as she struggled to reign in the magic boiling to the surface. "Yes, I wanted to be a princess, but only if it meant I was Graham's princess." Her heart tugged at his name. "But that changed. Why do you even care?"

"That is exactly your problem. All you ever cared about was loving some boy." Water splashed as Leah tossed up her arms in exasperation. "You lived at a palace, with the royal family—"

"I know where I—"

"Don't interrupt me. You grew up surrounded by the people who decide the fate of others.They listened to you. Loved you. And you had magic! You had the opportunity to show the king and queen—hells, even your precious Graham—that magic is not evil. That mages shouldn't have to live in fear, hunted down and forced to live in one pocket of land."

"Magic is not forbidden in Solven," Audra said warily.

"I know, I was born there."

Audra reared back in shock. She knew that Leah was not born in Ymira and her parents had abandoned her once her magic manifested, but to come from the same kingdom as Audra? The knowledge that someone was treated so poorly in her homeland shamed Audra.

Leah pushed her advantage. "Magic may not be forbidden, but is it encouraged? Are mages respected?" Leah's face was flush from the heat of the water combined with her frustration.

Audra remained silent. Her life was an example of how magic was hidden in Solven.

"That's what I thought." Leah nodded. "I never hated that you wanted to be a princess. I hated that you never tried to be a princess *for us*. Over the years, Valeria continued to speak about your potential, crafting new letters to convince you to come live with us. But I always thought you were more useful to us in Solven. You could have used your relationship with the royal family to protect mages. But instead, you sat around in your pretty gowns, going to parties and daydreaming about a prince, while other mages were struggling to survive."

A tense quiet fell over the group. Eyes shining with disappointment, Leah pinned Audra in place with her gaze. Challenging her to refute the words. Perspiration clung to Audra's skin, the combination of the humid air and guilt heating her face. As much as it pained her to admit it, Audra knew that Leah had a point. It was a privilege to grow up in the palace, one that she was grateful for and worked hard to be worthy of, but she had lived in ignorance to the pain of her people. Despite the few times she had used magic accidentally, Audra knew that the royal family would not punish her. By hiding her own power, Audra unintentionally sent the message that magic should be hidden.

Lifting her gaze across the pool, Audra looked at Leah's flushed face. "You cannot blame me for not knowing that. Despite what you might think, I worked hard at the palace, striving to learn as much as I could to improve diplomatic relations and be an asset to Solven. You may not see it that way, but that is your problem, not mine. If you spent more time getting to know me, instead of assuming things about me, you would have learned that my life was not just parties and dresses." She took a steadying breath before continuing.

"I am sorry for what you and countless others have gone through, but I cannot change the fact that I knew nothing about mages and their suffering before coming here, and I do not even know if it would have helped had I done anything different. But what I can change is how I act going forward. Coming to Ymira and studying magic was not the future I had in mind—I will admit that—but now that I am here and know all of you, I am proud to call myself a mage. And I will do everything in my power to help make the kingdoms better for all of us."

"How?" It was the first time Taara spoke since the argument began. Both girls turned to face Audra as they waited for her response.

Taking a moment to gather her thoughts, Audra weaved her fingers through the water. "Well, to be honest, I spent my entire life preparing to help lead Solven. I know how to fit in with courtiers from different kingdoms, how to socialize and host them to build better relationships. What others may view as Ymira's greatest strength, our wards and protection, I see as our greatest weakness."

Leah's eyes sparked with interest and Audra hurried to continue before she could interrupt. "Yes, the wards have protected you from attack, but the mystery surrounding the practice of magic allows others to create stories for us. If we do not show them who we are, that we use magic for beneficial purposes, they will continue to imagine that we are evil and wicked."

"You have a point, but I don't think people will change their minds easily." It was reassuring that Leah did not immediately reject her idea.

"No, it will not be easy, but nothing in life that is worth doing comes easy."

"How do you propose we start?"

"We? You want to help?" This was definitely not how Audra saw the evening progressing. Originally, all she wanted was to soak her tired limbs. Now, she was forming an unlikely alliance to shift the narrative about mages.

"I may not like you, but I misjudged you and I'm sorry for that." Leah inclined her head, the ends of her hair dipping into the water. "But if you're going to try and improve things for mages, I want to help. I don't want any other children experiencing what I had to." On Audra's other side, Taara nodded in agreement.

"Thank you. We should probably keep this to a small group for now. That way Valeria does not find out before we can prove it will be successful."

Leah smirked and leaned back against the edge of the pool. "We can count on Eli and Silvan to help, they've both had issues with the restriction on non-mages in Ymira."

"Yeah, they won't be happy that we started plotting this without them. They're both such busybodies," Taara said and laughed.

"Silvan is going to be insufferable now, never letting us out of his sight just in case we plot something new." It was the first time Audra heard Leah laugh fully, and the light tone caught her by surprise. Their laughter echoed off the rocks and spilled into the quiet night air.

"It will be nice to have them help," Audra added. "To start, I can teach you all the basics of courtly manners and the customs for each kingdom."

"Does that mean you will teach us how to dance?" Taara's smile rivaled the brightness of a star.

"Yes, dancing is part of it."

Taara leaned forward in the water. "When do we start?"

NINE

Starting the lessons took longer than any of them expected. With Audra and Taara's individual magic lessons and the rest of the group's daily tasks, finding time to meet was challenging. Lessons in etiquette were taught over meals, and customs and traditions from the different kingdoms blended with daily chores. Audra smiled to herself as she remembered Leah's outburst when she made her balance plates on her head while washing dishes. Each dish that fell resulted in a curse from Leah's mouth, increasing in vulgarity and force as more plates fell. Eventually, Leah got so frustrated with the exercise that she flung the remaining plate at the wall, shattering it into pieces.

"This is ridiculous," she muttered while magically repairing the plate. "What's the point of standing perfectly straight? I just look like someone shoved a rod straight up my—"

"Language, Leah." Audra was glad that she was facing away from Leah so her smirk was hidden. The argument at the springs lessened the tension between the two, and they were slowly forming a friendship, Leah's dry humor and unfiltered opinions refreshing. "Posture projects confidence. When you stand tall and look straight ahead, you are telling people that you are someone important and worth taking seriously."

"I could send that same message by freezing them with magic."

"And then they would still be afraid of us, which is not the point."

"Fine," Leah grumbled, setting the plate back on top of her blue-tipped hair and continuing to wash the dishes.

For all her reluctance, Leah was progressing well in the lessons. The whole group was. Having grown up in Ymira, Eli found it particularly challenging to learn the customs of each kingdom, but he spent time practicing with Taara. Taara made up for any lack of knowledge with enthusiasm, peppering Audra with questions and reading book after book in the library to learn as much as she could.

Having spent more time outside Ymira than the others, with the exception of Audra, Silvan proved invaluable at assisting in preparing the group for life outside their home. Particularly due to his native knowledge of the kingdom of Kalmere. With the natural mountain border separating Kalmere from most of Solven and parts of Feldor, Kalmere isolated itself even more than Ymira had. Trade and diplomatic visits were rare, but one thing was known for certain. Magic was forbidden in the kingdom, and use or possession was punishable by death.

Fortunately, Silvan was able to escape Kalmere, and his journey through Feldor and Solven to reach Ymira gave him knowledge and experience with the other kingdoms. His natural grace and eye for design were critical to educating the group on traditional dances and attire for each kingdom. Once a week, the group pushed aside the tables and chairs in the dining room to create a dance floor where Eli would enchant instruments to play music based off of songs that Audra and Silvan hummed.

"I was thinking," Eli said as he sat side by side with Audra. They watched Silvan demonstrate the steps of a dance to Leah and Taara. The scuff of slippered feet on the floor and the swish of clothing as it curled around the dancers sent a stab of homesickness through Audra. She loved dancing. The euphoric feeling as her heart pounded underneath her skin, moving to the rhythm the instruments created. The sense of accomplishment at successfully completing complicated steps while the music poured into her soul.

"Mmmhmm." Audra nodded absently as she watched Silvan glide across the floor. Leah and Taara were struggling to mimic Silvan's movements. Taara's face was twisted with concentration, the tip of her tongue poking out one side of her mouth while Leah was scowling, a slight flush to her face from the exertion.

"Are you even listening?" Eli rested his hand on her arm to get her attention, his mouth turned up in a wry smile.

"Sorry, Eli," she said and turned to face him. "You have my full attention now."

"When are we going to start using these skills?" Eli asked the question that had spun in Audra's mind for weeks. Knowing how to prepare the group to interact with non-mages was one hurdle, but actually getting them out into the kingdoms was another. Night after night, she tossed ideas through her head, debating the merits of each one.

"If I am being honest..." Audra glanced to make sure the others could not overhear her and Eli. "I am stuck." Having a project to focus on helped her feel fulfilled and useful, a welcome distraction from heartbreak, but her lack of next steps worried her. What if she could not help improve the mages' image and others were left defenseless outside Ymira? What if the plan backfired and made things worse? Then she would be no better off than when she arrived, a failure at achieving her goals.

"Getting out into the kingdoms is not as easy as walking out of the ward and asking for an invitation." Toe tapping with the music, Audra continued, "At the palace, we did not have to ask for an invitation, we were always getting invited to house parties, dinners, and other events."

"What if the king and queen were trying to improve relations with an ally or another kingdom? What would they do then?"

"They would usually invite an emissary to stay at the palace and host a party in their honor. But with the wards up, that is not possible here."

Eli frowned. "No, I don't think so either. Considering that we are keeping this plan to ourselves, I don't imagine Valeria would be too pleased to have guests show up at the wards."

"Could you imagine her reaction? I do not know if she would kill them on the spot or cast an illusion to have them wander the mountain until they went insane."

"I'm imagining what she would do to us," Eli said and shuddered. "But let's not worry about that until we have to. Is there any way you could write to some of your old friends, see if they could invite you to visit?"

It was Audra's turn to frown. "The only real friends I had were the royal family, and I cannot imagine that they would be happy to hear from me based on the way I left." Although leaving was the right choice, Audra felt ashamed at leaving without saying goodbye.

Taara's laughter filled the air as Silvan spun her around. For several moments, Eli and Audra watched the pair spin around the makeshift ballroom while they thought of different ways to execute their plan.

"What about the merchants? They visit Ymira often enough," Audra mused.

"Sure, but they don't make it past the wards. Someone brings them our goods for trade outside the wards and purchases anything we might need."

An idea began taking root in Audra's mind. "How do you know when they are coming?"

"When they are a few days away, they send a message through enchanted paper to Valeria. She lets us know to gather anything we have for sale and to list any supplies that we might need from the outside." He turned toward her, eyebrow raised. "Why, what are you thinking?"

Audra beckoned the rest of the group over. When they were settled into a ring of chairs, she revealed her plan.

"The next time the merchant comes, one of us needs to leave with them."

Four faces looked at her with mixed expressions of confusion, apprehension, and curiosity. "What's that brilliant mind of yours planning?" Silvan looked the least concerned of the group.

"Magical goods are popular in Solven and Feldor, but they are sold by non-mages. If people are willing to purchase items made by mages, then they should get them *from* mages. The merchant acts as a go-between for us, but if someone traveled with them, we could sell directly and create opportunities to showcase our abilities in a positive light."

"What if people don't want to buy directly from us?" Leah stretched her legs out and crossed them at the ankles, the casual posture ruined by the tense set of her shoulders. She knew what it was like to be ostracized and discriminated against for her power. As much as Leah knew this next step was necessary, Audra saw the concern lurking behind her dark eyes, the desire to keep her friends safe always at the forefront of her mind.

"Then we learn what makes people hesitant to interact with us and do what we can to counteract it."

"How do we know we would be safe with the merchant?" Taara ran her hand repeatedly down one of her tight curls.

"We don't," Silvan answered for Audra. "The only way to guarantee that is if we had more power. But we knew it would be difficult when we agreed to do this. The person who goes needs to be strong enough to protect themselves. There is risk in going, but we gain nothing if we don't try."

The group was silent for several heartbeats. Audra looked at each person and rubbed a hand over her chest at the painful thought of any of them getting hurt. She did not know how to answer that. Life had taught her that nothing is guaranteed.

"I can't go," Eli said as he patted the arms of his chair. "I'm strong and can defend myself, but I don't know if the other kingdoms are as accessible as Ymira."

Taara rested her hand on top of Eli's and gave it a squeeze. "I don't think I should go either. I'm still learning to defend myself."

"That leaves me out too then." Audra knew she would be a liability if she went before she finished training. Besides, she barely had a grasp on basic magical concepts, nothing detailed enough to answer the myriad of questions non-mages would have.

"I'll go." Silvan sat up straight and met the gaze of each of his friends. "I have more experience outside Ymira and can hold my own in a fight. Besides," he said as he winked at Leah, "my shining personality is better suited to putting people at ease."

"I can't argue with that." Leah smirked and crossed her arms over her chest. "The bigger problem is Valeria. She'll stop us when she finds out."

"She cannot stop him if she does not know until he is already gone," Audra replied.

"How rebellious of you." Silvan punched her lightly on the shoulder. "Looks like our little group is starting to teach you something.

Once we know when the merchant is arriving, I can wait outside the wards for their arrival and persuade them to let me travel with them."

"Excellent idea. You can send a message once you are clear and we can tell Valeria."

"If she doesn't find out first, that is," Eli chimed in.

"It's a risk we have to take."

Two weeks later, as the air turned crisp and the scent of decaying leaves cloyed the air, word came from the merchant, and Silvan was gone.

TEN

Facing down a pack of halions—barb-tailed monsters with pincers and razor-sharp teeth—seemed more pleasant than walking to Valeria's office after Silvan's departure. Each footstep echoed in the stairwell like the knell of a death bell, tolling Audra's imminent punishment. Her hand grasped the railing to steady her assent, limbs trembling with nerves. Audra dreaded telling Valeria what they did. It was for the benefit of all mages, but she doubted Valeria would see it that way. Like the High Mages before her, Valeria believed she was protecting them by keeping Ymira isolated. But during her time here, Audra learned that many of the other mages did not agree with the ban on non-mages in Ymira and wanted to practice magic safely in the kingdoms they grew up in.

Taking a calming breath when she reached the top of the stairs, Audra smoothed her hair and cornflower-blue dress before knocking on Valeria's door. No matter the consequences, Audra was glad that Silvan left with the merchant and would begin improving relations with the people of Solven and Feldor.

"Enter." Valeria's voice was clear despite the wooden door between them, her tone giving no hint to her mood.

Audra grasped the worn handle and pushed open the door. Despite her previous visits to the room, the view behind the desk still gave her pause. Today, gray clouds filled the sky and settled over the landscape with muted light. Through an open window, a steady wind brought in humid air and the scent of coming rain, gently rustling the carefully organized papers on the desk.

Valeria sat on a plush armchair in an alcove with an unlit fireplace, a low table and second chair completing the small seating area. Her fingers drummed against the armrest, the firm line of her mouth revealing her displeasure.

"Please, have a seat." Gesturing to the chair across from her, Valeria summoned two cups and began pouring tea from a steaming pot. The scent of the tea evoked memories of orchards and spices.

"Thank you." Audra took the offered cup of tea and let its warmth seep into her skin. They drank without speaking and Audra knew better than to interrupt the silence before Valeria was ready.

"Am I correct to believe you know why you are here?"

"Is it to get my opinion on new fabric for the dining room chairs? Or perhaps you were looking at brightening your wardrobe? Burgundy would look exceptional in either situation." Since she had known her, which, admittedly, was not long at all, Audra had only seen the High Mage wear black, shades of gray, and—if she was feeling spontaneous— incredibly dark blue.

Cocking one eyebrow, Valeria regarded her over the brim of her teacup. "I expected better from you than hiding your dishonesty behind jokes. You and your friends broke my trust, sending Silvan beyond the safety of the ward, in the care of a merchant, all without consulting me."

Properly chastised, Audra fought against the urge to wring her hands together, a nervous habit since childhood. Regret and guilt burned down her throat. Believing that what her friends were doing was right, Audra still knew it was wrong to keep their plans from Valeria. As High Mage, Valeria was responsible for keeping them safe, and Audra and the others circumvented her authority. There would be conse- quences for those actions, but first, Aura needed to plead their case. She could deal with the punishment if it meant getting permission to continue their plan. "I apologize that we went behind your back, but it was for the betterment of all mages."

"Is that so?" Valeria's tone was cold as the frost that was beginning to gather on the windows in the morning. "And you didn't pause to think that what I have been doing, what the High Mages before me were doing, has always been what is best for all mages?"

Audra and her friends had prepared for this moment, debating every side of the argument to establish a solid rationale for their actions. Emotion would not sway Valeria, only precise logic would prove successful.

"We all hold you in high regard and know that every High Mage since Dyrun's fall did everything they could, with the resources available to them, to keep mages safe. But, with all due respect, times have changed and mages are failing to adapt to the new environment."

Gathering her courage, Audra fought to keep her voice even, breathing steadily through her nose to calm her racing nerves. "You say that you work to keep all mages safe, but that is not technically true. Any mage that cannot, or does not, make it to Ymira is left without guidance. Abandoned to struggle with their magic, or worse, defend themselves against ignorant people who seek to harm them.

"Even those that make it to Ymira can be harmed. If they have non-magical family, they are forced to choose between never seeing those they love ever again, or forgo instruction and carve out a life for themselves outside our borders. It is cruel and unkind."

"The world is cruel and unkind to mages." Valeria gripped her teacup tightly, eyes hard and weary of carrying the weight of their people's plight.

"I know it is, but that does not mean we can stop trying to make it better."

"Others before you have tried and failed, with much suffering and loss for our people. What makes you think you will do any better?" There was no judgment in her tone, only true concern and a hint of curiosity. It gave Audra hope that Valeria was willing to listen to what she planned and possibly agree with the course of action.

"I cannot guarantee that I will do better than them. But what I can guarantee is that I will not stop trying until the last breath leaves my body. Leading a kingdom, navigating politics, and building relationships was what I trained my entire life for. The palace taught me how commoners and nobility alike view mages and also gave me the skills to persuade people to change their views. I can advocate for our people in all classes of society in all three kingdoms. And I will not be alone. Not all mages will agree with me, and that is alright, but the more who are working towards a common goal the closer we are to achieving it."

Wind rustled her hair, cooling the skin that had grown warm with her enthusiasm. Despite Audra's impassioned speech, Valeria's expression remained impassive. The High Mage kept her emotions close to her chest, guarded like a precious treasure in a fortified vault. Audra's patience was tested watching Valeria calmly drink her tea when every fiber of Audra's body raced with the need for action.

"My father, Arne, was like you. Optimistic and full of hope. A dreamer. When others were content to remain in Ymira, he looked forward to the days when a merchant would come, giving him the opportunity to leave the ward and see what treasures came from the other kingdoms." Valeria smiled wistfully. "Sometimes, he would take me with him, selling the enchanted clothing we made for new thread and fabric. He loved showing me the paths through the mountains, pointing out the landmarks we could see in Solven—that was where he was from, before moving. If he was feeling particularly adventurous, we would go to the bottom of the mountain and pick flowers."

Silent, Audra let Valeria share her story. The High Mage was usually tight-lipped about her personal life and Audra relished the idea to learn more about the woman.

"I often wonder if my father would have moved back to Solven if not for me. His magic was softer, easily hidden, while mine would set fire to trees or knock shelves off walls. I had difficulty controlling it, but he was patient and never scolded me no matter how much damage I did. There was nothing I wanted more than to make him proud."

There was a sadness to the air, a bitter cold that pulled the heat from the room as Valeria continued, tears in her eyes. "He wanted to believe that not all people feared mages, that we could learn to bring outsiders into Ymira and live in the kingdoms with non-mages, and he died believing that. Unbeknownst to even his closest friends, my father had made several trips to a nearby farm in Solven, wanting to prove that mages could live alongside non-mages. One day, while I was studying, he went to visit his friend and was attacked. Someone had seen the trips he was making from the mountain and considered him an easy target."

Tears slipped down Valeria's cheeks. "He wasn't a fighter and didn't have enough magic to defend himself. I was so angry at him for leaving the ward, but even angrier at the people who hurt him. Can you understand now why I am angry with you? I know you think that what you are doing is right, but there are very real risks, Audra. Risks I am not sure you and your friends fully understand."

Softly, Audra rested her hand on Valeria's, bringing warmth back into the cold digits. "I am so sorry that happened to your father. That kind of loss is never easy." Audra knew all too well how the loss of a parent lingered. "I understand why you want to protect the mages of Ymira from harm, but just because the world can be cruel does not mean it cannot also be wonderful. I would not ask anyone to take the risk who was not fully aware of the potential consequences. Eli, Silven, Leah, Taara, and I have all faced hardship and understand the risks better than most. All we are asking is an opportunity to try."

Valeria slowly stirred her new cup of tea, drawing out the moment for one breath.

Two.

Three.

Audra waited for her answer.

"It won't be easy to convince others to change their ways. But, I am willing to give you a chance."

"Thank you! We will not let you down." Audra leapt up and gave Valeria a swift hug. The elder mage's arms remained stiff against her side, unaccustomed to displays of affection.

"Don't thank me yet. You and your friends are still assigned extra chores for your insubordination, and I expect you to keep me apprised on your decisions and progress. Make no mistake, this may be your idea, but I am still the highest authority for mages."

"Of course, and I am happy for your guidance."

One side of Valeria's mouth inched upward. "Being a leader isn't an easy path, Audra. Success and failure offer their own challenges and opportunities, but always remember that you're not alone. Your greatest strength comes not from the magic in your blood, but the power of those you surround yourself with."

"I will not forget it." Practically skipping down the stairs, Audra nearly collided with her friends where they anxiously waited in the corridor below. She was glad to see them all, their support giving her courage.

Catching herself before she tumbled into Taara, Audra put a hand to her chest as she sighed behind pursed lips. "Hells, warn a girl before you startle me like that, lurking about in the corridor like thieves."

"Sorry, Audra! We were just so worried about what Valeria would say and waiting in our room wasn't helping. Leah said that we would get answers faster—"

"Don't drag me into this." Leah tried to remain aloof, but the way she was rapidly braiding and unbraiding a section of her hair revealed her apprehension. She cared more about the outcome of the conversation than she wanted to let on.

"If you didn't want to be involved, you wouldn't be waiting here with us," Eli chimed in, trying to lighten the mood. One hand tightly gripped the armrest of his chair, hinting that he, too, was nervous.

Not wanting to keep the group in suspense any longer, Audra recounted her conversation with Valeria. As she did, Eli released the breath he was holding and Leah relaxed against the wall.

"So, what's our next step?" Leah pushed off the wall as the group began making their way to the library.

"I thought you would never ask. Next, we go to a party."

***

The party in question was the annual harvest day festival. Much like the harvest in Solven, the farmers of Ymira sent word to the townspeople when the harvest was ready, and all available mages went to the fields to help harvest the crops. Unlike the crops in Solven and the other kingdoms, which could ripen on different days, causing a fluctuation in when the harvest was celebrated, magic created a reliable schedule, dwindling down a week or two of work into several days.

Scents of hardy vegetables, sweet fruit, and herbs bled into Audra's clothes as she helped gather food. It was rewarding to gently grasp and pull each ripe plant from its cradle in the earth, knowing that her labor would feed the mouths of her people for months to come. Warmth blossomed in her chest at seeing each basket filled and transported to homes and storage centers, and Audra paused to thank each person for their hard work. Dirt was embedded beneath her nails and speckled across her skin, plastered with sweat, by the time the sun set each day. On the final day of work, Audra was beginning to think that the dirt was now a permanent part of her body, particles of it finding their way into the most inconvenient places.

"Is it like this when you work with your plants?" Audra asked Eli on their way back to Rauha. He had found his own way to help with the harvest, rigging a barrel to the front of his chair to assist with carrying the produce to the villagers.

"I'm used to getting dirty." Realizing the hidden meaning behind his words, Eli flushed a color red that would rival some of the flowers he nurtured. "O-on my hands, I mean. My hands get dirty. Not anything else." Covering his face with remarkably clean hands, Eli continued to speak, though it was muffled. "Now you probably think I'm some kind of pervert, coming onto you like that."

Seeing the normally composed mage flustered was cute, but unlike Leah, Audra did not want to tease Eli further. "I know you did not mean it that way, Eli. I was just curious how you manage to remain clean after working with plants all day when I look like I have gone to battle with the earth." Gesturing to the marked difference in their clothes, Audra laughed at herself.

"Oh, well, the plants in the greenhouse are more contained and require less soil movement than crops. After the initial planting—and any repotting that occurs when the plant grows—my herbs, flowers, and medicinal plants only require harvesting and maintenance. Not a lot of battle in that process." Eli gestured to the greenhouse as they passed it. The small, rectangular structure was created with walls of mageglass, keeping the climate inside the appropriate temperature for the plants. Additional mageglass walls created sections within the greenhouse, allowing Eli to establish multiple climates within one structure, an invention that he was particularly proud of. Rows of colorful plants were visible through the tinted glass, beads of moisture running down the panes.

"I also keep a sink in the greenhouse, in addition to the watering mechanisms. That way, I can wash any dirt from my hands before I return to the hall."

"You will have to teach me your secret then. There is no amount of soap in the world that can remove the dirt under my nails."

"Oh, that's an easy fix. Ask Taara if she has a spare brush for under your nails. She made one for me and it works great."

"Ask me for what?" The girl in question came bounding down the stairs, meeting them at the base before continuing back up with Audra. Linking their arms together, they waved goodbye to Eli and agreed to meet him after changing to go to the party in the village.

"Eli mentioned you might have a brush to help get the dirt out from under my nails?" Audra stretched her fingers out to show Taara, wincing at the caked on dirt. Despite loving to play outside and not being afraid of getting dirty as a child, she had always enjoyed being clean after.

Smacking her forehead lightly, Taara laughed. "I can't believe I didn't think of that sooner. You must feel so gross."

"Well, if I did not before, I do now."

"Sorry, sorry. I should have a spare in my room. I made them after my first harvest here."

When they entered their room, Leah was exiting the washroom, skin dewy from the damp air trailing out behind her.

"Good, you found her." Leah sent a gust of wind up from her hands, drying her hair with magic. Using magic for something so frivolous filled Audra with envy. She was still learning to harness her magic for simple tasks, and worried that attempting something like drying her hair would end with more tangles than a nest. "Hells, you smell like vegetables and sweat, go get clean or we'll leave for the festival without you."

"You did not smell much better after today, and I hope you at least left some warm water for me."

"Learn to heat it yourself and you won't have to worry about it." Unlike when they had first met, Leah's words no longer held the mocking condescension that they once did. Now, she found ways to support Audra, often taking advantage of Audra's competitive nature to goad her into testing the limits of her power.

Infuriating, but successful.

Leah had also learned to apologize, in her own way, for her harsh tongue. Like the emerald green dress that lay on Audra's bed after she bathed. Embroidered with golden leaves across the hem of the scooped neckline, the long-sleeved dress cinched at the waist before flowing to the ground in a pleated skirt. "It was one of my old dresses. I didn't need it anymore and thought you might want something new to wear."

"She embroidered it, too. Spent all night working on it," Taara chimed in from her seated position on her own bed before Leah threw a pillow at her. The younger girl was wearing a similar-cut gown in a yellow that matched the grain they harvested, complementing the rich color of her skin and accenting the line of her throat with its low collar. One half of her hair was pulled back with a clip made from a leaf dipped in metal.

Noticing where Audra was looking, Taara patted the leaf and smiled softly. "Eli made it for me. Do you like it?"

"It suits you beautifully." Audra returned the girl's smile. Although Audra was sure that Eli gave her the gift as a friend—he was several years her senior after all—she did not want to discourage the crush. The fragile hope of her own first love still beat in Audra's chest.

Clapping her hands together, Taara jumped from her bed and giggled in delight as she spun in a circle towards Audra. "Your first autumn festival in Ymira. Aren't you just so excited? I'm sure it's not as grand as a royal party, but I think you'll find our food and music better than any court! We have firecakes and wine while we dance by the bonfire."

Joining in the other girl's merriment, Audra grabbed Taara and Leah's hands and spun them in a circle. She did not know how fulfilling female friendship would be. A warm feeling, like liquid sunshine, filled her soul as she looked at the faces of her friends. When she first arrived in Ymira, Audra thought that the bitter agony of losing Graham would prevent her from experiencing any joy in her new home. Slowly, Taara, Leah, Eli, and Silvan had pulled her from the dark place of her thoughts and provided her with new, happy memories. Pulling them into a tight hug, Audra hoped her actions revealed the emotions that she could not put to words yet. Two sets of arms squeezed her tightly in response.

Leah let out a small cough to hide her embarrassment at the uncharacteristic display of affection before saying, "Yes, well there won't be much food left if we waste all our time in this room. Sit at your desk and I'll dry your hair. The frost will be upon us if we wait for you to do it yourself."

The resulting hairstyle was something much simpler than Audra was used to at court, a wave of soft brown curls down her back, with two braids pulling back the front of her hair to showcase her oval face. Simpler, but somehow more suited to who she wanted to be.

"Thank you, Leah. If we had more time, and I had my cosmetics, I would return the favor by showing you how to accent your eyes with kohl."

"It's a good thing you don't have any then."

"You never know what Silvan and the merchant might bring back."

"And what money would you purchase it with?" Leah smirked at her win.

Without being able to use her magic for a tradable skill, Audra was stuck unable to purchase new things. She sighed at the prospect of purchasing new clothes or books, ones that she could not find in the academic library of Rauha. Once again, Audra was beholden to the goodwill of others to provide her with necessities. Between the second-hand clothes, shelter, food, and other items gifted by Valeria, Audra longed for the opportunity to own something of her own. Helping with the harvest and daily chores alleviated some of the guilt at receiving everything when she could not pay for it, but Audra desired the ability to provide for herself.

Outside, the leaves were a blaze of changing colors, like a living fire throughout the forest. At the center of the small town, long tables were arranged around the perimeter of the square with plates of food stacked on them. Steam rose from platters of smoked fish, the scent of char lingering in the air. Weaving from table to table, sampling food and filling mugs till foam dribbled over the top, mages were gathering. Their mingled conversations sounded like a discordant symphony, voices calling out across the square at friends, people laughing at stories and working to be heard over the growing crowd. It was one of the most beautiful things Audra had ever heard.

Her people were vibrant and enthusiastic in their celebration. Here were people that gathered with each other because they enjoyed each other's company, not to petition for favor or build relationships built on what you could gain from the other person. Their small group joined the square, stopping to receive hugs and warm greetings from those they passed. As the newest mage in Ymira, Audra was peppered with questions and hesitant smiles as the other mages were introduced. Not wanting to be rude—and understanding that the other mages were using this as an opportunity to assess how she would fit in—Audra gave each person her undivided attention, allowing them to talk with her as long as they wanted before she continued on. Luckily, Isik provided a focal point for conversation, endearing himself to everyone they met, and giving Audra an exit from the conversation when he moved on.

"I thought I was going to have to send a rescue party for you," Leah said when Audra joined her and Taara at a table. They had excused themselves earlier, Leah loudly proclaiming that she would die of starvation if she waited for the princess to be free of her adoring public.

"Rescue would imply that I was not exactly where I wanted to be. This is my home now and I care about knowing the people who live here. Besides," Audra said with a furtive glance around, "if we hope to get assistance from other mages, I need them to like me."

Taara placed a warm hand over Audra's. "Just be yourself and they will come to like you just as much as we do. If they don't, then they aren't worth your time."

Warmth blossomed in Audra's chest and tears pricked at the edges of her vision at her friend's words. Years of needing to look, act, and appear perfect were all she knew, and Audra was still learning who she wanted to be outside those boundaries.

"Speak for yourself," Leah added. "I'm still working out if her nagging about posture and etiquette is worth it."

"I do not nag. But since you mentioned it, elbows off the table." Audra looked at her pointedly, but her mouth quivered at the corner as she suppressed a laugh.

Throughout their meal, more mages stopped at their table to meet Audra and converse with all three women. Eventually, Eli approached their table with a middle-aged couple. The taller of the two, Eli's mother, Myra, had strong arms and close-cropped red hair. Standing at her side was a man who could only be Eli's father, his blond hair and wide smile copied on Eli's features. Zackary and Myra owned a blacksmith's shop, selling tools and intricately detailed weapons.

"Your shop sounds lovely. I hope that you will allow me to visit one day."

"Stop by anytime you like. We love having Eli's friends over." With his deep laugh, perpetual smile and the twinkle in his eye, Audra believed that Zackary meant it and was not offering the invitation merely to be polite.

"Eli told us that you are from Solven. How has your transition to Ymira been?" Myra's voice rumbled like it was pulled over the coals in the kiln.

"Wonderful. I miss Solven, but this is quickly becoming my home. Everyone here has been welcoming and kind, which makes it easier to adjust."

"Although it has been many years, I remember what it was like leaving the only home I ever knew to reach Ymira." Myra glanced down at her son's chair and pain flickered in her eyes. Magic made adapting to life in a chair easier for him, but the world outside could be cruel and inaccessible to those who were different. "We were fortunate that Eli never had to leave home."

The look that passed between Zackary and Myra revealed a deep-seated sense of relief at their fortune as well as empathy for other parents who were not as fortunate. Magic was rare and Ymira's small population meant that magically-gifted children were uncommon. Like Audra's mother, children born without magic left Ymira when they reached adulthood, something Audra hoped to change. Glancing at the two parents, Audra wondered if she could count on their support, even if it meant the possibility of their son leaving.

Zackary pulled his wife close to his side. "Indeed, we were."

"What if we wanted to change that for other parents? Make it so that they did not need to be separated from their children to study in

Ymira?" Audra clasped her hands in front of her waist to prevent nervously fiddling with them.

Sharing another look with her husband, Myra turned and looked at Audra and her friends, measuring the determination in their faces. "That would be a welcome change, but not without its trials."

"Ymira is our home," Zackary continued, "and we won't leave it, but should you need help here, will we provide it."

"Thank you father, mother." Eli wheeled close to hug his parents. Over his shoulder, Myra locked eyes with Audra.

"Just be safe. All of you." With one final squeeze, Myra released Eli. As happy as Audra was to meet Eli's parents, watching the obvious affection between them caused a stab of longing for her own parents. She could no longer remember what it felt like to be held by them and it renewed her commitment to prevent that pain for mages.

"We will," the group responded unanimously.

"Now that that's settled, we'll leave you younger folk to enjoy the party." Zackary laced his fingers with his wife's.

"But it's still early! You should stay and dance with us." Taara bounced on her heels, eager to join the groups around the bonfire.

"Thank you, but Myra and I can dance at home." Zackary winked at his wife, causing Myra to laugh and Eli to flush.

"Dad!" Eli groaned and tried to push his father away.

"What? There is nothing wrong with me expressing my love for my wife."

"There is when you do it in front of my friends."

"Don't embarrass him further, honey." Myra gave Eli a kiss on the cheek before offering the others a small wave. Physically turning her husband in the opposite direction of the group, she said, "We'll leave you all to your evening. Enjoy yourselves."

Eli cleared his throat. "Sorry about them. My dad could probably use some of Audra's lessons on what's appropriate conversation in public." The group shared a laugh.

From the corner of the courtyard, a small group of musicians played the final chord to their song, the notes reverberating through the space. Audra let the music wash over her, each note sinking into her soul. Although she had never demonstrated an aptitude for playing an instrument, she appreciated the expressive way the group performed. The musicians swayed and tapped their feet to the beat, smiling and laughing with each other as they played for the sheer joy of it. Mages spun around them, dancing freely without any coordinated steps or patterns. It was the same way that Taara moved during their dance lessons, enjoying the moment instead of worrying about how she looked. Unlike Audra, whose love for dancing was hindered by a need to execute each movement correctly and had not experienced the unfettered joy that shone on the dancers' faces.

"Come dance with me." Taara tugged Audra towards the group, taking advantage of the pause between songs to find a space for them. Eli took up a position with the musicians, tuning a violin while Leah sat at a table nearby with a cup of mead.

Audra tried to pull her hand away, but the younger mage's grip was strong. "Thank you for offering, but I cannot."

"Sure you can! It's just like the dances you taught me."

"But I knew those dances," Audra whispered fiercely, embarrassed that the other dancers might hear her. "I do not know how to dance like this, without steps to follow."

"Then I can teach you. You've done so much to help me learn, it would mean a lot to me to teach you something for once." Those damn eyes, round and pleading, would be the death of Audra. How could she say no to that look?

"Alright, show me what to do."

"Yay! Okay, so, the most important part to remember is that there are no rules. Just feel the rhythm and move however it feels right."

Audra's body was stiff as the music started again. It felt like every eye in the courtyard was watching her, judging every stilted movement. Heat filled her cheeks and Audra glanced left and right at the other dancers. They made it look effortless. *You can speak four languages, dancing should not be this difficult.* Audra gave herself a mental pep talk.

Twirling in circles with her arms in the air, Taara nudged Audra with her hip. "Relax. Don't worry what other people are thinking."

"Easy for you to say." Audra tried to match Taara's movements, knowing that the look of concentration on her face made it seem like she was not enjoying herself.

"It's not easy for anyone. But what's the point of being here, living life, if you aren't enjoying it?"

Watching her shadow dance along the ground, cast from the flickering firelight, Audra contemplated Taara's words. Had her life become so focused on fitting a mold, working to create the perfect image, that she stopped enjoying the process? Reading, riding, even studying had lost the glow that came from experiencing them unless it was tied to achievement. When they were merely tasks to complete, it felt hollow once she checked it off her list.

How depressing.

Lifting her face to the sky, Audra vowed to herself that she would start enjoying her life again. Starting with this dance. With each song that played, Audra felt her body loosen, opening herself to the music and joy of unrestrained movement. She danced with Taara and other mages, as well as by herself.

Her movements were still slightly stiff and she could not completely stop worrying about what others thought, but it was fun. And that was enough.

Eleven

During the frigid months of winter, where outdoor activity was limited to one's endurance for the cold, Audra had little else to entertain her other than practicing magic. When the weather was bearable, Audra, Taara, Eli, and Leah visited friends in the village and helped out where needed. When they were indoors, the three women would play games, read together, and stay up late competing to come up with the most frightening stories they could imagine. Leah usually won and they would have to keep a low-lit lamp on to combat the shadows morphing into terrifying shapes in their imaginations. Audra loved those nights spent with her friends, the small moments bonding them together through laughter.

On one of those nights, Leah tossed her head in the direction of the kitchen door with a curt, "Follow me." Intrigued, Audra followed her into the crisp evening air.

The moon was glowing softly in the sky, the purple crescent acting as a guiding light from Hellig. It was the same moon that Safrina wrote about when she and her sisters cast the enchantment over Bria and the first Guards. The reason for the sigil of Ymira.

We have been betrayed, Safrina wrote, pages of journal entries detailing the initial signs of Dyrun's descent, agitation, lack of eating and sleeping, and threats against non-magical people, finally coming to a head. *I was blind to Dyrun's ambition, mistaking his thirst for knowledge and power as a sign of friendship. He lured us in with kind words and a love of magic. For weeks, he has urged us to use our magic to punish those whose crimes he considered unforgivable, using honeyed-words to persuade us that we were given power to guide non-magical people. Annika never agreed and Pennifrin followed her lead, but I was foolish and believed Dyrun knew better. That changed when I saw him in the forest today. I knew he was searching for a way to grow his power, but I kept it a secret from my sisters. Today proved just how naive I was. I found him kneeling in the glen, blackened grass and ashen plants around him, like life was leached from the soil. He did not sense me, so focused on his task, that I hid behind a tree to watch. His black nails dug into the earth as the circle grew, stretching out in front of him like a corpse. To my horror, a shape began to take form from the dead earth. Thick liquid bubbled from the ground, pulsing and twisting as it rose into a misshapen form as tall as Dyrun. Even without a face or distinguishable characteristics, my body froze, sensing an evil presence that had no place in this world. The forest around me was silent, nothing dared go near the vile creature. Then, before my very eyes, it surged over my one-time friend and consumed him. As quickly as I saw it appear, it was gone. How mistaken we were when I told my sisters of what I saw and they agreed that Dyrun met his end at the hands of whatever darkness his magic conjured.*

"...Audra. Hello! Are you listening to me?" Leah faced her with hands on her hips.

Blinking, Audra realized they had walked a large distance without her noticing. It was the same path that led to the bathing pools, but instead of following the slope down, Leah led Audra to the right, following a steady incline that led to an opening in the mountain. Flushing in embarrassment at being caught not paying attention, Audra murmured a quick apology.

Waving off the apology, Leah moved next to Audra to walk together up the path towards the entrance to a cave. "I was asking if you finished Safrina's journal. With the moon in the right phase tonight, I wanted to show you something."

"Oh, yes, I did. Sorry that I have not returned it to the library yet. I was hoping to study it more." There were still questions Audra had, and she wanted to re-read the pages to see if she overlooked the answers.

"Keep it as long as you need." Leah nudged her shoulder. "I thought you might have some questions. You know, since the only books you cared about before were on a certain prince."

Her guarded manner was loosening somewhat, her hostile tone gone as Audra got to know her better. After months of time together, Audra now knew that Leah's dry humor and critiques were her attempts at friendship, and her honesty—though sometimes brutal—was something Audra came to appreciate.

"You are just jealous that I have read more books than you," Audra teased back. "But I did have some questions about Safrina's journal. After witnessing Dyrun creating the first netvor, she mentions that they began hearing tales of horrific monsters appearing across the land and that several mages attempted to defeat them with no success. Then she writes about feeling hopeless in the face of such creatures, and that they were out of options trying to defeat them, so they prayed to Hellig for guidance. After that, the handwriting changes."

Dark rock walls surrounded them, jagged with age and the rough wear of the elements carving a natural opening into the mountain. Tools or magic had expanded the path that was barely visible from the light at the entrance. Audra's voice echoed through the small space, filling the cracks and accompanying the occasional drip of water from stalactites that punctured the roof of the cave. It still struck Audra as strange that the last entry in the journal was written by someone else, an anonymous source.

"What happened to the sisters?"

Turning from the last light, Leah's face was somber. "Come feel for yourself."

Confused by the odd choice of words, Audra stepped into the cave. At the end of the tunnel, bathed in the warm glow of mage crystals studded throughout the rock, was a sunken circle in the ground. By sight alone, the room was nothing special, just a continuation of the dark, sturdy rock from the entrance. But Audra felt a steady thrum in her veins when they crossed the threshold into the room. Like the vibration after plucking a stringed instrument, the resonant frequency of *something* filled the air and very ground that they walked on.

"What is that?" Her voice was barely a whisper. No sound emerged from the presence, but it felt familiar to Audra, like a dream that she could not remember after waking up, and it seemed disrespectful to disturb the quiet.

"That is Annika's magic." Leah stopped at the edge of the circle. "Years after mages settled in Ymira, someone found this cave and the letter waiting in this room. It was written by the same person as the final entry in the journal. Irene, Safrina's daughter, wrote that Hellig blessed the sisters with a vision of a warrior who was leading her clan to eradicate the netvor. They were shown a place—this place—where the warrior would meet them, and it was here that the sisters would need to cast a spell to gift the clan with enhanced abilities to fight netvor. As they cast the spell, Pennifrin was the first to tire, fatigue weakening her muscles until she passed out from the drain on her magic. When Safrina began to tire, she urged Annika to stop, saying that they needed more mages to cast the spell. But Annika knew that they only had one chance. Apart from her sisters, Annika was shown a vision that if Dyrun was not defeated by the next lunar cycle, he would drain the earth of enough power to be unstoppable. There was no time to gather other mages. So, Annika made her choice. Knocking Safrina unconscious, Annika used the last of her power to complete the spell."

Audra shivered as Leah told the story, imagining the sisters gathered on the floor of the cave, casting what had to have been the most powerful spell in existence under the guiding moon of Hellig. She thought of how afraid they must have been, and how desperate they were to save the world they loved.

Leah stepped around the circle, never entering it. "When Safrina and Pennifrin woke up, they found their magic nearly depleted, their once impressive capacity for magic reduced to a trickle of power. But while they mourned the loss of their power, it was nothing compared to looking across the circle to see their eldest sister gone. By using up all her power for the spell, Annika gave up her life, fading back into the earth. That is why you feel remnants of her power so long after she died, because draining her magic fed it back into the earth, and now it lives here like an imprint of her soul."

Humbled by the weight of Annika's sacrifice, Audra dropped to her knees on the ground. Moments later, Leah joined her, their heads bent in somber reflection.

"Why did you bring me here?" Audra whispered.

"Because you need to know our history. That even though we may not have a king or a crown, what we do here matters. What *you* are doing here matters. And even if the world forgets that, Hellig gave us a place among the stars."

Lifting her face to the ceiling, Audra could imagine the three stars that shined brilliantly alongside the moon, guiding light to the lost and hopeless. Three stars for three sisters. The completed emblem of Ymira.

TWELVE

"Silvan...is coming...back!" Audra looked up from the book she was reading on the foundations of magic as Taara skidded to a stop on the midnight blue rug in the library, arms braced on her knees as she gulped down air.

Draped over the arms of an overstuffed armchair, the silver twin of the one Audra was sitting in, Leah set down her own book and regarded Taara upside down. Though the weather was warming with the first signs of spring, lingering frost necessitated the crackling fire in the room, maintained by Audra's magic.

To strengthen her magical endurance, Valeria had Audra using magic for every task around the hall, pushing her to exhaustion at the end of every day as she stretched the limits of her power. As if that was not enough to have her fall into deep sleep the moment her head hit the pillow, Leah was also training her in magical combat. Each afternoon, they met in the empty hillside and sparred. Audra still landed on her ass more than she would like, but Leah said she was almost passable in a fight, the closest to a compliment she would give.

"Just remember that your greatest advantage in a fight is distance," Leah told her the week prior. "Most weapons are designed for close range. Disarm your opponent before they can reach you and you'll be safe."

Though it had only been a few months, the group felt Silvan's absence like a link pulled from a chain. His flirtatious banter and confident attitude were missed, and Audra knew they all worried for his safety. Especially with recent reports of attacks from Kalmere increasing.

"Deep breaths, Taara." Audra uncurled her legs, earning a glare from Isik as he was dislodged from his curled position behind her knees. "Start from the beginning."

"Well, I was with Valeria practicing my potion making. I was working on a new idea I had, something to help soothe stomach distress. You know how sometimes a particular food upsets your stomach, but not because it went bad?" Her face crinkled thinking about it.

"Yes, I am familiar with the sensation." Audra was used to Taara's conversational tangents by now and knew if she tried to divert her back to the original topic, Taara would need a few moments to recall what they were talking about. It was quicker to allow her thoughts to continue down their path until it looped back around.

"Great—or not great if you are in pain—but I thought that I could make an antidote that would target a person's stomach to ease the discomfort. They would still need to avoid the food that caused distress, but at least they wouldn't be in pain."

"Very considerate, Taara."

"Thank you. So, I was with Valeria when a letter arrived from one of the merchants, letting us know that they would be here in two days, along with a note from Silvan!"

She waved the paper over her head like a victory banner.

"Are you going to read us the note, or shall we guess what it says?" Leah leaned sideways to scratch Isik under his chin when he nudged her leg with his nose. Never one to stay mad for long, the fox was quick to receive attention from whomever was willing to give it.

"I'm getting there! Geez, you're worse than Audra at waiting."

"Hey! I have been very patient." Not that the anticipation was not killing her waiting to hear what their friend wrote.

"Please," Leah breathed out the word with a snort. "Don't pretend like you weren't five seconds away from grabbing the letter out of her hand and reading it yourself." Audra's hands twitched where they were holding on to the edge of the chair. She was not going to admit how accurate Leah's assessment was.

Hands on her hips, Taara gave them both her best approximation of a stern glare, failing to achieve the desired effect based on the smile pulling at her lips.

"You two are arguing like children. If you don't quiet down, I can't read you the note." Both women quieted immediately. "Good, now, here's what it says." Taara unfolded the paper and read aloud.

> *Friends,*
>
> *Did you miss me? Of course you did. You will be glad to know that I am doing well and am returning to Ymira in two days with a representative from the merchant guild. I have so many stories to share with you all, and I expect tales of your escapades in return. Plan a large feast for my return! See you all soon,*
>
> *Silvan.*

A small smirk played on Leah's face at the end of the note. "At least we know he didn't lose his flair for the dramatic while he was away."

"No, that he did not." Standing up, Audra put away the book she was reading before putting out the fire. "Come along then," she pulled Leah up off her chair.

"Where are you dragging me to now?"

"The kitchens. We have a feast to prepare."

Isik perked up at the word kitchen, having quickly learned the word for where meals and snacks came from, and padded after the friends.

"What do you think the merchant brought this time?" Taara picked at a frayed seam on her sleeve while they walked down the corridors. It felt like a lifetime ago that Audra was getting lost in these halls. Now, the tapestries and paintings guided her path.

"Probably the usual assortment. Fabrics, seedlings, artwork, and crafting supplies," Leah replied. "Was there something you were hoping for?"

"No. At least, not for me." Taara averted her gaze. "Eli was hoping to get new plants to study."

"Plants, huh? You have an interesting way of flirting."

"F-flirting? No, no, no." Taara's voice began to squeak as it raised in pitch, her hands fluttering nervously in front of her as she tried to deny it. "You have it all wrong. Eli's just a friend."

"Sure, keep telling yourself that." Leah's laugh rang out through the hall as she pulled Taara into a side hug. "Between your and Audra's love lives, I'm glad I don't have to worry about any of that for myself."

Not wanting to draw the conversation onto her own dismal attempt at love, Audra quickly pivoted back to the arrival of the merchant as they stepped into the kitchen. "Hopefully, the merchant brings fabric. It would be nice to own clothes of my own." Not wanting to hurt Leah's feelings she quickly added, "Not that there was anything wrong with the ones you gave me."

"Black really isn't your color anyways. What were you thinking of getting?"

Audra's only parameters for clothing were the pastel dresses from Solven and the black or earth-tone ensembles from Ymira. Clothing was something that was given to her, not something she ever had the chance to select herself. When she admitted as much, Leah slowed her steps so that she and Audra were several paces behind Taara.

"Just pick whatever feels most like you," Leah urged her. "Not what anyone else expects you to wear, but what you want."

Audra looked at her from the corner of her eye before quickly averting her gaze, tucking her head into her shoulder. "What if I do not know what that is?"

A hand on her forearm stopped Audra before she turned into the kitchen. Leah's deep eyes met hers, unflinching. "Then take as much time as you want to figure that out. Clothes are an expression of who you are. If you want to wear a different color every day of the week? Do it. Pants, dresses, flowing robes, or armor, it only matters if it is what *you* want. I can sketch some patterns if you want? See what speaks to you."

Gratitude flooded Audra and threatened to choke the words in her throat. Though she meant well, there was an image that Queen Isadora projected, and Audra wanted so desperately to be like her, that she never questioned the queen's choices in wardrobe. She liked pastels and the beautiful dresses that she got to wear, but there was a part of her that wanted to wear something...more. None of it ever felt right, like she was an actor in a play, her costume turning her into the princess she never would be. With magic, Audra unlocked a part of herself that was raw and honest, and she longed for a way to express that internal growth externally. Cut free from the strings of what it meant to be a princess, Audra could be herself, wearing whatever felt right. Deeper, richer colors and luxurious fabrics. As well as comfortable pants and tight shirts that made her feel confident and powerful. The prospect of getting to explore new colors and fabrics was exciting, and Audra was ready to step out of her old shell and show the world who she was, magic and all.

Pulling Leah close, Audra whispered, "Thank you."

Returning the gesture, Leah tucked her head into Audra's shoulder. "That's what friends are for. You deserve to be yourself. Everyone does."

They hugged for a moment, before Audra pulled away with a sniff, wiping away the moisture from her eyes. With a nudge from Leah, Audra continued into the kitchen, turning the conversation back to Silvan's arrival.

Two days later, Audra, Leah, Taara, and Eli waited at the edge of the wards, staring down the winding path for the first sign of Silvan. From their vantage point, Audra could not see past the bend to the kingdom below, but she knew that spring would be in full force in Solven. Where winter was slowly relaxing its hold on Ymira, the ground thawing to soon allow the planting of seeds for the harvest and melting snow filling the river, the base of the mountain would be decorated with new plant growth, bursts of color from wildflowers surrounding tilled earth for crops. Audra recalled walking through the castle's gardens with Graham when the first flowers began to bloom. There was something special about being the first person to view the new life, touching the velvet-soft petals before they were battered by the wind, sun, and rain. Each year, when she returned to her room after their walk, Audra found a single flower waiting on her dressing table.

The rattle of a heavy pack and scuffle of feet broke Audra from her thoughts, the bright sun preventing her from seeing more than a shad-owed figure approaching.

"I'm back!" Silvan called out in a sing-song voice, waving like a returning royal. Per Valeria's instructions, the merchant was waiting at the base of the mountain—far enough away from the ward—where mages would conduct trades. Originally, the group wanted to invite the merchant into Ymira to trade, but Valeria shut down the idea with stern authority. Letting a mage out of the ward was one thing, a risk that an individual alone took, but letting someone in risked every person in Ymira. A risk Valeria was not willing to take this soon.

Alone, Silvan came into view, his hair longer now, brushing the shoulders of his flowing tunic and pants that were popular in Feldor. "Hells, I forgot how cold it would be this high up."

Catching a flash of color as Silvan's hands moved to emphasize his words, Audra reached out to grasp his hand between hers. Decorating each nail were bright splashes of yellow paint, making his fingers look like flowers.

"Do you like them?" Silvan wiggled his fingers. "I got the idea from a performer in Feldor. They painted their nails to match their costume. Imagine all the colors we could create with Eli's plants."

"They're so pretty! Can you paint mine?" Taara took Silvan's hands and placed the nails next to hers to see how the color would look against her skin.

"As if I could deny you anything, Taara. We'll make a night of it. Wine, snacks, and pampering as we swap stories."

"Glad to hear you have your priorities straight." Leah jerked Silvan into an approximation of a hug, surprise clouding his face at the gesture.

"I missed you too," Silvan replied, squeezing Leah tighter.

"All right, make some room. Best friend coming through." Eli nudged Leah aside with his chair. Anxiety over his friend's status was a constant companion to Eli the past months, the stress etched on his face and the tight draw of his shoulders. Running an assessing gaze over his friend, Eli smiled when he saw his friend healthy and happy. "It's good to have you back," Eli said as he pulled Silvan into a hug.

For a moment, Silvan allowed his head to rest on Eli's shoulder, shifting the burden of its weight onto his friend before straightening.

"Audra." Silvan turned to address her warmly with open arms, and she walked into his embrace. Holding him tight, Audra breathed in the smell of his spiced-orange soap. It was remarkable that he could travel for days and not reek of sweat and grime. "Did you just sniff me?"

"Of course not. That would be inconsiderate." Audra flashed him a playful smile. "Although, now that you mention it, I am curious how you managed to stay so clean after months travelling."

"Allow a man to keep some of his secrets, Audra, dear."

Audra carefully examined his face, noticing the slight shadows under his eyes and the pronounced cut of his cheekbones. "Are you well?"

"Of course, mother." Silvan laughed with a smile that failed to reach his eyes. "Tired and hungry from the journey, but not every aspect of travel is luxurious."

Eli cheerfully clapped Silvan on the back. "Let's get you home, then. I hope you weren't planning on resting soon, because it will be hours yet with the feast we planned."

Violet and pink rays chased away the last brilliant orange of the sky by the time Audra was able to meet privately with her friends. Tucking a bottle of wine in her elbow while her hands gripped the glasses, Audra waved the door to her bedchamber open. Laughter poured through the open portal, the happy sound bringing a smile to Audra's face. It was reassuring to hear the light notes of Silvan's laugh meld with Eli's deeper rumble, Taara's rich twinkle, and Leah's scratchy chortle. Throughout the evening, Audra caught moments where Silvan looked somber, as if drawn deep into thought, his lips curving into a frown and eyes hardening. Something on the journey was causing those thoughts and Audra was determined to find out what. Hence the wine.

Small vials of colored liquid lay scattered across the floor with brushes and bowls of green, tacky mixtures. True to his word, Silvan was currently painting Taara's toenails petal pink, her fingernails drying on her knees where she was sitting on the floor. After slathering the green substance on their faces—the newest beauty trend in Feldor—they each selected a color to paint their nails.

"Audra, look!" Taara squealed as she wiggled her fingers in Audra's direction. Choosing to get her nails painted last, Audra had gone to get beverages for the group. "Aren't they pretty?"

"Very beautiful. That color suits you perfectly," Audra said after setting down the wine and glasses to properly admire Taara's nails.

"Thanks! Silvan made it with one of Eli's flowers."

"Yes, my genius knows no bounds. Now quit wiggling or I'll never finish."

Leah began pouring the wine and passed the glasses around, handing Taara a glass of water. "So, what else did you learn on your trip?" She gestured with her glass. "Or was it all a relaxing spa trip for you?"

A year ago, Audra would have thought that Leah was acting callous and unkind, but now she knew that Leah hid her worry behind sarcasm and dry humor. In Silvan's absence, she had taken up the habit of picking at her nails when stressed, something Silvan had chastised her for as he painted her nails blue to match her hair.

Arching a manicured brow at her, Silvan replied dryly, "Tactful. I'll remember that next time I bring home gifts." Reclining against the foot of Audra's bed, he took a swig of wine before continuing. "The trip proved valuable in more ways than one. It was incredible to see more of the kingdoms than I ever had before. Traveling with a merchant, Cellan, opened more doors than I would have received otherwise."

Eli leaned against the chest at the base of Taara's bed, his blue nails running through the fur of Isik's head on his lap. "How so?"

"People recognize and trust Cellan. As an outsider, they were already suspicious of me, but most were willing to listen once Cellan introduced me as his traveling companion."

"Most?" Audra knew that mages would not be welcome everywhere, but she needed to know exactly how and where opposition lay so that they could adjust their plans accordingly. Silvan turned so their eyes could meet, a flash of pain quickly masked.

"Cellan and the other merchants are familiar with what towns and villages want mage products, so those were our primary destinations. Some places would trade with us, but banned me from staying there on account of 'what I am.' Others drove us away, wanting nothing to do with a mage. I knew that not everyone would be receptive, but it still hurt to see how much they hated me without even bothering to get to know me. They called me horrible names and threatened me. Some even bragged about the vile things they had done to mages before."

A somber weight fell over the group like a blanket. Audra wrapped an arm around Silvan's shoulders and pulled him close. "I am so sorry that you had to go through that. You did not deserve to be treated that way. No one does." The others vocalized their agreement, scooting closer to hug Silvan. "I appreciate you sharing that with us."

"Of course. We all need to be prepared for what is out there. I never felt unsafe. Threats by people hiding behind cloaks, too cowardly to show their faces, are nothing against magic." With a forced smile, Silvan opened his palm to send sparks of light into the air.

Audra froze. "People behind cloaks? Silvan, are you okay? If things are too risky, you should not go back out." They could change their plans if it meant keeping each other safe.

Shaking off her concern, Silvan minimized the incident. "It was nothing I couldn't handle, and few were bold enough to approach me directly. Most just ignored me if they did not want to interact with a mage. There were plenty more who were interested in trading with us, or just pretending to so they could stare at the unusual sight. People definitely want what we have to offer. After the first few months, when word started getting around that I was with Cellan, people came to us with requests. I helped as many as I could, but some required traveling beyond the route we were on."

Some of the light was returning to Silvan's eyes, his posture softening as he shared details for a few of the requests he had accepted.

"We need more people, more power, out there." His expression was more serious than Audra had seen before. "There was a young girl in a town near the edge of Feldor, who I suspect has magic. We did not stay long enough for me to verify my suspicions, but if we had other mages traveling, one of them could have stayed with her. Taught her if she did not want to travel here."

Helping the mages who lived outside Ymira was just as important as helping those within. But, they had to be tactful.

"I agree," said Audra, "but it was difficult enough not knowing where you were. If more people leave, we need a better system for sending messages."

"What if they were instructed to check in with enchanted paper?" Eli asked.

"That only goes one way. Without knowing where they are, I could not send a return message to any of them."

"At least they could keep you updated with their progress and any concerns that you need to address."

Eli had a point. A better solution than they currently had, and Audra could ask that if they needed a response, that the mage provide a location for a reply.

"All right. Silvan, what other ideas do you have?" Apprehension filled her when Silvan flicked his eyes away, rubbing his lips together as he pondered the best way to share what was on his mind. Whatever it was, Audra knew she would not like it.

"To start, more mages need to travel with merchants to broaden our reach. Even still, we lack the influence and connections that are truly needed to make change. We need invitations into the courts, where decisions with real power are made. If the nobility accepts us, public opinion will follow."

Audra's breath quickened as she connected what Silvan left unsaid. She clenched the fabric of her skirt in her fist.

"Please do not ask that of me, Silvan." She could hear the tremble in her voice. "I cannot see G—" Audra paused. "Them," she corrected herself. She was not going to make this about Graham.

"You cannot hide from them forever, Audra." Silvan's words had a harsh edge, his fists clenched against his thigh. "You wanted to help us. This is how you help us."

Leah offered her an understanding smile. "You're the only one with a connection to the palace. Without you, we wouldn't even make it past the gates."

Anger lanced her chest at the thought of seeing Graham again, magic swirling in response. Distanced, the pain of his rejection was a dull pain now, like a bruise, but Audra did not trust her reaction if she saw him happy with someone else. "They may not let me through the gates either. Not with the way I left." Isik sensed her discomfort and padded over to rest in her lap, offering what comfort he could. Embarrassment heated her cheeks at the thought of the royal family turning her away.

"How you left may not have been great, but they were your family. Perhaps they might understand better than you think." Taara rested her hand on Audra's ankle. It was easy to forget, with her cheerful demeanor, that Taara had emotional intelligence beyond her years. "And we'll be with you, too."

This was the difficult part that came with being a leader. Painful as it was to face, her friends were right. Logically, she knew it was the right decision. Her personal connections to the royal family would open doors for alliances and resources for her people. She just had to find a way to do that without damaging her healing heart.

"Alright, I can start with Kasteel." He was the safest choice. "But I will need to take things slow. Rebuild the relationship before I can ask for his assistance with the king and queen."

Patting Audra's knee, Silvan stood up with a clap of his hands. "Good. Now that that's settled, let's solve the problem of your dry skin. We can't have you meeting royalty like that. Everyone, clean off your faces. It's time for step two!"

Laughter filled the room once more as Leah groaned. "There is not enough wine in the world to put up with this."

The next morning, Audra rose early, stepping over Eli and Silvan's sprawled limbs on the floor. After consuming more bottles of wine than was advisable, they were too drunk and tired to make it back to their own room and used spare pillows and blankets for makeshift bedding on the floor. With a wave of her hand, Audra used magic to cover Silvan with a blanket and moved Eli's chair closer to him in case he needed it. Taara was facedown in her pillow, snoring softly with her arm wrapped around Isik, while Leah was lying straight as an arrow, blankets hardly rumpled from her ability to sleep without moving. Taking a moment to observe her friends while they were completely relaxed, Audra smiled. She loved them all fiercely and would do anything to keep them peaceful and safe.

Starting with reconnecting with Solven's royal family.

Thirteen

Creaks of wooden beams finding their homes and thuds of stone being set atop stone filled the air of Ymira. After a lengthy discussion with Valeria, families would no longer be separated to protect mages. Any new mages coming to the ward could cross with their family, and all Ymira's current citizens could invite their family to live with them. Per Silvan's suggestion, three additional mages departed with him when he left with Cellan. That way, if they found someone who wanted to study magic without leaving their home, a mage could stay and train them.

With the anticipated influx of newcomers—including Taara's fathers and siblings—mages were hard at work carting supplies from the forest and mountain to finish adding new dwelling areas to existing homes and building new cottages. Days were longer now, providing additional daylight to work through, as well as warmer, which necessitated breaks during the peak of the day to rest in the shade. Audra watched the progress from the open window in Valeria's study, letters and their responses crowding the desk behind her.

Including one from Kasteel. Through the network of merchants, Silvan had managed to get Audra's letter delivered, and the reply sat atop a pile of correspondence. It was there when she arrived that morning, silently mocking her cowardice every minute it sat unopened. For a while, Audra was able to ignore its presence, focusing on requests for supplies and building plans. Now that there was nothing else to preoccupy her time, Audra reached for the letter.

"Just like pulling out a splinter. You have to get it over with," she tried to tell herself. Breaking the seal, Audra unfolded the paper, hastily scanning over the few lines of text. Reading and writing at length gave him headaches, so Kasteel's letters had always been brief.

> *Sprite,*
> *Glad to know you are not dead. I miss you and have big news.*
> *Come visit my estate in Nabura and we can talk more.*
> *Love,*
> *Kasteel*

"It must be good news then, if you are smiling like that." Valeria was quiet as Isik when she entered the room, managing to get by undetected.

"It is. Kasteel invited me to his home."

"You sound surprised."

"To be honest, I was unsure how he would respond to my letter." Audra's fingers toyed with the letter, dragging along the folded seams as she gathered her thoughts. "With how I left things, I was...anxious that he would be angry or ignore me, which I would have understood. But, I am glad he did not."

"From what you have shared of your friendship, he sounds like someone who respected your choices, even if he did not agree with them." Valeria sat in her favorite armchair, warming a pot of tea and arranging cups, sugar, and cream with magic. "Do you want to see him again?"

"It would be the right thing to do for Ymira. Having Kasteel as an ally could open doors to other noble houses."

"That was not what I asked."

Sighing, Audra crossed her arms over her chest, staring at the pattern of Ymira's emblem on the rug beneath her slippered feet. Hellig's crescent moon and the three stars for Annika, Safrina, and

Pennifrin. A reminder of her legacy. "I miss his friendship and do want to see him, but not if it means seeing Graham again."

Valeria hummed noncommittally. "You cannot avoid him forever, you know. If you continue pushing mages out into the world, your paths will cross eventually."

"I know." She dropped into the chair across Valeria, holding her head in her hands. "But not just yet. I want to...be someone when I see him again."

"As opposed to what, a figment of our collective imaginations? You have always been someone, you just had difficulty seeing who that was."

Maybe that was true. For years, Audra worked to be someone that fit with the royal family and the life they gave her. She dressed in the clothes they gave her, did activities they suggested, learned what they thought she should know, and acted in a way that would not dishonor them. Not that they meant any of it maliciously. No, they did love her. But she had spent so much time being who she thought she should be that she had to relearn who she was.

Seeing Kasteel was the first hurdle. As soon as time permitted, she would arrange a visit with him. Her responsibility to her people meant waiting until the families arrived in Ymira, but once they were settled, she could travel. For the first time since Audra left, seeing a member of Solven's royal family did not fill her with dread. The dark places inside her that grew after her departure were lightened by cautious optimism. With the prospect of reconciliation fresh in her mind, Audra scrawled a quick reply, folding it into a swan and opening the window to allow magic to carry it to its destination.

Nestled on the border of Solven and Feldor, Nahura was a collection of bright white buildings with domed ceilings and pale, stone structures with tiled roofs. Shuttered windows were open to allow mild breezes to cool the rooms and dry the laundry hanging on lines. Taking advantage of warmer weather than she was used to in the fall, Audra had the windows of the carriage open, wind playing with strands of her loose hair as she watched the streets pass by. Tarps colored in bright yellows and pinks, rusty oranges, and teal billowed in the sky above her, covering the street in shade where they connected one collection of buildings to another.

This was her first time in Nabura and Audra was enchanted by the gently sloping streets and brightly colored doors. Though they were still in Solven, voices speaking Feldorian and people dressed in the bright colors of the neighboring country filtered through the streets. The relationship between the two kingdoms had always been strong, and people around the borders often had heritage from both. It was curious that Kasteel was given an estate here. Traditionally, the noble that oversaw Nebura shared both Feldorian and Solvenian ancestry, connecting them to the people and land they governed on behalf of the crown. Despite being born in Cordille, Kasteel was raised as the king's son and was as much part of Solven as any born citizen. He had no connection to Feldor.

Audra got her answer as the estate came into view. Situated at the crest of a small hill overlooking the town was a two-story manor built with the same light stone as the surrounding homes. Short, thin-limbed trees were arranged around the home, providing shade amongst a collection of garden beds filled with short, prickly plants and sand-colored pebbles. Twin pools of water lined the path to the door, large pointed flowers floating on the surface. Audra watched as the door opened and Kasteel stepped out, a smile on her face at the sight of her old friend. Her joy morphed into delighted surprise when a woman stepped out after him, linking their hands together as they watched the carriage roll to a stop. *So this must be the big news,* Audra thought as she looked at the couple. They complemented each other beautifully, Kasteel's olive skin and rugged countenance pairing well with the woman's bronze tones and elegant features. A sense of recognition tingled in the back of Audra's mind as the couple stepped forward with warm smiles.

"Audra," Kasteel opened her carriage door before hugging her tightly, dangling her feet off the ground as he swung her in a circle. Mirth bubbled in her chest before escaping via laughter.

"Put me down, you brute." Audra wriggled as she half-heartedly tried to escape. Dulled by memory, his features were different than she remembered, silver flecks in his long hair and hints of wrinkles on his forehead. But his warmth and love she remembered perfectly.

"Sorry, Sprite, but I missed you too much." Holding her at arm's length, Kasteel scanned his eyes over her. "Look at you. All grown up now."

She wondered what he saw when he looked at her. Would he notice everything that was new, her longer hair lightened by the sun and the aura of magic that followed in her wake, or did she still resemble the girl he once knew?

"We need to work on your compliments, my love. That is no way to greet a friend." Memories of that rich, melodic voice danced in Audra's brain when the woman spoke. She sounded just like...but it could not be...could it?

Kasteel kissed the woman's round cheek, barely having to lean over to reach. "You're right, as always. Audra, you look lovely."

"Thank you, it never hurts to hear it." She laughed at the look of surprise on his face. In the past, Audra would have demurred at the compliment, but Leah had taught her to own who she was.

With a gentle nudge from the woman next to him, Kasteel remembered himself. "May I introduce my beautiful wife, Princess Esha of Feldor."

Audra nearly choked on the confirmation. She knew the woman looked and sounded familiar. Curiosity to learn the story of how Esha went from dancing with Graham at the ball to marrying Kasteel warred with Audra's ingrained manners.

"A pleasure to meet you, Your Highness. I look forward to learning more about the woman who managed to capture Kasteel's heart." Audra was surprised to find that she meant it.

In her youth, she had unfairly resented Esha for the humiliating events of the ball. Quickly, she realized the blame was misplaced, because the princess had no way of knowing the significance of that dance to Audra. Whatever led them to be together, Audra was truly happy for their marriage.

"Please, call me Esha. Kasteel has told me so much about you that I feel as if I know you already. I am sorry about the circumstances around our initial meeting, but I hope that we can become friends."

Esha's sincere smile and open affection for Kasteel endeared her to Audra's heart already. "Then you must call me Audra."

With introductions out of the way, the group made their way into the house. Audra gasped in awe at the contrast between the simple exterior and the intricate details inside. A stunning, tiled mosaic patterned like ocean waves covered the floor of the entryway, casting the room in a cool glow as the sun reflected off it. Matching tiles covered square alcoves, decorating the wall in place of paintings. Sunlight and fresh air poured through the open-air courtyard, glinting off a reflecting pool and swaying the fronds of small trees. Low chairs and couches covered in brightly colored pillows with gold beaded embroidery were placed in shaded areas. Pillars lined the edges of the path, supporting the second floor and allowing guests to view the space in its entirety.

"Beautiful, isn't it?" Kasteel looked more relaxed in this space than Audra had ever seen him. "We based it on the palace Esha grew up in."

"It is magnificent. Your home must be breathtaking."

"Feldor is a wonderful country. This is my home now, but having the reminders of my past makes it easier to be away from my family."

As Audra looked around, she recognized the influence of Kasteel's heritage in the banister scrollwork and carved ceilings. It was incredible to see how they took parts from each of their lives and created something of their own. Their tour took them through the sitting room, dining room, study, and music room before continuing upstairs to the private rooms. They gave Audra a room patterned in shades of blue, bidding her farewell so that she could rest before they met for dinner.

The room reminded her of the coast. Sky blue walls were broken up by windows open to a view of the town. The stuffed chair and bedcover were deep blue and were tufted in wave-like patterns. Seashells were embedded in the wall, creating a swirling pattern that matched the shell-woven baskets holding magelights. Efficient as ever, staff had already unpacked her bags, placing her cosmetics on a distressed-wood table and her clothes in the matching wardrobe. Disrobing, Audra fell onto the lightweight sheets and drifted off to sleep.

"What are you doing?" A boy with unruly brown hair stared at Audra, legs hanging over a branch of the tree she was sitting under so that his body dangled upside down. She had just moved to the palace and

remembered that this boy was the oldest of the two princes. Surprise had her brain scrambling to remember his name. It was something tricky, with sounds that got jumbled on her tongue. All Audra recalled was that it reminded her of a fish.

"I'm reading," she wiped her runny nose on the back of her sleeve.

"Really," the boy tilted his head to the side, "because it looked like you were crying." In a feat of acrobatics that seemed impossible to Audra's young mind, the boy curled inward before flipping forward off the branch, landing on the grass without stumbling.

"I wasn't." The tears currently leaking from her eyes betrayed her.

"Crying is our heart's way of letting out the sadness." His long legs stretched out next to hers in the grass. "I'm sorry about your parents. It's okay if you miss them and you don't have to hide if you need to cry. I won't tell anyone."

"Y-you won't?" Audra hiccuped and rubbed her tear-stained face with her sleeve.

"Nope. And if you are feeling sad, you can come play with me and my brother. We can be your family now."

Waking in the darkened room, Audra stretched and went to the washroom to prepare for dinner. Dressed in a topaz gown that Leah designed, the light and breathable fabric suited the warmer climate, and the short sleeves and scooped neckline rimmed with lace that matched the overskirt were inspired by Ymiran fashion. Styling her hair in a thick braid that fell over one shoulder, Audra added a touch of cosmetics to complete her look before making her way to the dining room.

Hanging lanterns illuminated the white walls with multi-colored lights, making the room look like the inside of a tent. More tiled mosaics lined the space, tall windows spaced evenly along the two outside facing walls, their shutters open to the night air. Kasteel and Esha sat together on a cushioned bench at one end of the low table, their heads bent together in intimate conversation. When they saw Audra, they rose to greet her with smiles on their faces.

"Your gown is stunning, I adore that color on you." Esha kissed her cheeks after Kasteel wrapped her in another hug.

Audra gave a small twirl. "And here I was envious of your outfit. Want to trade?" Dressed in a teal, wrapped shirt and pants that billowed before tucking at the ankles, Esha managed to look regal and casual at the same time.

"Deal. Although, if all your clothing is that beautiful, you might end up leaving with none of it."

Bringing his wife's hand to his lips, Kasteel placed a kiss on the back, laughter in his eyes. "My love, you do not need to rob my friend of her wardrobe. If you wish for new garments, we will have them made. Audra, I don't suppose you would share the name of your seamster?"

"Of course, I am always happy to help a friend."

At that, a melancholy look passed over Kasteel's face, his lips turning down slightly as he ran a hand up and down the stem of his glass. Years apart had not changed his nervous tick. Something that she had said was bothering him. Unwilling to sit in uncomfortable silence, Audra asked what was wrong and braced for the worst.

"After everything that happened, I worried that you would no longer consider me a friend."

Shame slid like molten lava down her throat, burning the backs of her eyes and threatening to spill free. Though Kasteel still called her a friend, Audra was angry at herself for letting him think that she no longer considered him one.

"You were the first friend I ever made, and I will always consider you a true friend. I am so sorry that I ever caused you to doubt that." Her eyes were locked on his, urging him to see the sincerity pooling in their depths.

A warm, calloused hand settled over hers. "I forgive you, but it hurt when you left. I was worried when we never got another letter from you, and wondered if I should have done more to stop you. But I love you, the sister of my heart, and you will always be welcome in my home."

"And you in mine. Both of you." Audra reached out her other hand to grab Esha's, their connected hands forming a triangle over the table. It felt like another hole had been sealed in the dam of her grief, the love of her friend more soothing than any balm magic could make.

Giving her hand a squeeze, Esha apologized as well. "I am happy that you consider me a friend as well, and am sorry for my part in your heartbreak. Kasteel told me about your childhood with Graham. Had I known what that dance meant to you—what Graham meant to you—I would not have danced with him."

Audra knew there was no reason for Esha to apologize, as a visiting princess it would have been unthinkable to refuse a dance with Graham. "There is nothing to forgive. You could not have known, and even if you did, it was not just the dancing that broke my heart." Clearing her throat, Audra glanced away and quickly breathed out the rest. "I heard what he said that night in the kitchen, Kasteel. That he did not want me to love him. That was the reason I left."

His cheeks darkened with embarrassment, and Kasteel reached for Audra's hand to return her gaze to his. The couple looked at her with empathy and kindness, not pity like she feared.

"He never should have said that, Sprite," Kasteel's voice was steady and reassuring. "You may not believe me, but Graham was not himself that night. I know he did not mean what he said. If—"

"I would rather not talk about him," Audra interrupted. Her heart may be mending, but hope had the power to destroy her all over again. Nothing could come of it anyways, she lived in Ymira now. "I would much rather hear more about how the two of you met."

Laughter eased the tension as the couple shared the story of their courtship, passing parts of the story between each other like a dance. Apparently, Kasteel fell in love with her almost immediately. Esha initially married him to get help with a netvor problem in Feldor—and escape an arranged marriage—but Kasteel used that as an opportunity to court her and she quickly fell just as deeply in love with him. As they spoke, Esha began removing lids from covered dishes, Kasteel spooning food onto her and Audra's plates first before serving himself. Succulent meats simmered in curries, their aroma complementing the roasted vegetables and steamed saffron rice that filled each plate.

"From the moment we met, Kasteel showed me that he cared. Making sure the kitchens prepared some of my favorite foods, taking care of my horse after we went riding. Once I got him to open up, I knew I found someone who understood me. Who would choose me, every day, and love me even when things were difficult. And I knew that I could love him the same way." Esha cupped Kasteel's jaw, bringing his face closer to share a kiss.

"You deserve the world, my love." Kasteel brushed her hair off her face. "I am just glad that you chose to be my world."

Hells, the tender way the pair looked at each other bordered on sickeningly sweet. Feeling like she was intruding on a private moment, Audra averted her gaze to the window and remained quiet. Of course, that was the moment her stomach rumbled with hunger. Waiting for her hosts to start eating, Audra had yet to take a bite.

Kasteel set her plate in front of her. "Glad to hear you have the same appetite."

"How kind of you to remember," she teased. How easy it was to return to their sibling-like teasing and squabbling. "I see yours has not changed either. Though I have heard that old men like you need to keep up their strength."

"Old? Did you hear that, my love? She wounds me." Clutching playfully at his chest, Kasteel burrowed his face in Esha's shoulder in mock despair. Audra smiled broadly. As long as she had known him, Kasteel had a jovial disposition, but seeing him like this was especially touching. Every movement spoke of adoration for his wife, constantly touching her just because he could, eyes softening whenever he looked at her, and the lightness of spirit that radiated from him in her presence. And Esha mirrored those emotions.

Happy as she was for her friends, envy twisted its way into Audra's heart as she watched them, wishing for that kind of love in her life.

As the evening wore on, drinks were continually filled and food was cleared from the table. Peels of laughter flowed out the open windows as Audra and Kasteel shared stories of their childhood with Esha, both determined to make the other more embarrassed. In return, Esha shared stories of her own childhood and the mischief her siblings and cousins got into.

"There was one time, after a bard had visited the castle, that I tried to run away to Ymira."

"No! How old were you?" Wine buzzed pleasantly in Audra's veins, and she spoke louder than she intended. Setting the glass down, she decided that she had probably had enough wine for one night.

"Practically an adult! Or, at least that was what I thought at ten years old. The bard told such fantastical stories of dark enchantments and curses, and I was determined to find out if they were true. Of course, I was not as clever as I thought and immediately got caught when I asked my lady's maid to pack a bag for me."

Audra laughed so much she gasped for air. Imagining a young Esha listening in rapt fascination as storytellers wove tales intended to frighten and alarm. "Your parents must have been pleased about that."

"Oh, they were. I received a lecture after that attempt. But, it never curbed my interest in magic. As long as I did not try to run away again, my parents allowed me to read books about mages. For years, I ran around the castle pretending to use magic, taking cooking powder from the kitchen and flinging it around like I was casting spells."

The image of a smaller Esha prancing around and making a mess was too adorable. Audra was intrigued by the tale. How rare that a princess of Feldor would find magic fascinating, not fearful. From her endless lessons with tutors, Audra knew that Feldor, like Solven, lacked laws regarding mages. Neither prohibited nor supported, mages who lived in either kingdom had to take care of themselves.

She wondered if that fascination extended to other members of the Feldorian royal family. Perhaps their understanding of mages was uninformed, and that if they knew more about magic, they would better protect the mages who lived within their borders.

Proceeding with caution, Audra asked, "Has your sister, Queen Soraya, ever met a mage?"

"Not to my knowledge. She became queen at a young age after her father died, and her time was dedicated to learning how to rule a kingdom. My younger siblings and I, on the other hand, had a more flexible education because we are not directly in line for the throne. A few years after the king's death, our mother remarried my father, a commoner whose distant cousin had magical ability, which meant he was more open to magic. He did mention that several mages were traveling through Feldor with merchants recently. Was that your doing?"

Audra nodded. "Would she like to meet one?"

Tipping back the last of his wine, Kasteel watched her with a mischievous grin. "Why do I get the feeling that your trip here wasn't just to rekindle old friendships?"

"Because it was not."

"Sounds interesting." When he started to sway to one side, Esha pushed him upright, steadying herself before tugging Kasteel up. "It appears that my wife thinks I should head to bed now. Probably for the best, our conversation should take place with clearer heads anyways."

"Hells, you are getting old if you cannot hold your alcohol anymore."

Kasteel laughed with his whole body, head thrown back and white teeth blinding against his tan skin.

"Goodnight, Sprite."

"Goodnight, Eel."

ONE INCREDIBLY DISAPPOINTING feature of the decorative wooden shutters, cut out in geometric patterns, and the gauzy curtains in Audra's room was their lack of ability to sufficiently blot out the sun's rise. Watching the sun's assent through the sky, peachy rays of pink and orange piercing through the inky sky, usually brought Audra joy. When she had the time and energy, Audra would complete her morning exercises while the mist covering the ground evaporated. Today was not one of those days. Hours spent talking with Kasteel and Esha meant that she had gone to bed much later than she should have, and Audra glared at the light for waking her before she was ready. Wishing for the thick curtains from her room in Ymira, Audra rolled over and covered her head with a pillow, willing her mind to return to sleep.

When she woke a second time, Audra felt more refreshed and ready to see where the day led. Stretching as she rose, Audra padded over to the washroom, finding a set of pants and shirt that matched the one she had complimented Esha on, only this version was violet. Thank Hellig that Audra had remembered to alter the ward on her room so that she was not woken by someone dropping off the garments. Now, her magic would only alert her if someone who wished her harm entered the room, a safeguard that Valeria insisted on. It was thoughtful of Esha to send this to her, and Audra gave herself a mental reminder to leave behind the dress she had worn the night before as a gift, along with sending a new gown for the princess once she returned to Ymira.

Feeling more human after washing and dressing, Audra returned to the dining room, stopping to admire the mosaics along the way. Compared to the colorful tapestry of light that painted the dining room walls before, the clean white walls of the room were particularly harsh in the full light of day. After a light breakfast with Esha and Kasteel, they made their way into the town. Audra was eager to see more of Nebura beyond the narrow view the carriage provided. Clusters of buildings wound their way down the hill, larger and with more space between their neighbors than the closely packed quarters at the base on the hill. Narrow streets bustling with people separated the taller buildings.

"As a border town, we see a lot of trade and travelers." Kasteel pointed out various shops, pubs, and inns, and waved to the people that greeted him. "Most residents choose to live above their shops, or further up the hill if they have land to tend."

A practical solution when space was tight, and Audra wondered if she should start encouraging that in Ymira, where workshops were adjacent or within the home. Depending on how many people continued to move to her kingdom, it was smart to build up instead of out to accommodate the influx of people without destroying the beautiful land they lived on.

They stopped in several businesses after one of them spotted something that caught their eye. In a small bookshop, Audra noticed a collection of fabric-bound journals, each colored to match the various flowers and plants pressed in the fabric. Running her hands over the choices, she selected one for each of her friends. At Esha's insistence, Audra also purchased one for herself, a silver cover pressed with light blue flowers.

"To start keeping a record of all your adventures," Esha said with a wink.

The closer they got to the center of town, the louder and busier it got. People walked faster, and hawkers yelled louder to be heard over the ambient noise. Which made sense once Audra stepped into the square. The town center was based around the mouth of the river, workers loading and unloading crates of goods from boats into waiting carts. Vendors selling fresh fish, produce, grains, and spices called out to passing shoppers.

"So..." Kasteel turned to her with a grin. "What do you think?"

"It...it's...*chaos.*" Her eyes barely knew where to look, flitting from baskets of precariously arranged spices to the beady eyes of fish laid in rows. "I love it!"

Diving into the crowd, Audra walked along the rows of vendors, absorbing the experience into her soul. There were so many textures, scents, and creatures to look at, far more than she had seen before. Even when she lived in the palace, Audra had never been in an area so filled with life. Merchants operated stalls in the palace courtyard on market days, and traveling merchants visited often, but it was never on this scale.

"Just let me know if you see something that looks good. Most of the stalls will prepare the food in front of you to keep it fresh."

Right as Kasteel said it, Audra noticed people receiving sticks of food from the stalls. Skewered fruit and fish grilled and seasoned to perfection. Letting her nose and stomach guide her, Audra began sampling a variety of food, passing off anything she did not enjoy to Kasteel, who had a bottomless pit for a stomach and was never picky about what went in it. Graham had not been either, saying that Guards had to be prepared to eat whatever they could find when hunting a netvor. She wondered what he thought about Nebura. Would he have enjoyed walking through the stalls with her, absorbing the sights and sounds of people and things from all over the kingdoms? Life as the crown prince acclimated Graham to large amounts of socializing, but Audra knew he found the noise and crowds draining, and she could always find him somewhere quiet and alone after interacting with a lot of people.

Shouts of alarm sounded beyond the crowd in front of them, causing anyone in the vicinity to turn towards the commotion. Like moths drawn to a flame, people never could resist watching something dramatic unfold. Shouldering his way through the crowd, Kasteel was hindered by the veritable sea of people that were filling the small walkway, all eager to reach the exit to the square where the sound originated.

"Move," he shouted. It was no use. Between the slow shuffle of bodies and his own need to protect Esha, Kasteel was barely progressing through. "Let the Lord and Lady of Nebura through!"

"They cannot hear you," Audra shouted in vain, her voice drowned out by a chilling groan of wood. Frustrated and more than a little panicked over the press of bodies against her, Audra shoved past Kasteel and pressed her palms together in front of her.

The edge of panic prevented her from reaching her magic instantly, and Audra breathed deeply to steady her nerves. Wind howled as she separated her hands, parting the crowd and preventing anyone from moving past the barrier she created. Mouths gasped in shock as bodies moved against their will, barreling into each other and stalls, eyes searching for the source of the magic.

Now they had a clear path to the exit. Looking over her shoulder to motion Kasteel ahead, Audra paused when she saw how he was standing. Before, he had one arm wrapped around Esha's shoulders and the other in front of his body to part the crowd. Now, both his arms were at Esha's waist, positioning her behind him. The spark of fear in Kasteel's eyes was enough to tell Audra that his hand would be on his sword should she turn her hands towards him.

"Audra." How many times had she heard her name said like that? At the ball, Kasteel whispered her name just like when her control over her magic was threatened. A warning laced with concern and fear.

She was foolish to think anything would have changed. He knew she was a mage. Knew what she had gone to Ymira to learn.

He knew *her*.

Maybe he did not really know her at all.

When Kasteel made no move to use the path she created, Audra turned away, keeping the flow of magic rushing from her hands. They wanted to be afraid of her, *fine*, but that would not stop her from helping. Stalking forward, Audra allowed the wall of wind keeping the crowd back to caress her hair and clothes, billowing them like a siren rising from the sea. Was it necessary?

No.

But damn did it make her feel powerful. And with the splinter of pain digging under her skin from Kasteel's look, Audra wanted to cloak herself in that power.

Exiting the row of stalls, Audra found the square more crowded than before, but at least the majority of people were traveling in the same direction. Following the rush of movement with her eyes, Audra searched for the cause of the chaos.

There.

At the edge of the docks, workers struggled with a crate that was suspended in the air by a series of ropes. Their muscles strained as they held the ends of the rope taut. One of the ropes connected to a corner of the crate had snapped, the disproportionate balance pulling unevenly on the remaining ropes, one of which was currently fraying.

"Out of the way!"

"Lower it slowly!"

"It's lost, let it go!"

Voices of the workers and surrounding crowd created a cacophony as they argued over the best course of action. But the workers were already struggling to maintain their grip on the ropes, losing precious time to make a choice.

With a horrifying snap, the frayed rope broke, and the large crate fell towards the ground.

People screamed in terror and struggled to dive out of the path where the crate would land. Some would not make it in time. Once more, Audra thrust her hands out. Calculating the rough size and weight of the crate, she knew what she was going to do would hurt. Magic shot from her, rushing to catch the rapidly descending box as she sprinted forward, shortening the distance her magic would stretch.

Closer.

A young boy tripped and fell to the ground, crying out as he watched the crate descend to crush him.

Audra grunted as her magic cushioned the bottom of the crate, relief at catching it in time quickly eclipsed by the drain on her magic.

"Get out of the way!" Audra shouted. The foolish people who were previously scrambling to get away from the crate were now staring at her in shock, standing in the way of where Audra planned on lowering the crate.

Her muscles screamed along with her voice. "Now!"

If they stood there any longer, Audra would not be responsible for their injuries.

A burly worker was the first to snap out of it, tugging on two other workers as she hustled out of the way. Once enough space was cleared, Audra lowered the crate to the ground. Fatigue settled in her limbs and her knees wobbled as Audra tried to take another step. It was surprising how quiet the previously noisy square became, mixed looks of curiosity, gratitude, and distrust watching her. Audra wondered which one would win out.

The center of the crowd parted, and the same worker that had moved first now walked towards Audra. Well over a head taller than Audra with thickly muscled arms and legs, the woman looked like she could snap Audra in half. Tensed in preparation to be run out of town, like Silvan had experienced, Audra drew more magic into her shaking hands to defend herself.

"That was you, right? Who saved us?" The worker's voice was softer than Audra imagined, more like a spring rainfall than the rumble of thunder. Audra nodded in response, saving her energy.

"We owe you a life debt. Thank you." Huge arms wrapped around her like tree trunks, pulling Audra into a crushing hug. It took Audra's brain a moment to catch up to what was happening, relief and pride filling her with warmth as she returned the gesture, albeit with significantly less force. More surprising was the cheer that went up through the crowd when Audra was released.

If the crowd was stifling before, it was nothing compared to how people gathered around her to thank her, pressing her hands to weeping faces and lips in gratitude from family members and friends of those who would have died. Audra wanted to collapse into the nearest chair, but she forced herself to remain standing, knowing how important it was for each person to have their chance to speak with her. She had watched the royal family do just that time and time again.

Just when she thought that the crowd would never die down, Audra felt a hand press against the middle of her back.

Esha stepped up next to her and began guiding her through the crowd, calling out, "Thank you everyone for your kind words and appreciation for our dear friend. After such a heroic feat, my husband and I would like to take her home for a well earned meal and time to rest."

Unwilling to contradict their princess, the crowd stepped back and offered any remaining thanks as they passed by. A carriage waited for them at the edge of the square, and Audra was too tired to wonder how it got there.

"Thank you for the exit. I was beginning to think that was more exhausting than stopping the crate."

"You deserve every bit of gratitude and praise from them. As well as ours." Esha's eyes were wet with unshed tears. "Without you, those people would not be alive. From the bottom of my heart, thank you." Esha clasped Audra's hands between hers, squeezing tightly.

"I could not just stand there and let it happen when I had the power to stop it."

"And what impressive power it was!"

Audra laughed at her enthusiasm. "Not quite the image of terror the old bards warned you about?"

"Terror? Incredible is more like it." The look of awe on Esha's face was flattering.

Audra frowned when she remembered Kasteel's reaction. "I am glad you think so. Not everyone is as understanding as you are."

Audra knew it was too much to hope that she could avoid Kasteel, especially since she was staying in his home. Apparently, thinking about him was enough to summon his presence. The carriage shook slightly as the door opened and Kasteel stepped in. Awkward silence filled the space as Kasteel settled into his seat and the carriage began moving. Noting the change in atmosphere between the two friends, Esha glanced between them.

"Audra, I—" Kasteel began.

"It is fine. Nothing to worry about."

"Don't say that. I hurt you when you did nothing to deserve it. Especially not when you were trying to save my people."

"Kas." Esha adjusted in her seat so that she could reprimand her husband while facing him fully. "What did you do?"

"When Audra parted the crowd, I acted out of fear. Instead of trusting her, I worried that she might hurt you and moved you out of her way."

He should have known her better than that. "I would never hurt either of you, nor anyone else who was not threatening me or my people."

"Please believe me when I say that I know that. But when I first saw your magic, it reminded me of all the times you struggled to control it. My worry was not that you would intentionally harm us, but that it would be an accident. I would do anything to keep Esha safe, even if it meant having to hurt you."

Audra could hardly fault him for that. Just because he knew that she was training did not mean he had seen her control it before today. Especially when her magic came as a surprise, in a moment where panic surrounded them.

"I forgive you. I can understand how knowing about my magic versus seeing it are different realities."

"Thank you. I hope that one instance does not deter you from using your magic around us again. You should feel comfortable being yourself in our home."

Seeing a powerful display of magic inspired a myriad of emotions, even in mages. Fear and awe were often two sides of the same coin.

Audra leaned back with a sigh. "I appreciate that. Getting your help spreading awareness about mages was actually one of the reasons I came to visit."

Kasteel brightened, sitting up straighter in his seat. "That's right, we were supposed to discuss the reasons behind your visit today. I'm glad you brought it up as it had slipped my mind."

Audra laid out her ideas for how they could help her, adjusting the original plans to include Esha's influence in Feldor. With all the dinners they hosted or attended with other nobility and gentry, the royal couple could share their experiences with magic and ease the way for mages to visit high-ranking households. Esha and Kasteel listened intently, the latter rubbing his lower lip with his thumb in a sign of concentration. When the carriage reached the manor, they continued their conversation in the sitting room, reclining on low couches as suggestions and adjustments were added to the plan.

"Based on the events of today, I wager that word of your heroic act will spread fast, doing more good than we ever could." Esha had a small notebook in her lap, writing down names of people she wanted to send invitations and letters to.

Pouring tea for the group, Audra nodded. "Among the merchant class, yes, but we have already been making headway with them. Without the support of those in charge, who are more than happy to buy from us, we are still barred from certain towns. We need acceptance from all levels of society so that my people will be safe."

"Perhaps we are not thinking big enough then." Esha tucked her legs up on the couch, smile widening in excitement.

Kasteel watched his wife with fondness, tucking a lock of hair behind her ear. "What are you thinking?"

"I cannot believe I did not think of it before. Remember how I mentioned last night that my sister might have interest in learning more about mages?"

Of course, Audra remembered. How could she forget such an interesting fact?

"If you want to establish your credibility as a kingdom and build relationships with other kingdoms, you need ambassadors to act in your stead. Send one of your mages to meet my sister, and if it goes well, they can stay at court and advocate from a better position than we can."

It was a thrilling proposition. As an ambassador, whoever Audra sent would be a set of eyes and ears in Feldor's palace, offering aid to the royal family and bolstering the impression of mages in Feldor. They would even be in a position to address changes to the law regarding the practice and treatment of mages who chose to live there.

"You would help facilitate this?" Audra did not want to take advantage of her friends' generosity, as much as she did need the help. She did not want them to think that her friendship was solely based on what they could do for her.

Kasteel gave his wife a questioning look, responding on both their behalfs. "We'll do everything we can to help you. You're family to us, and I deeply regret that you had to spend a large part of your life hiding who you are. Working together, we can prevent that from happening to anyone else."

Audra leaned over to meet Kasteel for a hug. He squeezed her tightly before pulling away to continue. "Once my parents learn about what you are doing, they will be eager to help as well."

Panic surged, tightening like a vise around her lungs. Audra thought his previous silence on the subject meant he understood that her wish to remain anonymous on this trip included the royal family.

"Please do not tell them about me."

"Why not?" His brow wrinkled in confusion. "Surely it would help your case more if I were to share that the mage seeking to improve relations with Solven is none other than our long-time friend."

Audra's hands twisted in the fabric of her dress. So much time had passed. They would want to see her again and she could not bolster her courage enough to face Graham. Not yet.

"I need more time. Please." She begged him with her eyes.

"Okay." Kasteel gave her a cautionary look. "But your paths will cross again one day, Audra. Graham hasn't been himself since you left, and I know you had your reasons, but I think it would help you both to hear him out. Not now, but someday."

Was it wicked of her to be glad that Graham was impacted by her absence? Maybe. Did she care? No. And that alone was reason enough for her to continue to stay away. Until Audra could control her emotions around him, it was better to focus on building her new life.

Once again, the group found themselves talking into the late hours of the night. Kasteel regaled them with tales of previous hunts, gesturing wildly as he swiped at imaginary monsters, sending the women into fits of laughter as he used his hands to create false fangs and horns. In return, Audra told them about her mishaps when first learning magic. Tears leaked out of Esha's eyes as she gasped for air when Audra relayed a particular instance where, intending to clean the floors, Audra had filled the hallway with bubbles, causing a veritable waterfall down the staircase as she struggled to scoop them out the windows.

After a week, the time spent with friends restored Audra's spirit and she was ready to return to her responsibilities in Ymira. With promises to visit again soon, Audra hugged her friends goodbye and climbed into her carriage, now laden with more trunks than before to transport the gifts she received. Esha and Kasteel stood side by side, waving to her until their figures grew smaller with distance. They now had a stack of enchanted paper, and Audra was eager to have the connection to them across the distance. Once she could no longer see them, Audra checked the ward she had placed around their estate one last time. One could never be too careful.

Fourteen

As much as she enjoyed visiting her friends, a reassuring calm settled over Audra as she neared the wards to Ymira. One of the mages on duty waved for her to halt, and Audra smiled when she saw Leah's distinct blue-tipped hair. Hardly waiting for the carriage to slow, Audra leapt out the door and ran to her friend, tackling her in an enthusiastic hug.

"Careful, now, can't have you injuring yourself before anyone else gets to see you." Despite her general dislike of physical affection, Leah squeezed Audra tighter, the small gesture revealing how much she had missed Audra and worried over her return.

"I missed you too," Audra whispered.

Releasing Leah, Audra waved the carriage forward. After hours spent seated, the walk back to Rauha would feel good. "Did anything interesting happen while I was gone?"

"Not particularly. One or two letters arrived from families planning to move here, and a group of angry farmers tried to reach the ward, but nothing I couldn't handle. How was your trip?"

Audra suspected there was more to the story, and she arched an eyebrow to convey that she would bring it up again later. Despite receiving an overwhelming amount of appreciation in Nabura, there were a few people who avoided crossing her path in town or spat out derogatory names in her direction. The fact that the group of farmers—if that was even what they were—got close enough to the ward for Leah to engage, meant it was more than just a verbal confrontation.

"Informative and enjoyable. We can meet when your watch ends. That way Taara, Eli, and Valeria can all be there and I will only have to tell the story once."

"Fair enough. I'll let you head back to get some rest. Taara will likely keep you up all night with her questions."

That was fine with her. When Taara's family moved into a cottage near the forest, she joined them, and Audra missed her lively roommate. Any extra time they could spend together was precious. Since it was early afternoon, most of Rauha's inhabitants were tending to their daily chores, and Audra encountered few people on her way back to her room. Just a few steps past the arched entryway, Audra was greeted with short yips of joy and the blurring figure of Isik racing towards her. Kneeling on the ground, Audra opened her arms to receive him, running her hands through his soft fur as he rubbed against her and flopped to the ground.

"Hello, my sweet. Did you miss me?" Isik yipped again, nuzzling her hand. "I missed you, too. Have you been good? Yes? Let's get you a treat then."

Laughing at Isik's abrupt change in attitude, bounding away from her in the direction of the kitchen, Isik looked back at her every few feet to ensure Audra was still following. After giving the wily creature some of the fish in the cellar, Audra went to rest in her room, penning notes to Eli, Taara, and Valeria requesting a private dinner where they could discuss the events of her trip.

Fortunately, Valeria was willing to use her private study as the setting for their dinner. A large table was set with chairs, plates of food and glasses of sparkling wine glimmering in the light provided by the moon and magelights. Stepping into the room, Audra found her friends already gathered.

"Audra!" Taara was the first to greet her, sailing across the room to hug her tightly, bouncing up and down. "How was it? What was Nebura like? My fathers passed through on their way here and they said it was lovely. Did you get to see the shops? Dad said that he had never seen so many things for sale."

"Yes, I did. I brought you back some gifts as well." Audra laughed when Taara's grin widened at the mention of gifts. Ever since her fathers and siblings moved, Taara was happier than ever, radiating joy at having them all near. As happy as she was before, there were subtle changes to her demeanor. Now, she looked more relaxed, the subtle strain of worrying over her family gone.

Audra was not the only one to notice the change in her friend. Eli watched her closely, eyes brightening when Taara smiled and dimming with concern if she was sad. He was the next to greet Audra, wheeling over so that she could hug him.

"Glad to have you home safe."

Dressed up for the occasion, Valeria wore a black tunic and plants with the Ymiran crest embroidered in deep purple thread on the lapel. "Ymira was not the same without you." Valeria did not hug her, it was not her way. Hidden in her words was the implication that she had missed Audra. Gesturing to the table, Valeria sat first, the rest of the group following suit.

"So, tell us everything!" Audra admired Taara's restraint at holding back until everyone had taken a few bites.

Anticipating the numerous interruptions from the group, Audra recounted all that had happened on her journey, starting with the news that Kasteel was married to Esha.

"Does that mean Graham never married?" Curse Leah for voicing Audra's innermost thoughts.

"He did not." Esha let that tidbit slip during a walk around the grounds of their home. One of her and Kasteel's many attempts to warm her up to reuniting with the prince.

Smirking like a smug cat, Leah resumed eating. "Interesting."

If Audra were a petty person, she would jinx Leah's fork so that it missed her food each time she took a bite. But her friend was only meddling because she cared. Leah and Taara were the only ones besides

Valeria who knew the depth of Audra's love for Graham, and her struggle to let go of the pain he caused.

When Audra got to the incident at the docks, Valeria sat up straighter in her seat, steepling her fingers in front of her face. "How did the people react?"

"Some were shocked, but most were appreciative. Once they saw that I was using magic to help them, and no one got hurt, I was swarmed. Esha had to pull me out."

Eli raised his glass in a toast. "You were a hero, of course they wanted to fawn over you."

"How did you feel after?" Valeria gave nothing away with her gaze. She could either be worried that Audra had displayed a huge amount of magic in public, or pleased that it was a success.

"A little tired, some stiffness in my muscles, but nothing a nap, water, and light meal could not fix."

"Good. That means your endurance is improving. I'm proud of you. You did well, remaining calm and helping those people."

With how happy she felt at receiving praise from her mentor, Audra would not be surprised if her skin were glowing as she beamed with pride. Knowing that she had done the right thing was reward enough, but it felt great to impress Valeria.

"Thank you. But that was not even the best part of the trip. The reason I wanted to meet with you all together is because of an opportunity Esha presented me with." That got the group's attention, each of them leaning forward slightly in interest as Audra explained the plan to send an ambassador to Queen Soraya's court.

Silence settled over the room, utensils and glasses frozen on their way to and from mouths. This was obviously not what they expected to hear. Audra understood their surprise. Their plans for Ymira were moving faster than they hoped for. Having an ambassador was a huge step toward keeping mages safe.

"Well...that's..." For the first time since Audra met her, Valeria was at a loss for words.

"A wonderful opportunity," Leah finished the thought. She looked pensive, setting her chin on her hand.

Valeria shook off her surprise, flinty eyes staring at her. "Indeed. Did you have someone in mind?"

"I was hoping you all might have some suggestions."

"Whoever we send needs to be powerful, intelligent, and able to hold their own against courtiers." Valeria tipped her head back, mentally cataloging each mage within Ymira or currently traveling.

Those were all traits Audra had thought of in addition to needing someone who knew enough of Ymira's inner workings to advocate for changing laws. Someone willing to live somewhere where they knew no one and create a new life for themselves.

Someone Audra could trust.

Leah met her eyes across the table and Audra's heart dropped to her stomach.

"No."

"I'm the perfect fit, Audra. You need me to go."

"Not as much as I need you here."

Audra could not lose her. Not now. Leah was her best friend. Audra relied on her for advice and Leah's brutal form of encouragement. Like the kind she was offering now.

"You don't *need* anyone, Audra. When we first started this journey, you told us yourself that you were raised for leadership. You've been preparing for this moment your whole life. And you cannot do that if you don't have people in positions to support you. It was hard when Silvan left and when you sent out more mages. Just as it will be hard now."

The rest of the group was quiet as the two friends watched each other.

"And it would be good for me too," Leah continued. "I've spent too much time angry at the world for how I ended up in Ymira. I want to change that. You've inspired me to leave my mark on the kingdoms."

How could Audra argue against that? She was proud of her friend for wanting to spread her wings and grow outside the boundaries she had set for herself. Keeping Leah behind just so that she did not have to live without her best friend would be selfish. Opportunities like this would not come around often and Leah sounded genuinely excited about it.

Blue eyes so dark they were nearly black questioned Audra's damp, green ones.

Audra's voice shook with a combination of pride and apprehension. "Promise me you will write all the time, letting me know how you are and if you need anything."

"So much that you'll be sick of me."

Audra gave Leah a watery smile, dabbing the corners of her eyes to remove any stray tears. "Impossible."

"Don't forget to write to me too." Taara squeezed Leah's arm. "Everyone but me gets to go on adventures."

A laugh rumbled out of Eli. "Be careful what you wish for. Adventure follows Audra wherever she goes."

Recently, it certainly seemed that way. Hopefully, there would be less adventure in the next few months as they prepared for Leah's departure. While they waited, Audra took advantage of spending as much time with her friend as possible. Taara joined them on trips to the hot springs and girl's nights spent playing card games or reading around the fire.

Sooner than Audra wanted, when the first snow began falling, a letter arrived from Nebura with news that Queen Soraya was ready to meet the new ambassador. Instead of sending Leah off on her own, Audra and Taara volunteered to accompany her to Nebura before sending her the rest of the way. For Leah's safety, they rationalized.

This time, when the carriage bounced up the road to Kasteel and Esha's manor, the bouncing was largely due to Taara. Her leg was tapping a rhythm on the floor of the carriage that only she could hear. Being confined to a small space was difficult for her, and they stopped frequently to let Taara stretch her legs.

"You're beautiful," Taara blurted out as she exited the carriage, wide eyes landing on Esha. "I mean, Audra said you were, but meeting you in person...wow!"

"Taara, manners," Audra chided as she followed the younger woman out. Kasteel and Esha greeted her with warm hugs.

"Do not listen to Audra. I will always accept compliments in lieu of a proper greeting." Esha's smile was bright against the gloomy backdrop of the sky, her arms wide as she pulled Taara into a hug like they were old friends. After everything Audra had told them about each other, perhaps they felt like they were. "Welcome to our home."

"Thank you, Your Highness. I appreciate you letting me stay here. My fathers and Audra told me a lot about Nebura and I am excited to see it with my own eyes."

Kasteel pulled Taara into his own hug. "We'll have to give you the grand tour tomorrow. As long as the weather holds up."

"Even if it does not, I am sure we will find some way to entertain ourselves." Audra stepped to the side. "May I introduce the final member of our party, Ambassador Leah?"

They had debated the appropriate way to introduce Leah on the way to Nebura, but as the expert in courtly politics, Audra got her way. If Leah was going to act in an official capacity for Ymira, she needed to adjust to having a title. Titles garnered respect and would establish her place in society.

"It's a pleasure to meet you both, Your Highnesses." Leah bowed first to Esha then Kasteel.

Taking their approach from Leah, Kasteel and Esha nodded instead of opening their arms for an embrace, respecting her desire for personal space.

Esha clasped her hands beneath her light jacket. "We are pleased to have you. Audra told us so much about you, and my siblings are looking forward to meeting you."

"Only the interesting things, I hope." Leah's mouth twitched on one side, the closest she would get to a smile before she was comfortable around someone new.

"As if there is anything else," Audra teased, nudging her friend with an elbow.

Kasteel missed nothing, observing the interaction between Audra's friends with a reminiscent smile.

Ever the gracious host, Esha thought of every consideration. "Would you like a brief tour of our home, or would you like to rest in your rooms first?" When Taara and Leah expressed interest in a tour, Esha led them through the door, a tray of warm beverages waiting for them. A slight tug on her elbow stopped Audra from following. Kasteel's hand wrapped around the curve of her jacket, his face pensive.

"May I have a word in private?"

Concerned over what he would need to say without an audience, Audra frowned. "Of course."

Ever observant, Leah noticed that they were not following and gave Audra a look over her shoulder to ask if everything was okay. With a reassuring smile, Audra waved her on. She could handle whatever Kasteel wanted to discuss. He guided her into the study, sliding the doors closed behind them before retrieving a wrapped parcel from the desk.

"It's good to see you again." He leaned against a chair, shifting the parcel from hand to hand.

"You too. But surely you did not request privacy just so you could tell me that."

"No, you're right." He rubbed a hand along the fresh growth of hair along his jaw. "The thing is…What I wanted to talk to you about…" His sentences remained unfinished as he paced.

"Eel, you are making me nervous. Whatever it is, you can tell me."

"Shit, sorry, Sprite. I didn't mean to make you nervous. It's nothing bad. I just don't know the best way to tell you."

Barely restraining the urge to shake it out of him, Audra sat in one of the armchairs, trying to settle her growing nerves.

"I spoke to my parents about you—"

"Kasteel, you promised!"

"I didn't mention you by name, just that a high ranking mage visited us, saved some of the villagers, and was interested in developing a relationship between Ymira and Solven." Seeing her open her mouth to interrupt again, Kasteel held up a hand. "We'll get back to that later. I need to finish telling you what I brought you in here for."

Briefly chastised, Audra settled into the chair.

"Graham was the most interested in improving relations with Ymira. He asked me to give this to the mage the next time I saw them. So that they could deliver it to you."

He handed her the wrapped package.

"What you do with it is up to you, but I wanted to make sure you had a choice. I'll make sure you are left alone, so take as much time as you need. We can discuss everything else later."

Focused on the rectangular object sitting in her hands like it would bite if she took her eyes off it, Audra hardly registered Kasteel leaving, closing the doors softly behind him. The package was larger than her hands, its gentle weight suggesting it was a book. Her curiosity would always get the best of her when it came to Graham, and after a moment's hesitation Audra pulled back the wrapping.

Her heartbeat increased at the familiar binding.

Embossed on the front cover was the royal seal of Solven, a sword driven into the ground with small, blue flowers growing around it. The shiny gold-leaf imprint was dull after many years of use, the red leather creased and worn with age. It was a journal Graham gave her when they were younger. Tied to the front was a letter with her name written in Graham's familiar handwriting. Audra traced each letter of her name while her heart and brain warred between wanting to know what Graham wrote and keeping herself safe from future disappointment. With a steadying breath, Audra broke the seal and unfolded the letter. There was no way to know what he wanted without reading it.

> *Audra,*
>
> *When Kasteel mentioned meeting a mage, I knew that I could not let the opportunity to try and reach you pass. Not a day goes by that I do not regret how I treated you and I am deeply sorry that my behavior drove you out of your home. As proud as I am that you finally get to use your magic, I wish that I could see you again. If this letter reaches you, I hope that you might agree to meet. You deserve to hear what happened in person. In the meantime, I thought you might want your journal to document your new memories.*
>
> *Yours Always,*
> *Graham*

Rubbing her thumb along the letters of Graham's name and *yours always* left an unsettled feeling in Audra's stomach. What could he mean by that? Was there more to the story than she knew? Unfortunately, answers would have to wait. She was busy integrating mages into the world, and her heart was not ready to face the past. Holding the cover of her journal open, Audra flipped to the first page. There, in black ink, was a simple inscription:

For days when you cannot take off the mask.

They were in those awkward years between childhood and adulthood, stretching the boundaries of their world and struggling to fit the molds they would need to grow into. Light from the windows of the palace glowed in the darkness, the clank of dinnerware mingling with voices of courtiers. Audra found Graham at the training grounds, flinging daggers at targets mounted around the circular pit. With more fury than aim, he brought his arm back time and time again to flick his wrist and send the dagger flying, burying the blade deep into the wood. Flashes of silver were all she saw before the dagger pierced the target, never in the center, but Graham did not seem to care.

She watched him in silence, seated at the edge of the pit with her legs folded beneath her.

"How can you stand it?" Graham's voice was heavy with frustration that matched his throws.

"The party?"

"Yes. No." His arm dropped to his side, head tipping back with his eyes closed to the sky. "Not the party itself, but the pretension and false sincerity dripping from those people like venom." Graham looked lost as his eyes met Audra's. Searching her face, Graham's next words sounded frantic and almost desperate. "That was not you in there, not the real Audra. How can you do it? Be someone you are not?"

Audra tucked her knees into her chest, wrapping her arms around them as she replied. "Because they do not want to see the real me. I suppose that is part of living in this world. Sometimes, we have to put on a mask to keep our real desires and self hidden. That way they cannot use it to hurt us."

Walking to the edge of the pit, Graham bracketed Audra's legs with his arms, hands digging into the dirt next to her. "Promise me something, Audra."

"Anything." The word was breathless, holding on for whatever came next.

"Promise me that when we are alone, when it is just you and me, that we will never wear masks. I could not bear it if you were fake around me, and I want you to always see who I really am."

"I promise." Audra raised one hand to cradle Graham's cheek, hoping to soothe the frantic energy that raced behind his eyes. "I see you. No masks between us."

A blank journal arrived in her room a few days later, the brief note on the first page reminding Audra of Graham's skin against hers.

She wondered if Graham somehow knew that she needed the journal now, to remind her that even when she had to make difficult decisions, she could be true to herself and that there were people who loved her exactly as she was. Sinking back into the cushion, Audra read through several of the journal entries before heading upstairs to prepare for dinner.

When the weather cleared days later, they loaded trunks of gifts for Queen Soraya on the carriage along with Leah's clothing and personal effects.

"You have everything? Funds for any stops you make along the way and lighter clothes for when you arrive?" Audra fussed over the carriage, triple checking that everything was secure and fit for travel, avoiding direct eye contact with Leah.

"Yes, *mother*," Leah chided, grabbing Audra by the shoulders to stop her from continuing to pace around the carriage. "I'm going to be fine and so are you. It's time."

Unfortunately, it was. Sailors reported another storm blowing in from the south that would hit within a few days, meaning that Leah, Audra, and Taara needed to leave if they wanted to beat the storm. As sad as the friends were to separate, there was an excited air about them as Leah prepared to embark on her own adventure, one that would mean great things for all mages.

Pulling Leah close, Audra hugged her tightly. "Be safe, and for the love of Hellig, do not forget your manners."

"Please," Leah hid the crack in her voice with a chuckle, "I'm always on my best behavior. Don't go back to being boring while I'm gone, princess."

Smiling fondly at the old insult, Audra opened the door for her friend. "For the last time, I am not a princess."

Audra stepped away from the carriage after closing the door, losing the fight to keep from crying until Leah was out of sight. As the wheels rolled into motion, the horses tossing their heads as they began walking, Leah pulled back the window curtain and leaned out.

"You're right. You aren't a princess," she called out from the window. "You're our queen."

FIFTEEN

There were moments in the two years since Leah's departure where Audra thought about Graham's letter, tucked safely in her journal, but with her responsibilities increasing, leaving Ymira became more difficult. True to their word, Kasteel and Esha—now expecting their first child—told others about their interactions with the mages, instilling trust and curiosity in the noble houses of Solven. Word among the kingdom's people spread like wildfire, tales from the dock workers and witnesses growing in exaggeration, positively building the reputation of mages. With Leah acting as ambassador, conditions were improving in Feldor as well, mages opening shops and learning magic in their homes.

Weekly, Audra received reports from the mages traveling through the kingdoms, providing updates on their locations and requests from citizens all over Solven and Feldor, addressed to the High Mage of Ymira, a position that Valeria has passed on to Audra. With the change in position came a move into the rooms of Ruaha's tower, a "perk of the job," as Valeria referred to it when she helped Audra move her belongings. Isik was thrilled with their change of rooms, taking particular enjoyment in racing Audra up and down the stairs, weaving between her legs in an effort to trip her.

Behind the desk in the tower's study, Audra pinned a large map of the continent to the wall with locations of known mages throughout the other two kingdoms. One mage that remained difficult to keep track of was Silvan. He had made it a personal mission to locate as many mages in hiding as possible, bringing them back to Ymira or contacting Audra to request a private tutor if the individual did not want to move. Helpful as it was, the nomadic lifestyle meant that Silvan often forgot to write to Audra, weeks or months passing between contact. What letters he did send were disconcerting, Silvan was taking risks that put him in danger and any attempt to sway him away from a course of action was brushed off.

Audra was worried, particularly now that Leah was gone as well. She knew that helping mages outside their wards feel safe and protected was critical, but she needed to remind Silvan that it was also important for him to stay safe and not take chances that put others at risk. Fortunately, Silvan was on his way home with a young mage, though he had not said where he had found the child.

"Moving up in the world I see." At the sound of a voice, Audra looked up from the letter to Queen Soraya that she was reviewing.

Silvan leaned against her open door. Dressed immaculately in polished boots, black pants, and a thick green sweater to match the current color of his nails, Silvan's attire gave the illusion of looking well. But Audra knew the smaller signs to look for. No amount of cosmetics could completely hide the slightly swollen, red rim around his eyes or the dark shadows underneath them. Though he gained back some of the weight he lost on those initial months of travel, the sharp lines of Silvan's cheekbones suggested that he was not taking care of himself as well as he should.

The letter floated down onto the stack on her desk as Audra rose to greet her friend. "Only in the literal sense. If I did not know any better, I would say that the rumors of mages flying were true based on the height of this tower."

Silvan's laugh was more snort as he pushed off the doorframe to take a seat and stretch his long legs in front of him. "If you think this tower is tall, you should see how tall they build them in Kalmere."

Audra doubted that she would ever get the chance to see them. The rulers of Kalmere had strongly opposed joining with the mages during the battle against Dyrun. They viewed all mages as evil, wicked creatures that should be destroyed along with the monsters their magic created. Any individual found practicing magic in Kalmere was immediately killed, no matter their age. To make matters worse, they actively encouraged the rulers of Feldor and Solven to follow suit, and agents from Kalmere were suspected to disguise themselves in the other kingdoms to hunt mages and recruit others to their cause. Audra banned anyone from traveling to Kalmere, the danger far outweighing the cost.

"I will have to take your word for it." Waving over the tea set, Audra watched as Silvan warmed his hands with the cup. Concerned that he caught a cold on the journey, Audra lit the fire to give the room additional warmth. "How was your trip?"

Isik, who was sitting in his basket, rose and stretched leisurely before moving towards the pair. Sniffing around Silvan's feet, Isik crinkled his face like he had smelled something unpleasant. Jerking away from Silvan's outstretched hand, Isik trotted out of the room. Audra kept her face neutral as she pondered the strange behavior. Usually, Isik was not one to turn down attention, particularly from a friend, but he must have smelled something from Silvan's travels that irritated his nose.

"Good. Better than good actually." If Isik's rejection bothered him, Silvan did not show it, and his words drew Audra's focus back to the conversation. "Travelling within Solven and Feldor is easier now that more people are willing to accept help from mages. I heard about what you and Leah are doing with Feldor, congratulations." He raised his cup in a toast.

Audra shook off the feeling that it was more mocking than congratulatory. "Thank you. I was actually working on a treaty when you came in. If all goes well, soon mages in Solven and Feldor will be protected under law, making it legal for their citizens to practice magic openly."

"And what are we giving them in return?"

"An alliance. Should they need our help, Ymira will send aid. The treaty also stipulates regulations for traveling within the kingdoms."

Silvan crossed his arms and shook his head. "Aid? They don't deserve our help after leaving our people to fend for themselves. Does traveling between kingdoms include Ymira?"

"In time," she said, biting back her frustration. "It is only fair since we have been traveling and trading in the other kingdoms. There will be safety measures, a slight alteration to the wards, but it is the logical next step."

Silvan was silent for a moment while he pondered her words, his fingers drumming on the armrest. "Alter the wards how?"

"By removing the condition that only those with magical ability can find Ymira. Those approaching with malicious intent will still be diverted by the wards."

"And what about those with malicious intent outside our borders?"

Pausing mid sip, Audra lowered her cup to the side table. "What do you mean?"

Something like resentment flickered in Silvan's eyes. "There are still a few pockets where people outright oppose magic in the other kingdoms, not to mention all of Kalmere. People attacking and killing mages. What are you doing to protect them and punish those that hurt us?"

The vehemence in his words caught Audra by surprise. No one outside the ward reached out to her with reports of attacks. Even instances of getting barred from establishments or towns were fewer. Much as she would encourage anyone, mages knew to defend themselves if attacked and to step in if they saw someone else getting attacked. But, they did not provoke fights.

"We do not have power to punish citizens of other kingdoms, that responsibility lies with their rulers. Which is why we need alliances, so that I can protect our people when they travel to other kingdoms as well as safeguard mages who live outside Ymira. Taking action in another kingdom—without consulting their leader—is a grievous overstep of power, one that would offend other rulers and could make things worse for mages. We are building relationships, not destroying them. Did something happen? I can help."

"Help? With what, friendship and treaties? While you are busy working on those, perpetrators are roaming free, living without any consequences." Silvan's voice rose as he spoke, a wild look in his eyes. "No, thank you. I prefer to take care of things myself."

Betrayal welled in Audra's chest, tightening her lungs in its vice-like grip.

"Silvan, you once supported our plans here. What happened to change your mind?"

"You haven't seen what I've seen, Audra." Silvan ran a hand through his hair in agitation, revealing threads of white scattered amongst a sea of black. "Do you remember the girl I told you about, the one living on the border of Feldor and Kalmere?" Audra nodded. "I went back to find her, but she wasn't there. Do you know what I found instead?"

Audra shook her head, swallowing thickly. Based on the despair in his voice, it could not be anything good.

"They killed her. Tied her to a tree in the forest and let a netvor devour her. Said that it was only fitting that a monster kill another monster." Silvan slammed his hand down on the table, knocking his teacup to the floor where it shattered. "They were the real monsters and I made sure they regretted every vile thing they said about her."

Bile rose in Audra's throat along with the disgust and fury over what happened to the girl. Death at the claws and fangs of a netvor was gruesome and painful, something that only the vilest of people deserved. She was so focused on the tragedy of the girl's death, that she almost missed the last part of what Silvan said.

"What did you do?" The air was charged with magic, practically sparking as it flowed off of Audra in raw waves. Her voice was deathly calm, and if Silvan was smart, he would heed the warning in her voice.

He did not.

"I followed them into Kalmere. Tracked down each one of the people responsible for her torture and made sure they experienced the same agonizing death that she did." A grim smile curled Silvan's lips, eyes unfocused as he recalled the punishment he dolled out.

Every nerve in Audra's body felt frayed. This one action from Silvan could jeopardize everything they had worked for. Mixed with the disappointment was empathy for his actions, and there was a wicked part of her that wished she could have been the one to exact judgment for the lost mage, but the logical side of her prevailed.

"I cannot believe you did something so reckless." Feeling more than a little reckless herself, Audra made sure to keep tight control over her magic as it thrashed under her skin. Controlling her magic was always more difficult when her emotions were running high.

"I was only—" Silvan tried to speak, but Audra did not want to hear it.

"Do not excuse your actions to me. Believe me, I want nothing more than to punish those people after what you told me." Silencing his continued attempts to speak with a raised hand, Audra continued, "What you did puts every mage across the continent at risk. Not to mention the risk you put yourself in. If anyone in Kalmere realized that you were there, knew what you did, they would report you to King Balor and he could view it as an act of war. Do you think he would understand that you were seeking justice? He views magic as a scourge on the land and wants to kill anyone possessing magic. Should he learn that a mage travelled into his kingdom to kill his people...hells."

Her power rose with each sentence, gathering in the room like a storm. Silvan's own power rose in response, wrapping around him for protection. As if she would ever hurt him. Audra just needed him to understand the seriousness of the situation and that her wrath was just as impressive as Valeria's.

"Now, we can only pray that King Balor never finds out. It will already be difficult enough to explain the situation to Queen Soraya so that she can increase protection at the border without alarming her that vigilante mages might start attacking her people. This is bad, Silvan."

"What did you expect me to do, nothing? I am not a coward!"

"I never said you were! This is different than protecting yourself or others when you witness an attack. But hunting people down? That makes us no better than them. You once asked for my help guiding Ymira into a better future. So let. Me. Lead." Her eyes bore into his nearly unreadable face.

They mirrored each other in opposite seats. Legs braced on the floor and arms resting on the chairs, anyone looking at them would imagine they were relaxed, but tension coiled between them like a snake preparing to strike. Maybe he had spent too much time away from friends and other mages. Silvan had been alone or in the company of non-magical people for years. Perhaps that distance put too much pressure on his shoulders and made him forget their goals.

Forcing herself to relax with a silent exhale, Audra knew that she had to make a difficult decision. "For the time being, I want you to stay in Ymira. You do not look well and need to rest. Hopefully, the time here will remind you of all the good we have done and we will continue to do, the right way."

The wooden armrests groaned as Silvan released his clenched fists from the curved ends. "I'm not sorry for what I did, but I am sorry that I did not think through the implications of my actions. That does not make you right though. No other ruler will care about our people the way we do. The only way to guarantee mages are safe is if we rule over everything."

Silvan stood abruptly, jostling the table with his leg. The remaining cup and saucer rattled and some tea spilled over to splash on the table. Before he swept out of the room, Silvan caught himself on the door-frame. Without looking over his shoulder, he said, "The boy I brought back. He was from Kalmere. I would like to train him, if that is alright with you."

"Yes, of course." That would be good for him. Reminding Silvan of all the good he was capable of.

Without another word, Silvan left.

Concern for her friend was at the forefront of Audra's mind. Rubbing her forehead, Audra worked on cleaning up the table while she thought. Silvan grew up in dangerous circumstances, hiding his power during his childhood in Kalmere. Living in Ymira had helped heal those mental and physical wounds. Perhaps returning to Kalmere and bringing back the young mage had stirred up old memories and that was why he was acting out of character.

Promising to check up on Silvan regularly, Audra decided to decompress by taking a walk with Isik around the lake. She just had to find him first.

SIXTEEN

"Is my friend somewhere in there, or did the pile of paperwork eat her?" Taara leaned against the doorframe to Audra's office. Taller than Audra now, Taara had grown into a confident young woman, long curls framing her heart-shaped face. One thing that never changed was the brilliant smile on her face.

Audra peeked around the enormous amount of parchment scattered across her desk in semi-organized piles. Requests for magical assistance piled together on one corner, correspondence from mages on the other, and various messages of gratitude or complaints fanned the length of the desk. Containing the potential to reinforce positive impressions or establish footholds for mages seeking to live and work outside Ymira, Audra had to dedicate time to each and every letter that crossed her desk. Just when Audra got caught up, a new batch of letters would arrive and the process would start all over again.

"Sometimes I wish it would eat me," Audra said with a hollow laugh. "At least then I would not have to respond to all of them."

Scooting the papers enough to look at Audra across the desk, Taara chided, "You can ask for help, you know." She knew better than to try and move them altogether or else Audra would panic about losing where she was in the stack.

Rubbing her tired eyes, Audra was grateful for the break that her friend provided. Busy running the newly formed kingdom, Audra often forgot to stop and appreciate the impact of the work.

"I know, and I appreciate the offer. But not all of it is bad. Esha gave birth to a healthy baby girl. Little Diana."

Shouting with joy, Taara jumped up and down. "We should celebrate! It's been too long since we had a party." Her eyes were bright with excitement, plans for the party already forming in her head.

Audra smiled fondly. "We celebrated your dads' anniversary just a few weeks ago," Audra reminded her.

"Yes, but that was with my family, Eli's family, their friends from the village, and so many other people. I want a night with just you, me, Eli, and Silvan. It won't be the same without Leah, but it is close enough to how things used to be."

Audra's face fell at the sobering reminder that their circle of friends had altered so much. There was a happy sort of sadness watching her friends growing and thriving in their lives. Miles away, Leah corresponded via letter and was only able to visit a handful of times since she left. Taara lived with her family now, and Eli spent more time in the village with his family or Taara's that he might as well live there. Although nothing romantic occurred between the two, Audra noticed they spent more time together than before. She was happy for her friends, truly, but Audra did miss spending time with them.

"Have you talked to Silvan recently?" He had moved back into Rauha, taking a separate room from Eli now that there were fewer mages residing there. Even though they lived in the same house, Audra hardly saw him, passing briefly in the halls or sharing quick meals together.

As he requested, Silvan had taken over training the mage he brought to Ymira, but he sent Audra a note that the boy wanted to stop training and return home. She was not thrilled at the idea of sending a mage back into Kalmere, but it was the boy's choice and she could at least allow Silvan to protect him for the journey. They had agreed that Silvan and the boy would leave after his shift along the ward ended that night, giving one last day to convince the boy to stay.

"A little." Taara rubbed the cuff of her sleeve between her fingers.

"Eli has spent more time with him, and he said that Silvan is getting better. He doesn't seem as angry anymore and I think being back has helped. I know you want him to talk to you, but we need to give him time and space."

Pursing her lips, Audra knew that Taara was right, but it still upset her. She wanted to take action to help her friend, not sit around and wait. But if that was what he needed, she would respect his need for space. All she could do was ensure her door was always open if he wanted to share the burden.

"You are too young to be this wise," Audra teased. "We could use a celebration though. Want to go check in on Eli and see if tonight works for him? Silvan's watch ends tonight so we can grab him and celebrate before he leaves again."

"That sounds great! Oh, this is going to be so much fun. Leah just sent me a new dress that I cannot wait to—"

The ground shook beneath them, toppling Taara and several stacks of paper to the floor. Audra braced herself against the desk as a shiver went down her spine. Steadying herself, Audra reached down to help her friend up.

"Was that...?" Taara trailed off, fear widening the whites of her eyes.

Audra's voice was tight when she replied. "Something breaking the ward? Yes, I believe it was."

Both women rushed out of the room, skipping multiple stairs in their haste to exit the tower. Audra's momentum almost caused her to ricochet into the opposite wall and she pivoted quickly to turn the corner at the bottom of the stairs, Taara close behind her. Cloudy sky greeted them as Audra pushed through the door near the garden.

She took a moment to survey the area, looking for the direction of the breach. The magical earthquake meant that something broke through the ward. The fact that it was able to get through at all meant that whoever had been stationed at that part of the ward was away from their post, or...

Audra could not let the other option distract her thoughts. She had learned enough battle strategy from listening to Graham train over the years that although she had not fought herself, outside of practicing with Leah, Audra knew that distractions could be the difference between life and death.

And she had too much going on to die today.

Taara pointed to a portion of the hills. "There!"

A dark ball was rolling towards the village, picking up speed as it continued downhill, trees cracking as bark and dirt shot through the air. From this distance, Audra could not make out what it was, but the fact that she could see it at all meant that it was massive.

Breaking into a sprint, Audra willed her body to go as fast as she could. But there was no way that she could run as fast as that creature was moving. Shouts of alarm rose from the town, people beginning to spill out of their homes and businesses to see what was going on.

"We have to get everyone to safety," Audra shouted to Taara just as another shock vibrated through the ground. This time, even Audra struggled to remain upright, calling on every ounce of muscle control she learned from Valeria. Her heart hammered in her chest and panic churned in her stomach at the sound of falling bricks and people screaming. Dozens of people began rushing away from the village, glancing behind them in panic.

"Head for the forest," she urged them. "Take cover in the trees."

It was their best option considering she did not know what type of creature had set upon them. She issued the same command to anyone that they passed on their way through the streets. Dust from debris rose in the air, providing a guide toward the attacker. Even without it, the people running away from one direction gave Audra a clear picture of where to go.

Stopping several mages who were rushing in the same direction as Audra, she urged them to protect the people fleeing, who had no magic to defend themselves. They hesitated, but Audra knew how to issue a command.

Streets with cheerful storefronts and homes with brightly colored doors passed in a blur as Audra and Taara rushed forward. The haze of dust impeded their view as they turned a corner. Covering her nose and mouth to prevent inhaling the particles, Audra sent a breeze down the street, clearing their way. The sight that it revealed caused her steps to falter.

One side of a building had collapsed, a gaping hole where solid walls once stood. Stone and wood cascaded down onto the street like a waterfall, shards of glass sparkling throughout. Underneath a large slab of flooring, a man was crushed, a small girl trying to pull him out. Tears ran down her dirty cheeks, her clothes torn and bloody. One of her legs was injured, yet she still tried to pull out the much larger body. Audra did not want to tell her that there was no point. The man was dead. Taara approached the girl slowly, murmuring soft reassurances as she held the child in her arms.

"Get her to safety." Audra knew that the girl needed comfort, but she had to continue on.

"I'll find you when I'm done."

"No, you do not know how to fight and I need your help with the wounded." She knew that Taara would not take the words harshly, it was just reality. Taara was better at healing than she ever would be in a fight.

With a look of concern, Taara nodded. "Be safe."

"You too." Audra hugged her friend quickly before making her way over the rubble.

Stone shifted under her feet and Audra had to move slowly to make it across safely. Wanting to keep up her energy before a fight, Audra had to traverse the damage without magic. This was near the edge of the town, where buildings were spaced farther apart, and the street led to an open field at the base of the hill. A few mages were scattered around the field, launching attacks at a round ball that appeared to be made of plated scales. More bricks, pieces of furniture, and roof tiles lay along the ground, like a child had pushed over a tower of building blocks in anger.

The mages in the clearing were primarily those who regularly protected the ward, more skilled at fighting than the average citizen. However, they rarely had to fight, and what practical experience they had was not enough against a creature near immune to magical attacks. Already, one mage lay motionless on the ground. Bile rose in Audra's throat and she had to force down the urge to be sick at the sight of the scales lodged into the mage's abdomen, cutting open flesh to expose blood, muscle, and bone.

Finished rolling in a circle to force the mages back, the creature uncurled onto six short legs, their narrow width covered in coarse hair. Pure black eyes stared at Audra over a long snout, the netvor—for that surely was what the creature was—sizing up its prey. The other mages continued to strike at the monster with magic, the attacks diluting when they hit scales, barely drawing the attention of the netvor.

"That won't work," Audra yelled to them.

She doubted any of them had received education on netvor, since their magic prevented mages from becoming the creatures and the wards acted as a natural barrier to keep the monsters out. Outside the Guards, there was little training against netvor anywhere within the three kingdoms. It was a mistake to forget that allowing non-mages into Ymira could increase the chances of a netvor getting in. Audra thought the wards would be enough.

"We need to draw it away from the town," she added. "Try to lure it toward the lake." It was the opposite direction of where the people were fleeing toward the forest, and the lake provided ample space to figure out how to defeat the creature without risking additional lives.

The three remaining mages nodded their understanding, but before they could make a move, the creature's back rippled. Layers of scales separated and fanned outward with a faint clicking sound. In a spray of projectiles, scales released from the netvor's back with a jerk, flung in the direction of the mages. They split the air as fast as daggers, their sharp points embedding themselves deep into anything in their path, including the wooden door Audra thrust in front of her as a shield.

A cry of pain rent the air and Audra let the temporary shield drop to the ground to see one of the mages clutch their side in pain. Dark red blood poured out of the wound where a scale sliced through cloth and flesh. Sensing that its prey was weak, the netvor faced the wounded mage. With a burst of magic, Audra sent the mage flying backwards, out of the path of the netvor and into the arms of another mage.

"Get them to safety," she shouted, beginning to launch broken bricks at the netvor to draw its attention. When one of the rocks connected with the creature's nose, it turned with a snarl that chilled Audra's blood. Tiny, pointed teeth peeked from behind a curled lip, and Audra never wanted to be close enough to see how many there were.

Backing away while facing the netvor, Audra was relieved to see the injured mage being carried away.

The remaining mage was breathing heavily, shoulders moving up and down with each breath, her freckles a stark contrast to the pallor of her skin. Audra recognized the signs of burnout and knew that the mage was close to the limit of her magic. With shaking hands, the mage sent a wave of magic into the ground, causing the earth to ripple and knock the creature onto its side. Hoping that the underbelly would be more vulnerable than the rest, Audra sliced her magic through the air. It created a shallow cut, but nothing more. Growling in frustration, Audra continued to put distance between herself and the netvor while she looked around for a weapon.

Thinking about weapons sparked an idea, and she turned to the remaining mage, who looked as if any remaining strength was dedicated to staying upright. Her ice-blue eyes held a glint of steely determination and Audra knew that she was willing to stay and fight, even though she would surely die without enough magic to protect herself.

"I need you to go to Myra's shop and get me a sword," Audra hollered across the open space between them.

The netvor's legs kicked against the air as its body lurched to get upright.

The mage's reply reached Audra's ears. "It's too strong. It will kill you if you fight it alone."

"Maybe, but it definitely will if I don't have a weapon. Go! Meet me at the lake."

Time was running out and the creature was starting to tip back onto its feet. Without a sideways glance at the other mage, Audra sent a line of fire to surround the netvor, discouraging it from moving towards the town and the people still escaping. Turning, Audra began running in the direction of the lake, trying to put as much distance between her and the netvor before she had to turn to face it again.

Her lungs burned from the effort, Audra's endurance tested by the speed required to reach the town and now turn back. Beneath her feet, pebbles trembled as the ground shook. Risking a glance behind her, Audra saw the netvor was once again curled into a ball and rolling in her direction. Magic swirled around her fingers as Audra pulled chunks of earth up to slow it down. She was almost clear of the village, near the slope that led in one direction to Rauha and the lake in the other. Time was what she needed, time to bring the fight away from her people.

The broken earth worked, but not in the way she expected. When the creature hit the raised dirt, the momentum propelled it a few feet into the air.

Audra cursed and dove out of the way of the descent.

Dirt and grass flew as the netvor hit the ground.

Gulping down lungfuls of air, Audra wasted no time continuing toward the lake.

"Audra, duck!" Valeria's warning came just in time. Audra flung herself to the ground, watching as scales flew over her head with a whizzing sound. Glass shattered as several struck the side of Rauha.

Pushing up to her feet, Audra whipped around to face the netvor. Menacing eyes glared at her, teeth gnashing in its fury. While it was frightening to look at before, the netvor now struck terror in Audra's veins. How the Guards faced creatures like this time and time again was beyond her.

Valeria appeared from around the netvor's side, racing to stand beside Audra. It was a relief to see her mentor uninjured. There were rips in her pants and shirt, along with smears of dirt and dried blood, but it did not look like any of it was hers.

"I was told to bring this to you," Valeria said as she handed over a short sword. She must have been in the town when the attack started and ran into the mage sent to get Audra a weapon. Audra was glad that the powerful mage was by her side. Together, they could take down the monster, Audra was sure of it. They just needed a good strategy.

"We have to keep it off balance long enough for me to get close. Direct lines of magic won't work, but manipulating the elements does."

"Got it. I'll take the left side and you take the right. We can surround it."

They separated at the next volley of scales.

Weaving around the creature, Audra and Valeria cast spell after spell to distract it. As tense as the situation was, it was awe-inspiring to watch her mentor fight. Valeria moved with precision, her magic striking its target over and over again. She used the environment around them to creatively work around the netvor's natural resistance to magic. Water turned to shards of ice as tree roots wrapped around the monster's spindly legs.

Audra was equally as ferocious, using light to blind and chunks of rock to dent the thick armor. With each successive attack, the netvor grew agitated, darting toward each of the mages and releasing more scales, sacrificing accuracy for frequency. Many of the scales shot wildly past Audra and Valeria, colliding with more of Rauha Hall or falling harmlessly into the lake and forest. One hit the greenhouse and Audra prayed that Eli was long gone.

When Audra was finally close enough, an attack from Valeria drew the netvor's attention and Audra lunged with the sword. The weapon was heavy, the unaccustomed weight pulling her arm lower than where she was aiming. Metal opened the tender flesh at the netvor's neck and black blood slid from the wound. Triumph swelled in her at the successful hit.

Rearing back in pain, the netvor twisted to search for the source of the injury. Aiming to slash the sword again, Audra was knocked backward as its scaled torso hit her. Airborne for a moment, Audra struggled to breathe as the wind was knocked out of her. Her vision blurred as she looked up at the cloudy sky, her limbs sprawled in the dirt.

Everything hurt, her nerves tingling as Audra tried to roll over. Clutching her side with one arm, Audra felt warm blood beneath her fingers. Cursing, she looked down to see a long gash below her ribs. A scale must have sliced her. Wincing at the pain, Audra pushed up onto her other elbow. She had to get up. Valeria was doing everything she could to continue fighting the netvor, but its rage-filled eyes were focused on Audra. Like a dying animal, the netvor was going to use its last strength to try and take her down with it.

Her ears buzzed, but Audra could see Valeria's mouth moving soundlessly as she motioned for Audra to get up. Distantly, Audra heard the shifting clink that signaled the netvor was ready to release more scales. This time, they would all be directed at her. Putting pressure on her leg sent a blast of pain up Audra's side, and she looked down to see a deep gash running up her thigh. Deep enough to damage the muscle, the pain of trying to get up nearly had her blacking out. Breathing through her teeth, Audra reached for her magic.

Her throat closed and her heart raced as panic set in at the realization that it would not be enough. Not yet drained, her magic struggled to respond to Audra's sluggish concentration. Valeria continued to attack, increasing the damage done by the sword. Watching the creature slow, Audra slumped back against the grass. She locked eyes with the netvor, determined to see it breathe its last.

If she was going to die, at least it was by protecting her people. Audra was at peace with that.

The final scale shifted into place. Audra watched as the projectiles hurtled through the air before the netvor fell to the ground, the life fading from its black eyes. Its aim was true and Audra was glad that her death would be quick. She whispered a goodbye to her friends, wishing them lives full of happiness as tears slid down her face. Closing her eyes, Audra allowed her mind to think of Graham, his roguish smile and piercing eyes a happy memory in her last moments.

Audra expected the initial pain to be greater, but when she heard the scales make impact, she felt nothing. Perhaps it was a small mercy from Hellig. But that deep grunt she heard definitely did not come out of her mouth. Her eyes flashed open, and for a moment, Audra thought she must have already died because her vision was filled with black. Focusing, the black sky shifted into the familiar sight of plain cloth.

Valeria stood in front of her, shielding Audra from the attack. Spade-shaped scales protruded from her legs, abdomen, and chest, her body riddled with bloody wounds.

"Nooooooo!" Audra screamed. Adrenaline pumped through her veins as she pushed past her own pain to kneel and catch Valeria's falling body.

Cradling Valeria's head in her hands, Audra brushed the dark curls away from her face.

Audra bit down on her lip to stop sobbing. "It's going to be okay... Tell me what to do..." Her hands shook as they moved down Valeria's shirt, the blood staining the fabric an even darker black. Fighting against the pain and lethargy plaguing her own body, Audra spooled magic into

Valeria's wound, frantically trying to knit back muscle and blood vessels that were speared by the scales.

It was not enough. Her magic pulsed faintly, the effort to remain awake and slowly heal herself battling against Audra's will to heal Valeria. Letting out a frustrated curse, Audra steadied one hand against the other, forcing her magic into Valeria's wound.

Not enough.

Why was it not enough when it mattered?

A wrinkled hand gripped Audra's wrist, the weak grip a mockery of her once formidable strength.

"Audra." Even weakened, her voice was rich and warm. "Stop. There's nothing..." Her words were separated by rattling breaths. "...You can do. This was my choice."

Audra's lungs seized in response, tears pouring down her face. "No, please don't go. I need you."

"I am so...proud of you." Valeria raised a hand to cup Audra's cheek. "And I have no regrets. You are everything our people need, but don't... forget you aren't...alone."

"I won't." Audra kissed her cheek. "Thank you for teaching me how to love myself."

Valeria smiled even as her chest jerked with a choked breath. "Thank you...for teaching...me." Each word was fainter than the last.

With another gasped breath, Valeria's chest stopped moving.

Grief swallowed Audra like a tidal wave. She wailed over Valeria's body, pain and sorrow ripped from her heart as she released the loss of her mentor, the mages outside the village, and countless others whose deaths she would learn about in the coming days. Bent over, she cried for what felt like an endless amount of time. This was her mentor, the woman who seemed like an unstoppable force, now dead. She would never get to share another pot of tea with Valeria or hear her advice.

Valeria was gone, and Audra had to figure out how to pick up the pieces.

That was how Eli and Taara found her, the muscles in Audra's legs locked in place from sitting in one position for too long. They said nothing when they saw Valeria's body, but their faces were lined with grief. Hugging Audra against her chest, Taara ran a soothing hand down her hair while starting to heal the wounds on her torso and leg. Audra's eyelids felt like they were weighed down and she wondered if Taara was using her magic to sedate her against the pain.

Sleep seemed so peaceful, where grief could not touch her, so Audra let her eyes close and drifted into unconsciousness.

Sorrow filled the days following the attack. Audra felt the weight of it dragging her down and all she wanted to do was lie in bed and hug Isik to her. But she had to show the people of Ymira that she felt the loss as deeply as they did, and sharing the stories of the deceased helped ease the pressure on her chest.

Once she was healed enough to walk longer distances, Audra went with Eli to investigate the location in the ward where the breach occurred. Studying the netvor had revealed no clues to where it had come from, but Audra had expected that since none of them had the knowledge Guards received on netvor. When they reached the ward, Audra and Eli were struck with another wave of grief. The body of the mage on patrol was bloodied and shredded almost beyond recognition. But when they saw the green tipped nails and probed for traces of magic, they both leaned into each other to cry again.

Silvan had been patrolling this portion of the ward. And now he was gone too.

Eli took the loss harder than the rest and was somber and quiet for weeks.

In the tradition of mages, Valeria and others who perished in the attack were buried in the earth under the night sky, the light of the crescent moon providing Hellig's blessing as the souls passed into the afterlife. Afterwards, everyone gathered in the village to share toasts to those who were lost. Leah was able to join them for the burial and subsequent celebration of life, and she promised Audra that she would stay for as long as was needed. Having her closest friend back was one of the few things helping Audra get out of bed and continue working.

After the attack, Audra wanted to keep the mages close. Knowing where everyone was and if they were safe was imperative. She could not lose anyone else. As soon as possible, Audra sent letters to all known mages living in Solven and Feldor, informing them of what happened, reminding them to be on their guard and take measures to limit potential for running into a netvor. Staying near areas with Guards was the first step. She also requested more frequent check-ins, the reassurance that they were safe easing some of the fear that tracked Audra like a shadow after the attack.

Unfortunately, the fear was not unfounded. Weeks after the initial attack, Audra stopped receiving communication from two mages, Avery and Leon. Subsequent letters went unanswered, and Audra knew that the worst was not yet over.

SEVENTEEN

Sunset was Audra's favorite time of day at Rauha. The soft shades of pink and orange bowing beneath the horizon as they bade farewell to the day, allowing the rich blues to overtake the sky with hints of purple from the moon. Watching the colors shift and fade from the windows of the library, her temporary office until the rubble of Rauha could be rebuilt, filled her with serenity. Knowing that the day was coming to an end, that they had made it through, was calming. Unlike the invigorating light of sunrise, the sunset was calm and gentle. Fading over the land like a blanket tucking them in safely to sleep.

If only it could stay that way forever.

"Are you going to attend?" Leah stood at her side, reading a parchment over Audra's shoulder.

Passing the invitation to Leah, Audra rubbed her brows.

To the High Mage of Ymira
King Keld and Queen Isadora of Solven cordially invite you to
the royal ball honoring the christening of their granddaughter,
Princess Diana. As our honored guest, we hope that you will stay at
the palace so that we may discuss the future of our two kingdoms.

"The timing is almost too convenient." Everything seemed suspicious to Audra these days.

When she was unable to glean anything from the body of the netvor, Audra had sent Kasteel a letter discreetly inquiring if he knew what type it was. His response was prompt, checking in on her safety and asking if Ymira needed assistance before letting her know that he had never heard of a netvor that looked like the one Audra described. However, he was quick to add, the royal library in Solven would have the book the Guard had compiled on all known netvor.

Leah put the letter down and crossed to the other side of the desk to sit, pushing her long hair back from her face. "Maybe, but you are close with Esha and Kasteel, an honorary aunt to Diana. With your inquiries about a treaty, it does make sense that the king and queen would combine a celebration for Diana with political talks."

"To be honest..." Audra got up to pour herself and her friend a drink. "I had forgotten about the treaty with everything going on. Between the rebuilding, extra patrols, and checking in on everyone, it feels like the least important thing on my list."

Leah watched her with scrutinizing eyes, and although Audra took great pains to look presentable and competent, her friend knew what to look for. The dark shadows beneath her eyes and tight pull of her brows gave away the tension and stress that was eating away at her.

"Still no word from Avery or Leon?" Leah's voice was neutral, but Audra could tell by the way she twirled the wineglass between her fingers that her friend was worried.

"No, and that is not like them," Audra said with a frown.

Avery had a shop set up in Oshea, a seaside port in Solven, and they sent updates practically every week with requests for items that Avery could not make themselves. Leon, by comparison, was hardly in the same place for long. Traveling where requests took him, Leon did not check in as often, but he made sure to write at least a note saying he was safe every other week.

When she took a seat next to Leah, Audra kicked off her shoes and massaged the back of her neck. She sighed with relief as a knot loosened and allowed the wine to relax her. So much of her day was spent putting on a brave face for her people, so it was a relief to be herself around Leah.

"This invitation might be beneficial for multiple reasons." Leah saw the calculating look on Audra's face and stayed silent, sipping from her own wineglass while she waited to hear what plan the High Mage had.

"Sending more mages after Avery and Leon is too risky. If they were just delayed in responding, then sending out a search party would cause unnecessary panic. But, if something is wrong, I cannot send anyone unprepared." Her fingers drummed against the glass. "I also cannot have the other kingdoms alerted to our problems, our relationships with them are too new to show a sign of weakness. With your position in Feldor, having you poke around will not raise any suspicions, and you are the only person I would trust anyways."

Leah scoffed. "I'd like to see anything try to get in my way." Leah was furious when she arrived in Ymira. The helplessness of being far away when the attack happened put her on edge. For days, ice-cold rage poured off her in waves of magic used to clean up the town as a cathartic release.

For a moment, Audra thought about how different the attack would have gone if Leah had been there, but she quickly shook off the thought. There was no point in dwelling on what ifs, she could only deal with what was.

"Solven is a different matter. Though they have allowed mages to open shops and live out in the open, it would look bad if someone was caught snooping around before the alliance is secured. Besides, there might be information on the netvor that attacked Ymira in the royal library." Swirling the wine in her glass, Audra thought about her return to Solven.

"I know that look. What put that scheming look on your face?"

"Oh, I was just thinking that it has been a long time since I went to a ball. I do hope I have something suitable to wear."

ONCE AGAIN, Audra found herself sitting in a carriage across from a scowling Leah.

"Hells. Are these things always so tight?" Pulling at the sleeves of her shirt, Leah twisted one way and then the other trying to loosen the fabric.

Smothering a laugh, Audra let out a small smile. "Stop pulling at it or it will rip."

With one last tug, Leah slumped against the back of her seat with a huff. "Good. Then maybe I can finally breathe."

"You are being ridiculous. Besides, you only have yourself to blame. It's your design." Clad in head-to-toe black, Leah's warrior-like ensemble would have looked severe on anyone else. Sheer sleeves curved from her shoulders, ending in a point on each hand, a delicate band holding them in place. The fabric continued across her chest, tucking into the velvet, corset-like top and forming a collar around her neck. Paired with snug, black pants, the simplicity of the attire highlighted Leah's fierce beauty. Her hair was pulled into two buns atop her head, a few tendrils allowed to curl around her face. Lacking any other accessory, Leah's one concession to color—a frivolous purchase she called it —was the ocean-blue heeled boots on her feet.

"A decision I regret more each moment." With a final shimmy, Leah slumped against the back of her seat. Complaining was a coping mechanism for her. The more she vocalized disliking something, the more Audra knew she was trying to hide what was really bothering her.

"It's going to be fine, Leah. We are honored guests. No one is going to hurt us." Allowing one side of her mouth to lift in a wry smile, Audra teased, "Besides, no one would dare try with you wearing that."

That got a small snort out of her friend.

"I know I can take care of myself." Blue eyes met green briefly before fixing on a spot out the window. "It's not me I'm worried about."

"Me?" Audra's brow furrowed in confusion. "This was where I grew up, raised on a diet of polite conversation and subtle backstabbing. I am not afraid of them."

"Which is exactly what concerns me. As far as we've come over the years, there are still those who don't want mages in places of power. You need to be careful."

"I will be."

As they drew closer to the castle, Audra felt like she was walking through a dream. Memories of traveling through the forest and up the dirt path played behind her eyes, shrouded in the slight haziness that came from the passage of time. She could remember how strong and imposing the stone walls appeared, but could not recall how it looked bathed in fading sunlight. Or how passing under the gates felt both like entering sanctuary and a prison. Members of the staff stepped forward to open the carriage door and lower the steps to help the ladies out.

Audra placed her ungloved hand in a footman's, the gesture both foreign and familiar. It had been years since Audra attended a ball, years since anyone had waited on her, and it felt slightly like putting on too-small shoes. Not at all like the fiery-orange heels that clicked against the staircase as Audra walked into the castle. Head held high, eyes forward. She had to look like she belonged here and that no one could touch her. Even if they had no idea who she was.

For now.

It was Eli's idea that Audra and Leah enchant the carriage to look like any other at the ball. Disguising their identities until the last minute would give them authentic reactions to their arrival and an alluring air of mystery. Couples and small groups gathered in the grand hallway, and Audra felt the weight of their stares as they passed, keeping her eyes forward and face impassive. Dressed in the colors of a Ymiran sunset, Audra knew she looked exceptional.

Thin straps made of dark crystal held up the heart-shaped bodice before crossing at her back to connect with the fabric on her hips. Near-black purple faded into amethyst, violet, and cobalt down the plunge of her neckline to the swell of her hips where it burst into blush pink and soft orange. Crystals sparkled in the light where they lay in strategic patterns to look like the rays of the sun fading into starlight. Painted on the exposed skin of her back was the crescent moon and stars of Ymira, enchanted not to smear or fade throughout the night.

Catching her reflection as she passed a mirror in the hallway, strategically placed for guests to check their appearance one last time before entering the ballroom, Audra glowed with pride. No longer was her reflection the nervous girl waiting to enter the room and become a princess. Now she would enter the room with the confidence of knowing exactly who and what she was.

A queen.

Stepping up to the ballroom door, Audra watched as the herald's eyes widened with shock when Leah gave their names and titles.

"The High Mage of Ymira, Lady Audra, and Ambassador Leah."

A hush rolled over the ballroom, surprised faces turning toward the open door. Standing at the edge of the raised balcony, Audra paused and allowed her gaze to sweep over the crowd. Now that she had their attention, she intended to keep it. This was her debut as High Mage, and she would sear this impression into their memories. In a world that valued appearances and wealth, she would make them fall to their knees in adoration. Dimming the lights clustered on tables and hanging on the walls, Audra focused the glow on herself, illuminating her descent like the setting sun. More than one cry of delight was heard when the crystals on her dress caught the light, scattering pinpoints of light across the room.

Once again, the crowd parted around her when she reached the base of the stairs. She recognized many familiar faces, none more so than those at the end of the path. Seated on his throne, Keld gave nothing away as he watched Audra's approach, new lines around his eyes and gray at his temple softening his features. Beside him, Isadora gripped his left hand with her right, moisture shining in her eyes. Her once ebony hair was now sprinkled with white, which only enhanced her beauty, and her eyes flickered between Audra and her husband, as if seeking reassurance for what she saw.

Audra kept her gaze on the king as she approached the raised dais, but her skin prickled with awareness at the presence beside him. A person she dared not look at yet.

"Good evening, Your Majesties." She nodded to each of them as Leah bowed behind her. "We are honored to attend this celebration."

"Audra?" Isadora started to rise from her throne before Keld placed a steadying hand on her shoulder.

"Is it really you? We thought we lost you." Keld's voice shook with hope.

Although she had anticipated their doubt and knew that hiding her identity was the right decision at the time, it surprised Audra how much guilt she felt over it.

"It's her, father," Kasteel's voice came from Audra's right, where he stood with his family on the side of the dais. Passing his daughter into the waiting arms of his wife, Kasteel stepped forward to hug Audra.

"Still hiding on the side of ballrooms?" Audra whispered into his jacket, absorbing some of this warmth to bolster her.

"Always, Sprite." Turning towards his parents, Kasteel held out his hand for Esha to join him. "Audra has been a guest in our home many times over the past years."

"You knew?" Hurt and anger laced a voice that haunted Audra's dreams, and she braced herself to look at Graham for the first time since she left.

The sharp lines of his face hit her like a punch to the stomach. Dark brows drew low over his storm-gray eyes. Confusion, anger, and —Hellig save her for hoping—longing swirled like a vortex in his gaze. His left arm was covered in black ink, the monsters he slayed penned into his skin in a violently beautiful pattern. Why could he not have gotten uglier over the years? Was it too much to ask that he lose some of his muscular frame instead of growing into it? It was almost cruel that his chiseled features sharpened more with age. His thick hair, cut shorter on the sides, was swept in a manner too artful to be unintentional.

Graham gripped his brother's arm tightly, drawing attention to the chords of his muscles. There was no reason for Audra to find that attractive. "You knew where she was, and you did not tell me?"

"I'm sorry that my actions hurt you, but it was Audra's wish to remain hidden." Kasteel glanced between them with worry.

"Sons, now is not the time for this discussion. We have guests waiting." The king spoke in a low voice, his reminder meant for only their small group. If their conversation continued much longer, it would draw more unwanted attention from the guests eagerly leaning forward to listen. In the moments since Audra and Leah were announced, no other guest had been introduced, the party quieting for the reunion.

"Of course, father, forgive us." Audra watched as Graham turned back toward her, no longer able to avoid meeting his eyes. He looked at her like he was staring at a mirage, his eyes wide with shock and lips parted slightly. "Hello, Audra." He spoke her name like an answered prayer. Lightning sizzled in her veins at the sound of his voice, rendering her breathless.

A pinch at her elbow drew Audra's awareness back into herself. She was not here to reprise her role of the besotted young woman making moon-eyes at the prince. Power hungry nobility would assume that she was here to try her hand at marrying Graham again. That she was weak and foolish. Audra was more than happy to show them what happens to people who assume.

"Good evening, Your Highness." Audra dropped her eyes and smiled wickedly. "The ballroom is as beautiful as I remembered it. I do hope you remember to save me a dance this time."

Before he could reply, Audra turned in a whirl of skirts and strode toward the side of the room, leaving a gaping Graham behind. Leah looked like she wanted to applaud, barely restraining a smile as she took her place at Audra's side.

"Damn. You cut him down at his knees. I'm impressed."

"Please." Taking the glass Leah passed her, Audra hid her smile behind a sip of wine. "I learned from the best."

"You're welcome." Their glasses clinked together, a small toast to celebrate the success of their arrival. But the hardest part of the evening was yet to come. Captivating the crowd was the first step, but next was navigating conversations designed to trap while planting the seeds of alliances. As ambassador to Feldor, Leah had established a good foundation for them to work with, but now that Audra had entered the game, players would begin jockeying for position and favor around her.

And so it begins, Audra thought to herself as an attractive man approached them.

"Lady Leah, a pleasure as always." Brilliant white teeth shone against dark skin as Prince Maxim approached. Leah had told her stories of the youngest prince of Feldor. Quick-witted and smart, his turquoise gaze missed nothing, an invaluable asset to his queen and ambassador.

"Your Highness." Leah bowed. "I would say the same of you, except it would not be true."

Dramatically clutching his chest, Maxim stumbled back a few steps, mirth gleaming in his eyes. "You wound me. How shall I ever recover?"

Shaking her head at the exaggeration, Leah patted Maxim's shoulder. "I'm sure you'll find a way. Audra, may I introduce Prince Maxim of Feldor?"

"A pleasure, Your Highness." Audra smiled at him, liking him instantly. Anyone who could work their way past Leah's walls and gain her trust was a friend to Audra.

"Please, none of this *Your Highness* business. Titles are so stuffy. Call me Maxim." His hands were soft as silk as he drew Audra's hand to his lips. A pang of homesickness filled Audra as she thought that Taara would want to know how he kept his hands so soft.

"You ladies certainly know how to make a splash. I cannot recall ever witnessing anything like it before. Everyone here wants to be you, kill you, or bed you. Well done."

Audra let out a peal of laughter. Maxim's frank assessment was refreshing and put her at ease. Rarely were courtiers so honest. "They will be incredibly disappointed then," she said.

Several guests took their laughter as an invitation to join the trio, breathing out sighs of relief after watching Maxim survive his encounter with the High Mage. Audra had to hold back a scoff as people who previously paid her little attention now greeted her like an old friend, expressing their joy at having her back at court. She wondered how much time would pass before they started asking for favors.

"Lady Audra, what a surprise to see you again." A portly man with cropped hair and a ruddy face approached the group, his beady eyes running down Audra's body. Suppressing a shiver at his calculating look, Audra peered down her nose at Lord Nadeen. A high-ranking noble in Keld's court, Lord Nadeen had vocally disapproved of Audra as a match for Graham, claiming her lack of land or foreign connections made her inconsequential. Of course, it did not help that Audra had never shared his opinions on policy or encouraged his favor with the royal family.

"Lord Nadeen, how curious that you would be surprised by my appearance. Anyone close to the king would know which guests were invited." Watching his face heat with embarrassment delighted Audra. Whatever favor he had in Solven was not worth coddling his ego.

"Of course, I was aware that his Royal Highness extended an invitation to the High Mage of Ymira, but even he seemed surprised to see you. One has to wonder at the reason for such secrecy. Weren't you once close friends?"

Straightening a hand down his jacket, Lord Nadeen recovered quickly, knowing precisely where to aim his poisonous words. But Audra was adept at masking her emotions, showing no hint of the bruised patches of her heart that flared to life at the reminder of the love she lost. Threading through the pain was a line of curiosity. His use of Royal Highness, not His Majesty, implied that Graham was responsible for the invitation.

Why would he have invited them? Why did he care? She could mull over the answers later, when she was alone. Now, the small crowd around them watched her closely, waiting to hear how she would respond.

Think. What would satisfy their curiosity without showing weakness? A single note from a trumpet saved her from answering.

All heads turned toward the dais as Graham stood. "Friends, thank you all for gathering tonight. It is my great pleasure to welcome you all to our celebration commemorating Diana's christening." Clapping echoed around the hall. "Born from both kingdoms, she represents a new generation of hope and prosperity between our lands. As we celebrate in the coming days, may we never forget the friendship our people share, and work together to build a brighter future." His eyes locked onto Audra's across the room, burning her from the inside out with the fierce possession of his gaze.

Speech concluded, Graham raised his glass toward Audra, drinking shallowly as the instruments began playing the opening strains of a waltz. Guests shuffled around as they found partners, moving towards the dancefloor. Audra watched the flurry of activity in front of her part suddenly, like a wedge was forcing them apart.

Striding confidently toward her was Graham, his eyes never straying from hers, despite several courtiers' attempts at catching his attention. The weight of his gaze pinned her in place, her legs melting. Audra's heart began to beat faster. Fragile hope wanted to take root, but she had to squash it. He had tricked her once before. If he insulted her this time, she would skewer him on the spot. Unless Leah did it first, based on the fire blazing in her eyes.

Still he came.

Closer.

Where did all the air go?

Audra's breath caught in her throat along with her hammering heart. The foolish organ refused to listen to her. Up close, Graham's intensity smoldered like hot coals. His body vibrated with restrained energy, as if the act of stopping steps away from her physically pained him. At least she was not the only one affected by their proximity. While Graham stored every inch of her appearance into this memory, she did the same with him.

Transfixed by the bob of his throat as he swallowed, Audra almost missed what Graham was saying. "This is several years late, but it would be a great honor if you shared this dance with me."

So this is what it felt like to get something you always wanted. Delicate hope, tentative joy, and a murky undercurrent of fear. Shifting her gaze from his outstretched hand to his eyes, Audra saw the mirror to her own emotions before she shuttered them. She could do this. Dance with the man who held her heart, and then crushed it, without giving away another piece of herself.

Graham breathed sharply when their palms touched, the pulse at his neck throbbing with increased tempo. For a moment, he simply stared at their hands, the thin band of gray glowing faintly around enlarged pupils.

"One generally needs to move in order to dance, Your Highness."

He chuckled softly, leading her into the center of the dancers before pulling her close. Music filtered into her brain like a distant buzz, the warm spread of Graham's fingers at her waist and hand drawing her attention as their bodies began moving to the music. Her dress caressed his skins as they stepped together, then apart.

"Audra, I—"

"It's Lady Audra now, Your Highness." Petty to require the title, but she needed the emotional detachment the formality provided.

Audra caught the wince on Graham's face before he masked it. "I deserve that and so much more for how I treated you."

They separated briefly as Audra spun out a in twirl, giving her a moment to determine how to respond before Graham pulled her into a dip, bending her back over his arm. Her hair nearly grazed the floor as Audra watched the dizzying swirl of dancers around her before Graham lifted her to his chest.

"It was a long time ago. We were both young and foolish back then."

"That is no excuse for my behavior. I—"

Coward that she was, Audra did not want to hear how that sentence would end. "Your family looks well. Kasteel keeps me updated on Diana, but I am astounded at how fast she grows each time I see her."

At the mention of his niece, Graham smiled brightly. "She's incredible and already so smart. Did they tell you that she started trying to say my name? It comes out more as 'Gam' right now, but it's a good start." Only half a year old, Diana's attempt was probably more babble than a conscious effort at saying his name, but it was sweet how excited Graham got.

"Sounds like she has you wrapped around her finger."

Another twirl spun her away from Graham, but Audra thought she heard him murmur, "She's not the only one."

A series of quick turns separated them again. Audra's body was flush with exertion, pumping blood through her veins that brought awareness to every exposed piece of skin. With a snap of his arm, Graham pulled her to him, her back flush against his chest. She could feel his quickened heartbeat through his clothes and the bare skin of her back and smiled at the knowledge that he was similarly impacted by their proximity.

"I missed you." Audra should have known that Graham would not let her avoid the conversation for long.

"It wasn't like I went missing. I left a letter saying where I was going." The ability to avoid his gaze made her bold. Five years had dulled, but not removed, the bitter disappointment that no one from the royal family had attempted to contact her in the initial days and weeks after her departure.

"I know." He sounded ashamed. "I am sorry for every moment of pain I caused you. By the time I put aside my pride and wrote to you, enough time had passed that when my letters were returned, unopened, I knew you wanted nothing to do with me."

"I never received any letters. Not beyond the one you sent with the journal." Maybe it was foolish of her to admit it, but there was something about Graham that always made her honest. If he was telling the truth, it was possible that either Valeria or the wards had prevented the letters from reaching her. Ymira was specifically designed to keep people out. Even after the changes Audra made, people and correspondence still had a difficult time finding Ymira without a magical escort.

"I wrote to you every damn day for two years."

Air left her lungs as Graham lifted her, turning them in a circle before lowering her to the ground, her body sliding against his as their eyes connected. Her dress caught along the side of his clothing, and Audra felt the contours of his muscles rubbing against her. Disoriented by the sensations creating havoc on her body, Audra failed to notice that the song was over until she heard the crowd clapping around them. Chest flushed, she stepped away to curtsy.

Facing Graham was a mistake. If she thought he looked intense before, the steely determination in her eyes changed her mind. He looked like he would tear apart the world before being parted from her again. Audra's mind warred between protecting herself and believing him.

Survival won.

"Thank you for the dance, Your Highness."

Walking away from him was more difficult the second time. Finding Leah in the surrounding crowd, Audra made her way toward her friend, not stopping even as Graham called for her to wait. Fleeing was not an option, not when the ball provided the best chance to meet potential allies in one place. But Graham was a Guard, a hunter, and she knew he would not give up pursuit. Eyes pleading for her friend to understand the predicament, Audra quickened her pace.

Risking a glance behind her, Audra found Graham much closer than she would like, his longer gait shortening the distance between them. Just as he reached out a hand to clasp around her wrist, another hand took hers.

"Lady Audra, I believe the next dance is mine." Hellig bless Maxim. The younger prince shot an apologetic glance toward Graham, who acknowledged being out-maneuvered with a nod of his head, his eyes following Audra.

"Thank you, Maxim."

"Anything for my newest friend." Maxim did not possess the same skills as a dancer, his movements rigid and cautious. "Though your prince did look particularly determined to keep you to himself."

"He is not *my* anything," Audra scoffed.

"Sure, you keep telling yourself that."

Despite Graham's hovering presence, or perhaps because of it, Audra found herself in constant demand as a dance partner. Her feet complained against the constant movement, but stopping was not an option. If she declined any dance, Graham was waiting at the edge of the dancefloor to continue their conversation. She knew she could not avoid him forever, but Audra needed time to process what he had revealed. That did not stop her heart from pulsing with joy each time she saw him decline an invitation to dance in favor of watching her, arms crossed with jealousy.

That plan was working well until a large hand clamped down on the shoulder of her current dance partner, the deep, familiar voice of the king asking, "May I cut in?"

Unwilling to offend the king, her partner bowed and placed Audra's hand in Keld's. The black of his sleeveless shirt contrasted sharply with the blue and green of his hazel eyes as his assessing gaze examined her. Audra felt like one of the plants Eli studied. She forced her spine straighter, refusing to lower her eyes to the man who was once like a father to her. Though Audra's position now made her Keld's equal, a part of her still wanted his approval.

"You've caused quite the stir with your arrival, Lady Audra."

"Have I? I had not noticed."

Keld's thick mustache twitched with humor. "Isadora will have my hide for this, but I've never been a man to mince words."

Audra swallowed past the lump in her throat. She knew that Keld was not dancing with her for the pleasure of it, he reserved that for his wife, but this was not a conversation she looked forward to having.

"When you left us, we were devastated. I know you had your reasons, but leaving without a proper goodbye broke our hearts."

Shame encouraged her to avert her gaze, but Audra owed it to Keld to address him directly. "I know. It was selfish of me to leave without thanking you for the kindness you had shown me. I am sorry for the pain I caused." It was one of the few things Audra regretted in life.

Around them, couples attempted to dance closer to them like gossip-hungry vultures. Keld deftly steered them away, maintaining distance between the other couples.

"It was never about you owing us a thank you. You were one of our own and we loved you like a daughter." Tears gathered in the corners of his eyes, threatening to spill. "Why did you never reach out? Why not reveal yourself in the letters you had Kasteel pass on?"

Audra's eyes watered. "I was afraid you would hate me. At the time, mages were regarded with suspicion, if not animosity, and I did not want your feelings towards me to cloud your relationship with my people."

Understanding softened his gaze.

"As a monarch, I commend your caution. You waited until your position was secure before acting. Something I hope you learned from my queen." He glanced toward his wife with fondness. Time had only strengthened their love for each other.

"She is an incredible ruler. Her influence guided me many times over the years." The song began to wind down and Keld guided them toward Leah. Mercifully, Graham was nowhere to be found.

"As an old friend, I will not lie and say that your mistrust does not hurt. But I respect your decision and hope you will grant us the opportunity to know you again as a friend and as High Mage."

"I would like that as well."

Before another guest could request a dance, Audra motioned to Leah to follow her out of the ballroom. Anyone that tried to approach them was quickly deterred by a quelling glance from Leah. Staff posted outside the ballroom doors snapped to attention when they exited and offered to show them to their rooms.

"How could you stand that? I am exhausted just from watching you dance and talk for hours." Leah shuddered in mock horror.

They spoke low enough so that they were not overheard. "Believe me, my legs and feet will protest in the morning."

When they reached the top of the staircase, Audra was surprised that they turned right, towards the family wing of the castle, not the left wing where guests usually stayed. Familiar portraits and artwork decorated the hall they walked down.

"Here we are, My Lady." A housemaid gestured toward the door to Audra's old bedroom. "The queen requested this room for you herself. Lady Leah's room is across the hall. Should you need anything, please ring the bell." With a deep bow, the staff departed.

The curved handle turned easily in her hand, the door opening soundlessly with a push. Audra braced herself to see her old belongings replaced with new decorations, but the room was frozen in time. Cleaned during her absence, everything was exactly as she had left it. Perfectly matching furniture with thin, fragile legs filled the room, pastel paintings framed in gilt decorating the walls. Gauzy curtains were pulled back from the large windows, allowing moonlight to spill into the room.

Leah looked around the room, brow furrowed as she examined the lilac wallpaper and dove gray fabric covering the bed and chairs. "This was your old room?"

"You sound surprised."

"It just doesn't feel like you. It's too...delicate."

Audra looked around the room with new eyes. The room had not changed in the five years she was gone. But she had. It all looked so breakable, items that were selected to fit the person she thought she had to be. Her rooms at Rauha were colored in rich browns and deep emerald tones to mimic the surrounding forest.

"It may not feel like me anymore, but it was a thoughtful gesture. And, look," Audra crossed to the sitting area, "they added wine. That was definitely not here before."

Crossing one leg beneath her on the armchair, Leah accepted a glass of wine. "Thank Hellig for that. With all the people crowding you, I could barely enjoy the food and drink tonight."

"You do not have to watch me like a hawk. I can protect myself, you know." Audra rolled her shoulders down her back and took a steadying breath to release the tension that had knotted her neck. She forgot how exhausting it was keeping a perpetual smile on her face and having a heightened awareness of every action she took. Although she enjoyed the ball, Audra was constantly focused on making sure that she presented a confident and friendly disposition befitting a leader. Massaging her sore cheeks, Audra sat in a periwinkle chair.

"Even still, the last time you had to defend yourself you nearly died. Let me worry about protecting you while I'm here." Audra sobered at the reminder that her friend was only here for a few days before she returned to Feldor with Maxim, tasked with investigating Leon's disappearance. "So, what are you going to do about Graham?"

Caught off-guard by the shift in conversation, which was likely Leah's intention, Audra hesitated. "I am not going to do anything about him. Our past is just that, the past. My visit here changes nothing and I plan on avoiding any unnecessary interactions with him."

Leah arched an eyebrow. "Next time, try to sound like you mean that. If you think I've been watching you closely, the prince was far worse. He looked at you like you would disappear the moment he took his eyes off you. I don't know what you talked about during that dance, but he seems far from done with you."

"He apologized for his behavior when we were younger." Audra hid behind the fall of her hair as she mumbled, "and he said he wrote to me when I was gone."

"He. Did. What?!" Leah sat up so quickly that her wine nearly sloshed over the rim of the glass. "Lead with that next time. This changes everything."

"It changes nothing, Leah. I am here to learn what I can about Avery's disappearance and strengthen alliances. What we shared was a lifetime ago and we are different people now, with different kingdoms to run. I will not give up everything I worked for to marry him."

Smiling like a predator that caught its prey, Leah said smugly, "I never said anything about marrying him. That was all you." Audra sputtered with indignation, face flaming at being caught sharing her secret desire. "All I'm suggesting," Leah continued, ignoring Audra's protests, "is that you give him a chance to explain. Where it leads is your choice, but with the way he was looking at you, I imagine that he will be *very* eager to make it up to you."

"You want me to sleep with him?"

"If he puts you to sleep, then he is doing it all wrong. But with the way he walks, he looks like a man who knows how to do it right."

"Leah!" Audra gaped at her friend.

"What? You know I'm right." She pointed a finger in Audra's direction. "And don't think I didn't see the way you were looking at him. I thought you would set the room on fire with all that smoldering heat."

A throw pillow sailed across the room, narrowly missing Leah as she laughed at Audra's murderous expression. "I thought you were supposed to be on my side."

Growing serious, Leah leaned forward, resting her arms on her knees. "I will always be on your side. But, I don't think you know what your side is right now."

Audra folded her legs on the seat, wrapping her arms around them so her chin rested on her knees. "I'm scared. He hurt me, and I cannot live through that again. I cannot lose myself in him again."

"I know. But you aren't the same person you were back then. You are the High Mage of Ymira. You built a kingdom and are fighting for our place in the world. Hells, you even fought a damn netvor. He hurt you, but you survived. Just like you survived losing Valeria and Silvan." Leah's voice cracked. "Last time, he broke you because you made him the reason for your existence. Don't give him that power this time. Nothing can break you if you don't give it that power. The Audra I know and love is strong enough to withstand anything."

Tears were flowing freely down Audra's face. It meant everything to have the love and support of her friend. Setting aside her glass, Audra hugged her friend. "I love you too," she whispered into Leah's hair.

With a final squeeze, Leah released her, subtly dragging a finger beneath her damp eyes. "I almost forgot, Maxim told me the wildest story while you were dancing."

Subject changed, the women drank and talked for another hour before Leah pronounced she needed sleep. As Audra prepared for bed, she thought about what her friend said. She could not avoid Graham forever and, at the very least, she might gain closure from what he had to say. Getting close to him could also reveal something about Avery's disappearance. Pleased with her new plan, Audra went to pull back the duvet, ready to sleep away the events of the evening.

She froze.

Nestled between two pillows was a netreus flower, its obelisk-shaped petals open over folded parchment. Inhaling the fragrant scent, Audra placed the white flower on her bedside table, reaching for the parchment with shaking hands. Her name was written across the front in Graham's curved handwriting, the parchment dry and creased from travel. When she read the first line, her legs gave out, falling on the bed with a soft thud.

It was a letter. Written half a year after she reached Ymira.

Audra,

The netreus are blooming again. Do you remember the first time we saw them? We waited months for them to bloom, running into the garden each morning to check on them. We were so young. I remember how disappointed you looked each day the flowers remained shut, how I wanted to wipe away your disappointment and spent hours in the library trying to learn anything I could to get the flowers to bloom. We were playing cards one night when the answer came to me. It was dark, and when I mentioned getting another light, you laughed and told me we had all the light we needed before pulling back a curtain to let moonlight spill over the table. That was the first time I noticed how beautiful you were, as if all I needed was the right light to finally see you, and that was when I realized the flower might be the same.

It makes sense that they would bloom now. As if they wanted to remind me of you. Little do they know...everything reminds me of you. I know I hurt you and it kills me to know that you left because of me. For months, I lived in denial that you were gone, naively thinking that you would return, and I am ashamed that it took me this long to reach out. You deserve better than an apology in a letter, so I will keep it until I see you again, no matter how long I have to wait.

-Graham

Eighteen

A soft, wet nose sniffed hers, jolting Audra awake.

"Go away, Isik," she grumbled, pulling a pillow over her head when Isik began nudging her with his snout.

It was later in the morning than she was used to sleeping, courtesy of the ball, and her head and body were complaining about it. Yipping near her ear, Isik pawed at Audra's chest, incessantly demanding that she wake up. Pushing herself up into a seated position, Audra glared at her pet. He stared back innocently, head tilted to the side.

"Fine, fine, you win. I'm up." Her muscles protested when she stretched before swinging her legs over the side of the bed. Following her movements, Isik padded to the edge of the bed, stopping to sniff the netreus on her nightstand, preserved with magic so that it stayed fully bloomed. Running her fingertips over the petals, Audra's thoughts drifted to the letter as she prepared for the morning. The contents of the letter contradicted what Audra thought she knew about Graham's feelings for her. Why give her the letter now, after all the years apart?

Shaking her head at the direction of her thoughts, Audra knew that staying in her room would yield no answers. Nor was she certain that she was ready for those answers yet. She already had to uncover the mystery regarding the netvor attack on Ymira and the disappearance of two mages. Anything else would have to wait.

Knowing that the rest of the guests would likely sleep past noon, Audra dressed for her morning exercise. Fastening a cape over the sleeveless, flexible top that crossed over her front and tight pants, Audra exited her room, casting a ward to prevent access to anyone who wished her harm. The corridor was quiet around her, beams of sunlight creating a crisscross pattern on the floor. It felt bittersweet to run her hands along the worn bannister, recalling all the times she had done so in the past. New rugs ran down the hall and staircases, a pale blue that matched the flower on the royal crest. Audra sighed at the impractical beauty of it. Cleaning the carpet would be an endless task, something Audra was now familiar with after her time at Rauha.

Chuckling to herself, Audra missed the tall figure turning the corner towards her.

Large hands grasped her biceps as Audra nearly bounced off the firm chest covered in dark gray fabric. Audra followed the line of the sleeve until her gaze snagged on the patch of tan skin exposed by the open collar of the shirt, a hint of brown hair peeking out of the opening. A soft exhale ghosted over her brow, the air scented with cinnamon.

"Good morning, Lady Audra. I hoped to run into you today, but I did not mean it literally."

For a moment, Audra wanted to remain with Graham's hands around her, the heat of his body warming her skin, but that would only invite trouble. Audra needed to keep her distance while she determined exactly what Graham wanted from her, and what she wanted from him.

"Good morning, Your Highness. I should have been paying better attention to where I was going. I did not expect to find anyone else up at this hour."

"Neither did I. Although I should have guessed you would be awake. You always were an early riser. Are you still?" He asked the question hesitantly, as if he were worried that the girl who once knew him better than he knew himself was now a stranger.

"Yes. Although, not for the same reasons." At his questioning glance, Audra continued. "Mornings are now the few hours that I have to myself before the concerns of Ymira occupy my time."

"A ruler's work is never done. Would you—" A blur of white fur nudged Graham's knee, knocking him forward with the unexpected force.

For a member of the Guard, being caught unaware could mean death and Audra saw the flare of alarm in his eyes before it shifted to surprise. She was flattered to know that Graham was so focused on her presence that he had not noticed Isik sneak behind him. Leaning down to look the fox in the eyes, Graham and Isik regarded each other.

"Hello, Isik. Do you remember me?" Isik took his time sniffing Graham's offered hand before sniffing anywhere else his nose could reach. The greedy little thing was probably searching for a treat. "I will take that as a yes. Are you looking for food? I am afraid I do not have any on me at the moment."

"That is a pity. If you did, I would be able to leave Isik with you and return to bed."

Watching Graham run his hands through Isik's fur sent a tendril of irrational jealousy through Audra.

"Then I am glad that I do not."

"Oh, and why is that?"

"Because I can think of no better way to start my morning than seeing you." Graham's wink sent heat rushing to her face. It was too early to withstand the full force of his charm.

"Well...I..." Clearing her throat, Audra tried to form a coherent sentence. "We had better get going. Isik gets surly if he has to wait for breakfast."

"Sounds like someone else I know."

Audra started down the stairs, not slowing when she heard Graham's steps behind her. "I do not know what you are talking about."

"May I join you? I know you rarely get time to yourself, but if you do not mind the intrusion, I would like to spend more time with you." His proximity was already causing havoc on her system and any additional time would only dig up old wounds.

"I do not think that is a good idea."

"Why not?" He winced at the glare she cast in his direction. "Shit, sorry, that was a thoughtless thing for me to say. Audra—Lady Audra," he corrected himself at her look of reproach. "Please give me a chance to apologize."

They reached the door to the garden and Graham grasped her hand in his. Isik looked up at her as if to ask if she would be okay on her own. At Audra's slight nod, the fox bounded off in the direction of the forest, sliding out the gate to hunt.

"After the way I treated you, I understand if you never want to speak to me again. I deserve that and more. But will you at least hear what I have to say before you make your decision?"

Thinking it over, Audra decided there was no harm in letting Graham speak. She nodded and his shoulders lowered with relief.

"I treated you terribly, spurning your hard work and ignoring you on what should have been one of the happiest days of your life. The Hunt was—" He swallowed visibly. "—more than I was prepared for. It brought emotions to the surface that I was not ready to face, and I took that out on you. I am not looking to excuse my actions, but I do wish that I could take back every moment of that horrible day. I should have trusted that you would have listened to what I was going through and understood me. Instead, I tossed away our friendship and any hope for a future with you."

Shoulders pushed back and head high, Audra's emerald eyes held his in an unwavering stare. "I heard you that night, when you argued with Kasteel." Audra watched as awareness washed over Graham and he hung his head in shame.

"Hells, Audra. You never should have heard that, because I never should have said any of that."

"Then why did you?"

"Because I was drowning, and instead of reaching out for help, I lashed out and pulled you under too. I know that I hurt you, and I will always have to live with that. But I am not the same person that I was, and although I cannot promise I will not make more mistakes, I can promise that I will work every day to earn your trust and affection again."

Audra paused, sensing that he was not revealing the entire story. But his eyes could never lie to her and she searched them for the truth. Cool, silver pools watched her closely, allowing her to see the open honesty reflected in them. Graham meant every word he said, and the pain of his actions cast shadows in their depths.

"I forgive you." She watched as hope flared in his eyes, and her heart skipped a beat as her own hope rose in response. "But, what you did hurt me. You embarrassed me and made me feel used and unwanted. So, even though I forgive you, I cannot go back to how things were. Perhaps the easiest thing for us to do for our people is to start anew and let the past stay where it belongs."

"Liar," a voice whispered in her ear, sounding suspiciously like her conscience. Audra knew in her heart that she had forgiven him years ago, not wanting to let her anger and hurt poison her spirit by holding on to grudges.

"Maybe it would be." Audra felt some of the tension in her body release as Graham spoke. "But I have always found that the harder I have to work for something, the more rewarding it is in the end. Our history shaped us, Audra, melted us down and forged us together into something unbreakable, and I do not want to forget it. Before, I made the mistake of not showing you how much I wanted you, and that is a mistake I will only make once."

He lifted her hand to his lips, pressing a kiss to the back as he stepped away from her. "You do not trust me yet, but I will prove myself to you. Better prepare yourself. I do not plan on losing you again."

Unable to comprehend what just happened, Audra was only able to stare at Graham's retreating back as he walked into the castle. His confident swagger was distracting as she struggled to process what he said. When his words finally filtered through her brain, frustration filled her as she called out, "I never agreed to that!"

But he was too far away to hear her. Was this what it was like to have the full force of his attention? If so, Audra did not know if she would survive it.

Fuming, Audra's shoes crunched over the pebbled walkway as she made her way through the garden. Silently repeating every word of their conversation, Audra tried to make sense of it as her fingers brushed along the petals and leaves of plants. *After all this time*, she thought to herself, *he decides that now is a good time to reveal his feelings?*

She could not return to the castle with her emotions in upheaval.

Besides, Audra reasoned, she had originally journeyed outside to stretch her stiff limbs, and no prince would disrupt her morning routine. By the time Audra worked her way through the series of poses that Valeria had taught her, her muscles were relaxed, her mind clear, and a layer of sweat covered her skin. Feeling rejuvenated and more like herself, Audra returned to her room to bathe before heading towards the breakfast room.

Now that sleep had swept away the lingering effects from a late evening, a few guests were seated at the long table. Steaming dishes lined the sideboard, fresh fruit, bread, and salted fish beckoning Audra closer. Conversation halted as she entered the room, people watching like she was a performer on display, waiting to see what she would do. Smiling mischievously, Audra decided that if it was a show they wanted, it was a show they would get.

Servings of food floated through the air, gathering on the plate that drifted beside Audra. Gasps sounded from the table, and one guest dropped their silverware with a clatter. They acted as if they had never seen magic before, and Audra wondered how many had. It was not as if the mages were still hiding away.

Seated at the table, Audra smiled behind her cup at the range of shock, envy, and animosity directed her way. Based on the shifting eye contact and tensing of jaw muscles as they tried to find the right words, Audra guessed that no one wanted to be the first to break the silence. Gossiping about the presence of mages in their drawing rooms was one thing, but to sit across from one left them clueless. It was delightful to watch them stare, transfixed, as her knife spread jam over toast without Audra lifting a finger. As if she was performing a miracle. She briefly wondered how they would react if she showed them a glimpse of her real power. Perhaps they would scatter like frightened rabbits.

Alas, she would not find out. Terrifying them would only cement their belief that mages were monsters and would counteract everything she and her friends had worked on for years. Still, little reminders of their ferocity never hurt to remind people that they would defend themselves if provoked. Realizing that her table partners were too proud or scared to start a conversation with her, Audra scanned their faces for the best candidate to liven up the morning.

Several chairs down the table was a short, auburn-haired woman who was grasping her fork tightly in her chalky grip. Audra remembered her from her time at court. Although they had never conversed at length, Lady Matilde had always been pleasant and respectful. If her memory was correct, Matilde had two children around Audra's age.

"Lady Matilde, it is a pleasure to see you again. How are your children doing?"

The woman briefly startled. "They are doing well, thank you. The eldest, Petra, is slowly taking over the management of the family business, and the youngest, Tyler, joined a crew on a merchant ship. Both are married and Tyler and his spouse have two children of their own now. They live with my husband and me while Tyler is at sea."

"That must be lovely, having a full house again."

"Oh, it is. Our grandchildren are absolutely darling, the cutest children in the world." Her posture relaxed as she slipped into a long story about one of her grandchildren. "Goodness, listen to me ramble. I could talk about my grandchildren for days."

"I do not mind," Audra reassured her. "Before becoming Diana's godmother, I had little interaction with children, but I can appreciate how they quickly become the center of your world."

"They certainly do. Are there many children in Ymira?"

Audra knew that asking the other woman about her children would work to open the door to further conversation. Reminding people of what they had in common made the mages relatable and less obscure. She may not have much experience with children, but she did know that people loved to talk about them.

"Not yet. We have a few younger families, and more families are planning on moving there."

"What's it like?" A balding gentleman with a thick mustache and eyebrows framing his leathery face joined their conversation from his place between Audra and Lady Matilde. He was unfamiliar to Audra, but if the charmed ring and crystal adorning his ear were any indication, the man enjoyed the benefits of magic. From the way the other nobles at the table were leaning slightly forward in their seats, they were curious to hear what Audra had to say.

Pitching her voice so that it was alluring and projected through the room, Audra lured them into her story and dazzled them with vivid imagery of the people and places in Ymira. She painted a verbal masterpiece of the wonderful and practical uses of magic, describing the fields, flowers, and forests, laying the foundations for future conversations.

Leah entered the room as Audra was sharing the experiences of her first harvest festival, placing a note beside Audra's plate. Surreptitiously looking at it, Audra found an invitation to join the queen for tea. Politely excusing herself with promises to share additional stories, as well as a potion for joint pain for Matilde, Audra swept out of the room with Leah.

"That looked like it was going well," her friend remarked.

"Not at first. They barely spoke to me when I joined them, but I managed to win them over."

"You always do." Leah followed Audra's lead as they strode through the hallways that Audra remembered well. "So, tea with the queen. Do you think we should change first?"

Dressed in soft pants and a long-sleeved shirt covered in a leather vest—all black of course—Leah looked more suited to her patrols on the ward than the delicate tableware and dainty food served at the queen's private tea service. But if Isadora still hosted in the same manner as Audra remembered, what Leah wore would not matter.

"No, it is not as stuffy as you are imagining. This is not a formal tea with other nobility. When Queen Isadora invites someone to her private garden, it is more casual. Or, at least it was."

Audra took a moment to look at her own ensemble. Her floor length coat was cut to look like a dress, tucked in at the waist with crescent buckles and a deep neckline to reveal a lace undershirt. The amethyst fabric complemented her coloring and brought out the lighter strands in her hair. With shimmering silver pants and heeled slippers, she looked like the night sky. Decadent enough to showcase her status while remaining comfortable.

Magic prickled the tips of her fingers in response to the nervous energy flapping in her stomach as they drew near the queen's private rooms. Located apart from the royal apartments a floor higher, Isadora's sitting room was on the ground level to accommodate access to her garden. Two soldiers stood outside the wooden double doors, carved with various flowers and birds, and they moved as one to open the doors as the mages approached.

"The High Mage of Ymira, Lady Audra, and Ambassador Leah, Your Majesty." The soldiers bowed and exited the room, closing the doors behind them.

"They act as if I did not remember exactly who I invited to my room." The queen sighed in fond exasperation. Isadora looked as beautiful as she had the night before. The soft fabric of her dress settled around her ankles as she stood, the simple cut of the empire gown striking on her curved frame. With her hair pulled back in a loose bun, long pieces framing her face, she looked youthful, and it complemented the lines around her eyes and mouth.

"Thank you for the invitation, Your Majesty." This woman had once been a maternal-figure to Audra, but after leaving without saying goodbye to her face, Audra was uncertain how to greet her.

"My darling girl, there is no need to act like strangers." Tears shimmered in Isadora's eyes as she approached Audra. "I thought my mind was playing a trick on me yesterday, but here you are."

"Here I am." When Isadora opened her arms, Audra stepped into them, allowing the hug to heal some of the cracks in her heart. Over the years, Audra had convinced herself that Isadora would forget her after her departure, replacing Audra with a true daughter-in-law. But as much as Audra had viewed the queen like a mother, Isadora had seen Audra as a daughter, and the pain at losing her must have been devastating. "I am sorry for leaving like I did, without a proper goodbye. And for not letting you know I was doing well."

"We both made mistakes. I should not have pinned all my hopes and dreams on you and let you choose your own path in life. I want you to know that I always viewed you as a member of this family, whether you married Graham or not."

Tears streaked down both their faces when they released each other from the hug. Wiping her face with a handkerchief, Audra let out a watery laugh. "At least some of your hopes for me came true, I am a queen now, in my own way."

"An excellent one from what I have heard." Isadora's eyes jumped to Leah, who hung back near the entrance to the room to give them as much privacy as possible for their reunion. "Lady Leah, my daughter-in-law speaks highly of your work in Feldor and I look forward to getting to know you. Will you be staying with us long?"

They made their way through the tall, glass doors that opened to a covered patio, deep purple blooms twisting along the pillars. Atop a metal table sat three tea settings, a towered tray filled with small treats positioned in the middle. Looking at it sent a pang of sadness through Audra, the contrast between the fine porcelain and practical set owned by Valeria made her miss her mentor.

"I'm afraid not. My work in Feldor can't be delayed, and I return with Prince Maxim tomorrow."

"What a pity." Isadora shook her head and began pouring the tea. As if no time had passed, she remembered how much cream and sugar to add to Audra's cup before asking Leah for her preference.

"Perhaps you can visit us again one day. If Audra can spare you."

Audra smiled with pride, happy to brag about her friend's accomplishments. "The better question is if Queen Soraya can spare her. Leah is a valued member of their court and magic is quite popular with the royal family."

Isadora waved her hand with a flourish, a large ring on her finger catching the light. Recognizing that the ring was crafted in Ymira, Audra sent a line of magic towards it, concerned that the queen might need magic for an ailment. Her shoulders relaxed when it was just a charm to prevent hair loss. "I cannot say I blame them. You have done a miraculous job at proving just how useful it can be. We were hesitant at first when Kasteel first approached us with a proposition from the High Mage, but even without knowing it was you, you convinced us to give your people a chance. You should be proud of what you accomplished."

"That means a lot for you to say. I learned so much from you. Though you never did tell me how exhausting it all would be."

Isadora's laugh rumbled like thunder. It always surprised Audra to hear it because it was so different from the refined way she usually carried herself. "You shadowed me so often that I thought it was obvious." Her face softened with fondness. "Leadership looks good on you. You look confident, more sure of your place in the world. Are you happy?"

Audra lifted a shoulder. "Most days. I learned so much about myself while I studied magic, and the privilege of ruling is not something I take lightly. Having a close circle of friends helps make everything bearable."

"But?" Isadora was as good as Valeria at sensing her hesitation.

"Sometimes it can feel a bit...lonely. And I feel ungrateful to say that because I have so many people supporting me." It felt insulting to mention it in front of Leah, but her friend looked at her with understanding. As ambassador, Leah dealt with tricky politics and navigated conversations laced with hidden meaning well, but at the end of the day, she still went to Audra for final decisions.

Isadora sipped her tea before responding. "Support is not always the same as having someone to shoulder the burdens with you."

Audra had not thought of it from that perspective. Keld and Isadora ruled as equal partners, sharing the burdens of leadership and the choices they had to make. In Ymira, Valeria had ruled on her own, taking counsel from other mages when needed, and had instructed Audra in the same way. As much as her friends were there to lend a hand, they did not always understand the limitations and responsibilities of leadership. How reassuring would it be to have someone that *understood* it? Who knew firsthand the crushing weight of keeping people safe, happy, and thriving.

Isadora tried to sound nonchalant, but the wry tug at the corner of her mouth and avoidance of Audra's gaze gave her away. "Graham never married after you left."

Swallowing too quickly, Audra choked on her tea. Muffling her cough behind her napkin, she attempted to regain her composure. "That ship sailed a long time ago. I am sure there are plenty of eligible ladies that would delight at the chance to court him." Despite what Graham said to her that morning, Audra doubted that she would be here long enough to keep his interest.

"If you say so, dearest. Though I remember saying much the same when I traveled here to meet Keld. I thought that he would not be interested in a widow, much less one with a young son, and look how wrong I was."

Continuing that circular conversation was pointless, since both women thought they were right and would never come to an agreement.

When she set her mind to something, Isadora was tenacious and stubborn. Audra knew it was easier to pivot the queen's focus to another topic that interested her than get her to change her mind. Casting a pleading look in Leah's direction, Audra shoved a cucumber sandwich in her mouth.

Barely restraining a laugh at Audra's predicament, Leah chimed in, "The gardens are beautiful, Your Majesty. Audra told me that you maintain them yourself. Do you have a favorite plant?"

Audra gave Leah a grateful smile. Besides her children, and now her grandchild, Audra supposed, there was nothing Isadora liked talking about more than her garden. Many of the plants in the beds were cultivated from cuttings sent across the sea from her former home in Cordille.

The trays of food were nothing but crumbs by the time Isadora finished sharing details of her favorite plants with Leah, her face flushed from her energetic motions. Declining the invitation to tour the garden, Audra bid farewell to Isadora and Leah with a promise to see them at dinner. She had to leave before she did something foolish.

Like ask why Graham had not married in their years apart.

Nineteen

The once empty hallways now held collections of people, staff going about their daily responsibilities and guests strolling arm-in-arm on their way to other activities. Knowing that the lawn and pond were most popular for partner sports, where nobility could show off their talents in the hopes of impressing a potential spouse or bedmate, Audra followed a route to the library, greeting passing groups with a nod.

It was a shame that more guests did not take advantage of having access to the expansive array of books at the palace. Generations of history lined each of the three walls, connected by spiral stairs that climbed each of the four floors before they reached the ceiling. Skylights illuminated the space and magelights provided additional lighting in the darker recesses of the space. Books were arranged by genre, time period, and author, their bindings as varied as the topics. Coarse paper and supple leather pressed together—tall and short, thick and slender—and all had their place of honor on the finished oak shelves. They lined the walls like soldiers, waiting to be called into action. Audra and Graham had spent hours here together, curled up in armchairs or window seats leisurely reading, or hunched over tables with stacks of books between them as they studied for lessons. A fireplace lined the back wall, rocks from the riverbed encasing it and flowing up to meet the ceiling as its crackling flame warmed the room's inhabitants.

Her fingers danced along the spines as Audra walked down each row, savoring the smell of parchment and possibility. Each book could transport her to a different time or place, allowing her to slip into the pages like a thief. History and philosophy, romance and mystery, the library held thousands of choices. What she would not give for the seemingly endless time of childhood to explore each book, weightless from responsibility. Maybe Audra could persuade Solven's royal family into lending her several hundred books to bring back to Ymira. Sighing at the dream, Audra knew she would be hard-pressed to find time to read a few books, let alone dozens, once she returned.

Though she wanted to disappear into the shelves for days, Audra focused on finding the book she was looking for.

As tall as her forearm and nearly as wide as her thigh, the tome containing records for every known netvor was bound in wood with metal latches. It hit the desk with a thud, and Audra used magic to open it without a sound, frequent use keeping the metal well lubricated. There were hundreds of pages, each with a drawing—quality varying—depicting the netvor along with a writeup of the name, known origins, powers, and weaknesses. An attempt at order was made by categorizing the netvor into land, water, and air dwelling creatures, though that marginally helped with a book of its size.

"Well," Audra said to the still air, "no where else to start but the beginning."

Page after page of nightmare-inducing monsters. Some came close to what attacked them in Ymira, but none were a perfect match. Shadows lengthened in the room and magelights began glowing brighter as the sun descended in the sky. Audra closed the book forcefully, disappointed that she had not found what she was looking for. If mention of the creature was not in this book, where could it be?

Happy as she would have been to continue looking, her stomach chose that moment to grumble, reminding her of the dinner she was expected to attend. Glancing down at her now rumpled attire, Audra hurried out of the library to change in her room. She was in such a rush that she almost missed the wrapped parcel on her bed. Changing could always wait for presents. Tucked into the ribbon holding the gift closed was another letter, this one dated for a past ageday.

> *Happy Ageday Audra,*
>
> *The first time I met you, it was your ageday and we have rarely spent one apart. Are they celebrating you in Ymira? I would have sent your favorite cake if I believed it would reach you. As it is, I am not sure that even this gift will reach you, but I had to send something.*
>
> *Do you remember when I accidentally cut your hair showing off my new sword? You were distraught when your lady's maid had to cut the rest to match how short it was. I hated myself for making you cry. When you were finally able to joke about the incident, you told everyone it was your own fault for not wearing your hair up like a lady. After that, you rarely wore it down. I used to imagine how it looked flowing down your back, the breeze catching it so that I could tuck it behind your ear.*
>
> *This gift is ten years too late, but I made these combs so that you could wear your hair down without it getting in the way. Selfishly, I also wanted you to have something that would remind you of me when you wear them. Although it does not matter how your hair is styled, you are always the most stunning person in the room to me.*
>
> *-Graham*

Nestled in the paper were two silver combs, gems placed along the handles in the shape of Ymira's sigil, honoring her new home. He must have made them after dozens of letters went unanswered, yet he still fashioned them into a style fitting the life she chose, not the one she left behind. They were stunning, but what touched her heart was the fact that Graham made them himself. A skill he must have learned during their time apart. One that he was remarkably good at if the combs were an example of it. Audra caressed the points of the moon, the rich color sparkling in the light. She would need the perfect outfit to complement it.

Luckily, she had just the thing.

The occupants of the drawing room turned as Audra entered, timing her arrival to ensure maximum impact. If she was a burst of radiant sunset the prior evening, tonight she was muted, wearing the dusky color of clouds before a storm. Each step she took rippled the satin fabric from the tips of her jeweled shoes to the cinched waistline. Eyes followed her movement across the room as Audra made her way to the center, greeting Keld and Isadora before accepting a drink from a server.

She could feel the heat of one gaze in particular track her around the room. Licking a drop of wine off her lip, Audra rolled her head over her shoulder in the direction she knew Graham was waiting. Eyes the same color of her gown burned as he drank in her appearance. When his gaze stopped on the combs pulling Audra's hair away from her face, Graham froze. Around her, Audra could hear the din of conversation, but the people around them might as well have stopped existing for all the attention Audra paid them.

It was like that whenever Audra saw Graham. Everything else ceased to matter. Only this time, he was looking at her the same way. She could see the moment he remembered to breathe and a smile that promised wicked things appeared on his face.

Hells, that dimple would be the death of her. Just a glimpse of it sent her heart thumping. But the entire thing? That set her body aflame. She would not turn into a pile of clay at Graham's feet, waiting to be molded by him. Not anymore. Two could play the game of flirtation.

Drawing his attention to her lips, Audra raised her glass, tipping back her neck to swallow the crisp wine. With her free hand, she gently pushed her hair off her shoulder, fingers lingering on her collarbone to trail along the neckline of her gown.

Graham watched every movement like a predator stalking its prey. When Audra wiped away a stray droplet from her lips and licked it off her finger, Graham clenched his glass so hard his knuckles turned white. Clasping a hand on the shoulder of the man desperately trying to keep his attention—Lord Nadeen by the look of it—Graham strode toward Audra, never breaking eye contact or allowing anyone to stop him from reaching his destination.

"Good evening, Lady Audra." He took the hand that touched her lips and pressed his own against the back. "You take my breath away and outshine everyone in attendance tonight."

Audra lowered her lashes playfully. "Thank you, your highness. The credit goes to my jewelry. A new talent of yours?"

"I believe you will find I have many talents that you do not know about."

Damn. He really was not holding back anymore. It reminded Audra of their long-ago promise to not hide their true selves from each other. This side of him was intoxicating, as if she had drunk more than a single glass of wine already. How long had it been since she enjoyed flirting with a man? Too long if she had to think hard about it. Besides, this was not just any man.

This was Graham. He was once her everything, and she could not deny that there was a large part of her that was curious to learn what type of man he had become.

"Perhaps you can show me," Audra said with a coy smile. With the way Graham's eyes lit, Audra was surprised the room was not on fire with the heat they gave off.

"Only if you share yours as well." The thought of showing Graham everything she learned in Ymira filled her with a mix of elation and trepidation. Never again would Audra hide who she was—the power rolling inside her—but if she saw fear in Graham's eyes when he saw her use magic, it would destroy her.

Silence that used to be comfortable now surrounded them like an itchy blanket. Playful banter would not close the chasm that had grown between them over years. They were like two halves of a ripped tapestry that was slowly being stitched together again.

Still perceptive of her shifting moods, Graham's face turned serious. "Do you find it very different from what you remember?" He gestured to the room. A thick metal cuff on his wrist caught Audra's eye as his sleeve rose. Based on the scuff marks, the band was not decorative, but Audra could not determine any other purpose for it.

"None of it seems as important as I remember. It is not that the castle or court changed, but me. I outgrew this life. These people never cared about me beyond what I could offer them—that has not changed —but I no longer care. Here, I never got to be myself, not completely. In

Ymira, I have a purpose, people who rely on me and respect me based on my actions. No longer do I feel the need to play courtly games, pretending to be anyone other than who I am. Do you know what I mean?"

"More than you might believe." Something dark passed over Graham's face, shadowing his eyes in a memory, before he blinked it away. "From what I have seen so far, I think I am going to like Audra the High Mage just as much as I did Audra of Solven."

"I am quite magnificent now."

Heads turned in their direction to see what caused the crown prince's deep laugh. "Confidence is a good look on you. Though I think you could make anything look good."

A lock of hair curled onto Graham's forehead and Audra was overcome with the urge to push it back. She was saved from temptation by the interruption of a young noble. They greeted Audra and Graham with a bow, their shoulder-length silver hair slipping in front of their smiling face. Dressed in a cream robe that tied over vermillion pants that sharpened their tan, Noble River was one of the few people Audra tolerated from her old life in Solven.

Taking Audra's hand and spinning her in a slow circle, River said, "Good evening, Lady Audra. Your return has made quite the splash at court. I, for one, am glad to finally see you ruffle some feathers." Direct honesty was one of River's best qualities, one of the few nobles at court with that quality.

"Noble River, a pleasure to see you as well. Have you been well? Your family and tenants?" Catching the eye of a passing server, Audra set down her empty glass and retrieved a plate filled with an assortment of appetizers.

"I wish that I brought happier news on that front, but I actually came over to discuss a matter with Prince Graham."

That was her cue to leave. As she walked away, Audra heard River mention an attack near their estate that was different from any netvor attack they had heard of. Brows narrowed in concern, Graham led River to the side of the room for privacy, but not before Audra heard River mention that they knew Graham was investigating a new strain of monsters that were appearing across Solven and Feldor.

That must be why the netvor that attacked Ymira was not in the book in the royal library. It was something new. Something Graham was researching. And if Graham knew something that could lead Audra to what attacked her people, then she had to find out. Strolling slowly around the room, Audra stopped periodically to chat with acquaintances and small groups, exchanging pleasantries and promising to look into their magical requests as she made her way toward Leah.

Breaking away from Prince Maxim without an excuse, Leah looped her arm through Audra's and proceeded to walk with her.

"Graham may know something about the disappearances and netvor attack," said Audra.

"Is that what the two of you were talking about? With the way he was undressing you with his eyes, I could have sworn your conversation was far less serious."

Shushing her, Audra quickly filled Leah in on what she overheard, their voices quiet. With many pairs of eyes watching them, the two mages kept their faces neutral, not wanting to risk attracting more attention.

Turning down the side of the room leading towards the door, Leah asked, "What do you plan to do?"

"Any information would be in his private chambers. While everyone is down here, I need to go search for answers. People will grow suspicious if we are both absent, so I need you to stay here."

"And if anyone asks what happened to you?"

"Tell them I had a headache." Not much of a lie when constant stress dug into her skull daily. At this point, the dull throb behind her eyes was a given.

"Good luck," Leah said, timing their strides so that Audra could slip out the door just as a trio of servers entered with refreshments.

Since most of the castle's staff were helping at the party, the hallways leading to the royal family's wing were empty. This part of the castle was accessible by invitation only and Audra muffled the sounds of her footsteps with magic to prevent anyone nearby from hearing her. Formal portraits of the family and their ancestors lined the dim hallway, their eyes tracking Audra's movement ominously. Audra blamed Taara for the irrational sense that the portraits were watching her. The younger mage had a knack for weaving frightening tales at night that would keep Audra up for hours, her imagination conjuring monsters out of the shadows.

Hearing the sound of soft footfalls, Audra wedged herself behind the curtain of a tall window, casting a shimmering haze around herself so that she could peek out without being seen. Her heart pounded in her chest as a shadow appeared down the corridor, drawing closer with every shallow breath. It was smaller than she expected, and as her eyes strained to make out the shape, Audra sighed in relief.

"Isik," she whispered as she stepped out from behind the curtain. "Did you come to help me?"

Soft white ears tilted to the side, sharp dark eyes regarding her as if it was obvious that she needed help. Slipping into step beside her, Isik padded silently to check the path ahead, ensuring they did not run into trouble.

The outer door to Graham's chambers opened silently, the latch clicking into place behind them as they slipped through. Decorated in cream and the pale blue of the royal crest, the sitting room was devoid of any personal touch. Elegant, yet simple, furniture surrounded the fireplace to create a formal sitting area, and bookshelves flanked the stone fireplace. Spaced in rows along the side walls were paintings of the major cities of Solven, and a sheet of metal pressed with the royal seal hung over the mantle. Functional, yet sterile. Graham's favorite books were not even on the shelves.

A nondescript wooden door was tucked between two bookshelves, not quite hidden, but discreet enough to offer privacy.

"You stay here and let me know if anyone comes in." Isik looked up from where he was sniffing and chuffed, turning in a circle before settling onto the rug. It was as close to an agreement as Audra would get. Hopefully she would find what she was looking for quickly, in and out before anyone knew she was gone.

TWENTY

A wave of longing hit Audra as she stepped through the door. The other room belonged to the crown prince, but this room was all Graham. Compared to the practical simplicity of the sitting room, this room was sumptuous and decadent without being ostentatious. Rich navy fabric covered dark wood furniture, the plush armchairs and settee placed in a manner that invited guests to sink into them and linger. The scents of cinnamon, smoke, and the earth that Audra had always associated with Graham blended with the scents of leather clothing and dusty books. Papers covered a small writing desk by large windows that opened onto a private balcony, and books lay on every available surface. One book was placed on the chair diagonally opposite the fireplace, pages open as if the reader was returning at any moment. Despite the clutter of books, the rest of the room was meticulously clean—a compliment to Graham's training no doubt.

Running a hand down the soft counterpane embroidered with gold thread, Audra's body heated at the thought of laying down on the fabric, sliding across it as her body entwined with another's. Shaking her head at the wayward thought, Audra continued her perusal of the room, refocusing on her goal. Isik would warn her when Graham was returning, but that could be at any time and she had to learn what he knew about the netvor before that. Unfortunately, being in Graham's private room was incredibly distracting, pieces of him reminding Audra of the past and urging her to discover more about the man he was now.

Each item in the room uncovered facets of his personality, from the meticulously organized drawers of weapons to the assortment of grooming tools. There was nothing logical about the way she wanted to linger over these personal items. Graham was part of her past and Audra needed to keep her mind firmly in the present. Her people were counting on her. Internally chastising herself for wasting time in places that were unlikely to hide the information she wanted, Audra crossed to the desk and began sorting through the stacks of papers. Waving her hands over the desk, Audra lifted each paper with magic and kept it suspended in the air so that she could return them to their original place and leave no trace of her presence.

Halfway through a stack of loose papers, Audra found a map of Solven, Graham's curved writing cluttering the page. A cry of triumph left her lips at the discovery. Dates and locations were circled on the map.

One date and location matched when and where Avery had gone missing.

Audra's magic rifled through drawers so that she could locate a blank sheet of paper as hope bloomed in Audra's chest. After months with nothing to go on, she was finally closer to finding out what happened. While the pen copied the map, Audra continued to search the rest of the desk. A heavy thud came from the corner of the desk as a pile of papers was moved. Curious, Audra peered at the space between the top of the desk and a drawer and saw a glint of light flashing off metal.

Graham's crown, Audra thought to herself as she puzzled over why the crown was on a desk of all places.

Images of Graham tossing the crown off his head while he ran his fingers through his hair floated through Audra's mind as she carefully lifted it off the desk. Made of silver, the metal circlet was decorated with depictions of the royal flower along the band and points that resembled the pommel of Guard swords peaked along the top. For years, Audra dreamed of wearing this crown's counterpoint. The impulse to try on the crown, just once to fulfill the childhood fantasy, came over Audra.

No one would know, she reasoned. Cold metal settled on her head, resting at an angle. Wearing this small piece of Graham filled Audra with possessive delight, as if it made him hers.

"It looks good on you."

Gasping in surprise, Audra whirled around to face Graham. He leaned against the closed door, arms crossed as he watched her.

"When did you get here?" *And how did you get past Isik,* Audra thought to herself, sending out a thread of magic to ensure her companion was safe. The little traitor was resting peacefully in the other room.

"I should be asking you that. Of all the times I imagined you in my room, fully-clothed and rifling through my desk was not what I pictured. Although, the crown is a nice touch." His suggestive smile had Audra's toes curling in her shoes, the hint of pleasure behind his gaze more than tempting.

Feeling bold under his scrutiny, Audra cocked a hip and spoke in a voice laced with desire. "Believe me, Your Highness, if I wanted to be in your bed, you would know it."

"What little imagination you possess if you think I want you only in my bed." Rendered speechless by the shocking confession, Audra could only stare at Graham as liquid heat pooled between her legs, nails digging into the flesh of her palms to resist the urge to reach for him. Audra watched in rapt fascination as Graham pushed off the door and began walking towards her, eyes catching on how the tight fit of his clothing stretched over powerful muscle with each step. Damn the man for looking so good.

"If you are not here for me, then why are you here, Audra?"

"To try on your pretty crown, of course." Audra kept her head high, unwilling to yield. "I have been thinking of getting one of my own and thought I would try yours for comparison." Her breath quickened as Graham rounded the desk. Attempting to distract him from looking at the papers sliding into place, Audra took a step back, glancing quickly at the pen to ensure it was finished writing.

Looking at the pen was a mistake. Graham took one look at the desk and immediately honed in on the duplicated map. Stepping towards Audra, Graham's features hardened with mistrust. "You came here to try on my crown, did you? Then why do you need a map of Solven? Has it been so long that you forgot the kingdom you were born in?"

Caught, Audra shifted on her feet as her pulse leapt in her throat. "Please, as if I would forget a single river. I was always better than you at cartography."

"Then I ask again. Why. Do you. Need. This. Map?" Each of Graham's words was punctuated by a step forward.

Cold glass met Audra's back as she retreated, the temperature shocking her warm skin. Pinned by Graham's gaze, Audra knew she was trapped when Graham's forearms came to rest on either side of her shoulders. The lines of tattoos peeked out from his shirtsleeves, revealing the strength that Graham had at his disposal. But Audra was not afraid, not of Graham. Instead of holding her wrists—thereby removing her ability to wield magic—Graham created a cage with his body. If she wanted to escape, she could. Audra's heartbeat slowed as she realized that he wanted to trust her and was giving her an opportunity to trust him.

Relaxing in his hold, Audra shared her concerns. "We were attacked several months ago by a netvor. It was unlike any I knew of, and Kasteel did not recognize it either. Earlier today, I checked the library to see if there was a record of the creature, but that was a dead end. When I heard you talking to River about investigating new netvor, I thought you might have more information in your room. That is why I was searching through your things."

He nodded for her to continue.

"After we were attacked, two mages stopped reporting. When my letters continued to go unanswered, I knew I had to investigate. Avery was working in Solven, and one of the locations you identified matched where they were living and the date matches the estimated time they went missing."

"And you thought the two might be connected." A muscle in Graham's jaw flexed. "I wish you had brought your concerns directly to me instead of sneaking around my room."

"I did not know if I could trust you."

Graham's eyes closed as he hung his head, sighing softly as he pushed away from her. When his stormcloud-gray eyes met hers, Audra saw pain shining in them, as if Graham was hurt by her words.

"I deserve that after what I did to you," Graham said after a breath. "Words are not enough to atone for my actions, but I am truly sorry for the pain I caused you. I hope that in time, I can prove to you the sincerity of my affection and gain your trust again. You were my closest friend and I do not want to lose you again."

Audra tried to keep her tone light and unconcerned. "Just your friend?"

Graham reached out a hand, moving slowly to give Audra the opportunity to reject his touch, before cupping the side of her face. The rough calluses on his palms dragged against her skin. His eyes simmered with heat as he stepped forward, bringing their bodies a breath apart.

"You were never *just* anything. You have always been more than I deserve, but I am selfish enough to keep you anyway. So, yes, I want your friendship, but I also want your heart."

Their faces were so close, Audra could feel every exhale on her lips. Graham matched her breaths, inhaling when she exhaled as if she, not air, was keeping him alive in this moment. The rise and fall of Graham's chest was intoxicating, a dusting of light brown hair visible in the open neckline of his shirt. What would it feel like to touch him there? To run her fingers across his smooth skin or kiss her way to the spot where she could feel his heartbeat. Every inch of her skin vibrated with the urge to touch him.

But then she remembered the pain of losing him. What if Graham's desire for her was just a passing fancy, brought on by the novelty of her return? She needed time to discover if this was nothing more than pretty words meant to seduce, or true intention. When her palms pushed against his chest, Graham stepped back and let his fingers trail down her cheek as he dropped his hands to his sides.

"I can be patient, Audra. I am not going anywhere. While I wait, I will help you find answers for what happened to Avery."

Blinking in surprise, Audra replied, "You will?"

"Of course. Your concerns are my concerns."

"Thank you, Graham."

Picking up both copies of the map, Graham led Audra to the settee by the fireplace. After pouring them each a glass of wine, Graham joined her, sitting close enough that his knee rested against hers.

"So, a mage disappeared from each of these locations?"

Studying each location on the map, Audra shook her head. "No, there were only two mages that went missing, one in Solven and one in Feldor."

"When did you first suspect something was wrong?"

"Later than I should have. Unless something urgent arises, mages that live outside Ymira only check in with me once a week, letting me know how they are faring or providing a report on any project I have them working on. Avery operated a shop and Leon traveled for assignments, so it was not uncommon for them to communicate infrequently."

"Did you talk with any of the villagers? See if anyone saw something?"

"I planned to do that after making sure that you had nothing to do with the disappearances." Audra felt no shame or embarrassment at admitting her suspicions. Protecting her people was her primary responsibility, and her feelings towards Graham would not change that.

Graham was unbothered by the thinly veiled accusation.

"What would the crown gain by capturing mages? Magic is not forbidden in Solven and my family harbors no ill-will towards your people."

Her voice rose with stress. "I don't know. When I found the map, my only thought was to copy it, look for other useful information, and then study it later. All I know is that my people are missing and I don't know how to find them."

Worry and fear over the mages was ever present in her mind, knotting her stomach. One of Graham's arms wrapped around her shoulders, pulling her against his side. The weight of his arm and warmth of his skin provided a reassuring comfort that quieted her fears.

"We will find out what happened to them, Audra. I vow it." He pressed a kiss to the top of her head. "Know that whatever caused their disappearances, my family had no part in it."

"Then what do the marks on the map mean?"

"Recent netvor attacks." He sighed in frustration. Audra felt the tension tightening his body and wondered if Graham's shoulders had as many knots as hers. "There have been a high number of attacks spread across the kingdom over the past few months. More than is typical. I have been scouring record books to see if there is a pattern behind it."

"Do you think the two could be related? Perhaps..." Audra held back tears as she continued. "Perhaps Avery and Leon were killed by netvor."

"That is always a possibility, but unfortunately there is no way to know for sure." Graham twisted in his seat so that he could face Audra before continuing. The worry she saw in his eyes caused a tendril of fear to snake down her spine. What could be bad enough that Graham was worried to tell her?

"Netvor do not leave corpses. Guards usually only find gruesome hints of attacks. Shreds of clothing, blood, maybe a bone, but nothing that is enough to identify a person."

Her mind whirled like a spinning top at the thought. Nothing to identify them? Impossible. Without confirmation, Audra would never know if the mages were killed by a netvor, taken by mage hunters, or any number of other possibilities. There had to be a trace of something...

That's it! "A trace!" Audra leapt from the settee, dislodging Graham's arm so quickly that he had to brace himself before he tumbled to the ground. *She would have to go there herself, see the place where the attack happened, but it could prove successful*, Audra paced in front of the fireplace while she thought.

Raising an eyebrow, Graham watched Audra with unabashed delight. "Care to inform me of what is going on in that brilliant mind of yours?"

"Mages leave behind an imprint, or trace, when we use magic. Like a magical calling card, each one is unique to the mage."

"So you can track them?"

She shook her head. "Not exactly. If I am at the location of the attacks—and it was recent enough—I can send out a pulse to sense any magic in the area. The mages would have defended themselves against a netvor and—based on the aura of the trace—I might be able to determine if they were killed or not."

Graham watched her with a look of fascinated wonder on his face, as if she had admitted to being able to create stars. "Incredible."

Blushing, Audra waved off the compliment with her hand. "Simple magic, really, nothing too impressive. But it does require that I be close to the location. Can you take me?"

"There are a few arrangements I need to make here first, but we can leave the day after tomorrow if that is agreeable." Audra nodded, the crown sliding on her head. She had forgotten it was there. It did not bode well for her heart that she was already growing accustomed to the weight of it.

Removing it, Audra held out the crown for Graham. "Here, I believe this belongs to you."

Frowning, Graham took it from her grasp and set it on the nearest shelf, as if he resented its presence. "The crown belongs to the kingdom, as does the one who wears it."

Audra had never heard Graham talk about his birthright in that manner. He might have been flippant about his royal duties in the past, but this new emotion felt heavy, like a boulder pressing on his chest.

"Graham, I—," Audra was interrupted by Isik's sharp yip. Both their heads turned towards the door. "Someone is coming. I need to go."

A playful smirk replaced the somber look on Graham's face. "Worried about someone finding you in my room?"

After his earlier confession, Audra was willing to take his flirtation seriously and match it in kind. "Caught fully clothed and not a hair out of place? You should be worried about what will happen to your reputation as a lover when your uninvited guest sees me."

The smile that lit Graham's face nearly melted Audra on the spot.

"Rest assured, Audra. When I finally have you, I will make you scream my name so that the entire kingdom can hear how well I pleasure you."

There was not enough air in the room to fill Audra's lungs as desire quickened her breath. Her breasts rubbed against the fabric of her dress, stimulating the sensitive tips. It would only take a few steps to reach Graham. To drag her nails across his chest while he mapped every inch of her skin with his hands.

"Your Highness?" A muffled voice, followed by a short knock, broke the spell that held Audra and Graham motionless. As one, they moved toward the door. Lord Nadeen's eyes widened in surprise as Audra brushed past him. "Lady Audra. How...unexpected to see you here."

Audra settled a mask of cool indifference over her face. Lord Nadeen was a pompous ass and their interactions always left her feeling unsettled. "Lord Nadeen. A surprise indeed. I do not recall Prince Graham inviting you here."

Puffing out his chest, the older man ran a hand down the oversized gold necklace that reached his large stomach.

"As a member of the king's council, I hardly need an invitation to speak with the prince." Insufferable man. He cared more about status and lording over others than actually helping.

"Ah, so you think that grants you access to my *private* rooms?" At the sound of Graham's hard voice, Lord Nadeen flinched, then turned to face the prince.

"Of course not, Your Highness. I meant no disrespect. There was an urgent matter—" A glare out of the corner of his eye in Audra's direction left no question what the "urgent matter" was. "—that I wanted to consult with you on. I'm afraid it cannot wait."

"Fine. We can discuss it out here." Graham shut the door behind him and gestured toward the sitting room. "Lady Audra, I am afraid we will have to continue our conversation another time. Enjoy the rest of your evening."

"Good evening, Your Highness. Lord Nadeen." Audra inclined her head toward both men and watched as Lord Nadeen bristled at her lack of curtsy. Just before she stepped out the door, Audra heard Graham call out to her.

"Oh, and Audra?"

"Yes, Your Highness?"

"Everything you do is impressive."

Twenty-One

Traitor that he was, Isik found Graham again on their way out onto the castle grounds the next morning. Graham joined them for as long as he could, walking alongside Audra and asking her questions about their time apart, before he was pulled away for official business. As she watched him walk away, Audra found herself wishing for more time with him, eagerly anticipating the uninterrupted time they would have when they left.

During the day, Audra poured over the books in the library, hoping to find something that she had overlooked before. Several members of the castle staff and guests sought her out to solicit magical enchantments and spells. She freely helped those who genuinely needed it and charged for frivolous requests. Anyone seeking aid at the expense of another was met with magic that caused itchy skin, warts in unmentionable places, and other infections. After one particular instance—involving a lord who found himself without the use of his favorite appendage when he asked Audra to "take care of" a situation involving a pregnant maid—Audra found herself summoned to the king's council room.

Pushing open the heavy wooden doors with magic, Audra found Lord Nadeen sitting at a table with a man and woman, the gray-haired couple wearing matching scowls that complimented their dour clothing and ashen skin. Lord Nadeen sat back in his chair, one arm draped over the side while the other rested against his bent knee, a thick wool coat parted around his rotund form. Audra wanted to tug the chair legs out from under him and see if that wiped the smug look off his face. Clearly, Lord Nadeen thought that he had caught her in some crime that he could punish her for. As if he had any authority over her.

Several of the seats around the table were empty, including the ones for Keld and Graham. When Lord Nadeen gestured toward an open seat across from himself and the other council members without standing to acknowledge her presence, Audra raised an eyebrow.

She returned his gesture with a pointed look at the king's empty seat. "Should we wait for the others to join us?"

"There is no need, Audra. It will just be us." The disrespectful lack of title was not lost on her.

"Oh, is that common for the council? It was my understanding that the king or crown prince were required for any meeting of the *king's* council."

The older couple bristled at the mention of the king.

"This is not a formal meeting of the council. With an entire kingdom to look after, we do not want to bother the king or prince with trivial matters," the pinched-faced woman replied with disdain. It was a wonder she could keep her head up under the weight of her own self-importance.

"How interesting." The cool edge of Graham's voice froze the table's occupants. "It was my understanding that the king and crown prince care about every issue in their kingdom, even *trivial* matters. Fortuitous that Lady Audra had the foresight to let me know about this meeting."

With a hand splayed across her back, Graham led Audra to the seat next to his, pulling it out for her and drawing a hand down her arm as he pushed her in. More than a polite gesture, Audra knew that Graham was establishing her importance by placing her at his side. Lord Nadeen was fuming from his end of the table. If he had any ounce of magic, Audra had no doubt that he would have skewered her with any available projectile. With the way Lord Nadeen's hands fisted at his sides, Audra knew that magic or no, he would not hesitate to hurt her if the opportunity presented itself. She would need to remain vigilant during the rest of her stay at the castle.

"Your Highness," Lord Nadeen bit out, "we meant no offense. An issue came up regarding this witch—"

Graham spoke sharply. "Mage."

"Pardon?"

"The proper address for magic users is mage," Graham continued, his tone deceptively calm. "I suggest you remember that. Lady Audra is the High Mage of Ymira. Refer to her in such a disrespectful manner again and you will not like the consequences."

"Of course, Your Highness. Given your personal connection to her, we thought to settle the matter privately so you would not be distressed."

"Well, then," Graham propped his elbows on the table and rested his chin on his steepled hands, "proceed."

Clearly the leader of the group, Lord Nadeen barely spared a glance at the other council members. Their presence was meant to bolster his claims and intimidate Audra. How pathetic. They relied on their titles and positions to create an illusion of power, as if she should be afraid of that.

"We received claims of Audra using magic to harm others. Attacking those who displease her, unprovoked. I myself have yet to see evidence that her magic can do anything good. Based on the accounts, it is clear that she is deceiving the royal family and everyone in Solven."

A snort escaped Audra's lips and Lord Nadeen narrowed his eyes in disgust.

"You think this is funny?" Lord Nadeen turned in his chair to offer Audra his back. "See, Your Highness, she mocks the testament of victims, showing how wicked she is beneath her lies of peace and friendship."

The air snapped with magic. "That is the second time you have insulted me, and you will find that I do not react well to insults. Do not mistake my being polite with being a pushover. You asked if I find this farce amusing? I do. You invited me here—under false pretenses I might add—and hurl accusations at me like a criminal. I am not the villain in this story."

Audra's back was straight as a rod, her tone unyielding as she used the full weight of her stare to pin down the table's other occupants. It was a trick she learned from Valeria, the look guaranteed to make the person squirm in their seat. A feline smile curled her lips when she saw the hunched over lord start to fidget.

"Let me ask you something, were you going to ask me why I did it, or were you going to judge me without hearing both sides of the story?"

Not a word from the council members.

"How unfair," Audra said with a mocking pout. "You would not even let me defend myself? Fortunately, I do not need your permission."

Lord Nadeen was clenching his jaw so tightly that Audra could practically hear his teeth chipping. It must gall him to no end that she was putting him in his place. Out of the corner of her eye, she could see a hint of Graham's dimple as he fought a smile. He did not bother hiding the pride on his face, more than happy to let her take control of the conversation.

"Although I do not owe you an explanation, I will correct your ignorant misconceptions. These 'unprovoked' attacks, was it Pomroy and Kendra that brought them to your attention?"

A tight nod was her answer.

"And when they told you that these attacks were unprovoked, did you ask any additional questions?" She silenced Lord Nadeen with a raised hand when he opened his mouth to answer. "That was a rhetorical question. Your actions today make it painfully obvious that you did not have the slightest inclination to discover the truth. Not that I believe either of them would have told you the truth anyways."

Spittle flew out of Lord Nadeen's mouth as he spat out, "And we should believe you? How can we trust a creature that can manipulate others against their will?"

Power slid across the room like a snake, striking Lord Nadeen and the nobles next to him, binding their limbs together. Audra watched as they fought against the magic, willing their arms to lower as she attempted to raise them.

"Can you feel that? Magic is a physical presence. If I was manipulating someone, they would know it and could fight against it. People, not magic, are responsible for their actions. Do not blame something just because you do not understand it."

When she released them, the older couple watched her with dilated eyes, their skin pale with fear.

"When I happened across Pomroy, he was cornering a maid in a corridor. Kendra was beating a horse with a whip. Both were *unprovoked*, not that it would justify their actions either way."

Graham's eyes cut to Lord Nadeen, fury turning them a stormy gray.

His voice was low, rumbling across the room like thunder. "Where are they? They should be facing punishment for their crimes, not Lady Audra."

"We did not know, Your Highness," Lord Nadeen lied smoothly, confident in the knowledge that they could not prove otherwise. "Kendra and Pomroy were distraught when they came to us, barely able to get out their testimonies before they left the castle in fear. Had you seen how upset they were, you would have believed them too."

"You had no right to let them go. I expect you to take responsibility and bring them back for judgment."

"Oh, I do not think that is necessary." Audra ran a hand along the grain of the table, unsure how Graham would react to what came next. "They will not hurt anyone again. I took care of that."

"You do not have the authority to distribute punishment in Solven." Lord Nadeen was grating on her nerves.

"You are correct on that count." He brightened at the prospect of having caught her on a technicality. "However, given that the victims were unable to defend themselves, I considered my actions necessary to stop Kendra and Pomroy. Surely, you are not suggesting that I walk by while the maid and horse were being assaulted? Magic or no, I would not stand by and let someone harm another person or creature."

"But—"

"Enough." Graham slammed his hands on the table, sending a tremor through the wood. It was easy to forget the strength he held on a tight leash. Instead of frightening her, as it did the cowering council members, Audra felt her magic brightening in response. He would never use that strength to harm her, only protect her.

Pushing back his chair, Graham stood. "I have heard everything I need to. Lord Nadeen, counselors, you have crossed a line. Not only did you presume to act on the authority of the king, but you insulted an honored guest and allowed perpetrators of crime to walk free. Rest assured, I will not make the same mistakes. My father will learn what you did and will mete out your punishment."

Pride burned behind Audra's chest as Graham defended what was right. When she first let him know about this surprise summons, Audra was uncertain if he would believe her or the counselors. After all, Graham had not seen her in five years and interacted with Lord Nadeen and the others regularly. But Graham knew Audra's heart, and his trust in her meant everything. She could not shake the feeling that this was what it would feel like to have someone rule at her side as an equal.

Holding out his hand, Graham helped Audra stand. When they reached the threshold, Graham looked over his shoulder. "One last thing. Get out of my father's chamber."

The door closed with a resonant thud behind them. Not wanting to speak again till they were somewhere private, Audra let Graham guide her, smiling when they approached his chambers. After ensuring she was comfortable on a chair, Graham rolled up his sleeves and leaned against the fireplace mantle. The lines of tattoos on his arm and curling hair flexed around his muscles in a tantalizing manner.

His fingers curled through his hair in frustration. "That prick. Hells, I am sorry that you had to deal with him."

Audra waved over the tea set, summoning water to heat while she set out the cups and saucers. "We have both had to deal with worse. Part of the role."

"How are you so calm?" Graham rolled his head to face her. "Knowing that those attacks happened in my castle, and those people tried to blame you? I want to destroy something."

"Feel free. I can clean up anything you ruin." She was happy to put a smile on his face at the jest. "Only the knowledge that they got what they deserved is keeping my anger at bay." That, and the torrent of magic she unleashed in the forest after doling out the punishments.

When he saw the cup Audra held out for him, Graham thanked her and downed it in one gulp. Refilling his cup, he chose to sit adjacent to her instead of resuming his post at the mantle. Their knees touched when he adjusted so they were facing each other.

"What did you do to them?"

She did not regret her actions—both people deserved what they got—but she did not know if Graham would see it that way. "Since Pomroy cared more about his dick than another person's boundaries, I made him impotent." Taking a sip of tea, Audra murmured around the cup, "and gave him an incurable rash."

Graham's cup froze halfway to his mouth, not moving for a breath. With a sudden motion, he fell back into the cushions with a laugh. "Hells, that is fitting. He deserved that and more. Make him suffer for the rest of his life."

"He should be grateful that I did not make it fall off. At least this way he can still piss." She let out a dry laugh.

"And Kendra?"

Laughter died at the memory of watching Kendra strike a horse with her whip. "That spell was particularly tricky. Any time she attempts to even raise a finger against another person or animal, even if she commands someone else to carry out the act, Kendra will find herself the recipient of the pain."

"You can do that?"

She nodded, waiting to see the glimmer of fear that entered people's eyes when faced with the enormity of her power. It was logical to fear something that could harm you, but it chipped off a piece of Audra's heart every time it happened. Magic was part of who she was and she would not hide it or pretend that she was less powerful than she was.

"Does that make you afraid?" Better to get a direct answer than wait for the inevitable.

"Never." Graham looked at her like he could not believe she was real. Like she was the answer to every question he had ever asked. There was not a hint of fear to be found.

Powerless against the surge of emotions, Audra grabbed the front of his shirt and pulled him towards her. Sparks fired where their lips met, sizzling through Audra's brain and wiping away any thought. This was everything kissing someone should feel like. The lightheaded rush that left her dizzy and breathless, like bubbles were injected straight into her veins. Graham's surprise morphed into a groan as he softened into the kiss.

Strong hands gripped Audra's hair, holding her in place as Graham tilted his head to better align their lips. Turning, Audra slid her knees between Graham's, each brush of their bodies igniting the fire burning beneath her skin. Too many layers were between them, the fabric of their pants preventing Audra from feeling his skin against hers. Her body was a contradiction, somehow wound tight while achingly loose at the same time. Like she was untethered from the ground yet firmly planted in sensation.

More. More. More, her body pleaded. Years of imagining what this would feel like had nothing on the reality. She wanted to drown in the sensation of his warm lips melding with hers.

"Audra." Her name was a prayer on his lips. Everything in her softened at the sound of it, liquid heat melting her bones. The fabric of his shirt was soft under her hands and her fingers curled against it with each drugging pull of his mouth against hers.

Their kiss was a gentle exploration, giving and taking in equal measure. Countless minutes were spent slowly learning the other person, resting their foreheads together when they paused for air, unable to completely lose contact.

She never wanted it to end.

The press of his tongue against the seam of her lips had Audra opening her mouth on a moan. Graham's answering groan sent a shiver through her. Magic was singing under her skin, begging for release. Too caught up in the moment to fully control it, a thread of magic shot from her fingertips, rushing down Graham's chest. He jolted in surprise, hands tightening around her face as his mouth opened on a gasp. When he opened his eyes, they were glowing faintly.

"Sorry," Audra whispered against his cheek.

"I'm not." Graham pressed a soft kiss to her lips, pulling away when she tried to deepen it. "That felt incredible."

Closing his eyes, Graham breathed in deeply, working to calm his racing heartbeat. When Audra tried to bring his lips back to hers, Graham gently held her back.

"I don't want to rush this." He chuckled at her put-out expression, kissing the tip of her nose. "We are still re-learning each other and I do not want to move so fast that you regret it...or me. As much as I want to continue, I want you to be completely sure. I know you, Audra, and can see the doubt lingering in your eyes."

His heart was a steady beat under Audra's hand where it rested against his chest, determination written across his features. Of course, the moment she decided to give in to the attraction between them, Graham had to be romantic. They knew each other too well and he could tell that although she was ready to remove their physical distance, the emotional wall between them was still too high.

His eyes were too intense, the deep pools of silver staring directly into her soul. "Take all the time you need. Just know that I will be waiting for you at the end."

Jerking her head out of his hands, Audra folded her hands in her lap to resist touching him. "Now I want to destroy something."

At her mutinous expression, Graham burst into laughter, tugging her into a comforting embrace.

TWENTY-TWO

Dawn was breaking over the horizon when Graham met Audra at the stables. After finalizing the preparations for their departure—additional letters and small gifts finding their way into her room—they were ready to leave for Oshea. Under the pretense of checking her horse's saddle, Audra surreptitiously watched Graham approach.

How inconsiderate of him to look so attractive first thing in the morning, especially when Audra was still shaking off sleep's embrace. He exuded a powerful confidence, each motion effortless as he strode through the door, light striking the golden-red hues in his hair. Reinforced dark blue leather covered Graham's chest over his riding gear, weapons secured in the sheaths along his thighs, back, and side. The metal cuffs that Audra had glimpsed before were now on full display, curved daggers clipped into slots along the inner arm with chains connecting them to the cuff. Trained to use any weapon with ease, Guards gravitated toward specific weapons that felt like extensions of themselves. It was the first time Audra had seen Graham fully outfitted in a Guard's armor. He looked dangerous, like a barely contained storm.

Audra shivered in delight.

"Cold?" Graham tracked her movement, a smirk playing on his face.

"If you are..." He pulled the edges of her cloak closer together, his knuckles grazing her chest and heating her body. "...you can always ride with me. We could keep each other warm."

Just the thought of sharing a horse with Graham, his body enveloping hers so that Audra could smell his enticing aroma and brush against his muscles with each step, was enough to set her ablaze.

"Tempting," Audra's voice purred as she pressed a hand against his chest, "but we will travel faster with two horses."

Graham kissed her hand. "You know where to find me if you change your mind."

The door to the stables groaned open, a flash of blue against midnight black catching the morning light.

"Should I come back, or is it safe to look?" Leah called out, one hand covering her eyes playfully. "You two should come with a warning. Disgustingly cute this early in the morning."

Audra laughed when her friend gagged in jest. Stepping out of Graham's orbit, she walked over to sling an arm over Leah's shoulders. Smiling, Audra rested her head against Leah's. "You only have yourself to blame. No one said you had to get up this early."

Wrapping her arms around Audra, Leah gave her a quick hug. "And let you leave without a proper send-off? Never."

The two friends had dined together the night before, saying their goodbyes before they both prepared for separate journeys. Leah would return to Feldor with Maxim to search for signs of what happened to Leon while Audra went in search of Avery. Between the two groups, Audra hoped that they would find the answers they needed.

Worry wiped away the smile on Audra's face. Logically, she knew that Leah was one of the best fighters amongst the mages, but logic had little power over concern for a loved one.

"Be careful, okay? No unnecessary risks."

Leah gripped Audra's hand, face serious. "I promise." She pulled a protective charm from her pocket, tying it around Audra's neck. "You know, I would tell you to take care of yourself, but I think Prince Muscles has got that covered."

Some of the tension in her chest lessened as Audra laughed. Behind them, Graham coughed, the tips of his ears pink.

"You!" Leah pointed at Graham. "Keep her safe."

Audra huffed at the implication that she could not protect herself, a small part of her pleased when Graham placed a hand on the curve of her low back and said, "We'll protect each other. You have my word."

The way Leah brightened at his response made Audra realize that she had been testing Graham. Her suspicion was confirmed when Leah pat Graham on the shoulder, wishing him well on their journey before bidding them farewell. Checking the straps on Audra's saddle one final time, Graham adjusted his own saddle bags.

"Do you have everything you need? The journey to Oshea is a few days and it will not be comfortable."

Due to the urgency of finding information on Avery, Graham had explained that traveling light and avoiding towns would be the best option for them. Stopping in populated areas meant risking someone recognizing Graham, causing delays from the inevitable requests that would follow. Instead, they would spend long days in the saddle and nights sleeping in the open.

"You do not need to coddle me, Your Highness. It might surprise you to know, but I have stayed in barns and cooked my own food when responding to requests for magical aid. I can handle some discomfort."

She did not see the need to tell him that most of those trips were taken with a carriage and that the residents of Rauha permanently banished her from the kitchen for her abysmal cooking. Any amount of discomfort was worth it to find her people.

"I am sure you can, but if you need to stop for any reason, let me know. There is no sense in injuring yourself just to prove a point."

He watched as she put a foot in the stirrup, the fabric of her riding pants stretching as Audra lifted herself into the saddle. A muffled groan followed and Audra turned to find Graham staring at the curve of her hip. Realizing that her cloak was tossed to one side, allowing what must have been an exceptional view of her backside as she mounted the horse, Audra lowered her gaze and smiled.

"Like what you see?"

"If we did not have urgent business, I would drag you off that horse and show you just how much I liked it." Graham's gaze was like a phys- ical caress, sweeping from the toe of her boots to the top of her head, lingering on her eyes. Without breaking eye contact, he mounted his own horse. "But I do not think you are ready for that yet. Luckily for me, I have time on this trip to change your mind."

"Do not hold your breath on that, it might be a long wait."

Their horses were side-by-side, facing opposite directions so that Audra was face-to-face with Graham. Even seated, he was still taller than her and Audra tilted her head up to see how he would respond. She was baiting him, testing to see if he would still want her if it was not an easy pursuit.

Cupping her jaw with one hand, Graham made sure her eyes were on his as his face grew serious. "Oh, Audra, I would wait forever for you."

The leather of his glove was softer than she imagined it would be as it traced her lower lip. Audra felt her eyes flutter shut as she leaned into his touch with a sigh. Warming at the memory of their kiss, Audra was grateful that her cloak hid the flush rising up her chest. At least she would not have to worry about the cold. The heated look Graham sent her showed that he also wished they had time for more lingering kisses. At this rate, they would never make it out of the castle.

Urging her horse into a trot, Audra made her way out of the stables. Informed in advance, the soldiers had the gate opened for their departure. Keeping a steady pace, Audra and Graham rode in silence, content to be in each other's company without the pressure of conversation. Birds called out to one another, their twittering and chirps filling the leafy canopy above their heads. As part of the forest that led to Ymira, the familiar smell of mossy soil, bark, and pungent leaves soothed Audra. So far away from home, she was hit with a wave of longing for the feel of Rauha's lawn beneath her feet.

"Did you miss this?" There was too much emphasis and hesitation behind the word *"this"* that Audra suspected Graham actually wanted to ask if she missed *him.*

"Solven was my home for ten years. My heart broke when I had to leave." She turned in the saddle to watch him, seeing the moment her words hit and the pain in his eyes. "But I do not regret the life I had here. Without it—and everything I learned—I never would have met my friends and been able to create the life I have now." A complicated answer, and perhaps not the one he was expecting, but she owed him the truth.

The humming of insects, forest critters scurrying through the trees and brush, and huffed breathing of their horses were the only sounds for several moments. If Audra was going to give Graham a second chance for anything between them, she could not cower and hide her feelings.

"I missed you every day though." Her voice was low enough that Audra almost hoped he had not heard it. Even after the sharp pain of his rejection had settled into a dull ache, she never stopped missing him.

From his saddle, Graham took a ragged breath of air. It sounded like someone had snatched it directly from his lungs. Maybe her admission had.

"As much as I hate that I was the person to drive you away, I think we both needed the time and space to grow on our own. The man I was back then was not good enough for you."

"And you think you are now?"

He flashed a rakish smile her way. "You get to be the judge of that."

Birds scattered into the air at the trill of her laughter. "I will keep you updated." Growing serious, Audra continued, "Something I learned in Ymira is that you should never let others determine your value."

"Sounds like you had wise teachers."

"The very best." Her voice wobbled as she thought of Valeria. Memories of all their lessons, her no-nonsense approach to life, and her almost smile when they shared a cup of tea flashed in Audra's mind.

Grief came like a wave, rolling over her and threatening to drag her under its current. She had not been able to prevent Valeria's death. What was the point of all her training and the immense cache of power that she possessed if Audra could not even protect her friend and mentor? What hope did she have of finding out what happened to Avery if she could barely stop the attack on Ymira?

A heavy hand pressed down on her thigh, pulling Audra out of her thoughts. Pulling up alongside her, Graham leaned his head down to meet her eyes, concern pulling his brows and mouth down. Their horses stopped, shifting their weight from side to side. Leaning over so that he could bridge the gap between them, Graham cupped Audra's face in his gloved hand. The soft leather smelled like him and Audra drew it in with a deep breath.

"Do you want to talk about it?"

She shook her head, hair falling around her shoulders to cover her face. "I am fine."

If Graham had looked at her with pity, it would infuriate her and solidify the plan to keep her feelings to herself. Instead, he watched her with understanding, the way only someone who knew the inner parts of your soul could. Audra wanted to lose herself in his gray eyes, sunlight brightening their color and highlighting his dark eyelashes, instead of having a conversation.

"No hiding, remember?"

They urged their horses into movement again, early afternoon sun warming their skin. Sad that they were not traveling this beautiful path under better circumstances, Audra gave herself a moment to enjoy the scenery while she gathered her thoughts. Talking about Valeria was not easy.

Graham tossed her some bread and dried meat from his saddlebags, and Audra caught a whiff of her favorite pastries. Knowing that he packed something he knew she liked brought a smile to her face.

Pulling his waterskin out of his bag, Graham took a long swallow. "I always thought I was fine, too. Killing netvor was what I was born to do. I saw it as my duty to be okay, no matter what injuries I sustained or what horrors I learned the monster enacted before I could get there." His hands tightened on the reins. "But, I was struggling. After spending more time around the other Guards, I learned that no one expected me to be fine. Not after what we saw. Talking about it never erases what we experience, but it makes the burden lighter. Knowing that other people have experienced what you have makes it easier to carry."

When the burdens of Ymira became too much, Audra would share with Leah and Valeria. All those mornings spent finishing chores or practicing magic with a flow of conversation between them had provided an outlet for Audra to share whatever weighed on her mind. As children, Graham and Audra had shared life's high and lows with each other. He never judged her and had offered good advice in the past.

Without the intensity of his gaze directly on her, Audra thought it might be easier to share what was bothering her.

"My mentor, Valeria, died when a netvor attacked Ymira."

"Hells. Audra, I am so sorry that you had to go through that."

"It was..." She took a breath as tears threatened to choke her. "...one of the worst experiences of my life. And it was my fault."

Once again, Graham halted their horses. But this time, he leapt off his, allowing the gelding to graze a nearby meadow while he approached Audra.

"What are you doing?" She gasped as he lifted her off the saddle, pulling her into his body with a hand cradling the back of her head.

"Holding you. There was no way I could let you continue reliving that moment alone and I could not comfort you from atop a horse."

Sniffing, she nuzzled into the warm leather of his vest, arms clutching his waist tightly.

"It was not your fault, Audra."

"You were not there. It was my fault."

"Impossible. I know you, and you would never intentionally hurt someone you love."

Burrowed into Graham's chest, Audra described the netvor's attack. "Maybe it was not intentional, but it was still my fault. The final blow was meant for me. Those final scales were meant for me. I could not move. My leg was injured and I was drained after using so much magic. I was ready to die, at peace with knowing I had done what I could to protect my people. And then she just jumped in the way. Covered my body with hers so that the scales hit her instead of me."

A shuddering sob wracked her body, shoulders curling inward to protect her broken heart. In the aftermath of cleaning up Ymira and then traveling to the ball to formalize their alliances, Audra had little time to process her grief and mourn. Doing so in the middle of a forest while she was investigating the disappearances of two mages with her first love hardly seemed like the place for it, but here she was. Graham's calm reassurance surrounded her. The firm press of his chest against hers and the squeeze of his arms letting her know that he was a safe place to fall.

"I-I miss her," she choked out between sobs. "It should have been me."

The hands on her back tightened, his cheek rubbing against hers as Graham moved to press his lips against her forehead. "No. Do not ever say that. You diminish your own worth and her sacrifice by even suggesting it."

Graham pulled back so that he could look Audra directly in the eyes. "I may not have known her, but I know she must have loved you fiercely to make that choice. The pain may never go away, but if you let me, I will always be a shoulder to cry on and someone to talk to."

Nodding into his chest, Audra let Graham fold her back into his embrace, wrapping her arms around his frame to squeeze, letting her actions show the appreciation she could not voice. They stood like that for countless minutes—heartbeats pounding against each other—content to take comfort in each other's company.

When Audra was ready to continue, Graham wiped her tears with his thumbs before retrieving their horses and lifting Audra onto her saddle. "Would you tell me a good memory you have of Valeria? I want to know more about her."

"She was infinitely patient, but also fiercely protective. No matter how many times she had to teach me something, she never lost her temper or stopped pushing me to reach my potential. But if we broke a rule or put Ymira in danger, her wrath was legendary."

Graham raised one eyebrow in her direction. "Breaking rules? You? I do not believe it." Obviously, he recalled the many instances in their adolescence where they stole sweets from the kitchen or snuck out of lessons to play outside with Kasteel.

A zap of magic flicked his side, jerking him in the saddle. "I am the model of decorum, Your Highness." She imbued every ounce of haughtiness she learned at court into her voice. "Everyone knew it was your idea to cause trouble in the castle." That earned a laugh, his hair flopping back as his head tilted toward the sky.

"Valeria and I used to drink tea together every afternoon. It was the only time I ever saw her indulge herself. For a woman who only wore black or dark gray, the amount of sugar she added was astounding. Sometimes we would sit in silence—watching the lake or other mages at work—and other times we would talk about magic and Ymira. We often disagreed on how things should be done, but I miss being able to ask for her opinion. She made it look effortless."

Sometimes, if Audra was mulling over a decision, she would set up the tea service in her room for two and pretend that Valeria was still with her. Imagining her offering advice on whatever was bothering Audra. Maybe it was foolish, but Audra could swear that there were times she could feel the other mage's magic in the air.

"I am glad you had her, even if it was only for a short time."

"Me too. There was one time—"

The rest of the day passed like that, Audra and Graham sharing stories of their time apart interspaced with periods of silence where they enjoyed their surroundings. Falling back into a comfortable rhythm was as natural as breathing, the past a small undercurrent that did not disrupt the ease between them. When the treeline began to thin, indicating they were nearing the rolling hills that would continue their journey to Oshea, Graham found a location for them to set up camp. Enough sunlight still filtered through the tree canopy for them to work with, but it would set soon.

Dismounting, Graham started untying his saddle. "We should make camp for the night. Netvor prefer darkness and it is unsafe for us to continue. I want to get us settled and establish a perimeter before the sun sets." Graham moved with efficient movements, following a pattern that he created after years of setting up similar camps.

Audra did not know how he could move like that when her muscles were screaming at her. She was an active person, but a full day in the saddle stiffened formerly loose limbs. What she would not give for a warm bath. Knowing that stretching would help, Audra groaned as she lowered herself to the ground.

Steel-gray eyes snapped to hers at the sound of her groan, darkening with desire before he recognized the sound as one of pain, not pleasure.

A smile tugged at the corners of his mouth, now covered with stubble. "Everything okay over there? Were you not the one to tell me you could handle some discomfort?"

"Shut up." Placing her hands on the small of her back, Audra arched backwards. "I just need to stretch for a moment. Let me know what I can do to help set up camp."

Smothering a laugh at the way she walked slightly bow-legged toward him, Graham pointed to the horses.

"If you can take care of the horses and get started on the fire, I will see if I cannot catch us something fresh to eat. I heard a stream nearby."

Watching until he disappeared into the trees, Audra resisted the urge to rest on her bedroll for a moment. Once she sat down, there was no way she was getting back up. Taking care of the horses, Audra gave them each a treat for their hard work before letting them graze. With a few flicks of her wrist, Audra had a low fire burning and their bedrolls set up.

Graham must have thought the tasks would take her longer, because he arched an eyebrow in surprise when he returned to find her bent in half, midway through her stretching routine. While she finished, Graham prepared two fish, seasoning and grilling them on sharp metal sticks over the fire. Tired after the long travel, neither of them spoke during their simple meal, content to watch the steady flicker of flames.

As they prepared to sleep, Graham laid out his weapons so they were easy to reach. "I can take the first watch."

"No need." At Graham's incredulous look, Audra waggled her fingers. "Magic. Remember?"

Focusing on the area around them, Audra created a domed ward, the iridescent shimmer the only sign it was there. Within the ward, the sounds of the forest were slightly muffled.

"There, now nothing can get to us." Turning toward Graham with a smile, Audra saw stark awe and desire looking back at her.

His breath fanned her face as he pulled her into a kiss.

"I will never get tired of watching you."

Twenty-Three

If Audra thought Nabura was the busiest place she had visited, Oshea proved her wrong. The seaside city was bursting with life, throngs of people rushing from one location to the next. Perched on top of their horses, Graham and Audra were protected from getting jostled by the crowds. Even still, they found it difficult to navigate through the crowded streets, watching carefully to make sure they did not trample anyone. Sharp scents of saltwater and pungent fish and other sea creatures fought for dominance, coalescing into an overwhelming smell that had Audra pulling her cowl down and releasing a breeze of magic to clear the air in front of their noses.

"Thanks." Graham's face was covered by the hood of his cloak, preventing anyone from recognizing him until it was necessary. "The smell will not be as bad the further away we get from the market. There is an inn that I have been to before. They can watch after our horses while we start making inquiries."

As the primary port city for Solven, Oshea was a curious mix of sturdy warehouses lining the docks, and opulent homes and public buildings at the center. Even the smallest homes and oldest businesses displayed their wealth and prestige with decorative glass windows and carved awnings. Audra took in the sturdy structures, designed to weather storms and stand up against salty air, marveling at the etchings of Hellig's crescent moon on the doorframes. Here and there, Audra could sense magical objects, enchanted to protect a home or bless a catch. Superstitious by nature, seafaring folk often gravitate either towards or away from mages.

The inn that Graham led them to was well appointed, the gilded sign and immaculate exterior boasting an expensive clientele.

"Well, this is certainly roughing it, Your Highness." Audra got perverse joy at the blush that crept up Graham's collar. If she was being honest, after several nights spent sleeping on the ground, Audra was looking forward to a soft bed. She knew herself well enough to accept that her love of expensive sheets and pillows was one of her vices. One Graham clearly shared.

"I wanted you to have the best."

Well, damn. Her defenses were lowering with each sweet gesture.

A stablehand came to collect their horses, passing their bags to a valet with assurances that the horses would be well cared for. Audra was glad to enter the building, the polished wood floor and sand colored walls creating a space that felt calm against the chaos of the marketplace. Immaculate paintings of ships sailing calm seas and artwork made from driftwood and sailors knots were spaced along the wall between vases made of seaglass. Behind the polished desk stood an innkeeper, a slender man who barely reached Audra's shoulder. His bristly beard covered toffee-colored cheeks, a warm smile crinkling his eyes as he greeted them.

"Welcome, m'Lady and m'Lord," he said, as he tucked away the rag he was using to shine the pristine desk. "Thank you for choosing The Seahorse for your stay. How many rooms will you be needing?"

Staying Graham's response with a hand on his arm, Audra answered for them. "One room please."

Curious gray eyes met light-green resolve. Graham had not pressured her to move faster than she was willing, and it seemed a waste to have two rooms when they had slept near each other in the forest. Her conscience snorted at the rationalization, letting her believe whatever she wanted as long as it put her closer to Graham.

In front of them, the innkeeper was rambling on, letting them know that the staff was prepared to see to their every need and offering recommendations for places to visit in the city. Lost in each other's gaze, Audra and Graham listened with a margin of their attention. His eyes asked if she was sure of her decision, the heat of his gaze warming her skin as she silently communicated her response. The slide of a key across the desk popped the bubble of intimacy around them, the innkeeper offering to show them to their room.

Graham declined, grabbing the key with one hand and Audra's hand with the other. "Thank you, for everything. Please send two plates of food to our room. We will let you know if we need anything else." His authority was clear even with his face concealed by the start of a beard.

"Of course, m'Lord." The innkeeper bowed. "Whatever you need."

"There is one other thing." Audra pulled the cowl off her head, smiling warmly at the innkeeper. "Can you tell us where we can find mage Avery?" Startled by the beautiful woman standing before him, the innkeeper stumbled over the directions to an address at the edge of the city.

Their room was moderately sized, a table for two sharing space with a four-poster bed, chest of drawers, and wardrobe. Audra groaned at the sight of the washtub in the attached bathroom, wishing that they had the time for her to luxuriate in the warm water. With a laugh at her wistful expression, Graham prodded her into the bathroom, magnanimously allowing her the first use of hot water while he waited for their food to arrive. There was something rejuvenating about having hot water to bathe with after days spent stooped over cold rivers.

Quickly drying off once she smelled creamy soup and hot bread, Audra joined Graham at the table. Ravenous after traveling for days, their only words were about the quality of the meal. Once they sopped up the last bits of soup with their bread, Graham excused himself to bathe before they left. With nothing else to occupy her time, Audra set about putting away her clothes, creating a pile for the inn to launder. Her jewel-tone cloak and riding habits hung next to Graham's blue and gray vests and overcoat. Their earthen scents mingled as Audra ran a hand along the fabric, admiring how good the clothing looked together.

A creak of the bathroom door had her turning, her thoughts blinking out of existence.

Damn.

Clothing was a disservice to Graham's toned body. Miles of muscles and tanned skin were visible above where his towel was slung above the sharp lines of his hips. The long slash of a healed wound across his chest and scattered scars along his arms and legs added to his animal magnetism. Powerful thighs peeked out below the towel before meeting his calves, hair matted from the water. This was the first time she had seen him in so few clothes, and it was doing delicious things to her body. Droplets of water dripped down from the hair that draped over his forehead, falling to his chest before clinging to each curve before they disappeared into the towel.

Overcome with the intense desire to lick the water from his skin, Audra's mouth went dry. Pupils blown to absorb every tantalizing motion, she watched while Graham pushed the hair off his forehead, the flex of his arm drawing attention to the tattoos on his arm.

"Sorry, I forgot to bring in a change of clothes." His smirk suggested otherwise.

"Isssokay." What were words? Who needed them when her brain was disconnected and her mouth wanted to be occupied with other, less cerebral, pursuits?

Caught in the hypnotic pull of his stare, Audra stood frozen as Graham approached, shuddering when his bare arm grazed her chest to reach into the wardrobe. She vowed to exact revenge for the movement the moment she could think clearly. That seemed farther and farther away as Graham bent to retrieve a shirt and pants, the fabric of the towel stretching across his backside. Hells. Why did every part of him have to be firm?

With a wink, he sauntered back to the bathroom, the air in the room returning with his absence. Inhaling sharp lungfuls of air, the haze surrounding Audra's brain lessened.

"Fiend," she muttered at the closed door. If that was what he meant by using everything in his arsenal to win her over, Audra worried for her sanity.

By the time Graham finished changing—no less handsome armed in a myriad of weapons and leather armor—Audra's body had returned to its normal temperature and her satchel containing several essential potions and crystals was prepped. After warding their door, Audra and Graham left the inn. Restored by the warm meal and clean clothes, the noise and scents of the city bothered Audra less. Following the directions provided by the innkeeper, they soon found themselves at the outskirts of the city. Here, the crowds were thinner and the buildings were spaced apart at intervals, the lack of shops allowing families to spread out.

When they turned down an alley crowded on both sides by tall buildings, Audra frowned. Compared to the cheery houses with flower boxes and painted shutters, this area of the city was uninviting and dim in comparison. A mysterious liquid seeped down the cracks of the pavement and Audra was careful to step around it, not wanting the smell to linger on her boots or skirt. The few people that they passed kept their heads down, rushing past them in a blur of suspiciously stained clothing.

How did Avery find themselves in this part of the city? Money was of little concern—the mages had a cache of precious jewels in addition to the funds procured through their newfound popularity with wealthy clientele. If Avery needed additional funds for a better shop, Audra would have been more than happy to provide it. Lost in thought wondering what led to Avery's presence in this part of town, Audra almost bumped into Graham when he stopped walking, barely catching herself from falling where she skidded to a stop.

"What the hells?" Audra fumed at the sight before her.

Despite living in a less established part of town, Avery had clearly done their best to decorate the shop so that it was warm and inviting. Quality craftsmanship shown in the detailed carvings and diamond-paned windows that were now smashed. Anything that could be reused —including the missing door—were gone, pilfered by desperate people. Stepping through the broken frame, Audra's boots crunched over broken glass. Dust motes floated through the air before settling onto the thin layer already gathered on the counter and shelves meant to display potions and charms that were now gone or lay in tatters on the floor.

Clenching her jaw, Audra wordlessly took in the damage. Decaying herbs and spoiled potions with a hint of orange spice perfumed the air, causing Audra to wrinkle her nose against the odor. Fury built under her skin, her magic rising in response. Behind her, Graham unsheathed the daggers at his wrists, eyes beginning to glow as his Guard abilities surfaced. Allowing the smallest amount of magic to release, Audra confirmed that whatever wards Avery set were long gone. Her eyes burned, tears building at the loss. If Avery planned on leaving and intentionally released the ward, they would have taken their supplies with them.

Death of the caster was the only other way to release a ward.

"You won't find Avery 'ere." Audra whirled around to find a stocky woman in homespun clothing at the doorway, a plump child on her hip. "Left weeks ago and 'aven't seen 'em since."

Audra regarded the woman with caution. "Do you know where they went?"

Flaxen hair pulled back into a sharp bun, the simple tailoring of her dress matched the mother's practical features. While the dark circles under her eyes and pallid skin suggested the woman's life was not easy, her voice rang with honesty. Whatever her motives in approaching the shop, Audra kept her guard up. Someone had done this to Avery and the shop.

"Saw 'em walking to the sea cave one day and never saw 'em again," she replied with a shrug, jostling the child in her arms. "Pity, too. Good people 'ey was. 'Elped out those less fortunate wi'out asking for anything in return."

Audra returned the woman's smile, knowing that Avery would have appreciated being remembered in a kind light. As one of the first mages to leave Ymira, Avery faced hardships in those initial months in Solven, approached each challenge with tenacity.

"Do you know why Avery set up shop here?"

"Only place 'ey could. Magic's a bit like a mistress, if you get my meaning."

Audra did. Despite all the progress they had made, people were still reluctant to allow mages an equal place in society. They were more than happy to benefit from it, but would not support it in the open. The weight of how much work she still had to do was a constant pressure on Audra's mind.

"Thank you for your help." Audra pressed a few coins into the woman's. "Do you know who did this to the shop?"

Her eyes shuttered, glancing around furtively before responding. "Some people would do anything for a quick coin, m'Lady, 'specially when it's magic."

Empathy gentled the rage in her blood. With Avery gone and the shop's wards removed, everything in it would be fair game with no other mage in the area to protect it. If they had attacked Avery to get to the items, Audra would have left no stone unturned bringing the perpetrators to justice. She was still angry that they had gone through Avery's personal items as well, but she could understand them taking advantage of an easy opportunity, particularly with the rarity of magic. Bidding the woman farewell, Audra stepped out of the shop, sending out a pulse of magic on the minuscule chance that a trace of Avery's magic lingered when they left the city.

Nothing. Too much time had passed.

"I am so sorry, Audra." Graham was a solid presence next to her, wrapping her into a quick hug. Sensing her despair, Graham knew that Avery was gone without her having to say anything. "This never should have happened. I cannot bring your friend back, but I promise to work with you to make Solven a safer place for mages—for all our people."

"Thank you." She pressed her face into his chest, allowing herself a moment of comfort before they had to continue. "Did you sense anything in the shop?"

"Nothing that would suggest something attacked them at the shop. Too cramped for most netvor. Unfortunately, the cave the woman mentioned matched the description of where a netvor was reported. Though I am curious as to why Avery would go there."

"Me too. Avery was not a fighter, so I doubt they would have gone after the netvor."

Not wanting to deal with the noise and chaos of the docks, they made their way to the closest gate out of the city, asking the soldiers for directions to the cave. It was odd that Avery had gone this far away from the city, the coarse sand and sparse plant life incompatible with most spells and potions Audra knew. Besides, Audra had seen boxes in the shop windows with remnants of herbs that Avery would have used. Why would they come here for any reason besides gathering supplies?

Perhaps they enjoyed the feel of the sea breeze and came here to relax. Listening to the crash of waves and the call of birds, Audra could see the appeal. If she remembered correctly, Avery had grown up in a hill town, and this might have been their first experience with the ocean. All mages had an instinctive draw to nature, and the rhythmic ebb and flow of the waves relaxed Audra. Even the cave itself had a rough beauty to it. The rock surrounding the opening formed an uneven circle, the bottom worn smooth by the crashing waves. Mismatched rocks popped up from the sand, like plants rising to the sun that peeked through the small opening in the roof of the cave. After they searched the cave, Audra thought it might be a nice place to take off her shoes and run her toes through the sand.

Until Graham tensed beside her, head tilted to one side while he threw out an arm to indicate she should stop moving. Quieting her breath, Audra strained to hear what he did. All she could hear was the crash of waves and—

"Move!" Graham tackled her, turning as they fell so that they rolled across the sand.

Grunting as she rolled over her satchel, Audra was glad the glass was enhanced with magic. Her side, however, was not. She could already feel the bruises forming. With lightning fast reflexes, Graham was on his feet, daggers in hand. Scrambling to her feet, magic primed in her fingertips, Audra searched for the source of his alarm.

There.

Burrowing under the sand was a creature that had Audra's stomach churning. A long, serpentine body slithered into the ground, the flat edge of its snout acting like a shovel. Before it disappeared, Audra caught sight of a split tail, sharp points on each end. The ground trembled beneath them, vibrating up the soles of her shoes and setting her teeth on edge.

"Friend of yours?" Humor might keep her from giving into the panic that set in at the sight of the monster's slitted red eyes.

"I wish." Graham kept his eyes on the ground, watching for a sign of movement. "That was unlike any netvor I have ever seen." Beneath the concentration that tightened his jaw, Audra could tell that the lack of knowledge bothered him. He had studied every netvor known to the Guard, and knowledge was power. Particularly when it was kill or be killed.

The last time she had faced one of these monsters, it nearly killed her. A combination of quick thinking and a healthy dose of Hellig's blessing kept her alive the last time, but Valeria was not here to save her again. And like hell would she let Graham fight this thing alone.

"Tell me what to do."

"We need to split up. There are some similarities between this one and others, and I suspect it can sense movement in the ground. Together, we are a single target, but separate..."

"We can surround it and take it down."

Flashing her a quick smile full of pride, Graham started moving away. "Try not to talk, it can sense those vibrations too. Watch its movements and do not put yourself in unnecessary danger."

She wished they had more time to prepare, time to practice and learn each other's movements and fighting style. Hells, she just wanted them to have more time in general. Praying to Hellig to keep them both safe, Audra watched as Graham submerged himself in instinct—grey eyes glowing blue—his Guard ability flooding his system better than adrenaline ever could.

Just in time too. The ground shivered, sand cascading into a hole near Graham's feet. He jumped back in time as the creature burst from the ground at a rate that was almost too fast for Audra to see. She realized her mistake too late, focusing on what was happening near Graham. Only part of the netvor was visible. Slashing at Graham in a double-pronged attack was the tail of the monster.

The head burst from the sand in front of her, knocking Audra off her feet and sending her flying into a rock. Glass and crystal shattered against the rock, the items in her satchel no match against the force of the attack. Dazed, Audra felt her shield fade, the impact sapping away the magic that protected her. Taking stock of her body, Audra was glad there were no broken bones. A mistake like that could not happen a second time.

Movement in her periphery spurred her into action, diving to the side as the beast locked its hinged jaw on the rock she was just against. With a thunderous crack, the rock crumbled beneath the pincers on each side of a wide mouth. As if Audra needed any other reminders to avoid getting caught between those sharp teeth.

Trying to put as much distance between them as possible, Audra sent a wave of magic at the creature. Like the armored netvor that attacked Ymira, the magic had little effect, pushing it back without causing real damage. She cursed Dyrun for creating a creature that could withstand magic.

Keeping a close eye on her target, Audra scanned the cave for anything she could use to fight back. Her eyes caught on the remnants of the rock. Lifting several pieces, Audra pelted the creature. Growling with frustration, Audra watched as rocks bounced harmlessly off the serpent's scales.

Her attack faltered when the head struck for her again, catching the way its neck coiled just before striking. Rolling out of the way, Audra and the netvor began a strange dance. Always moving, Audra launched pointed rocks at the creature before jumping out of the way of an attack. In the distance, she could hear sounds of Graham fighting.

Come on, come on! Audra thought to herself. There had to be a weak spot somewhere. She was running low on smaller rocks and it would take some maneuvering to break away one of the larger rocks. Time that she did not have to waste. On her next volley of rocks, Audra watched the serpent swerve to take the hits on its neck instead of its face. Aiming a rock at the creature's left side, Audra gathered water from the ocean behind her, waiting until the creature swerved to send a spear of ice into its eye.

A shriek of pain reverberated off the cave walls, loosening chunks of the ceiling and sending them plummeting to the floor. Her minor victory was short-lived. Dodging the debris, Audra watched in horror as the creature flailed its head, growing taller as its body slithered out of the hole to face her completely. Remorseless red eyes watched her, black blood flowing from the injury while its tail twitched in agitation. Scales that shimmered like oil slid along each other, each tip razor sharp to slice into its victim as it squeezed them to death. Its mouth opened on a hiss, displaying the pincers on each side that would pierce flesh before swallowing a human whole. She only had a moment to process the full image of the creature before it struck, faster now that its focus was no longer divided.

Urging magic into her legs, Audra had just enough speed to get out of the way. Sand sprayed around her where the creature's head landed. Rolling quickly, Audra dodged first one half of the spiked tail, then the other, the sharp tips glancing off her shields when she was not fast enough to avoid the repeated attack.

Dark blue leapt across her line of sight. Graham slashed at the creature's tail, black blood oozing from the wound, distracting the creature enough to give Audra time to get back on her feet. Her breathing was labored, the constant movement and pain from the hits she took taking their toll on her body. A thin sheen of sweat shown on Graham's face, his chest rising with increased inhalations. With a quick glance to make sure she was alright, Graham launched into an attack. Daggers shot from his hands, the chains that connected them allowing him to pull them back quickly, inflicting more damage where they dragged along scales.

Audra unleashed a barrage of magic, sending more spears of ice to pierce the creature's flank along with clouds of sand to distort its vision. It was difficult to time her attacks now that she had to work around Graham. Several times, one of her spears knocked his dagger off its course or Graham's weapon disrupted the sand. More often than she would like, Audra's attack nearly collided with Graham and her heart skipped a beat as she rushed to dispel the magic.

Without the luxury of practice, they had to adjust as they went, dodging the creature's increasingly erratic attacks. A hailstorm of rocks sent Audra to the ground as the creature let out another ear-piercing shriek. Winded from getting knocked on her ass, Audra was too slow to avoid a falling rock, the broken edge cutting her leg.

"Audra!" Graham growled when he heard her cry of pain, a feral look in his eyes as he raced to reach her.

"Behind you," Audra shouted as the creature dove for Graham's exposed back.

With a twist, Graham leapt over the creature's head, narrowly missing getting trapped in its jaws.

Spinning on his feet, Graham dove for the soft skin under the creature's neck. From her vantage point, Audra could see what he could not. He wasn't moving fast enough. The two ends of the tail were united as one, aiming for Graham's heart.

He would not make it in time.

Dread turned Audra's veins into fiery ice. Not again. She would not let someone she loved die again.

Acting on instinct, Audra's arm reached for Graham, a thread of magic racing through the air to strike his chest. His body shuddered at the impact. Then it surged through him like lightning. Graham's skin hummed as the magic pulsed through his veins, giving him the added speed to slide underneath the creature, tail striking the ground behind him. With one thrust, Graham drove his daggers into the creature's skull, pushing the head to the side as it collapsed in death.

When he turned to look at her, chest heaving and muscle bunched, Audra gasped. Was this how he felt when he saw her use magic? This heady combination of awe and pride as she took in the power he wielded to defeat a monster. Black blood covered his body, splattered across his face and hair from the final blow. Once they were clean, she would have to check his body for injuries.

Attempting to stand, Audra felt lightheaded, her leg throbbing with pain and nausea churning in her stomach now that the adrenaline was wearing off. Seeing her wince and topple back into the sand, Graham sprinted to her. Sliding to his knees, he cradled her head in his hands, propping Audra up in his arms.

"You better not...get any of that disgusting blood on...my clothes." Audra tried to breathe around the pain, body clenching around a spasm.

"I'll buy you new ones," Graham replied, running his hands along her body to find the source of her pain. "Can you tell me where it hurts?"

"Leg." She tried to gesture to the leg in question, but her arms felt so heavy. No matter how hard she tried to move even the slightest bit,

Audra's limbs were not responding to her commands. Graham also looked fuzzier than she remembered. "Numb."

"Shit. The tail had venom. Did you get hit?"

She just needed to nap for a moment. Then she could answer all his pesky questions.

"Audra, I need you to stay with me. You can't go to sleep, Elske—"

His voice was so lovely. She wanted to listen to him, she really did. But his arms were just so comfortable. And she was just so tired.

Twenty-Four

Muffled voices that sounded like they were coming from beneath the ocean roused Audra. Turning towards the noise, she groaned when the motion pulled on tight muscles. Why did her body hurt so badly? While she stretched her legs out, Audra tried to recall what she had been doing that made her so tired and achy. Based on the lack of light behind her eyelids, it was either late evening or the room she was in had exceptionally good curtains. Prying one eye open, Audra saw a vaguely familiar room lit only by a crackling fire. She remembered the wardrobe across the room and the patchwork quilt currently snuggled around her shoulders.

The inn!

Oshea.

Fighting the netvor.

It all came back with a rush as Audra gasped, looking frantically around the room for Graham.

"Hey, easy now. I am right here." Graham hurried over from the doorway, setting a tray with two steaming bowls on the table on his way. "You are safe. Do not sit up too fast." His face was lined with worry, exhaustion weighing on his shoulders and mouth.

Propping one knee on the bed, Graham leaned over Audra and

helped her sit upright. After fussing with her pillow to make sure it was supporting her head, he ran his fingers down her hair, eyes tracing each familiar feature. Hair damp from bathing, the removal of dried blood allowed Audra to see the scratches and bruises that were beginning to form on Graham's face and arms. Relieved that he suffered no major injuries, Audra slumped back into the pillow.

"How are you feeling?" Graham's voice was hoarse from exhaustion.

"A little sore and tired, but otherwise better than I expected. How long have I been asleep?"

"Just a few hours, but it felt like eternity." Stormy eyes closed, Graham rested his forehead against hers, taking comfort in her presence. "I thought I was going to lose you. I gave you an antidote as soon as I could, but with an unfamiliar netvor, I was not sure it was going to work." His voice cracked on the last words.

Audra wrapped her arms around him, pulling him in until he moved his whole body onto the bed, pressing against her side. Remembering her panic thinking that Graham was going to be killed in the final moments of battle, Audra understood how he was feeling.

"Are you hurt? Did you take care of your injuries? Were you with me the entire time?"

He looked at her like she had asked a ridiculous question. "Of course I was. I left you briefly to bathe and change—you did mention not wanting me to get blood on your clothes—but only once I knew the antidote was working. Nothing will take me from your side."

Unbalanced by the events of the day, Audra's heart clenched. Keeping her emotions detached was getting more difficult each day, especially when Graham was so sweet. But there was no point in imagining what could be when she was busy dealing with what was. She had made that mistake before.

"Graham, you have to know that no matter what you feel, there is no happy ending for us. We had our chance when we were younger, but we both have responsibilities now. Ones that we cannot walk away from. Why not just enjoy this for what it is, no expectations?"

"I want you to expect things from me. I know that I messed up, and that I cannot undo that hurt, but I want you to know that this." He linked their hands and pressed them against his steadily beating heart.

"This is forever. I am not asking you to give up anything to be with me, just do not give up on us. Please. Not before we even have the chance to try."

"Okay," Audra said in a voice barely above a whisper. There was no guarantee that anything between them would work, but the secret places of her heart wanted to try. Besides, Audra knew firsthand that nothing was guaranteed in life.

At her tentative smile, Graham leaned in to press his lips against hers. While their previous encounters were filled with passion and longing for more, like they were stealing time together, this moment was soft and slow. It was a time of reassurance and exploration, learning the pressure and pace that the other person enjoyed and reveling in the simple joy of their presence. Teeth nipped at plush lips and tongues soothed the sting. Audra marveled at the soft texture of Graham's hair compared to the coarse texture of his beard, growing in during their travel. In return, Graham's hands massaged the nape of her neck, fingers kneading into the tense muscles.

When he found a particularly tender spot, eliciting a moan from Audra, her hands moved to his biceps, gripping them as a bolt of pleasure rushed through her. Grinning against her mouth, Graham moved his hands lower, continuing his massage down her neck and across her shoulders. His hands were magic, melting her muscles and relaxing her body. Audra thought it could not get any better. She had never been happier to be wrong than that moment, because Graham followed the path of his hands with his lips. Open-mouth kisses pressed against her jaw and neck as Audra tilted her head in invitation.

Desperate to feel more of him, Audra pressed her hands into his back. Graham hissed between clenched teeth, tensing underneath her hands. Immediately, Audra removed her hands and sat up, focusing on the pinched expression on his face.

Audra pawed at his shirt, trying to find the best way to remove it without causing more pain. "You are hurt! Let me see."

Large hands stilled hers. "I will be okay. Guards were made to withstand the pain. My priority is helping you get better."

"And it will help me if I know that you are healed too. Let me see."

Just because he would live with the pain did not mean he needed to. Healing may not be her forte, but she was not useless.

Agreeing, Graham gave her a look that said he was only allowing it to appease her as he pulled off his shirt. Even though she had seen his naked chest before, Audra took a moment to appreciate the flex of muscle as the fabric ran up his chiseled form before getting tossed to the ground. If he was always this amenable, she would have to find more reasons for him to take off his shirt. As gracefully as she could when her muscles ached, Audra slid off the bed to retrieve her satchel, indicating for Graham to lie down on the bed.

With his back on display, Audra saw the full extent of his injuries. A mottled blue and purple bruise covered half of his lower back, stretching from under his left ribs to his spine. Audra hoped the damage did not extend to any organs or bones. In addition to the large bruise, Audra spotted another, smaller bruise, on his right shoulder along with several scratches on both arms.

"May I?" she asked with her hands hovering over his skin. Receiving his consent, Audra set about determining the extent of his injuries.

Heat rose up to meet her hands as she pulsed magic into him. Confirming her estimate that the smaller bruise and scratches were minor, Audra fed cool threads of magic to soothe and heal the areas. Her palms tickled as the magic stitched up the wounds and Audra had to resist the urge to scratch them. As each injury was healed, Graham relaxed further into the bed. Despite his claim that his body was built to endure netvor attacks, it was obviously still uncomfortable to live with it.

Once she finished with the little wounds, Audra focused her energy on the large bruise. She coaxed her magic around the injury, assessing the extent of the damage. Unfortunately, two of his ribs were bruised, but fortunately not broken. Flipping open her satchel, Audra was glad that at least one or two energy-boosting potions survived the fight. At full strength, such an injury would pose no problem, but the fatigue combined with her recovering magic lessened her focus and could lead to a mistake. Taking the potion meant she could heal some of the bruises on her own body after healing Graham, but replenishing her magic would take more rest.

Repairing the damage to his ribs and surrounding muscle took her complete concentration, and Audra had to shush Graham twice when he tried to tell her that she did not need to exhaust herself to heal him. Unless they planned on getting attacked a second time that evening, there was no point in holding on to her magic when it could help them. Sweat began to form on Graham's back as the damaged blood vessels, muscles, and bone began to heal. Low groans slipped out from his sealed lips, and Audra knew that Graham was too stubborn to admit that he was uncomfortable. Urging more magic into relieving the discomfort, Audra felt sweat bead on her forehead from the strain. Blowing a strand of hair out of her face, Audra was relieved that she was almost finished. Just a few more minutes, healing a few areas of strained muscle on Graham's body before she was done.

Hands shaking slightly as she lowered them to her side, Audra leaned her body heavily against the headboard. Allowing herself a few minutes to rest before working on some of her own injuries—notably the gash on her leg and the large bruise that undoubtedly formed as a result of getting knocked into a rock—Audra watched as Graham sat up and began to stretch his muscles. When he turned to look at her, his eyes were full of wonder, a wide smile splitting his face.

"Thank you." He grasped her face gently, pressing a firm kiss to her lips. "You are incredible." Another kiss. "Selfless." Another. "Mine."

If she had the energy, Audra would have laughed at his behavior. Instead, her stomach chose that moment to let out a long rumble.

"Shit. You are hungry and tired, and here I am keeping you from food. I promise that I ordered the food with every intention of giving it to you immediately, but something distracted me." He sent her a wry glance before rolling off the bed to get the food. Graham winced when he reached the tray, his hands feeling the bowls and finding them cold. "I will ring for fresh bowls."

"No need to do that. Bring them to me."

"Audra, after everything you have done, the last thing I am going to serve you is cold food."

She giggled, amused that he was pouting over a meal. Graham had always made sure she had the best of everything—even as children—

making sure her food was cooked the way she liked it and that her favorite desserts were served as often as possible.

"We are not eating cold food." She giggled again at the look of confusion on his face as he looked between her and the bowls. "Magic, remember? I can reheat the bowls so that the food does not go to waste."

"Brilliant and beautiful," he said as he brought the bowls over. When he saw the way she was still slumped against the headboard, Graham paused. "You are exhausted and should be resting, not fixing my mistake."

Audra wiggled her fingers at him. "Give me the food, Graham."

Reluctantly, he handed over the bowls. Warming the food to a bearable temperature, Audra smiled up at Graham's worried face.

"See? Nothing to it." Even she could hear the sluggish rate of her words.

She did not realize her eyes had drifted shut until she felt the press of a spoon against her lips. Graham was slightly fuzzy as she watched him bring a spoonful of soup to her lips through bleary eyes. Too tired to protest, Audra opened her mouth, allowing him to feed her slowly. Were it anyone else, she would have felt pathetic and weak, but with Graham, it was always different. It reminded her of the times she was sick and Graham snuck into her room to take care of her. When Audra told him that, his face softened with a look that she was hesitant to decipher.

When she got sick as a child, it was drastic, which Audra now knew was caused by repressing her magic. "I was always surprised that you managed to get into my room even after your parents forbid you from visiting me."

Fear of illness spreading meant that whoever was sick in the castle was isolated until it passed. Yet, every time, Graham managed to sneak into her room, climbing the trellis beside her balcony or finding a way around the doctor and staff stationed in her hallway. Bringing books that he would read to her or stories about his training and studies, Graham remained at her side as long as he could.

Brushing hair away from her face, Graham looked at her softly. "As if that would stop me. I worried about you, stuck in your room by yourself with only a doctor as company. Not getting to see you for days on end made me feel restless, though I did not know why at the time."

"It helped, you know, having you visit. Everything was more bearable when you were around. Even though I worried about you getting caught."

Graham had finished feeding her, setting her bowl to the side before starting on his own. While he scarfed down the first few bites, he watched her as if debating whether to tell her something. Coming to a decision, he swallowed. "Mother did catch me once, when I was climbing down the trellis. We were older and you were worse off than normal."

Audra remembered the instance he was talking about. Years of suppressing her magic caused her body to fluctuate between hot and cold, spasming and rejecting food as it tried to process the magic that was pressing against the cage she had placed it in. With nowhere else to go, it was wreaking havoc on her body, Audra's mistaken attempts to hold in the pain only making it worse. For hours each day, Graham would change the cool cloth on her forehead and tell her stories about his training to make her laugh.

Now, Graham watched her intently. "When she threatened to tear down the trellis to prevent me from going to see you, I told her the truth."

"Which was?"

"That if I wanted to be a husband worthy of you, I had to support you at your lowest as well as your highest. If I could not take care of you when you were ill, then I did not deserve you. You should be cherished and loved. Always. And I wanted to prove that I could do that for you."

Audra felt her resolve cracking, the wall fortifying her heart crumbling to dust beneath Graham's honesty. Had he really felt the same depth of emotion that she had for him their whole lives? It was too much to think about when her body felt like it was moments away from falling into the warm embrace of slumber. Watching her eyes flutter to fight off sleep, Graham pressed a kiss to her forehead, setting aside his bowl to lower Audra to the mattress.

"Rest, sweetheart. We can talk when you are feeling better."

Before letting her eyes drift closed, Audra let her magic pool in the worst of her injuries, repairing the damage so that her body could fully rest.

WHEN HER EYES OPENED AGAIN, the first thing Audra saw was an expanse of tanned skin rising and falling. Burrowing into the warmth beneath her cheek, Audra inhaled the scent of cinnamon dusted trees. A scent that managed to heat her blood and calm the initial feeling of disorientation at waking up in an unfamiliar place. Even when her brain was still shaking off the cobwebs of sleep, Audra knew that Graham was safe.

He was home.

A voice rough with sleep responded to her cuddling.

"Good morning. Did you sleep well?" Graham pulled her tighter to his body, the sight of his broad chest and tattoos waking Audra up better than any cup of tea.

At some point after she had fallen asleep, Graham had removed his shirt, and—if the low slope of the sheet was any indication—his pants as well. Respectful of her consent, Graham left Audra in the clothes she fell asleep in, which both warmed her heart and caused her to wish for a lack of barrier between them in equal measure.

Extending her legs as far as they would go, which was still barely to Graham's calves, Audra allowed awareness to creep into her body. Several muscles were still stiff, but not unbearably so. Cringing at the way her day old clothes and sweat-dried skin felt, Audra squirmed away.

"I did, but now I feel gross." As she got out of bed, Graham watched her through sleep-heavy eyes. With the promise of food by the time she finished, Audra rushed through getting washed and dressed. Graham was waiting at the table—fully dressed to her disappointment —with a plate of her favorite breakfast food.

While they ate, they devised a plan for the day. They would visit the merchants and local alehouses to inquire if anyone knew why Avery had gone out to the caves and if there had been anyone suspicious at the shop. Graham was also going to ask for more information about when the netvor first appeared, his tattoos on full display to encourage attention. People felt safe around Guards and relished the opportunity to talk with one and share their own stories. Whether those stories ended up yielding useful information would remain to be seen.

The market was just as busy as Audra remembered, people pressing in from every side. Just as she suspected, the merchants knew very little about Avery's personal life. They were more than happy to purchase charms and potions from them, but otherwise ignored the mage living in their city. A few expressed their disappointment in losing access to the profitable goods that Avery created, which boiled Audra's blood in anger at their selfishness. Locals at the alehouse were slightly better, sharing stories of their visits with Avery and the good they had done for the city, but they had no recollection of any incidents that would cause Avery to visit the caves. One suggested that maybe Avery found out about the netvor and wanted to get rid of it, but that made no sense. After the incident in Ymira, Audra made sure all mages knew that their power had little impact on the monsters.

Fists curled into balls, Audra weaved her way through the crowded streets. She knew it was unlikely that anyone would have useful information, but it was frustrating. Graham was able to learn that the creature had appeared a few weeks prior, around the same time that Avery disappeared, but that was information they already knew. Unlike most netvor, the one from the cave had no discernible pattern to its attacks, no lure that it used to draw in its victims. One silver-lining was that the netvor never left the cave, and as long as people did not venture near, they were safe.

Running a hand over his stubble, Graham said, "We might learn more from the cave itself. There is a slim possibility that the netvor left remains or tangible evidence of its victims."

Frankly, it felt like they were grasping at straws, but it was the only lead they had left. Body tensing as they approached the cave entrance, her heartbeat raced and breath quickened, remembering what happened the last time they were here. Magic burned for release in response. The salt air was spoiled by the smell of rancid meat and Audra covered her mouth as her stomach rolled. Waving her hand, she summoned wind to blow fresh air through the cave.

Beside her, Graham grimaced. "Damn. I forgot how bad they smelled. This is why we burn them."

"Good idea," Audra replied with a spark of fire at her fingertips.

"Wait." He thrust out an arm to stop her. "I want to get a sketch of the netvor before we burn it, that way we can add it to the book."

Of course. It made sense to share their knowledge so that others would not be at a disadvantage if they found such a creature again. While Graham walked around the limp body, jotting down notes and drawing rough impressions of the features, Audra walked the perimeter of the cave, trying to detect traces of Avery's magic. Near a small group of rocks, Audra paused.

So faint she almost missed it, a brush of Avery's magic lingered. It felt different than most traces of magic, clinging to the rocks like a starfish instead of slowly dissipating into the air.

"Graham," she called out. "Avery was here, but it is strange. Almost like the magic was put here on purpose, but any other magic from the attack is long gone."

Too much time should have passed for Audra to detect any magic. This residue felt out of place, like the ground absorbed the magic unlike the way it typically floated through the air before dispersing. Something about it was familiar, and any answers they found would mean that Avery's death was not in vain. Perhaps it would even bring a semblance of peace over the guilt of losing another mage. But she could not place her finger on why it was familiar.

Kneeling on the sand, Graham ran his hands on the rocks. "No marks from an attack either. I expected to find something belonging to Avery, or even any of the other victims. But the cave is bare. There is nothing to find. Your friend deserved better."

Audra did not want to give up, her mind grasping at ideas for where else they could search. They could not pull clues out of thin air, and if both she and Graham had searched the area, there was nothing to be found. She came all this way for answers, hoping to return home with good news. Now she had to tell her people that Avery was dead. Leah would need to be notified as soon as possible, since she was searching for

Leon. Hellig help them all if something happened to him as well. One death could be attributed to a random attack, but two was a pattern.

Letting out a growl of frustration, Audra hurled a ball of fire at the decaying monster. There was nothing left for them here but questions and black-coated sand.

TWENTY-FIVE

Audra was agitated on their journey back to the castle. Hopefully, the letter she sent would have reached Leah by now, but she would not know if there was a response until they were back. Plus, she could not escape the tingle at the back of her mind that they had missed something. Again and again, Audra mulled over every response they received about Avery and the exploration of the shop and cave, forcing her mind to recall any detail that she had missed before.

With each recollection drawing up blank, Audra grew more frustrated. Graham tried to draw her out of her bad mood, starting conversations that were increasingly one-sided as Audra barely responded. Whenever they stopped to camp, Audra quickly set up their bedrolls and created a fire and ward, barely registering what she was eating before curling up to sleep. When the castle was finally in sight, Audra was so wound up that she could not return to her room. Sunlight was fading behind her as Audra left her horse to the care of a stablehand before walking off. She was not surprised to find that her feet carried her to the secret alcove that she had always gone to when upset.

It also should not have surprised her when the ivy rustled a few moments later, Graham following her into the dim space.

"Go away." She barely spared him a glance as he laid out a blanket on the ground and sat down. The exhaustion of the past weeks settled heavily on her shoulders, disappointment at what they found wearing down her nerves to brittle edges.

"I am not going anywhere, Audra. Especially not when you are hurting." He spoke calmly, arms open in a placating gesture.

But Audra was too angry to be calmed. No amount of breathing exercises or visualization of letting the emotion go would help her. Not when she wanted the anger to burn her to ashes. Anger was better than the guilt slowly eating away at her from having failed to protect Ymira and Avery.

Her anger needed a target, and Graham was right there.

"Ha," she mocked, "you're one to talk about something hurting me. Not after what you did." The bitter swirl of emotions sitting in her chest brought up feelings she had long gotten past. Or, at least she thought she had. There was no closure after killing the netvor, no further justice to achieve for Avery, and Audra needed an outlet for that. Their past was something that she could solve, hopefully giving her the relief she desperately needed to feel balanced again.

"You want to do this right now? Finally talk about us?" His lips pressed in a firm line. "Fine. Let it out. I can take it."

Well, fine. If he was asking for it.

"Okay. You want the truth? Here it is. I feel confused. You say you missed me and want to be with me now, but five years ago, you spurned me in front of everyone, saying that you could not know if what we felt was real because of how your parents encouraged us to be together. How can both be true?" She paced in front of him, turning sharply when she reached each edge of the small space. "And I'm angry. So angry with you. I was devastated! I offered you my love, my partnership—my entire world revolved around you—and you tossed it aside like it meant nothing!"

Audra was furious, her movements sharp and exaggerated. One hand ran through the strands of her hair while she gestured with the other. Her chest rose with each quickened breath, a rosy flush rising on the open skin above her dress.

"I am not nothing! I worked hard to move on from you, learning how to love myself for who I am and not what I can provide for another person. For so long, I wished that you would find me and tell me that you were wrong, that everything you said was a lie. But years went by, Graham. Years. Ymira is difficult to reach, but not impossible. Especially once we started increasing our presence in Solven and Feldor. I forgave you for the past—not for your sake, but for my own—because I could not live with the poison of hating you. But then you start giving me those letters and telling me you cared for me this whole time, and it brings back everything. Because despite it all, I still loved you!"

Graham waited while she purged the ugly mess living in her chest, the words coming out faster and higher. Completely still, his sole focus was her. White-knuckled hands were gripping his knees, holding back the emotions that clawed at him as he witnessed her pain.

"I thought it wouldn't matter, but I have to know why. Why did you reject me? If you wanted me, why did you let us go through that pain?"

He pressed a hand against the blanket next to him, urging her to sit. "It is not something I am proud of and the story is quite long. Before I left on my Hunt, I had every intention of proposing to you after the ball. Expectations from my parents aside, you were going to make an exceptional queen, and above it all, I loved you. What hurts me the most is that I made you doubt my love for you because I was terrified to tell you."

"Why would you be afraid of that? I thought it was obvious that I loved you."

"Maybe, but you never told me explicitly. There were times that I wondered if you loved me because it was expected of you, or worse, if it was because you loved the idea of being a princess more than being my wife. Which ties back to the Hunt. The assignment I was given involved incidents of villagers traveling through the woods and never returning. Anyone that went searching for them also failed to return. Those details alone are fairly common for all netvor, so I knew I had to be extra vigilant."

His eyes were focused on a point beyond her shoulder, recalling the day as if he were currently living it. Audra could see his muscles tense at the memories.

"If it makes you uncomfortable to remember, you can skip over this part."

"No, I want to. I *need* to tell you." Standing, Graham paced from one end of the blanket to another, his features tense as boulders. "We tracked the monster for days, following remnants of corpses on a bloody trail through the forest, getting closer to its lair. Puddles of water near the path. Little evidence of a struggle. It became clear what we were hunting. Endriga are cunning creatures that emit a haze that muddles the mind. No one knows what its true form is, because anyone who lays eyes on it only sees whatever they desire most, slowly leading them towards enough water for it to drown you before feasting on your entrails."

Shuddering at the thought, Audra wrapped her arms around her raised knees to keep warm.

"When we neared a pond in a small clearing in the forest," Graham continued, "I knew we were at the lair. Since I had to kill it alone, Kasteel waited with the horses, keeping watch and listening for a cry of help should I need it. If only he knew how close I came to needing it. The clearing was peaceful, sunlight casting rays through gaps in the trees with no sound or wind to disturb it. Until I heard it. Or, rather, until I heard *you*."

"Me?" Audra's look of bewilderment caused a temporary pause in Graham's pacing as he let out a distressed sigh.

"Yes, I was surprised as well to discover you—in the middle of the forest—standing with your ankles in the water, beckoning me to you. The rational side of my brain knew that it was a trick. You were safe at the castle, not wandering around a forest. But in my heart, hells, I wanted it to be you. It was your voice that called out, '*Graham, look how beautiful the water is. Won't you come play with me?*' I knew how much you wanted to join me in the Hunt, so I had to check that it wasn't you. That you hadn't managed to find your way to me. So I asked why you were there. '*I came to be with you, Graham. Don't you want to be with me?*' And then you were before me, cupping your hands around my head, pulling me down into a kiss. A kiss that felt like a drug. The very thing I had wanted for so long was finally within my grasp. You wanted me. *Me.* Outside the palace without titles or politics getting in the way.

And I could finally have you. My body felt like it was on fire, the need to possess you was so strong that I almost didn't notice my body being pulled toward the water. Years of training, preparing my entire life to kill monsters, and I almost let one destroy me instead."

He let out a strangled laugh.

"It was only when my feet felt the cold sting of water that I became aware of my surroundings again. When I pulled my sword on you, tears fell down your face like miniature waterfalls as you begged me not to hurt you. Each sob and plaintive cry shred my heart to ribbons. The tears only made it worse when the creature began fighting back. It was *your* hands and nails that fought back. Your beautiful skin that was injured. All while crying out my name and screaming at me to stop hurting you. The first cut of my blade on your skin felt like it was cutting my own flesh. And I had to do it again. And again. And again. The creature cursed me, using your voice to tell me all the wretched things I thought about myself. That you only wanted me because of my crown and that you could never love me without it. That I was trapping you into a life in a gilded cage, not caring about your hopes and dreams. It was only when I plunged my sword into your heart, cutting off your wails of pain, that I felt the hot sting of my own tears on my face. Time felt endless as I knelt by your body, my heart and mind at war with each other. I knew the thing I killed was a monster—made even more vile by claiming your features as its own—but my heart mourned the thought of hurting you. I haven't wielded a sword since."

At that moment, tears were falling steadily from Graham's unfocused eyes, the horrors of what he experienced as real in that moment as they were years before. Audra's heart broke for the pain he endured, knowing that the experience changed the course of both their lives.

Wiping at the tears, Graham continued, "Enough time passed for Kasteel to call out to me, wondering if I was alright. Hearing a familiar voice was enough to remind me of the task at hand, but not banish the pain. I burned the body so it could no longer taint the world, then returned to Kasteel. We didn't speak for two days. I tried to feel pride at the work I had done, ridding the world of an evil creature, but I couldn't stop thinking about the vision it presented. Endriga are created when a person so desperately wants something that they are willing to kill for it. Each kill taints their soul further and further until the monster takes over, cursing them to a life of killing others for their desires. I knew that I cared for you deeply, but to be my greatest desire? That was a level of affection I wasn't prepared to face. How did my desire for you make me any different than the monster I killed? And it would have been so easy for me to have you. You wouldn't have put up a fight, not after my parents filled your head with expectations of being my bride. How could I know if you being with me would be a choice you made willingly, or based on years of training? I could destroy you just by bringing you into a marriage that you did not want, slowly killing you just as I killed the endriga."

Rising up to meet him, Audra grasped his face within her hands and forced Graham to look at her. "You know that's not true. What I felt for you wasn't based on your parents' desire for us to marry. I loved you for who you are. That kind boy who brought me flowers when I was sick. That smart boy who talked to me about the books he was reading and asked for my opinion. The man who walked with me through gardens and shared life's burdens."

"I know that now. Remembered it soon after you left. But when I first returned home, I was still reeling from the emotions the Hunt brought out. We came through the gates, and there you were, practically gift-wrapped as my bride in your pale dress. And I resented it. Resented the way our parents pushed us together, blurring my ability to know if you loved me for myself or if our feelings were a manipulation. I resented you for going along with it and never pushing for what you wanted. Mostly, I resented myself for not being good enough for you. For almost dying before I even had the chance to protect you or the kingdom. So I pushed back like a wounded animal. I treated you horribly, ignoring you and pushing you away when I needed you most. I'm sorry, Audra. I'm sorry for the pain I caused you, making you feel unwanted and rejected. We lost years together because of what I did."

Graham pressed their foreheads together, their breaths mingling. The fragrant scent of netreus—the night-blooming flowers—carried on the breeze, the cocoon of the alcove keeping them safe in a world of their own. Memories of past pain were softened in the glow of the moon, and Audra longed to take away the pain Graham bore. "I forgive you."

When it looked like he was going to protest, Audra gasped his face, green eyes pinning gray.

"I. Forgive. You." Each word was punctuated with a small kiss. "You were right that I spent more time trying to make you and the king and queen happy, that I barely thought about what I wanted. It broke my heart having you shut me out and say such cruel things. But, as much as it hurt to leave, I never would have grown here. Learning magic, leaving my home, and making new friends and family allowed me to become the person I am now. Eventually, I came to realize that the time apart was the best thing that could have happened to us. I was finally able to love myself just as much as I loved you."

His eyes searched her face. "And now?"

"Now I am happy to spend time with you again, getting to know each other without the burden of losing myself."

"Never again. If you ever feel lost, I will find you and remind you exactly who you are. Powerful, loyal, giving, a queen. I'll give you as much time as you need. Just know that I plan to keep you this time. In whatever way I can have you, you're mine."

"And you are mine."

No other words were necessary as Audra pulled Graham's lips to hers, luxuriating in the feel of their warmth. Despite the hard lines of his body, Graham's lips were soft, yielding to her exploration. Tilting his face with her hands, Audra slanted their lips together. With a low groan, Graham plowed his fingers into her hair, tugging her head back so that he could nip at her jawline. His stubble scraped against her skin, causing her to shudder. Nothing had felt this good before. This kiss felt like fire in her veins and Audra gasped for air. When Graham ran his tongue down the curve of her neck, Audra grasped his shoulders to remain standing.

"Just imagine what that will feel like elsewhere," Graham growled in her ear.

Thoughts of his mouth on the apex of her thighs would haunt Audra's dreams. Desperate for more, Audra brought his lips back to hers, tugging his lower lip with her teeth. Their tongues tangled in an open-mouth kiss as Graham walked them backward toward the blanket.

Audra lowered herself onto his lap, thighs straddling his legs. "Too much for you to handle, Your Highness?" She delighted in the way his hands clenched around her waist at the title.

His hands traveled up and down her back, caressing her covered skin. "One of these days, I'm going to punish your wicked mouth."

"I'd like to see you try."

With hands trembling from excitement, Audra unfastened the buckles of Graham's vest and pushed it off his shoulders. Tugging his shirt from his pants, Audra smoothed her hands up his chest, feeling each curve of muscle as he leaned forward to press kisses against her neck. His skin was warm beneath her fingers, flexing with each new uncovered part. Once his shirt was completely removed, Audra leaned back to study him. Her fingers trailed across the broad lines of his shoulders, then down his chest, brushing through the dusting of brown hair. Graham's eyes watched her as Audra continued mapping the contours of his body with her hands. Knowing that he was hers, that it was her actions causing his breath to quicken, filled her with pleasure. When she reached the line of his pants, Audra watched Graham tense, as if any movement would halt her progress.

Looking into his eyes, Audra smiled and ran her fingertips along his waistband. His eyes were clouded with desire as she leaned forward to kiss each scar on his chest, never halting the movement of her hand.

"Please, Audra," he panted.

"Please, what, Your Highness?" Audra teased, knowing what the title did to him.

With a growl, Graham grabbed her hand and placed it over the length of him, squeezing their joined hands. Their lips met in a heated kiss and Audra molded her hand over him, caressing him through his pants. Eyes closed on a silent moan, Graham thrust his hips into her hand. Her own desire left her hot and aching, her breasts straining against her dress, begging for touch. Sensing her need, Graham wrapped one arm around her waist, cupping her rear and dragging her up his lap so that her center was over him, using his other hand to cup her breast, rubbing the fabric over the sensitive peak.

Audra's head tipped back on a moan, sparks of light shooting from the nerve endings of her pleasure. She needed more, wanting Graham to consume her. His mouth returned to her neck, sucking on the sensitive skin at the base before continuing down to her chest. In a pattern surely meant to torture Audra for her earlier actions, Graham kissed his way across the line of her dress, slipping his tongue beneath the fabric to tease, but never touch, the place she needed him most. Despite her attempts to move his head where she wanted him, Graham remained firmly in place, drawing out the sweet torture until she was writhing against him.

"Tell me what you need, Audra."

A desperate moan was her answer as Audra tugged on Graham's hair, still trying to move him. Cool air flowed between their bodies, pebbling her skin where Graham's warm mouth had been. A shudder rippled through Audra at the sensation.

"You can do better than that." Graham's voice was husky, speaking each word into her chest. "I will give you everything, you just have to ask for it."

"Use this," Audra pulled his bottom lip between her teeth, "to kiss me here." Adjusting her position, Audra sat up in Graham's lap so that his face aligned with her breasts.

"Gladly." Graham's eyes were liquid starlight as he captured her gaze. Torturously slow, he ran one finger across the dress' neckline, pulling down the fabric as he went. It was maddening to watch him, but Audra would not have it any other way. When the fabric bunched underneath her breasts—freeing them to spill over the top—Audra held her breath, waiting for the first touch on her bare skin.

Graham's hand slid up her body, mapping each curve and sensitive location on its way up. Gently, he traced the curve of one globe, a whisper of a touch that had Audra almost begging for more. If just this small touch caused her body to react strongly, she was impatient to find out what his full hand would feel like. Mercifully, Audra did not have to wait long.

With one arm stretched along her spine to hold her steady, Graham cupped his other hand around her fully, lifting her to his eager mouth. Hot, wet pleasure gripped Audra as his mouth closed over the peak. A throaty moan left her as she tilted her head back at the sensation. It felt like tiny bolts of lightning were landing everywhere his tongue touched. When Graham pulled the tight peak between his teeth, tugging just enough, Audra thought she would combust. Nothing had ever felt this good.

Audra began rocking her hips against Graham's, needing him to feel as exquisite as she did. Clutching his hair with one hand, Audra ran her other hand down the muscles of his back. Years of physical training served him well. Graham's muscles rippled under her hands and a low groan reached Audra's ears when her fingers dipped beneath the waistline of his pants.

"Not yet," Graham hissed between clenched teeth. "I need to see you come first. Five times at least."

"Five?" Her voice shook at the pleasurable prospect.

"One for each year we were apart." Grabbing her wrists, Graham pinned them behind her back with one hand. With her back arched to accommodate the new position, Audra felt her core tighten for balance, the sensation of teetering over a ledge heightening her senses. But Graham would never let her fall.

Hands that could wield throwing knives with deadly accuracy—strong enough to take down ferocious creatures—were gentle as they moved over her body. Though his grip on her wrists held her in place, Audra knew that if she truly wanted to go, he would release her.

Night air met bare skin as Graham used his other hand to draw her skirt up to her lap, rubbing circles on her leg. Each glide of his hand brought him closer to her center, tingles of pleasure trailing up her thigh as if guiding him to where she needed him most. Just as his fingertips brushed the crease where thigh met hip, Graham moved his hand to the other side, continuing the circular pattern down toward Audra's knee.

"Graham, please," Audra begged when his hand repeated the action as it reached her hip again.

"What, dearest?"

Too far gone in a haze of pleasure to chastise him for teasing her, Audra settled for grinding her hips down, seeking the pressure that would bring her satisfaction.

"Touch me."

The next time his fingers reached the apex of her thighs, they followed the path to its end.

Bliss.

One finger outlined Audra's center, stars shattering behind her eyelids as Graham claimed her lips. He swallowed each of her moans as his fingers explored her. Lightly at first, then firmer as her hips began to move over him eagerly. Audra wanted it to never end almost as much as she wanted to climax. Just as he had always known the depths of her soul, Graham also knew how to read her body. He studied her expressions and moans of pleasure, determining which movements sent her spiraling towards the peak, and just when Audra was on the precipice, Graham would slow his motions, letting her simmer before stroking her desire back to a boil.

It was madness. Pleasure. Perfect.

Leaning her head forward, Audra sucked on Graham's neck, needing a way to touch him with her hands restrained. She could taste the salt from sweat on his skin, and she licked a path from collarbone to jaw, earning a moan from Graham. Sure that he had left several bruises on her neck from his mouth, Audra bit the base of his throat, pulling the skin into her mouth to leave a mark of her own.

Something unleashed inside Graham when Audra bruised his neck. "Yes, claim me. Make me yours." He wanted to belong to her as desperately as he wanted her to belong to him. Wanted the entire world to know it. Swirling his thumb around her clit, Graham eased two fingers into her body. The slick glide of his fingers in and out were Audra's undoing. She came with a harsh cry, core contracting around his fingers while she rode out her release.

Words that felt too early to say tried to tumble out of her mouth, but Audra held them back by crashing her lips against Graham's, trying to consume him as pleasure flowed through her. When the aftershocks of her orgasm settled into small pulses, Graham pulled his fingers from her. Her body felt empty without him and Audra nestled closer to his chest to make up for it. Head tilted to face him, Audra watched a cocky smile form on his lips before he brought each finger to his mouth, licking her arousal from his hand.

"Next time I taste you, my mouth will be directly on the source, head buried between your thighs." Imagining gripping on to Graham's hair as he feasted on her flesh caused Audra's arousal to flame to life once more. "But that will have to wait. When I get my mouth on you for the first time, I will need more space than this alcove. I want to spread you wide and take my time."

"Promises, promises."

"My apologies, Audra mine. In the meantime, how about I get to work on those other orgasms I owe you? Four more, correct? I do not want you to think that I am not a man of my word."

After delivering on his promise, Graham straightened their wrinkled garments and carried Audra's limp body through the castle and into his room. Her eyes were fighting against sleep as he removed their clothing and tucked them both into the bed. With a sigh of contentment, Audra snuggled against his side, drifting off into a bliss-induced sleep.

Half-asleep already, Audra blamed her befuddled mind for imagining Graham whispering against her hair.

"I am never letting you go, Elskede."

Twenty-Six

"Audra, sweetheart," Graham mumbled into his pillow, "you know I find anything you do sexy, but licking my hand is a step too far." Sometime during the night, he managed to sprawl across the bed, one arm nestled beneath his head while the other dangled off the edge.

Audra propped up on one arm to admire the curve of his back, the sheet deliciously low, before responding. "We definitely need to discuss boundaries soon if you think that is something I would do."

It was comical how quickly Graham moved once he realized a creature was licking his hand. Eyes alert and body tensed, he bolted upright to look at what was on the ground. When Isik yipped and jumped onto the bed as if they were playing a game, Audra could not hold back her laughter. After being woken up in a similar manner many times, she knew how fruitless it was to try and stop the fox once he got riled up.

"Isik, shit, get off the bed." Trying to push him off only excited the fox more, and Isik began to dart around Graham, eager to play chase.

Tears in her eyes from laughing at the image of Graham trying to tackle the white furball, Audra put a hand on his arm.

"I can take him outside, he is probably mad that I was gone for so long and wants to play."

"Where did he come from? He was not in here last night and I remember closing the door."

She shrugged, unable to explain the fox's nature. "Isik is prone to all sorts of mischief. He probably snuck in when you got up to fetch us refreshments."

Audra rolled out of the bed, padding over to Graham's wardrobe. Before sleep claimed her, Audra remembered asking Graham to help her remove her dress, not wanting to sleep in the uncomfortable garments like she had at the inn. Though it helped her sleep better, she now had nothing clean to wear to take Isik outside.

"Can I borrow some of your clothes? Just until I can get back to my room?"

Distracted by her movement, Isik finally jumped off the bed to investigate. Graham followed, pulling out two pairs of shirts and pants.

"You can have whatever you want. Anything that is mine is yours."

Cheeks flush with pleasure, Audra slipped into the clothes, accepting the belt Graham held out to keep the pants around her hips.

"You do not have to come with me. I am sure you have things to catch up on now that we are back."

"We both do, but I wanted to try something that requires us to be outside."

"Oh? And what is that?"

He was frustratingly tight-lipped about it, refusing to give her any hints as they made their way outside. When Audra started to veer toward the gardens, Graham held her elbow and steered her towards the training grounds with Isik trotting beside them. The sound of clashing metal, shoes slapping against the ground, and creaking obstacles came to her on a breeze. It transported her back to all those days spent watching Graham train.

"Defense practice, Your Highness?" Audra teased, enjoying the way the tips of his ears turned pink at the memory.

"We both know that you are more than capable of defending yourself, which reminds me, you have earned a tattoo for killing a netvor. I would be more than happy to draw it myself if you want." His suggestive words heated her skin, the image of him focused on inking her skin more arousing than she thought it would be.

"Not really my style, but thank you. You can reward me with jewelry instead." She was joking, but his eyes warmed at the idea, roaming over her skin as if considering what he could make first. It was a way for Graham to mark her as his, and she loved it. Forgetting where they were and why they were there, Audra stepped forward, eyes lidded with desire.

Kissing her briefly, Graham stepped back and tucked her hair behind her ear. "Later. We have work to do and Isik needs to play."

"We could do that anywhere. Why here?" As fond as she was of the times Graham had taught her self defense, it was a rather boring place for Isik. He preferred tall trees and grass where he could hide and chase.

Taking her hands in his, Graham said, "I have been thinking about our fight in the cave, that final blow. Your magic...it was incredible. Like every sensation was clearer, each motion smoother. Without you, I would have died, but with you. With you, I feel like we could do anything."

"And you wanted to see if we could do it again," Audra exclaimed.

Excitement built in her at the prospect. She had never read anything about this and did not know if any mage had tried it before. But, it could have been how Safrina and Pennifren assisted the Guards against Dyrun.

Audra paced while she thought out loud, hands gesturing as she walked. "It could work...but we would need to be careful. Since you already have magic in your body—sorry, I suppose you did not know that. Guards were created by the original mages with magic." She would have to give him the full story later, but he did not seem overwhelmed by the information, which was a good sign. "We know that it is compatible with my magic. Still, only small amounts at a time. I do not want to hurt you."

Leaning against the tree that Audra used to sit under, Graham crossed his legs and watched her plan.

"Just tell me where you want me," Graham said.

Audra indicated that he should stand in the middle of the training circle, farthest away from anything that could injure him if the magic went awry. Then, she flexed her hands and wrists. Just like learning to lift the crystal with Valeria, she had to focus and direct her magic at Graham.

Cautious of hurting him, the first thread of magic fizzled out when it connected with his chest. Frowning, Audra wondered if it was too little. In the haze of fighting, she was not conscious of how much magic she used to give Graham the advantage over the serpent.

"Is that all you've got?" Graham was trying to get her out of her own head, goading her like he used to.

Smirking, she sent a larger burst of magic at him.

Knocking him flat on his ass.

"Shit, sorry!" She rushed over to him, angry at herself for getting carried away.

He smiled up at her while he caught his breath. "I...deserved...that," he wheezed out.

Helping him get up, Audra took a moment to assess what went wrong while Graham readied himself. It was more magic than the previous attempt, but not alarmingly high. Maybe the amount of magic was not the problem. Chewing on her bottom lip, Audra recalled the feeling when she let the magic out.

The answer clicked into place. She had pushed the magic *at* Graham, not *into* him. This magic was similar to charging crystals, not like wielding the elements. Graham was something her magic needed to flow through, not manipulate.

"There she is." Graham smiled at her when he saw that she had her answer.

This time, when her magic reached Graham, it seeped into him like sunshine, energizing his cells. Eyes closed as the power washed over him, they were glowing blue when he opened them.

"Let's see what you can do."

Reaching down for a stick that Isik found, Audra tossed it to Graham. After all, he had promised to play with the fox. Launching the stick farther than Isik was used to, white fur flew as he chased it. When Isik returned, stick clenched between his teeth, he refused to give it up, having earned it after running so far. With a burst of speed, Graham lunged, but Isik slipped from his grip.

Audra laughed as they repeated the game from the morning,

Graham chasing an elated Isik. Her magic allowed Graham to keep pace with the fox and she watched carefully to see how long it would last. Each time he began to slow, Audra sent more magic in his direction, learning which amounts were more effective. It was not perfect—a few times Audra sent too much or too little magic, tripping Graham or propelling him forward—but, the longer they played, the easier it got. Once Isik tired, flopping onto the grass to pant, Graham sat next to him, rubbing the fox's ears.

As much as she wanted to continue, Audra knew that she and Graham needed to rest. Plus, they had a meeting with his father and council later to discuss their findings and talk about the treaty. Since she had left with Graham soon after arriving, Audra had to set aside negotiating the particulars of an alliance. She could already feel the headache forming at the thought of having to deal with Lord Nadeen and his cronies.

The council room was exactly as she remembered it, a rectangular table taking up the majority of the space with portraits of past rulers hanging on the walls. Keld rose from his chair as they entered, a broad smile covering his face when he saw their joined hands.

"Welcome back," he said, his deep voice carrying throughout the room. When Audra and Graham rounded the table in front of him, Keld pulled Graham into a one-armed hug before scooping Audra up into a spine-popping embrace. It was the same way Kasteel hugged her, and Audra was happy to see Graham's half-brother sitting at the table.

"Isa and I are both happy to have you back safe," Keld whispered as he lowered Audra to the ground. Raising his voice for the rest of the seated council members, Keld asked, "Was your journey successful?"

Twining their fingers together again, Graham walked with Audra to the other end of the table where one empty chair sat. "More or less. We did confirm that the monster was one of the new types of netvor. I have notes and a rough sketch for the scribes. But we were unable to discover how or why it got there."

Audra was glad that Graham did not mention the loss of Avery. Even if their kingdoms formed an alliance, there were still matters that Audra wanted to keep private from the calculating minds of the council members. Stopping in front of the chair, Audra watched as Graham pulled it out and gestured for her to sit. When her eyes caught on what was carved over the royal crest in the back of the chair, Audra glanced at Graham for confirmation.

He nodded, a calculating glint in his eye, and gently pressed on her lower back to guide her onto the chair.

Above her head now sat the markings of the royal crown.

Several of the council members gasped and stared at the couple in disbelief, but Kasteel and Keld beamed at them from down the table. Beside her, Graham rested one hand on her shoulder and the other along the top of the chair. The tips of his fingers grazed the peaks of the crown, a replica of the one Audra had tried on in his chamber.

"I told you it looked better on you," he whispered in her ear.

"Your Highness, we can send someone to fetch another chair for the mage," Lord Nadeen said. Of course he'd be the one to bring that up.

"Unnecessary," Graham purred, "a queen belongs on a throne."

Ignoring Lord Nadeen's sputtered protests, Keld clapped his hands together. "Now that's settled, let's get to the matter we came for today."

"ARE you incapable of understanding me, or do you need me to illustrate my point again, Lord Nadeen?" Audra fought to keep her temper cool, resisting the urge to yell and appear as temperamental as Lord Nadeen wanted to prove mages were. He forgot that she was raised on courtly politics, and hiding her true feelings was second nature. It helped that Graham was currently rubbing his thumb along the back of her shoulder, hidden from view so that no one would notice the tension tightening her muscles while still offering support.

"What I believe Lord Nadeen is failing to articulate," River spoke up from their place at Audra's side, "is what reassurances you have that mages will not harm our people and unleash another version of Dyrun and the netvor?"

This conversation was going in circles, Audra and the council members going back and forth on the matter of an alliance between Ymira and Solven. There were several members who wanted the assistance of mages, either greedy for the power it could provide them or motivated by a genuine desire to have magic improve the conditions of their people. River was the latter, and patiently waited for opportunities to express their support by asking questions that allowed Audra the chance to persuade those who were afraid of change and wanted nothing to do with magic.

"What guarantee do we have that Solven would not send their Guards and soldiers to attack mages? That is the point of an alliance. We have to trust one another to make it work. Ymira would not benefit from creating another war. Look at where the last one got us, isolated and cut off from the other kingdoms. Do not forget that while one mage was the cause of countless losses, it was also through the work of mages that led to the defeat of Dyrun. Our people were allies once, and can be again. Prince Graham and I even discovered a way where magic can assist Guards in killing netvor."

This brought about exclamations of surprise and question. Even Keld sat forward in his seat, inquiring how that could be possible. With a nod from Graham, Audra fed a line of magic into him. Enough to only last a few moments, the magic changed Graham's eyes and allowed him to throw a dagger across the room with enough speed to garner gasps from the table.

"Incredible."

"Impossible."

"This changes everything."

The council members began speaking over each other.

"I was able to defeat the creature in Oshea with Audra's help. An alliance means we would lose less Guards fighting the netvor, particularly this new type," Graham's voice was rough from the lingering magic.

"Or it could be playing right into her hand," one of Lord Nadeen's supporters said. The lord nodded in agreement. "She could have created these creatures and made herself the key to defeating them in order to force us into an alliance."

"At what gain?" River spoke up again, more nobles agreeing with them than Lord Nadeen now. "Lady Audra admitted that one of these new netvor attacked Ymira, so why would she create something that would harm her own people just for an alliance?"

Why, indeed? Audra thought to herself as one finger began tapping a staccato on the arm of the chair. Mages are wealthy and powerful enough without the alliances, so the main benefit to Ymira was ensuring that all mages were safe, no matter where they lived. She was glad to see that more of the council members were starting to recognize that.

Sensing that he was losing support, Lord Nadeen glanced around the table, staring down his supporters to bully them into continued support and glaring at those who had switched sides. "How can we know the inner workings of a mage's mind? Any alliance with them could change on a whim."

"We could always form an alliance through marriage," Kasteel said with a wink towards his brother. "Solven and Ymira could unite, so that any action taken against one would hurt themselves."

Audra froze, her heart beating faster while, inconceivably, her body temperature plummeted. Marrying Graham, getting to spend the rest of their days together, was something she was beginning to recognize that she still wanted, desperately. But not at the cost of her kingdom. After years living in isolation, Audra would not allow the mages to get swallowed up by another kingdom, losing what made them unique.

"No."

Startled by the word that was poised on the tip of her tongue coming out of Graham's mouth, Audra turned to look at him. His face was firm, but his eyes were soft as he watched her. He spoke for the whole group to hear, but his words were meant for her.

"If Audra and I decide to marry, it will be for love. Nothing more. I would never ask her to give up her crown for me."

He turned to face his father.

"Our alliance should be based on enhancing both kingdoms' resources, knowledge, and prosperity."

Gaping at him, Audra felt the last resistance in her heart melt. Maybe not immediately, but someday, they would figure out a way to make this work without having to sacrifice everything that was important to them. Declaring it to those in the highest positions in his kingdom made her wish for privacy to show her appreciation for Graham's thoughtfulness.

"I agree," Keld's voice filled the silence that had descended after

Graham's declaration. "An alliance between Solven and Ymira will occur, because I trust the High Mage and her people."

"Your Majesty, surely you cannot—" Lord Nadeen began.

"Enough." The authority in that one word from the king was enough to force Lord Nadeen back in his seat. "Need I remind you that the council exists to *advise* the reigning monarch. Do not overstep and presume to know better than me. I have listened to your suggestions and opinions, but the final decisions in regards to this kingdom reside with me. Is. That. Clear?"

Humiliation stained Lord Nadeen's face and neck crimson.

"My sincerest apologies, Your Majesty. You are, of course, always the final say in our kingdom," he bit out behind a thin smile.

Holding his stare until Lord Nadeen lowered his eyes, Keld nodded to the group. "This meeting is adjourned."

Effectively dismissed, the gathered nobility began to rise and shuffle out of the room. One of the last to leave—blatantly hoping to catch the king for a private word—Lord Nadeen leveled a glare at Audra that was filled with icy venom. When Keld made no move to address him, Audra smiled with glee.

"With all the apologizing you have been doing recently, Lord Nadeen, I do wonder if it would be better for you to not speak at all? Something to consider." Audra added a wave of her fingers to bid him farewell.

It was a surprise that the door did not shudder on its frame as Lord Nadeen closed it behind him.

Before leaving the room, Kasteel walked to where Audra remained seated and clasped Graham on the shoulder while bending to kiss Audra on the top of her head.

"When you two do decide to get married, remember that it was my idea first."

"I think your mother would have something to say about that," Keld said as he rose from the table, smiling at three of the most important people in his life. "Audra, I want you to know that the alliance stands no matter your relationship with my son, but I know Isa and I would both be thrilled to finally call you our daughter."

Audra flushed, watching the king and his oldest son walk out of the room. A firm hand on her shoulder pressed her into the chair when she tried to rise. Rounding the chair, Graham pulled on the armrests to turn Audra towards him. Now that the room was clear of its occupants, Graham's mask dropped, the princely confidence giving way to a man who looked at her like she had the power to build him up or break him with one word.

She reached out to clasp his hands in reassurance. Letting the mask of High Mage slip off like an unfurled ribbon, Audra looked at him without holding anything back. Every feeling she had for him was projected in her eyes, silently pleading with him to protect the one thing she could not ward.

Her heart.

Gray eyes flashed with understanding, Graham's face reverent as he lowered a knee to the floor.

Time stopped as Audra watched him, her heart speeding like she had raced Isik around Maneseen Lake in the winter. Her stomach bubbled with a mixture of happiness and nerves while her eyes focused on the one-sided smile that lit Graham's face. This was hardly the ideal moment for him to propose—the tension from the meeting lingered in the room—and Audra had barely reached the conclusion that a future was possible for them.

With every emotion flitting across her face, Graham caught the panic that was brewing behind her eyes.

"I am not proposing, Audra." Was it wrong for her to be disappointed when she knew she was not ready? "When you are finally ready, you can propose to me."

Cheeky man.

"Oh, really?" Audra let out a shaky laugh, trying to regain her balance after the twist this conversation was taking and finding her footing through humor. "Quite presumptuous of you. Maybe I would deny you and have you wait forever."

"If it meant that I got to be with you, I would gladly wait. Consort, lover, call me whatever you want. My feelings for you will not change. I meant what I said to the council, when I marry you, it will be for love. You make everything in my life better. You make *me* better and I want to spend the rest of my life beside you. Easing your fears and burdens, supporting you in all your endeavors. Making you laugh, comforting you when you cry, and every moment in between. You taught me what it means to accept someone exactly as they are, even the broken pieces that we do not love about ourselves. When you enter a room, it fills with your presence and I am consumed. I kneel before you—not with an offer of marriage—but with a vow of love. I love you, Audra. And I will choose to love you even after Hellig calls me home."

A warm tear slid down her cheek and fell off the curve of her lip. Audra was smiling so hard that she thought her face might crack, but there was no stopping the expression as the love blooming in her heart tried to burst out of her. Trying to form words was pointless, every language she had learned vanished from her mind, replaced with the memory of Graham's "I love you" playing on repeat in her head.

Watching the love in his eyes dim when he took her silence as rejection jolted Audra's scrambled brain back into coherent thought. Caressing his face, Audra pressed their foreheads together.

"There was never a moment when I was not yours. Better than anyone else, you understand the deepest wishes of my heart and give me the freedom to be myself. I have known you my entire life and watched you care for your people with generosity and respect. You listen with compassion and understanding, and protect me without stifling me. Your soul matches mine. I do not need you kneeling on the ground as if I am your better. I want you by my side, equals in all things, always. I love you."

Their bodies crashed together, lips meeting feverishly. Audra's fingers dove into Graham's hair as his hands roamed across her back. Tilting her head to angle their lips better, Audra opened her mouth on a sigh. Graham pulled her bottom lip between his teeth before sweeping his tongue against hers.

It felt like she was lit from the inside with stars. Bright and luminous. Burning with need. Moaning, Audra pressed further into Graham, delighting in the feel of his hard chest against her soft skin. Her enthusiasm nearly knocked them over.

Breaking from her lips, Graham began kissing along her jawline.

"Do you. Think. We should. Move this. Somewhere. Private?" Wet kisses along her neck broke up the words.

Not wanting to separate long enough to get to one of their rooms, Audra pulled Graham back to her mouth. She would just have to show him that there was no reason for them to move. Lifting one knee, Audra tried to straddle Graham's thigh, only to get tangled in the skirt of her dress. Cursing, she started falling to the side before strong arms caught her.

"Maybe that would be better," she said with a laugh.

His face turned serious.

"I want you to know that if you change your mind, we can stop at any time. Either way, I want you to know that I take a contraceptive tonic."

Audra caressed his face. "So do I. And you can also change your mind and stop."

"Noted."

"Good. So, what are we still doing here?"

Audra laughed again as Graham hastily stood and picked her up off the ground, his rush to get them out of the room causing her laughter to follow them down the halls. At one point, Graham turned to her with a mischievous smile and a devious glint in his quicksilver eyes.

"If you have time to laugh, you are going too slow." With that, he wrapped one arm around her waist and lifted her over his shoulder. The world tilted as Audra was lifted and her laughter died in her throat as the new position gave her a close-up view of Graham's ass.

Still, she could not let him think it was that easy to keep her quiet.

"Your manners are slipping, Your Highness. This is not how you treat a queen."

She heard, rather than saw, the door to Graham's room open and close.

"My apologies," he said while sliding her down his body. Audra's dress rode up with the descent, and she hated the way the fabric prevented her from feeling every ridge of his body.

"You do not sound particularly sorry."

"No? Tell me how I can make it up to you."

His husky tone sent a shiver down her spine.

"Well, for starters, groveling is usually more successful when one is down on their knees." Smiling wickedly at him, Audra watched his face to capture the moment Graham's eyes darkened with desire as he caught on to her game.

Gracefully lowering himself to the ground, Graham gazed up at her through hooded eyes. His hands rested on his knees to mimic a pose of supplication. "Is this what you had in mind?"

"It's a start."

Graham leaned forward, his hands sliding past his knees to glide underneath Audra's skirt. At the first graze of his fingers against her skin, Audra shivered with delight, the back and forth of the pads of his fingers against her ankles causing pleasant tingles to settle in her core. Her skirt bunched over his forearms as Graham's hands circled upwards, head dipping down to kiss the spot his hands vacated.

"Forgive me," his lips murmured against her skin. Warmth followed as Graham's tongue traced a path upward. When he reached her knees, Audra leaned back against the wall, watching Graham's dark head move up her legs. One hand reached out to grasp the layers of her skirt, exposing more of her skin to Graham's questing mouth, and the other ran through his hair, clenching her fingers with each spasm of pleasure.

"Have I groveled enough yet?" Graham's face was inches from her undergarments, fingers toying with the ribbons holding them up. "No?"

He continued when Audra shook her head, untying the ribbon to pull the fabric to her ankles. "Guess I need to try harder." Each word was a warm gust of air against her center.

"G-Graham," Audra moaned his name as he pressed a closed-mouth kiss to her curls.

"You smell divine," he groaned between her thighs, pressing his nose against her skin.

"Less talking, more groveling," Audra panted, needing his mouth on her. Now. And Graham was all too happy to comply.

The first swipe of his tongue along her folds set her nerve endings tingling. It was like the sharp sensation that came when you stepped into a warm room after being out in the cold, a rush that electrified her entire body. Graham started with long licks along the outer edges, mapping her most intimate parts. His large hands pushed her legs apart, lifting one over his broad shoulder to tilt her hips closer to his mouth.

The new angle had Audra's knees buckling, and she was glad her weight was supported by Graham and the wall behind her back.

His mouth opened fully over her, flattening his tongue to slide over her in long licks. A deep hum of appreciation vibrated in his throat. "You taste so good. I want to devour you." Her body clenched around nothingness at his words.

"Yes...*oh...more.*" Full sentences were beyond Audra now. Thinking was too difficult, a haze of pleasure blocking out anything beyond the sensations Graham was creating. Pulses of red and white light flashed behind her closed eyes.

A firm nip on her inner thigh had Audra opening her eyes with a flash of indignation.

"Eyes on me." Graham's eyes were fixed firmly on her face. Desire enlarged his pupils, the thin band of gray glowing against his tanned skin. "I want you to watch as I make you come, knowing exactly who is bringing you pleasure." Without breaking her gaze, Graham placed the tip of his tongue against her bud, flicking roughly. Pleasure spiraled through Audra's body with each pass, coiling deep in her belly. It felt like the moment just before she cast a spell, the magic burning beneath her skin before she released it in a tide of sensation.

"So. Close...Please." The pleasure was so intense, yet not enough. Keeping her eyes on him, Audra chanted Graham's name, her tone begging for him to push her over the edge. She was so close, yet the peak eluded her. With a grunt, Graham eased her weight more fully onto his shoulder, freeing up his hand to stroke a finger inside her.

"Yes!" Audra's eyes rolled back in her head. This was the stimulation that was missing. Graham pumped his finger in and out several times before adding another, her body tightening around them. When he curled the fingers inside her, matching the pace of his tongue, Audra saw stars.

She shouted his name as she came, her body slumping forward as the lingering pulses faded, limbs wrung out from the force of her release. Dragging in ragged breaths, Audra watched through lidded eyes as Graham used the back of his hand to wipe his lips.

With a self-satisfied smile, he raised from the crouched position, hands around Audra's waist to keep her steady. Audra placed her hands on his chest, running over the planes of muscle while he leaned in to kiss her. A kiss far too tame for her liking. She wanted him as mindless with pleasure as she was.

Hooking one leg around Graham's waist, Audra pulled him closer. With her skirt still tucked around her waist by his hands, Audra felt the heat of him through the leather of his pants. Groaning at the contact, Graham lifted her other leg, holding her weight with his arms. Firm hands gripped her rounded backside, and Audra felt the lingering embers of her release start to build again.

Sighs and moans were lost in the tangle of lips and tongues. Audra groaned in frustration as their layers of clothing prevented her from feeling Graham's skin as she pressed her legs into his back to grind against him.

"Too. Many. Clothes." She nipped at his jaw, her sensitive lips scratching against his evening stubble.

Graham turned them towards the bed, steps steady until Audra sucked on the skin beneath his ear.

"Hells, Audra," he groaned, dumping her onto the bed before pouncing on top of her. Graham was ravenous, kissing every inch of skin he could while he worked on undoing the laces of her dress. His back was warm against Audra's hands, the muscles flexing as she worked her way down to the edge of his shirt. Working the fabric free from his pants, Audra started pulling it off.

Graham's hair was in disarray after the shirt was lifted off his body. Brushing the strands back, Audra smiled up at him. He returned the look, the glow of magelights reflected in his eyes. When he bent to kiss her, Audra lifted up to meet him halfway.

Magic tingled at her fingertips as Audra traced the muscles of Graham's back and chest. Now that she had seen him fight, Audra relished having his strong body caging hers on the bed. The thought of finally feeling the weight of him pressed against her had Audra squirming beneath Graham.

Breaking the kiss to focus on finishing unlacing her dress, Graham stared at her with barely leashed desire. Audra could see the faint glow to his eyes, his power close to the surface, and she wanted to see it unleashed. They hid nothing else from each other, and she refused to let him hide this part of himself from her.

The slide of fabric off her overly sensitive skin was a relief. Her breasts sprang free and Graham groaned in appreciation at the sight. Her hips lifted to allow the dress and undergarments to pull free and puddle onto the ground.

"You are so beautiful." Graham stood in front of her and Audra propped herself up on her elbows to watch him. He looked at her like she was the greatest gift he had ever received. Starting with her face, Graham's eyes worked their way down her body, looking at her like he could not decide which part he wanted to savor first.

When he started to lean down, Audra placed a foot on his hip and pressed him back.

"I want to see you, too."

The look he gave her was full of carnal promises.

"Never let it be said I do not give you what you want."

Long fingers went to the fastenings of his pants. With aching slowness, Graham released each fastening, hooking his thumbs in the waistband to glide the fabric down.

Audra's eyes were fixated on the movement. Nothing could distract her from this. The line of curled hair on his abdomen was a beacon to his hard length. Her core clenched as the rest of his body was revealed. The glimpse of him that she got at the inn was nothing compared to how exquisite his naked body was. She wanted to sink her teeth into the v that defined his hips and kiss each scar that marked his skin. Lust clouded her head, delirious at the thought of this man being hers.

With a predatory gleam in his eyes, Graham kneeled on the bed, bracketing Audra's legs with his. Pressing soft kisses against her hips and belly, Graham poured his love and adoration into each caress. Restless, Audra alternated between grasping his hair and smoothing her hands down his skin. Her hips bucked against his, seeking out the friction she wanted.

"Patience, Elskede. Let me savor you."

His darling. Audra had not imagined Graham calling her the affectionate title before. Hearing the word reserved for lifelong partners had her heart bursting with pleasure. Clasping his face between her hands,

Audra pulled him into a feverish kiss. He moaned into her mouth, the vibration in his chest reverberating through hers, sparking arousal from her breasts to her core. Noting her reaction, Graham began kissing and licking his way to her chest.

"Graham!" Audra cried out when his teeth pulled on one peak, his fingers teasing the other. Encouraged by her response, Graham worked his mouth and hands over her chest, pulling raspy sounds from her throat.

Mindless with pleasure, Audra wrapped her legs around Graham's waist to rub against his length. He groaned against her breast, his hips beginning to grind against her in steady motions.

"I need you." His breath was warm against her ear as he pulled the lobe between his teeth.

"Yeesss." Audra clawed at his back, trying to get him to move closer.

Raised on one arm, Graham reached over for a pillow to slide beneath Audra's hips. His eyes lowered to watch as he held himself steady and pressed into her.

Their moans merged into one as their bodies joined. With slow thrusts, Graham worked himself forward.

In and out.

Audra felt her body open for him with each advance and tried to clasp him in at each retreat. Each thrust allowed her body to stretch and accommodate his length. Above the point where their bodies were joined, Graham rubbed his thumb to increase her pleasure.

"Graham," she moaned once their hips met. Her hands linked behind his neck and she pulled his lips to hers.

His thrusts and kisses were measured, the glide of his tongue matching the movement of his hips. Audra's senses were overloaded, pleasure zipping along her skin. But, she could still tell that he had more to give.

"Don't hold back," she urged against his lips.

"Can't hurt you." His forehead rested against hers, the gray in his eyes overtaken by black. She wanted to see them glow blue.

"You won't. I can take it."

Magic pulsed against her skin and snapped into Graham.

His body shuddered with pleasure and his hips lost their rhythm for a moment. When his eyes opened to look at her, power glowed in them like heated metal.

The next snap of his hips rocked Audra backwards slightly, pleasure erupting in her core.

"Yes," she cried out.

Growling against her lips, Graham finally unleashed his full strength, surging against her in powerful motions. Audra clung onto him with her arms and legs, holding on as wave after wave of pleasure swelled. The rhythm was exquisite. His hands cradled her face, keeping her in place for his rough kisses. Audra loved watching his arms flex as he moved over her, careful not to hurt her even as he gave her what she asked for. She could feel her heart pressing against her ribs, pounding blood to her sensitive skin.

Breaking away from their kiss with a gasp, Audra panted as the pleasure mounted. Unlike the slow climb from her first orgasm, this one built like a tidal wave. Building and building until she was begging for release.

"Let go," Graham growled against her throat, moving one hand lower to rub circles above her core. "Show me how good you feel. Destroy me."

With a cry, Audra felt her body tighten. Then bliss. Pleasure rushed through her like liquid warmth. Her body clenched around Graham's, spasming around him as the pleasure subsided.

"Yes. Hells, you feel incredible. Never want to let you go." Graham's hips were moving erratically, chasing his own release. His eyes were glassy as they looked at her, pleasure clouding them as he thrust one last time. A deep moan came out his open mouth, and Audra raised her boneless arms to pull him into a kiss. Their mouths opened against each other as they worked to steady their breathing.

Collapsing on top of Audra, Graham rolled them both onto their sides. Her head rested in the curve of his shoulder, rising and falling with his breath. His heart was beating quickly beneath her ear and she pressed closer to hear it. Tracing random patterns across his chest, Audra smiled sleepily up at Graham.

His eyes were closed, one arm draped over his forehead as the other curled around her body.

"Just give me a moment and I will clean us both up." He sounded wrung out and Audra was pleased to know she was the reason for it.

Pleasure made her body soft and sated, Audra's muscles practically melting into the bed as Graham stood and retrieved warm cloths to clean them up. Laughing at her sluggish movements, Graham tucked her against his chest to lower the blankets before settling them both underneath. Using his arm as a pillow, Audra snuggled into Graham's side.

"I love you, Graham."

"I love you, Audra."

Twenty-Seven

"I have been thinking," Audra said over the paper she was reading. After a few pleasure-filled days spent primarily in bed— although Graham was clever with his use of other furniture and the large tub in his room—they had agreed it was time to return to their responsibilities. Especially now that a letter from Leah had arrived.

"Hmm?" Graham raised his head from where it rested between pillows. The sight of his sleep-rumpled form was almost enough to tempt Audra to join him.

Unfortunately, the situation with Leon was no better than Avery. Well liked and respected, Leon was traveling throughout Feldor when he disappeared. Leah and Maxim were able to interview several people who last saw Leon and their stories matched. They had not seen anyone suspicious hanging around and Leon was not acting out of the ordinary. He was on his way to assist a farmer with diseased crops and when Leon never arrived, the farmer went looking for him, worried about his safety. The farmer was able to take Leah to the location where she found Leon's abandoned cart, the horse set free. Leah could detect the lingering note of Leon's rainwater tinged magic that permeated a section of the ground near the cart. She also found several scratch-marks and broken tree branches that were evidence of an attack, likely another netvor.

The death of another mage chilled the happiness that surrounded Audra the past few days. Crumpling the paper in her hand, the edges turned to ash as she burned the letter. She could not make sense of the deaths. Anti-mage groups were still vocal in their protests, but those groups took pride in their attacks and often struck out in large crowds. Also, the threat of punishment in light of the new laws protecting mages had deterred much physical violence. If one of those groups was responsible, why would they eliminate any evidence of the attack? And why did the netvor appear in those locations too? There was no mention of a monster sighted where Leon was killed, but Leah did report sensing an acrid thread of magic that led away from the scene. She followed it for several miles, but eventually lost the trail.

Before she lost the connection, Leah noticed that it followed a path that would lead to Ymira.

"It is time for me to return to Ymira."

At the mention of home, Isik cracked open his eyes from where he was curled on the end of the bed. Graham had tried—largely as a matter of principle—to stop Isik from sleeping on the bed, but he was no match for the cunning creature. He would settle Isik onto a cushion on the floor and the fox would pretend to sleep until he knew that Graham drifted off. Then, Audra would feel the pressure of Isik jumping onto the bed before curling up on Graham's feet. Each morning, Graham would grumble about beds being no place for pets before scratching between the fox's ears.

"I agree," Graham said while rolling to get up. In the process, he dislodged Isik from his feet, earning a glare from the fox. Audra watched as both exited the bed, Isik trotting out the door in search of breakfast while Graham strode toward the table she was sitting at. "Your people will have questions about Avery and Leon, and without finding more answers here, the best thing is for us to go to Ymira and see what piece of this puzzle we are missing."

"We?" Audra raised a brow at Graham. She did not want to presume that he would join her, worried that their royal duties would get in the way of their budding relationship. As much as Audra wanted to show Graham her home, she knew that he had responsibilities to his own people.

"Did you think that I would want to leave your side? If you want me there, I would love to see your kingdom and your people." Picking her up, Graham sat in the chair with Audra in his lap. She adored the way he needed to constantly touch her. Whether it was holding her hand while they ate or sitting with her feet in his lap while they read, Graham was always connected to her. After years of separation, Graham said that he never wanted to take a single moment together for granted. She also suspected that after the news of another mage's death, he was reassuring himself that she was safe.

"Besides..." He nipped along the junction where her shoulder met her neck. "...if Ymira is going to be my home soon, I should prove that I have more to offer as your consort than just my handsome face."

Audra twisted on his lap so that she could face him, smirking when he groaned as she wiggled over his hard length. "Feeling that confident, are you?"

"That I will love you forever? Definitely." He pressed a lingering kiss on her lips.

"What about Solven and your people?"

"The people still have my father—Hellig willing—for many more years. I would never ask you to give up Ymira to be my queen, but I do not think that would be necessary anyways. When the time comes, you can continue to lead Ymira while I lead Solven, supporting each other as partners and allies. Or, if you do not like that idea, Kasteel or little Diana can take over the throne of Solven. They would lead with wisdom and strength."

"You would give up your throne for me?" Fathomless gray eyes, filled with love, met her gaze.

"No kingdom is worth having without you in it."

Pouring her love into a kiss, Audra tugged Graham's head back to bite and suck on his lips. His hands clenched against the thin fabric of her robe, the material parting as the tie loosened.

"Hells, Audra," Graham groaned into her neck when his hands found the naked skin beneath her robe.

Honestly, she did not know why he was surprised to find her naked beneath the robe. Clothes were pointless when they spent more time with them off than on. Graham was gloriously naked beneath her, not bothering to put on anything after rising from the bed.

Lifting to her knees, Audra gently lowered herself onto Graham. Sometimes, they connected with intensity. Rough touches and frantic motions, pushing to see how fast they could reach the edge before plummeting over. Other times, they prolonged the pleasure, pulling away just before they reached the peak, over and over again until Audra was mindless with desire. This time, their bodies rocked together gently, gradually allowing the pleasure to build.

Hands stroked over bare skin. Mouths opened on sighs breathed into each other. This time felt like coming home. Like slipping into the truest version of yourself knowing that you were safe in each other's arms. Audra slid into the sensations, feeling every touch and kiss reach her heart before expanding out.

When she finally went over the peak, Audra collapsed against Graham's chest, kissing the skin above his heart as he found his own release. They were content to bask in each other's arms for quiet moments, breathing in and out together to calm their racing hearts.

"Come with me, Graham."

"Anywhere, Elskede. Anywhere."

After cleaning up from their morning together, Graham drew a bath for her, kissing Audra on the forehead before leaving to discuss his departure with his family. As a guest and ruler of her own kingdom, Audra was free to leave whenever she wanted, but Graham needed to go over what his departure would mean for Solven. He would not be able to stay in Ymira long, a few weeks at most, but it was a start. Audra could finalize the details of the treaty from Rauha, but there were several points she wanted to talk with Keld about while she was here, in addition to providing him with enchanted paper to contact her. Once that was settled, she and Graham could depart.

Audra let the tension in her muscles relax in the warm water around her, bubbles floating along the top. Swirling her hand through the sudsy foam, Audra smiled in contentment. She was leaving Solven for Ymira again, but this time she was taking Graham with her. Just thinking about how he loved her and never wanted to be parted again sent a rush of warmth through her body. It took every ounce of restraint to not shout from the rooftops that Graham chose her, that was how happy she was. Their path together had not been easy, nor would the road be smooth ahead, but Audra was confident that they would face whatever challenges came their way together.

Showing Graham all the places that made her home special was something to look forward to in the midst of searching for new clues about the attacks. The weather was spectacular at this time of year, the sun casting brilliant light over the trees and lake, making them shine. By day, they could explore the land, hiking through the hills and visiting the townspeople, and by night they could curl up in Rauha Hall or venture to the hot springs.

Images of glistening water droplets running down Graham's body, reflected in the pool's water, sent a shiver down Audra's spine. As she discovered in his room, Graham was quite creative with water. It would be fun to see what was possible in the hot spring.

Trying to cool her thoughts, Audra dipped below the water's surface, submerging herself in the tub.

A sharp jolt of her magic had her heart skip a beat. Someone had crossed her ward.

Grasping the edges of the tub, Audra attempted to pull herself out of the water.

Something pressed down on her head, keeping her below the surface. Panicking, Audra thrashed against the weight, her hands slipping off the tub. Her heart pounded in her ears, the adrenaline spiking and causing her thoughts to spiral.

Think. She had to think. If she panicked much longer, she would drown.

Another hand came to her throat, squeezing in an attempt to get her to breathe in water. Clawing at the hand to remove it, Audra felt her strength waning. Her lungs burned from the need to breathe, and her head pounded from the lack of oxygen.

No. She was not going to die in a bathtub at the hands of some would-be assassin. Not today. Not after everything she had worked for and still wanted to accomplish.

Grasping the wrist of her assailant, Audra let her magic heat her palm, burning through the leather glove to the skin beneath her hand. The moment the assailant's hands wretched away from her in pain, Audra shot to the surface. Gasping in lungfuls of air, she hastily wiped water and hair away from her eyes, turning towards the attacker.

Dressed in all black—Leah would mock them for predictability—the figure stood taller than Audra, and from what she could tell from their padded-leather clothing, were quite muscular. Thinking that their stature would slow them down was a mistake, one Audra could not afford to make. Her brain was already fuzzy and her reactions delayed from the time spent underwater. Burning the individual had delayed further attack, but that would not last long. Behind a black mask with unrecognizable markings, pale blue eyes glared at her, calculating painful ways to return the injury.

Exiting the tub as quickly as she could with shaking limbs, Audra shot a blast of magic at the person, hoping to push them back and give her time to move further away to think before they attacked again. When the magic should have hit the individual straight in the chest, it dispersed across the leather instead.

Cursing, Audra realized the armor was not leather at all, but instead was the hide of a netvor. That eliminated her ability to attack from a distance. Based on the wound she was able to inflict, only the thicker parts of the padding were made of the hide, leaving smaller quantities of skin susceptible to her magic. Without another weapon handy, Audra would have to work with that. Orienting herself in a room that was still hazy at the edges was difficult, and Audra barely had time to throw up a shield as a dagger came at her.

She was not as fortunate to avoid the body that lunged at her while she was blocking the dagger. The impact knocked them both to the ground, jarring Audra's shoulder with pain that had her gritting her teeth. Remembering the training from Graham, Audra rammed her knee between the attacker's legs.

A low grunt of pain came from behind the mask. While they were momentarily distracted, Audra scrambled to get out from beneath them. Lifting her hand to the tub, Audra created a ball of water.

"Let's see how you like it," she said as the ball enveloped the assassin's face.

They clawed at the water, trying to create a pathway for air, but it was no use. Audra kept the water rotating. Whoever hired this assassin underestimated her talent. Although they initially surprised her—the hide allowing them past her ward nearly undetected—it was Audra's turn to go on the offensive. Magic could not penetrate the hide directly, but that would not stop objects manipulated by magic.

Realizing that their efforts were futile, the assassin changed tactics. With impressive speed, considering their loss of airflow, they reached for another dagger and threw it toward Audra. It was enough of a distraction for Audra's control over the water to falter. They managed to get free, but Audra knew that their movements would be hindered by the recent lack of oxygen.

Reaching out her magic like a whip, Audra hooked the assassin's ankles and pulled. Hard. Disoriented by the rush of oxygen entering their lungs, they were powerless to stop their descent, crashing to the ground with a thud. Not wasting her advantage, Audra leapt onto their prone body, using the attacker's dagger to slice at the protective armor. She was able to get through one of the arm braces before the body beneath her began bucking, attempting to dislodge her. Now that the hide was gone, Audra was able to use magic to pin their exposed arm to the ground, trapping one of the limbs fighting against her. Their superior strength was a problem, and Audra struggled to pin the remaining arm with one knee while the other dug into the assassin's hip as she cut at the remaining brace.

Hellig only knew what she looked like, dripping wet over the black clad body.

Once she had the assassin successfully pinned, Audra sat back, breathing heavily from the fading adrenaline and exertion. Ripping off the mask, Audra marveled at the overwhelming hatred that marred the features of the man in front of her. White hair pulled in a severe widow's peak above a strong brow. Those pale blue eyes that glared at her with hatred were now fuming.

"Witch," he spat at her.

Wiping her face, Audra made a sound of disgust. "Call me what you like, but at least I have manners."

Rising to her feet, ensuring that her knees pressed into delicate areas firmly, Audra checked to ensure the binds would hold.

"Now, since you decided to interrupt my morning, I am going to get dressed. Then, you and I are going to have a little chat."

She was tucking her shirt into a pair of pants when Graham burst into the room, daggers drawn.

"Graham!" Her heartbeat raced at the thought that someone might have attacked him too. "Is everything okay?"

"That is what I came to ask you. I was with my parents when Isik burst into the room, barking and pulling on my boots until I followed him. I was worried that something happened to you."

A white blur bumped into her, nuzzling against her legs and sniffing to make sure Audra was uninjured. Her sweet, loving companion. Isik must have heard Audra's distressed cries and been unable to get past the closed doors.

"Someone tried to kill me." Graham halted where he was, a murderous gleam in his eyes. "But I am relatively unharmed. My attacker is currently tied up in the bathroom, waiting to talk about why he is here. No one attacks me and gets away with it."

After petting Isik between his ears to reassure him that everything was alright, and thanking him for getting help, Audra stepped into Graham's open arms. They held each other close, and Audra breathed in the scent of forest and cinnamon that made her feel safe. She could take care of herself, but knowing that something could happen to either of them meant that each opportunity to be close was precious.

"Foolish of them to underestimate the High Mage of Ymira." Graham pressed his lips against hers. "I will destroy anyone who tries to hurt you. Whoever sent them will wish they never set their eyes on you."

Waving him forward, Audra turned in the direction of the bathroom. "Shall we go find out where your wrath is targeted?"

"After you."

<hr>

Audra was really starting to hate this room. Every time she was invited to the king's council chamber, it ended in venomous words spewed at her and ridiculous disagreements over petty grievances. When it came time to sign the final version of the treaty, Audra would insist that it take place in a different room, perhaps even outside Solven altogether. At least if they met in Ymira, she would not have to look at the beady-eyed man striding into the room.

Lord Nadeen.

A thorn in her side that Audra looked forward to removing.

"Your Highness." He bowed to Graham, flicking a quick glance in Audra's direction. Seated beside Graham, Audra watched as Lord Nadeen took in the empty seats around the table. "I was informed that this was a closed meeting. Where is everyone?"

"On their way." As if Graham's voice summoned them, the other members of the council began trickling in, taking their seats along the table.

Once everyone was seated, Keld walked into the room. When the council members looked toward their king and inquired what the meaning of the summons was, Keld gestured at Graham.

"I called you all together at the behest of Prince Graham. He will lead the meeting."

Nodding his thanks, Graham rose from his chair.

"Thank you all for coming. I asked you here to discuss a grievous matter that was brought to my attention. Something that threatens the stability of Solven."

"I do not think it wise to discuss matters of the kingdom in front of an outsider, Your Highness." Lord Nadeen looked at Audra pointedly.

"Of course you do not, you sanctimonious prick."

Several of the council members had to smother their laughter behind ill-disguised coughs while others gasped at the prince's tone. Pushed past the point of politeness, Graham was unafraid to show them his wrath. While he would not abuse his power, Graham was using this opportunity to remind the council that he was the future king and had earned the respect and deference that came with the position

"How convenient," he spoke directly to Lord Nadeen, "that you continually forget that Lady Audra was born and raised here. She saved the lives of people in Nebura and mages from Ymira have provided aid to Solven's citizens for years now. Time and time again, she has proved her love for our people and dedication to making an alliance work. Yet you persist in your attempts to degrade and insult her. Why?"

The calm, practiced mask that Lord Nadeen typically wore was peeled away with each of Graham's accusations.

"Because her kind does not belong here. The council has grown concerned over your actions of late, Your Highness." A pointed glance in Audra's direction left no question as to what actions the council had problems with. "We said nothing when she seduced you into her bed, but we can hold our tongues no longer. Allowing her into council meetings, sharing plans for the kingdom with her, it has become clear that she clouds your judgment. "

As frequently as Lord Nadeen was using the plural, he should have been paying better attention to the atmosphere in the room. Council members seated near him were subtly edging away from him, and even those who were his greatest supporters were avoiding his eye. Whether they agreed with him or not, they were not going to publicly side with him against the prince.

"I would choose your next words wisely counselor." An undercurrent of steel ran through the polite tone of Graham's warning, his arms braced against the table. Audra watched the subtle tightening of his biceps, poised to defend.

"You would threaten me? Over this *witch*. " Venom dripped from each word out of Lord Nadeen's lips.

Fast as lighting, Graham's arm shot out, releasing a curved dagger into Lord Nadeen's shoulder. His pained cry when Graham pulled on the attached chain sent a swell of grim satisfaction through Audra.

"Let me make myself painfully clear," Graham spoke as he stood. Each step echoed loudly in the quiet room as he circled the table, stopping behind Lord Nadeen. "That *witch*," he spat out the offensive word, "is the High Mage of Ymira, and you should feel lucky to stand in her presence. If there was any seduction, I was a willing participant. I gladly welcome her to my bed, my heart, and if she will have me, my crown. Audra is compassionate, loyal, brave." Bracing his weight on the lord's injured shoulder, Graham bent over to whisper the next word directly in his ear, "And I should end your miserable existence for suggesting otherwise."

"Please, Your Highness, I only ever meant to protect the kingdom from her wickedness. Protect you. Forgive me, Your Highness." Lord Nadeen's voice shook as he breathed around the pain.

"Don't apologize to me. Apologize to Audra."

"Forgive me, Lady Audra."

Graham twisted the dagger further into his skin. "Mean it."

Lord Nadeen's eyes were glazed with pain and fear. A wild urgency in his voice as he realized that the next misspoken word could be his last. "Please forgive me, Lady Audra. I was wrong. You will make an excellent queen. I remember when you were a young girl, always kind and pleasant. Surely you can forgive an old man for his mistake?"

"I am not so unfeeling that I cannot forgive a mistake." Audra used a thread of magic to pull the dagger free, watching Lord Nadeen sag in relief as it clattered against the table. "But, this was not the first mistake you made. No, your first mistake was your treatment of me and my people. Without ever meeting us, you treated us with disgust and disdain. As if our existence is worth less than yours."

Audra allowed her magic to fill the room, its weight almost suffocating. The remaining council members shrunk in their seats, trying to present as small a target as possible.

"Worth so little that I was better off dead. Tell me, Lord Nadeen, should I forgive that?"

He began protesting, babbling around the pain about how he knew nothing of what she was talking about. That he would never do anything to hurt her. A few voices questioned Audra's statement.

"Would you like to tell them, or should I?" Graham leaned over Lord Nadeen, not giving him a chance to reply as he pressed his fingers against the wound, blood seeping to the table. "This morning, an assassin attacked Lady Audra on the authority of Lord Nadeen. I interrogated him myself and what I learned he planned to do is too deplorable to repeat. Luckily for him, Lady Audra was more merciful."

Eyes wild with fear, Lord Nadeen frantically searched for an ally at the table. Desperately, he blubbered about making a mistake, that he thought he was doing what was right for the kingdom. Hoping to spare himself from a worse fate by confessing his guilt, Lord Nadeed was digging himself a shallow grave. One by one, each council member turned away from him. When his gaze landed on the king, Keld was unflinching.

"Please, Your Majesty," Lord Nadeen begged.

Keld shook his head.

"Our laws are clear. You sought to end Lady Audra's life out of malice, and the council will decide your fate."

Nodding to his left, Keld instructed Noble River to begin the vote.

"The punishment for murder is death. While the attempt was not by your own hand..." River's face was grave. "...hiring an assassin makes you equally as guilty. The council has heard your admission of guilt in your own words and will judge you accordingly."

One by one, the council voted, Lord Nadeen turning pale with each response.

Solemn, Noble River clasped their hands together on the table and faced the king. "Your Majesty, as you have heard, the council is in agreement to sentence Lord Nadeen to death."

Heavy silence filled the room, the weight of the decision striking Lord Nadeen harder than any blow. He writhed in his chair, sobbing as he begged for clemency.

"You chose this path for yourself with your actions," Keld said. "Lady Audra, should you wish, since the attempt was made on your life, the manner of his death is your choice."

A decision that Audra did not take lightly. Graham met her eyes over Lord Nadeen's head, unconditional love and support shining in his eyes. When Graham caught the direction of her gaze, understanding what she intended to do, his mouth twisted into a cruel smile—one that should have terrified her, but instead made her glad that he was on her side.

Audra's voice was steady as she delivered the final words Lord Nadeen would hear.

"People like you only care about yourselves and what power you can gain. And you will do anything to maintain your power, including hate and kill anyone that gets in your way. Call me a witch. Call me evil. Call me whatever you want. But the real monster here is you, and I will always protect my people from the likes of you."

Eyes locked firmly on Lord Nadeen's, Audra raised the dagger off the table with magic, ruby red blood glistening on the blade. Restrained by the weight of Graham's grip, Lord Nadeen thrashed against Graham's hold as he fought to escape his fate. But Graham was unyielding, pressing the man into the chair as the blade found its mark.

Blood bloomed on his shirt, right below his heart. Audra watched as the life drained from Lord Nadeen's eyes just as blood flowed from his chest. With a sharp movement, Graham pulled his dagger free, wiping it clean against the dead lord's shirt. Now that there was nothing keeping it up, the body slumped against the table with a thud.

The other council members sat, transfixed, in their seats. None of them dared speak after witnessing such a display.

"In case that was not painfully obvious," Graham returned to his chair, staring down each member of the council, "let me make myself perfectly clear. The mages of Ymira have the full rights of an alliance. Any actions taken against them are considered an act against Solven itself, and I do not tolerate threats against those I love. Treat them with respect, and you have nothing to fear. But if you harbor resentment or ill-will towards them for a gift at birth, then you have the choice to either get over it or get out."

No one moved. Minutes ticked by and Audra watched as each council member looked at her before bowing their heads in respect. It was hard earned, and Audra knew many of them gave it out of fear, but it was another step forward.

"Good." Graham nodded to the group. "Now, I have a kingdom to visit."

Twenty-Eight

"That must be some book you are reading," Audra spoke from her side of the carriage, the gentle motion rocking her and Graham side to side.

Graham looked up in surprise, so immersed in the book that he had not registered what she had said. Just like when they were younger, he made an adorable face when he was concentrating on something that puzzled him. His mouth was set in a firm line with a finger rubbing over his clean-shaven upper lip.

"Hmmm," he murmured when Audra repeated her question, his thoughts still half-focused on whatever he had read. "It is the one you lent me. I was hoping that it might shed some light on the netvor."

Turning the book so that the cover was facing Audra, she saw that it was, in fact, Safrina's journal. Having read it several times herself, she lent it to Graham in the hope that he would glean something out of it that she had never noticed. Though Safrina wrote about discovering Dyrun with the first known netvor, it was the only mention of the creatures in the journal. Some of the original written volumes from Guards—including second-hand accounts from Queen Bria—mentioned that a few mages helped detect what caused the physical manifestations of netvor, but otherwise it was widely accepted that mages were not involved in fighting them due to magical incompatibility.

Audra told Graham as much.

"Which is understandable," Graham said with a nod. "It would be a risk to go after something you could not fight against. But, I was hoping that Safrina would have mentioned how Dyrun was able to create the netvor. This is the closest anyone ever was to the first appearance of them, yet she does not go into any details about how his magic was able to create it. What magic could be powerful enough to continue to corrupt people years after his defeat? If we knew that, maybe it would explain why the new netvor are different."

When he put it that way, it was strange that Safrina and Pennifrin—nor any mages after them to Audra's knowledge—had studied how magic was used to create the monsters. Was no one curious? Logically, having the knowledge would enable them to teach generations of mages what to avoid so that they did not create something worse. Or, was that the point? To keep the knowledge hidden so that no one attempted it again.

Her blood froze when she realized what Graham suspected.

"You think someone, a mage, is creating the new netvor."

Graham's gaze was unflinching, calm resolve settled over his features. "I do. Hundreds of years without change, yet now, when you are working to bring mages out of hiding, the netvor are different than before. That cannot be a coincidence."

Shocked, Audra could only stare at Graham, her brain shifting through thoughts faster than she could process. Trying to make sense of what he said.

"But...what we have been doing is for the good of all mages. Improving our place in the kingdoms. Preventing violence against us. Discrediting rumors of our practices. Creating new netvor would only instill further fear and mistrust. Why would someone do that if it would make things worse for mages?"

He was right though, only magic could be changing the netvor. The evil that lurked in people's hearts was nothing new. But powerful magic had recently made its way back into the kingdoms. Had she inadvertently allowed a new source of evil into the world?

"Was there anyone who opposed your plans for mages? Or, someone who was overly eager to get out of Ymira?"

Quiet filled the carriage while Audra thought, the sounds of the forest muffled through the walls. Sunlight filtered through the trees, casting shaded patterns on their faces and the interior of the carriage. With the direction their conversation was taking, Audra's eyes began to trick her and turned the shadows into sinister shapes. As if the discovery of where the netvor were coming from would summon them instantaneously.

"There were a few that were hesitant to change, but not overly so, and no one was ever forced to remain in Ymira. Even when the wards were stricter, no one was a prisoner. If someone wanted to leave, they could, but the risks of leaving were not worth it."

Leaning forward to rest his forearms on his knees, Graham mulled over the new details. "Something must have changed after more mages began leaving Ymira. Even Dyrun took a few years to show his true colors. What was it that Safrina wrote?"

He flipped through the journal, searching for the passage.

"He speaks of our superiority over others, that Hellig gave us magic because we are better and we should not waste our gifts," he read aloud. "Dyrun has begun talking of how the world would be much improved—"

"—if mages ruled everything," Audra finished for Graham.

She felt the blood draining from her face in alarm. Her pulse beat furiously in her neck, and her eyes widened with alarm.

"Graham." Audra's voice was barely a whisper, not wanting to give voice to the words. "If Dyrun created the netvor as a means to control the kingdoms, that means—"

An ear-splitting screech rent the air moments before the top of the carriage was ripped off. Shards of wood flew through the air, buffeted by wind. Graham launched himself across the seat, moving to cover Audra and Isik from the projectiles. Caught by surprise, Audra raised a shield to protect them, but was too slow to deflect everything. Several pieces scratched their skin and clothing, a thicker piece piercing Graham's arm. With a hiss of pain, Graham pulled out the sliver of wood and crouched in front of Audra so that she was still protected while he took in their surroundings.

With the roof gone, Audra could see the canopy of trees above them. Remnants of wood fell through the air, and she kept the shield up to protect them and the horses. The forest around them was deathly quiet, any animals within the area silenced by the presence of a predator. Even the air felt still, as if nature was hesitant to breathe, lest it draw attention from the attacker.

Searching the tops of the trees and what patches of sky she could see, Audra tried to locate what had found them. Isik growled in her lap, and Audra wrapped her arms around him to keep him from darting into danger.

"When I say run, get to the tree line as fast as you can," Graham spoke in a low voice. "Whatever the hell that was, it has wings. We'll have an advantage with coverage."

The soft boom of wingbeats was the only warning they got before the creature dived towards the open carriage.

"Now," Graham yelled, throwing a dagger at the netvor.

Audra leapt out of the open door, pumping her legs to cross the distance to the trees while she held Isik. Somehow, the netvor had known exactly where to attack them. This part of the path was closer to the edge of the forest, and the trees had wider gaps between them, allowing its large, webbed wings adequate space to maneuver. Setting down her fox, Audra wrapped her magic around Isik, binding his legs so that he could not chase her into danger. Barking and thrashing against the binding, Isik was furious, but Audra was willing to live with his anger if it meant keeping him safe. So long as she had enough magic to restrain him, her beloved Isik would be unable to escape the binding.

Turning away from the fox, Audra looked for the winged beast and thrust a pulse of magic towards the creature, pausing its descent long enough to give Graham a chance to dive out of the carriage. Creating an arc-like thread of magic, Audra separated the horses from the carriage, urging them to get as far away as possible.

Halfway to her, Graham stopped and turned, swinging the chain of one dagger in his hand to build momentum before sending it flying towards the netvor. With impressive coordination, the creature tucked its wings and spiraled out of the way. Skin the color of a decaying corpse covered the creature's large body and round head. The wings, with sharp talons at the tips, protruded from an angular torso, two hooked legs with razor-sharp claws extending out from the body.

Rows of sharp teeth flashed menacingly as the netvor released another screech. Its voice alone was nearly debilitating and Audra's ears rang from the noise, her head dizzy. With his enhanced physiology, Graham was faring better, but Audra was not taking any chances with their safety. Tossing up shields around both of them, Audra knew Graham was grateful even if he did not take his glowing eyes off the blood-red eyes of the netvor.

Audra watched as it took off into the sky, weaving between several tall trees as camouflage. Taking advantage of the brief respite, Graham made his way to Audra.

"You okay?" Beyond the gash from the wood, Audra did not see any damage beyond scratches to his leather armor.

"Yeah. You?" She nodded. A few splinters nicked her skin, but it was minor. "What's our strategy?"

"Give it hell. It has the advantage in the air, so we need to focus on bringing it down. My daggers have enough reach, but it's fast for something so large."

"But you can be faster." Since discovering magic could enhance Graham's abilities, they had practiced together as often as they could. Audra hoped it was enough. Especially since their last attempt at fighting together had led to them getting in each other's way more often than supporting each other.

"Be safe." He pressed a too short kiss to her lips. "I love you."

"Forever," she replied.

Pushing magic to the edges of her fingers, Audra took a ready stance near Graham. Far enough to separate themselves as targets, but close enough to protect each other.

A crash sounded behind them as the ugly head of the netvor barreled out of the trees. Graham spun, dagger already flying towards its target. As the creature turned, Audra was there, vines shooting out to wrap about one of its legs. Thorns dug into the creature's leg, drops of blood flying as talons ripped off the vines.

As the vines fell to the ground, Graham was ready with his daggers, throwing them in rapid succession while the creature recovered. Slowed, but still incredibly agile, the netvor dove and weaved to avoid getting caught in the daggers' path. Several lines marred the creature's body where it was grazed.

Shrieking in anger, it dove again, separating Audra from Graham as she leapt out of the way. Audra felt the air move above her head, stirring her hair as she narrowly avoided injury. The earth was soft beneath her body as she crashed to the ground, leaves cracking and twigs snapping against her side. Rolling to face them, Audra saw the netvor dive at Graham, clawed feet extended.

Magic poured from her into Graham's body. Lightning fast, Graham tossed both daggers before sliding under the netvor. Metal pierced flesh and the creature cried out in pain. In a kneeling lunge, Graham pulled on the daggers' chains, dragging the creature to the ground with a thud.

"Well, now that is a neat trick," a velvety voice spoke behind her.

Audra froze, the scent of rotting citrus faint amongst the fresh scents of the forest.

No. This was impossible. The cry of the netvor must have damaged her hearing. That was the only explanation why she would hear that voice again.

In the distance, Graham was pulled from the ground by a sharp yank of the creature's wings. But here, in the corner of her vision, Audra saw a pair of boots walking towards her. Lifting her gaze, Audra followed the line of expertly crafted clothes to the soulless black eyes set against a sallow face.

"Silvan? But you died." Her heart ached at the memory of seeing the bloody clothing. His death haunted her dreams.

"Is that any way to greet an old friend? I thought you taught us better manners than that." The smile was pure Silvan, pulling the corners of his lips to reveal a set of pearl-white teeth. But Audra could now see the strain of it, the forced sincerity. How it was just a touch too wide to be natural, lacking any warmth.

Hesitant to take the hand he was offering, Audra stood on her own. "You will have to excuse me, greeting the deceased was never covered in an etiquette book." Regarding Silvan warily, Audra thought about how she could put more distance between them while she figured out what was going on. She had to trust that Graham was managing the netvor, her own focus on the threat in front of her.

"How is this possible? We saw the body, we mourned you."

He cocked his head with a mocking smile. "Did you though?"

Audra thought back to the attack on Ymira. They had found a body near the portion of the ward where Silvan was patrolling. Damaged beyond recognition, the lingering notes of Silvan's magic—combined with the clothing and location—had been enough evidence for Audra and Eli to determine it was their friend. Looking back on it, the damage that she thought was caused by the netvor could have been used to disguise the true identity. But no other mages were reported missing. Where could he have—

"The boy," Audra gasped. The one from Kalmere who Silvan had claimed wanted to leave. "You killed him!"

"I made him useful," Silvan corrected, gesturing with his hands. Without his usual polish on, Audra could see the black nails on his fingers. One of the signs of netvor corruption. "You were hardly going to let me leave Ymira without supervision. His loss was for the benefit of all mages."

"Is that what you tell yourself to sleep at night?" Audra laughed mirthlessly, gathering magic around her. "That killing that boy and others in Ymira was your way of helping us? I suppose you think that killing Avery and Leon was for their benefit too?" Silvan had to be the one responsible for their deaths. The timelines matched.

To know that mages were attacked and killed by one of their own enraged Audra. Once, Silvan had been a protector at the wards, dedicated to keeping Ymira safe. His treachery would not go unpunished. She struck out with a blast of magic, which Silvan deflected with his own. They danced around each other for several minutes, volleying attacks and defending in turn. Sparks of light flashed where their magic met.

Silvan's movements were as fluid as ever, precise and deadly. But Audra expected that. Protectors at the wards were always the best fighters. What Audra had not expected was the power behind his strikes. It was far more than she had ever seen from him. Had he been holding back when they knew each other, or was something more nefarious at play?

"Narrow-minded as usual," Silvan taunted. "So focused on your precious treaty that you failed to see the bigger picture. You weren't willing to sacrifice to reach our goals, but I was."

He launched himself at Audra with a flurry of attacks that had her backing up, every ounce of concentration spent keeping him at bay.

"Those were people's lives, Silvan! They made the sacrifice, not you. What purpose could their deaths serve, to create the netvor?"

It was the missing piece of the puzzle. The unanswered question.

"No, those were an unintended bonus. I killed them for power." Silvan looked deranged, eyes wild with madness. "The only way to get more power, more magic, is to take it. When they were unwilling to join me, I found another use for them, by taking their magic to enhance my own. Unfortunately, killing tends to taint one's soul, but when I sensed the dark magic trying to consume me, I released it, channeling it to create netvor just as Dyrun did. Mine are superior, don't you think? I look forward to seeing what monster I create after draining you."

That had to be the reason Silvan was so powerful, and why they were unable to find Avery and Leon's bodies. Now Audra realized what the residual magic in the cave reminded her of. Like Annika, mages drained of their powers faded back into the earth, leaving behind a remnant of magic.

Digging her feet into the ground, Audra leveled Silvan with a glare. As if she would let him kill her. He needed to be stopped before he hurt anyone else.

Circling each other, Audra and Silvan sent raw magic, as well as crafted weapons, at each other. Bark and branches were torn from trees as spears, rocks flying as deadly projectiles.

One struck, the other deflected. Again and again.

They were both breathing heavily, sweat matting their hair as energy buzzed around them. Each had landed several blows, but nothing fatal. Audra knew that it would come down to cunning and creativity, since they were both evenly matched. Preparing to use fallen leaves to slice Silvan like knives, Audra was raising her hand when she heard the cry.

Turning, she saw the netvor's teeth sink into Graham's arm, drawing blood and crushing his bones.

"No!" Audra screamed, sending the leaves towards the monster instead. She saw Graham clutch his bloody arm with the other, only one dagger around his wrist. Leaves tore into flesh where they met their marks. Audra started to run towards Graham, her instinct to protect him at the forefront, when a force struck her back.

Gasping out in pain, Audra hit the ground. Her back burned. It was careless to forget her enemy. Gritting her teeth, Audra urged her bruised body to get up, arms bent at her side, attempting to push up when another blast hit her.

This time, her scream rent the air. It felt like her entire body was prodded by a hot poker. She tried to escape the pain by curling into herself, but weight pressed her down into the dirt. Twigs poked at her cheeks and Audra had to keep her head turned at an odd angle to see.

"How touching. Reconnected with your one true love. Too bad it couldn't last." Silvan's knees dug into Audra's arms, pinning her to the ground while his weight rested on her back. "At least you can die together. I'll even let you choose." Black-tipped hands wretched her head forward, and tears swam in Audra's eyes. Now she could see Graham fighting against the netvor with one arm. Both were injured, blood streaming from their wounds.

"Would you like to watch as my pet kills your beloved prince before I drain you of your power, or would you like to be the first to go?"

Audra sobbed, her tears hitting the dirt in wet splotches. Filled with despair, Audra could only hope that Silvan would listen to reason. Somewhere inside him was still her friend. The person she danced with in the converted dining room in Rauha and plotted strategy over wine. Eli's best friend. "Silvan, please. Think about our friends. It isn't too late to stop. Killing us will only bring the might of Solven, Feldor, and Ymira down on your head."

The pressure on her back lessened momentarily at the mention of their friends, but before Audra could take a full breath, Silvan sent another electric shock of magic through her. "And I will kill anyone who gets in my way. Don't you understand, I am doing this *for* mages. No one will ever hurt us again once I make sure we rule over everything."

There was no shred of her friend left. Completely consumed by dark magic, there was no reasoning with Silvan.

"So you protect mages by killing them? You are deranged."

"I knew you would never understand. It's unavoidable. I need more power to protect them—to go against Kalmere and anyone else who would hurt us—and the only way to get more power is to take it. You were too weak to see that, but in the end, it will all be worth it."

Audra thrashed against the hold he had on her. Pinned as she was, her magic had limited mobility and she was unable to manipulate it well enough to free herself. Panic set in as she felt a hand against her back. Fire filled her veins as Audra felt her magic being pulled towards Silvan, burning like he was dragging a knife across her skin.

She fought against crying out, biting her lip hard enough to draw blood. She would not give him the satisfaction of her pain. In vain, Audra kicked and arched her back to try and get free, her body weakening with the slow drain of magic. Nothing she had experienced before felt like this, her very life-force pulling from her body. Like ripping apart seams from clothing, Audra felt the snap and tear of each tendril of magic.

Despite the soul-wrenching agony, her eyes never left Graham.

If this was how she was going to die, Audra wanted her last sight to be him. Maybe, even if she did not make it, he would. That hope was all she had left. Her fingers and toes were desensitized, and Audra knew that soon her whole body would be numb, shutting down as life was pulled from her.

Graham's movements were frantic, slashing at the creature while attempting to move back towards Audra. Even injured, he worked to defend her. In a brief moment where he had pushed off the creature long enough to make eye contact, Audra mouthed the words "I love you" to him.

He cried out and darted towards her, desperation clear in every line of his body, ignoring the threat behind him to try and save Audra. With a triumphant cry, the netvor rammed into him, pinning his legs to the ground with its talons.

Audra's heart felt like it was tearing to shreds as Graham hit the ground. Pain distorted his features, yet he still tried to reach for her.

Choking on her tears, Audra tried one last time to get her arm free, not to save herself—that was beyond hope—but to at least get closer to the love of her life.

"Say goodbye, Audra," Silvan mocked from above. "Maybe Hellig will have mercy and you will see Graham in the afterlife."

Her eyes were heavy with fatigue and blurred from tears. Her head was so heavy, but Audra fought against laying it on the ground. With her last breath, she would keep her eyes on Graham.

A blur of white shifted in front of her. Emerging near her shoulder, Isik leapt at Silvan's throat, jaw open in a snarl. With the grip on her magic lessened, Isik was able to push through the spell holding him back. In the moment where Isik was airborne, Silvan raised his arms to catch the flying ball of teeth, fur, and claws. He was too slow to prevent the impact from knocking him off Audra's back.

Arms free, Audra did not hesitate to send some of her remaining magic to Graham. The loss of power caused her head to spin and Audra knew it would be near impossible to stand. Rolling onto her knees, Audra watched as Graham used the burst of energy to twist his torso, slicing the netvor's head off its shoulders, blood spurting from the wound in a black shower.

Continuing the fluid motion, Graham threw the dagger in Audra's direction, calling out her name. Timing was crucial and Audra knew that her vision was too distorted to accurately catch the dagger. Fighting through the exhaustion and light-headedness, Audra called on her magic to guide the dagger into her hand. The leather hilt was warm as it hit her palm. Spinning on her knees, Audra saw Silvan fighting against Isik. A blast of magic sent her beloved pet sprawling and Audra let out a cry filled with hatred and anguish.

Launching herself forward, Audra took delight in the shock that filled Silvan's eyes as she plunged the dagger into his heart.

Pressing down with her weight, Audra felt the dagger shred through muscle and organ. Silvan scrambled to fight against her, but life was already draining from his body. Nothing could stop an injury to the heart.

As he died, Audra felt her stolen magic return, giving her back some energy. With a shove, Audra rolled off Silvan's lifeless body. Knowing that the moment she stopped moving, she would not be able to get up for a while, Audra dragged herself to Isik. He looked up at her with coal-black eyes and licked her hand while she checked him for injuries. Luckily, the fall only winded him and Isik was uninjured.

"Thank you, my brave little warrior," Audra said with a kiss to his head. Isik let out a small yip in Graham's direction, as if to let her know that he was okay and she could worry about Graham instead.

Groaning as she stood up, Audra made her way to Graham on wobbly legs. Having her magic drained was worse than using it until it was nearly empty. The latter was like pouring out a full glass of water, knowing that it could be refilled. The former was as if the glass had shrunk and now was regrowing as the magic returned. She fell to her knees when she reached the prone form of her prince.

He was still pinned at the legs by the netvor, knowing that the blood loss from pulling out the talons would cause more damage than leaving them in. Using as much magic as she could to ease the pain, Audra pulled one leg free and began to stitch the muscle and skin back together as Graham grimaced in pain. Once healed, she did the same to the other leg. It was a slow process and Audra was surprised that Graham only passed out once from the pain and blood loss.

Finished, both collapsed to the ground, chests heaving once she was done healing the most serious injuries. Audra lay as close to Graham as possible without hurting him, their sides pressed together. Smoke gray eyes looked at her from heavy-lidded lashes, conveying a wealth of love and gratitude, like she was the most precious thing in his life.

One of Graham's hands came up to brush hair away from her face.

"You are incredible," he said with a gravelly voice. "But let's never do that again, okay?"

"Deal," she replied.

Twenty-Nine

After spending the night in the damaged carriage, Audra and Graham burned the bodies of the netvor and Silvan. Audra wept again while they watched the ashes scatter into the wind, Graham standing at her side. They waited until there was nothing left behind before starting on foot towards Ymira. They were fortunate and encountered the horses grazing in a field a few miles beyond the site of the attack. With some coaxing, they led the horses back to the carriage and continued in the now heavily-swaying conveyance. Restoring her magic was taking longer than Audra was accustomed to and it frustrated her that she was unable to repair the damage enough to make the journey more comfortable. Graham had her tucked into his side, wincing when his injured arm was jostled, and repeatedly pressed kisses to her forehead, breathing in her scent and reassuring himself of her presence.

Audra understood his desire to remain as close as possible. Never again did she want to experience the despair of not being able to reach him when he needed her. They were silent on the journey, both processing what had occurred and resting their healing bodies. The rocking motion combined with the exhaustion from the events of the previous day had her falling asleep in Graham's arms, safe in the knowledge that he would protect them. She woke to the bright sun streaming through the open roof, warming her skin and causing her to squint against the light. In the midafternoon glow, Audra could see the start of the incline leading up the mountain into Ymira.

"Hells," she gasped, bending to rifle through her bag, "I forgot to let Taara and Eli know about the delay. They are probably worried sick and now we are going to arrive looking like we were mauled."

When her hands found the parchment and pen, Audra straightened and wrote a hastily scrawled note to Taara, letting her know their arrival was imminent. Hopefully, she would be in the greenhouse where Audra was sending the note.

"Elskede." Graham's eyes twinkled with amusement. "We *did* get mauled. And you are still the most beautiful sight I have ever seen."

Audra snorted. Her hair was guaranteed to be a mess, leaves and twigs likely tangled in the curls, and her pants and shirt were torn and smeared with dirt and dried blood. This was not the image she needed to present as the High Mage, but she was so focused on resting that stopping at the river to wash had not crossed her mind. Glancing down at her appearance, Audra wondered if it would be worth using magic to touch up her appearance before they arrived.

No, she decided. If they were careful, only the mages at the ward and Taara and Eli would see them before they could rest and change. When it was time to share the news of Silvan's betrayal and the deaths of Avery and Leon, Audra wanted to present an image of strength and confidence. Her bruises and lingering injuries would speak to the lengths she went to protect Ymira, but it would spark doubt in her leadership if she looked like she was one step away from death's door.

Casting an illusion around the carriage to make it look undamaged, Audra explained her plan to Graham as she pinned her hair back into a simple bun to not appear quite as disheveled. He smiled at her, but Audra could see the weariness behind it. He was recovering from more physical damage than she was and Audra planned to ask Eli for a restorative potion to take to the springs that evening.

"We would not want them thinking that you brought home a ruffian instead of a prince," Graham joked, gesturing to his own disheveled appearance. Dark circles sat under his cloud-gray eyes, fatigue dimming his tan skin and causing his body to draw in on itself. His legs were stretched onto the seat across them, next to Isik's curled form, to relieve the pressure on his wounds.

Pressing a kiss to his stubbled cheek, Audra tunneled her free hand into Graham's hair. "I would still choose you. No matter what."

That earned her a full smile, pleasure giving his cheeks a pink tint over his dimples. Graham leaned in to kiss her, and Audra met his lips halfway. The light pressure of his touch warmed her, their lips moving softly over each other. Just when she was about to deepen the kiss, Audra heard the call of the mage on duty.

"Lady Audra, welcome home!"

Audra opened the window to stick her head out. Just enough to verify her identity while blocking the worst of the visible damage on her body.

"It is good to be back. Anything to report?"

"We've had a few merchants and one or two families visit, but nothing out of the ordinary. Was your trip successful?"

The mage's tone was hopeful, the worry over the missing mages something that weighed on everyone's mind.

"It was enlightening," Audra hedged. "Once I am settled, I will call for a gathering in the square to inform everyone of what I learned."

Bowing at the polite dismissal, the mage stepped back to allow the carriage to proceed. Audra watched Graham as the ward's magic flowed over him. He had felt her magic before, but this experience was different, the blend of multiple mages' magics felt like multiple textures at once. It could be disorienting, but Graham rolled his shoulders as they moved through the barrier, adjusting well to the sensation.

He watched the passing scenery out the window, taking in the fields of flowers and lush forest that made up Audra's home. As he took in the town and farms, Audra watched him to gauge his impression of Ymira. When Graham closed his eyes in pleasure, letting the breeze caress his face from the open carriage, Audra squeezed his hand.

"What do you think?"

"I am lucky that you chose to share this with me. I feel more at peace here than I have in a long time, but..." He squeezed her hand back. "...that could be because I have you by my side."

"Do not get too adjusted to the peace and quiet. Once we reach Rauha I expect nonstop chaos. And that is just from Taara."

Audra could see her friend in the distance, waving frantically from the path near the greenhouse. Eli was seated next to Taara, one hand shading his face from the sun while the other rested on her hip. The greenhouse was one of the first structures restored after the attack, Audra giving her blessing to Taara and Eli to rebuild it however they thought was best. Compared to the pristine glass panels sparkling in the sun, Rauha was in shambles.

"I am embarrassed that you have to see the hall like this," Audra said sheepishly. "There was no time to review any plans for rebuilding before I left."

Most of the mages in Rauha had relocated after the restrictions were decreased, choosing to live with their families in town or leaving Ymira to travel the kingdoms. Which was good, because it meant that they were safe and comfortable enough to leave, but Audra was lonely living in the once-full building. She also found that the change in leadership structure created a slight disconnect between her and the other mages. Rauha was informally considered the seat of her kingdom, and Audra could admit that she was torn between rebuilding it the way it had been, or adjusting it to fit the new role both she and it played in Ymira's future. So, beyond clearing the rubble, Rauha sat as it was, missing walls and all.

"You know," Graham started, "I do know a thing or two about living in a castle. With your permission, I could help you rebuild it."

"That would be really nice." Audra leaned in to kiss him again. It was the first time she had verbally confirmed their shared future. When she thought about it as building their home together, the task of rebuilding no longer seemed as daunting.

"Audra!" The door opened with sudden force, swaying precariously on broken hinges, Taara's dark hair bouncing as she leaned in to hug her friend. Laughing at her enthusiasm, Audra hugged her back, breathing in Taara's scent of fresh flowers and sunshine.

"I missed you so much. We were so worried when you did not get back last night, weren't we Eli?" She barely turned to get his confirmation before continuing. "But here you are now! Oh my gosh, look at you! Are you hurt? Do you need healing? Eli, where's my bag?"

Eli chuckled, wheeling forward to tug Taara back. "It's in the greenhouse. Let's give Audra space to get out and let us know what happened before you drag her to the infirmary."

Isik jumped from the carriage first, sniffing around Taara and Eli's ankles before butting his head against them to receive pets. When Audra stepped down, she could practically see her friends scanning her for injuries, Eli assessing for potential damage while Taara ran through her mental list of potions and plants for healing. Smiling at their complimentary reactions, Audra hugged both her friends. They were perfect for each other.

"We are a little battered and bruised, but nothing major, I promise." She rushed to reassure the healers before they acted on the joke of taking her to the infirmary.

"We?" Taara peered over Audra's shoulder toward the carriage door that Graham was now stepping through.

"May I introduce his Royal Highness, Prince Graham of Solven." Graham shot her a wry grin at the use of his title. She could not help teasing him. "This is Taara and Eli, our best healer and potion maker."

"It is a pleasure to meet you both. Audra has shared so many stories of your time together that it makes me feel like I know you already. I am glad that she had your friendship over the years."

Even covered in grime and recovering from injuries, Graham stood tall and proud. He looked every inch a prince as he stepped forward to kiss Taara's hand and shake Eli's in greeting.

For once in her life, Taara was momentarily speechless. "Wow. Audra said you were handsome, but not this handsome."

The rest of the group laughed and Eli pretended to be offended by the statement. Mollifying him, Taara clasped their hands together and assured him that he was the only person for her. They made their way into one of the few remaining rooms in Rauha, the entry hall with plush couches around an empty fireplace.

After checking over their injuries, healing what she could and making notes for what potions and salves would aid the healing process, Taara was finally reassured that Audra was alright and settled with a cup of tea. Once they were all comfortably seated, Audra shared everything that occurred since she left Ymira, leaving out only the private details. Graham chimed in where appropriate, but largely let Audra guide the conversation. As expected, Taara and Eli interrupted to ask questions and were saddened at hearing the news of Avery and Leon's deaths.

Before getting to the revelations of the previous day, Audra paused to consider the best way to break the news. The betrayal still boiled underneath her skin with rage, and she fought to keep her magic from spiking out of control. Though they had all been friends with Silvan, he was Eli's best friend and Audra knew he would take the news the hardest. Next to her, Graham placed a hand on her knee and squeezed in a silent show of support.

After a calming breath, Audra revealed the truth behind Silvan's betrayal. Taara gasped in shock, covering her quivering lip with a hand. Tears gathered at the corners of her eyes as she processed the information.

Eli was deathly quiet. His hands gripped the armrests of his chair so tightly that his knuckles were white. With a burst of rage, the normally level-headed mage unleashed a targeted stream of magic to blast a hole in the damaged wall on the other side of the room. He grieved the hardest after Silvan's fake death and that grief returned with a swell of anger. If he needed an outlet, Audra was more than happy to let him break Rauha. It needed repair anyways, so what was an extra wall or two?

Pulse after pulse of magic hit the wall, dislodging bricks and creating holes with black scorch marks until Eli's shoulders heaved with the exertion. Taara placed a comforting arm around his shoulder and Eli turned into her arms with a sob. Audra felt like she was intruding on a private moment, but then Taara opened her other arm to motion Audra forward.

The three held each other as they mourned the loss of their friend, taking solace in their love for each other. Leah was missing, and they would need to lean on each other again when they told her, but for now, it started to heal the broken pieces in their hearts to know that some friends remained true.

Later, after Eli and Taara left Rauha to return to their homes, Audra led Graham to the springs, a basket filled with food, wine, and a restorative potion to pour in the water.

"Let me take care of you," Graham whispered in her ear when they reached the pool's edge.

He spread a blanket on the ground and guided Audra to sit between his legs, her back resting against his chest. Closing her eyes, Audra relaxed into his hold. Piece by piece, he brought fruit, bread, and meat to her lips, feeding himself while she chewed. Between bites, he trailed his hands along her body in an affectionate, not seductive, manner. When she tried to stop him, protesting that she could feed herself, he trailed kisses along her neck, whispering in her ear over and over again.

"Let me take care of you."

Setting the empty basket aside, Graham removed the pins from Audra's hair, running his fingers through the strands to gently detangle them. When the last tangle was undone, Graham dug his fingers into her scalp. Audra moaned at the pleasurable pain of having her head massaged. With equally tender hands, Graham removed her clothing. Turning in his arms, Audra undid the laces and buckles on Graham's shirt and pants, adding them to the growing pile of clothing that would need to be burned.

Wanting to be clean before they came together again, Audra poured the potion into the spring's water and pulled Graham to a small alcove with running water and soap. Calloused hands ran down her body reverently, taking care that every inch of her was unsullied by grime. Audra shivered under Graham's touch, the slow seduction warming her blood and sparking desire along her skin that settled in her core. As desperate as she was for him, Audra enjoyed letting Graham take his time. Once she was clean, Audra lathered soap in her hands and worked them over Graham's arms and shoulders, watching the bubbles drift down his chest with water. She traced each tattoo with her fingers, respecting the pain he endured to earn each one. Black blood tainted the water and Audra continued to scrub until the water ran clear.

Turning him around, Audra cleaned Graham's back, kissing the scar that ran from shoulder blade to hip. Crouching behind him, Audra gripped his firm calves and worked her way up to his waist. The evidence of his desire for her bobbed in front of her face when she tapped Graham's leg to have him turn again.

She looked up to see him watching her with heavy-lidded eyes, lust enlarging his pupils so that only a thin ring of gray showed. Washing the soap from her hands, Audra moved them up his powerful thighs, squeezing the muscle as she went. Leaning forward, Audra gave Graham a questioning look.

In response, Graham linked their hands together and led them to circle his length. Water flowed around them and Audra found that it made it easier to slide her hands along him, learning what made him moan and shake with pleasure. Her eyes never left his as Audra continued to stroke him. His chest rose and fell in rapid motions, a red flush covering his chest and cheeks from the mounting pleasure.

"Audra...I—hells. That's so good," he groaned. With one hand, he continued to guide Audra, moving her hand in a rough pace while the other grasped fistfuls of her hair. When she grasped him firmly, he gave the strands a tug that had Audra moaning with pleasure.

When his legs began to shake, Graham pulled himself away with a rough moan. "Need you," he growled, bending to pull Audra to her feet.

Audra leapt into his arms, grasping his face to pull him into a fierce kiss. She had never wanted anything like she wanted him. Water ran down their bodies, sliding them against each other as they fought to get closer. Strong arms wrapped beneath Audra's thighs as Graham lifted her. With this position, she could grind her hips against him while their mouths clashed. Desire sparked along her skin, igniting the magic within her. Graham pulsed against her when Audra allowed some of her magic to play along his skin.

"Do it again," he said and pulled on the lobe of her ear, nipping down her neck before soothing the bites with his tongue.

She did.

Graham's entire body shivered with pleasure, the power giving his eyes an unearthly glow. Like she weighed nothing, Graham lifted Audra higher, his hands palming her rear as his mouth moved to her chest. Pleasure shot from her breasts to her core and Audra threw her head back. He gave them equal attention and each tug and suck on her flesh had Audra writhing against him. When she attempted to wiggle lower to get much needed friction against her core, Graham gripped her tighter, keeping her in place for his delicious torment.

"Need something, Elskede?"

She whimpered in frustration and tried to move again. The power she gave him provided the extra strength he needed to keep her in place, and as much as it frustrated her, Audra was delirious with pleasure. Knowing Graham would never hurt her and was determined to give her more pleasure than she could imagine emptied her mind of thought.

"Ah, you know what I want," Graham said as he shifted so that one arm was holding her up, the other moving to drag his fingers from hip to hip. Teasing touches that had her body on fire. "I will give you anything you ask for. Just say the words."

Audra pulled his hair, earning a hiss of pleasurable pain, and forced him to look at her. "I need you inside me, please, *Elskede*," she spoke against his lips.

It was the first time she had used the term of endearment and it unleashed something in Graham. He claimed her lips in a possessive kiss and walked forward until Audra's back was pressed against a smooth wall. Warm water flowed along the surface, heating her skin as Graham shifted back to plunge into her.

"Graham!" she gasped his name at the flood of pleasure. Audra wanted to live in this moment, the feel of his skin beneath her hands and her legs clutching him to her.

Quick snaps of his hips brought Graham in and out of her, the sensation drugging her body. Pressure built with each thrust, until Audra was moaning his name incoherently, kissing every available inch of skin. As she climbed toward the peak, Graham leaned them further against the wall so that he could free one hand to rub the place that made her wild. A few caresses of his fingers had Audra shattering, light dancing behind her eyes. She cried out Graham's name as she came, and her release triggered his, shouting out her name as he came.

Hands ran along wet skin as they came down from their high, breathing deeply to slow their heaving chests. In the afterglow, Graham moved them to the pool, gently lowering them to soak in the water.

Tucked against Graham's chest, Audra groaned as he massaged the tight muscles in her body. He kissed the top of her head as she tipped it backward to rest on his shoulder.

"Audra?"

"Hmm?" Her body was relaxed, eyes closed in appreciation at being pampered.

"When I saw you fighting Silvan...I have never felt that kind of dread in my life." His voice was raw, the usual confidence missing. "I lost you once, and it nearly killed me. But watching you die? It felt like my heart was being torn from my body."

His arms tightened around her, and Audra had to shimmy to turn and face him. Wrapping her arms around his neck, Audra pressed her lips to his. Their tongues tangled for a few moments before she pulled back, pressing their foreheads together. Her emerald eyes met his slate-gray gaze.

"No matter what it takes," he continued, "I will fight with every breath in my body to keep you safe. Wherever you go, I will follow. I meant what I said before, whatever you ask for, I will give you. There is no version of this world that I want to live in without you in it."

"All I want is you." Warm tears slipped down her cheeks and Graham brushed them away.

"Then you shall have me."

EPILOGUE

Stepping into her room, Audra immediately felt his presence. The scent of cinnamon and earth filled the space and Audra could feel his eyes on her, even if she could not see him. A low fire burned, casting the room in a warm glow without the aid of mage-lights. The fireplace was a recent addition to the room, part of her grey-eyed prince's restoration project. After completing work on the communal spaces in Rauha Castle, and adding several new rooms—including a ballroom to Taara's delight, and a throne room to Audra's begrudging acceptance—Graham surprised Audra by redesigning their room. Her forest green couch sat alongside his dark-wood end tables, paintings of Nebura, the Weld Forest, and Maneseen Lake decorated the stone walls. Hidden in the darkness, Audra knew that their desks sat facing each other by the arched window, his daggers and her crystals shining in the moonlight. Every inch of this room, and their suite in Solven, was a testament to how Audra and Graham fit into each other's lives. Over the last year, it had been a challenge to find a balance between their responsibilities in both Solven and Ymira, but there was no one else Audra would rather face life's journey with.

Audra pretended like she was unaware of Graham's presence, going to her vanity to store her jewelry and brush out her hair after a long day of courtly politics. A representative from Kalmere had arrived with news that King Balor was dead and that the new queen, Nerine did not share her predecessors' views on mages and extended an invitation for the High Mage to visit Kalmere. Considering the tense relationship that currently existed between the two kingdoms, Audra was hesitant to agree, asking the emissary to return in a month's time to receive her answer. That would give her time to consult with her council and allies in Solven and Feldor regarding the best way forward. For now, she wanted to put aside her duties as High Mage and simply be Audra.

A low groan sounded from her bed when she removed the moon combs from her hair, the curls falling like water down her back. Graham loved her no matter how she dressed, but he often expressed how much her unbound hair aroused him. He enjoyed wrapping it around his fist to pull her closer or let it cascade through his fingers. Still, she pretended not to hear him.

Smiling, she placed the combs next to her crown, a beautiful twisting of metal with diamond-studded stars and an amethyst crescent moon at the center. A gift from Graham, she remembered the first time it was placed on her head, at the ceremony crowning her Princess of Solven. That same night, Graham told her to keep the crown on as he undressed her on her throne, swearing fealty in the way only he could. She shivered at the memory. And the memory of returning the favor when she presented Graham with his own throne in Ymira.

Now, as she ran the tips of her fingers over her crown, Graham felt inclined to announce himself. "It looks good on you, maybe even better than mine did. I might need you to try them both on again, for comparison." His voice was rough with desire, heating up her body better than any fire.

The reminder of the time Graham found her in his chamber gave Audra an idea. Feigning shock, Audra turned. "Intruding in a woman's private chambers, Your Highness?"

In the dim light, Audra could make out Graham sitting upright on the bed, hands resting behind his head where he leaned against the headboard. When he shrugged—catching on to the game when she referred to their room as *her* room—the sheet fell to his waist, revealing his naked chest. Shadows danced across the exposed skin, urging Audra forward.

"If I recall correctly, you were the first one to sneak into my chambers. I thought it only fair that I do the same to you."

Swaying her hips seductively, Audra toed off her shoes as she approached. "Did you now? Well, the rules in Ymira are different than Solven. Breaking in is a serious offense."

When she was close enough to the bed, Graham reacted with lightning-quick reflexes, snagging an arm around her waist to drag her onto the bed beneath him.

"And how shall you punish me? I am eager to atone for my actions."

"Hmmm." Audra pretended to think. "A punishment this severe requires equal repayment."

She momentarily lost all thought when Graham loosened her dress enough to begin sliding it down her body, kissing each new inch of exposed skin. When the dress was a pile of fabric on the floor, Graham repeated the process in reverse. Knowing the effect it had on her, he placed feather-light kisses along the column of her neck.

"My punishment?" His words were a caress on her ear, the sharp bite to her earlobe making her feel like this was punishment for her instead of him.

Twining her legs around his hips and arms around his neck, Audra lifted her head to kiss him fully. When he was sufficiently distracted, Audra pivoted, flipping them with a smile. Graham groaned, loving that the new position placed her firmly against him.

"Your punishment is a lifelong sentence." Audra rocked her hips once, causing them both to moan at the friction. Not wanting lust to overtake their brains for what she had to say next, Audra refrained from moving her hips again, lowering her face until she was nose to nose with Graham, hands cradling his face as the metal on her finger glinted in the firelight.

"You must love me forever. Even when we breathe our last and join Hellig in the stars."

The promise of years of choosing each other showed in his eyes.

"Forever, wife."

ACKNOWLEDGMENTS

A year ago, if you told me that I would be self-publishing my second novel, I would not have believed you. What started as a creative outlet has transformed into a passion, and reaching this point was impossible without the help of many, many people.

Thank you, God, for everything.

Richard, my amazing husband, thank you for being my loudest supporter and cheerleader. When I was stressed, tired, or overwhelmed, you were there with a snack, the best hugs to recharge my batteries, and a reminder that it's okay to take breaks. You make every day better and I am forever grateful to have you in my life.

Thank you to my sensitivity readers: Gretchen, Ruthie, Renita, and Alexia. Your thoughtful suggestions and valuable insight enhanced the fantasy world I am building and added to the authentic voices of the characters.

To my beta readers: Michelle, Nicole, Susan, Sydney, Madison, and Billy. Some of you read this very first version of this book...vastly different from the final version, right? That is thanks to you all. You don't shy away from pointing out plotholes or inconsistencies, and I appreciate that. Nothing makes me happier than having you send a text or comment on something that you loved in the book.

Mom, there are definitely parts of this book that you need to skip over, but I am so glad that you want to read everything I write. The way you brag about my books, even before you've read them, makes me so happy. Knowing that you are proud of me and love supporting my work means the world to me.

To my family and friends, thank you for the words of encouragement and support at each and every event! Knowing that I have you all in my corner makes it easier to put my work out there.

Cara, my fabulous editor! Your critical eye and analysis took this book to new heights. Thank you for loving my characters as much as I do, protecting them by offering feedback on ways to make their stories better. Bouncing ideas back and forth with you stretches my imagination and drives me to create the best version of my writing possible. Thank you for catching those pesky commas!

Beyond the actual writing, creating a book involves a lot of steps! Thank you to Becca, fairy plot mother extraordinaire, for talking through all my book-related questions. When I was stressed over naming this book, brainstorming with you eased my anxiety and provided the inspiration for the entire series. To Shauna and Becca at The Author Agency, thank you for working with me on promoting Audra and Graham to readers! Credit for the stunning cover goes to Azura Arts. Azura, you are so creative and I am in awe each time you send over a design. The Ymiran symbol on the front cover and netreus on the back...beautiful!

If you made it this far, that means you are my dedicated readers! To each and every one of you, thank you from the bottom of my heart. Knowing that you chose to read this story means more than you could ever know. As an author, having people choose to read what I wrote is surreal. Thank you. As a life-long reader, I know the power of storytelling and the impact it's had on my life. I hope that in some small way, the characters in this book connect with you.

About the Author

Hi! I'm Kristen, a contemporary romance and romantic fantasy author. A storyteller at heart, I love writing about happily ever afters and the journeys characters take to get there. When I am not writing (or reading), you can find me visiting aesthetically appealing restaurants and coffee shops with friends, dancing, or traveling. I live in Southern California with my husband and two cats.

You can find me on Instagram or my website (kristenjennings.com).